THE UNSEELIE KING'S REBEL

REALM OF DRAGONS AND FAE

ALISHA KLAPHEKE

Ebook and Hardback Case Illustration by Julia Dea and typography by Miblart

Paperback Cover and Hardback Jacket by JV Arts

Critique Partnering by Tessonja Odette

Beta Reading by my Dragon Divas—Kelly, Ali, Rachel, Sarah, Megan, and Erin

Editing by Jen Boles on Reedsy

Proofreading by my Typo Hunters

Map of Realm of Dragons and Fae world by Soraya Corcoran

Veilbury Song written by Alisha Klapheke and graphic by Abide Selah

❀ Created with Vellum

To my children, nieces, and nephews—thank you for your ongoing encouragement

LIKE A WILD STORM DESCENDS
FROM THE SKIES

A THUNDER AND POWER AND SILVER EYES

FLASHING AND SLASHING

AND TEARING THE WORLD

THE UNSEELIE KING

COMES FOR YOU

LIKE THE NIGHT CHOKES THE DAY

DARKNESS AND MAGIC AND CLAWS TO SLAY

BINDING AND TEMPTING

AND BLEEDING THEM DRY

THE UNSEELIE KING COMES FOR YOU

DON'T WALK THE BORDER

OR CALL HIS NAME

MIND ALL THE DRUMSTONES PRAY HE CAN'T SEE

THE UNSEELIE KING COMES FOR YOU

A VEILBURY CHILDREN'S SONG

❧ I ☙
AN UNEXPECTED MEETING

❦ I ❦
BRONWYN

The Temple of the Star Goddess was a very pretty prison. Four years ago when I applied to be an acolyte, I was a heartbroken fifteen-year-old. I didn't realize I had sentenced myself to a life spent caged both literally and figuratively. Now, at nineteen, every single day I longed to travel back in time and shake some sense into that young girl.

Condensation gathered on the window of the temple library. I wiped the cool moisture away to see the Gwer-hune, the Fae forest that darkened the distance beyond the temple's gardens. The dark green boughs of ancient oaks swayed gently in the spring breeze and the indigo lights that remained a mystery to us humans floated between the limbs and over the mossy earth. What scents filled the Fae forest? What creatures would I see if I managed to escape this prison and venture through the Veil?

"Your book, Sacred Sister Bronwyn."

Turning away from the window's dangerous temptation, I faced the librarian who held out a dusty tome with a red spine that read *The Old Ones and Their Sacred Sites*. I accepted it with a "thank you" and arranged the book on a support pillow at the table near the window. Page twenty-nine showed a drumstone and a holy well lost to the wilds of Fjordbok, the birthplace of the new Queen of the Fae. The illustration detailed piles of glittering snow and stretches of dark ice. None had been to the well in over a century. Ten pages after that, the author told the story of a long-ago pilgrim's journey to reach a former temple, not too different from this one here in Veilbury. Boasting three stone towers, a library, and gardens, this lost temple appeared to have once been a bustling center of worship. But the sea had eaten away the coastline, and the old temple had fallen into the salty waves.

"What is it about these old books that you adore so much?"

I jumped at Seersha's voice. "I just like imagining traveling to all these sites."

Seersha shook her head, the tasseled ends of her temple headpiece shushing over the shoulders of her priestess robes. Her wide sleeves fell back as she removed a slim scroll from the shelves at the end of the wall. She was pretty—dark copper hair and haunting eyes—but her attitude soured the effect.

"House Mother will put you in solitary again if you're late for the herb ceremony," she said.

My heart leaped into my mouth and I stood, knocking the greenwood chair to the flagstone floor. It landed with a bang that had the librarian hurrying over with a glare that could melt all the ice around that lost sacred well.

"Sorry, Librarian." I gave a quick bow then rushed through the hall of shelves and the scribes scratching parchment at their desks.

Hitching up the white acolyte robes that most traded for priestess robes in the length of time I'd been here, I walked as quickly as I could out of the library without openly running. Running was against the rules— as was being late.

One of five religious sub-sects in the Kingdom of Saxonion, the Order of the Star Goddess provided its host city a way to demonstrate the grace and purity of the Old Ones through rituals and dances handed down from generation to generation. No one knew exactly when the order had been established, but our temple was the most highly regarded in Veilbury.

I slid open the heavy oaken door of the center tower

of the three here at the temple. Floral incense pinched my nose. Two younger acolytes scrubbed the already gleaming wooden floors with lemons and hot water that steamed into the air. They each paused to nod respectfully my way, and I returned the gesture hastily. Winding stairs took me to the second floor where House Mother stood in the ceremony room. Crockery bowls of lavender, rosemary, pixiebane, and yarrow surrounded her.

House Mother never glared when angry, but her stoic, unblinking look was far more frightening than any expression. "You are late. Begin immediately."

Sweat drizzled down my neck and made my hair cling to my forehead under the gold beads and pearls of my three-pronged headpiece. I really hoped my perspiration wasn't smearing the runes charcoaled onto my upper chest and cheeks. If the servants had to apply the runes more than once a day, I was punished with four days in solitary confinement. The thought of that iron cage deep in the bowels of the library sent a shudder through me.

I sat cross-legged in front of House Mother, took a breath in a sad attempt to steady my shaking hands, and whispered the holy words.

"To the Star Goddess, we offer this bounty of our earth."

I lifted the bowl of lavender above my bowed head.

Setting it directly in front of me, I began the holy motions. I swept one palm across the floor to the right of the bowl, then repeated the gesture with my other hand on the left side of the offering. A strange prickling blossomed between my eyebrows. Maybe I was about to get a headache.

"What is it?" House Mother's voice cut through the quiet. Her gaze narrowed.

"Nothing." My heart ticked like a beetle stuck on its back.

House Mother sniffed disdainfully. "Don't frown like that and stop wiggling like a louse-plagued peasant. This is a symbolic clearing of the sacrifice area. It's holy."

I sighed in relief. I could handle insults just fine. "Yes, House Mother."

Next, I took the flint and striker from my pocket and lit the lavender so it smoked into the last beam of sunlight that streamed through the warbled glass of the low, wide windows. Once I had echoed the process with the other herbs and lined up their bowls in a precise arrangement, I took each smoking herb between my palms and crushed their ashes into my skin.

"I am your sacrifice, Star Goddess. With my blood, you receive our earth offering."

I rubbed my ashen palms over my jawline. House Mother held out the ruby-encrusted dagger and I accepted it, silently scolding the younger version of me who had stupidly thrown herself into this madness. The blade cut my chin easily, and I only had to make a small slice for the blood to drip.

House Mother was still staring at me, shoulders tight, and the knuckles of her clasped hands were white. "May the Goddess accept our offering."

My heart was empty. No jolt of power hit me or wave of awe-inspiring devotion. This whole thing was a sham, and in the four years I'd been here, the Goddess had done nothing to heal my loneliness.

House Mother waved in the servants who cleared up the ceremony items and tidied my hands and chin with warm water and salve. I began to leave, but House Mother's voice stopped me at the archway. She handed me a book of rituals.

"Study this. If you can learn the ritual of Sending in one hour, you may sleep in your bed tonight. Tomorrow, you will spend the night in solitary for tardiness."

My mouth went dry, and I struggled to keep from shouting. Of course, she made me wait a day so I could wallow in fear. I couldn't look at her, but I bowed my head.

"Yes, House Mother."

Heading outside, I wiped a tear from my eye before it could fall and smear my runes.

I sat in the front courtyard with my rituals book.

Ceremonies such as this one didn't come easily to me. Only the dances of our religion enchanted me. The rituals never gave me a sense of satisfaction or of serving some greater good. But it wasn't as if I had a choice but to learn and perform the rituals.

Drefan, now captain of the city guard, waved a hand, his genuine smile almost hidden in his blond beard. "Good morning."

Most men weren't permitted to speak to acolytes or priestesses, but the city guard were allowed due to the nature of their job. They protected the temple, not that it was ever in danger.

I lifted a hand in greeting. Drefan had come from the same rural village as me and we'd both ended up here in Veilbury around the same time though for very different reasons. I'd applied to become an acolyte, and he'd signed up for guard training. Once he'd been accepted, he actually spoke up for me as a personal refer- ence to Beanie, who'd been House Mother then. At the time, I hadn't realized Drefan held any real opinion of me. His reference had been a kind surprise.

"How are the chickens?" I asked, leaning over the low temple wall. The city guard had a small kitchen garden and a few animals for food on the outskirts of town. The city rose up behind Drefan like a crowd, the many windows like eyes.

He glanced at the tower behind me and walked as

close as he dared. "Are you all right?" he whispered as his gaze slid over the bruise House Mother had left on my hand. She'd struck me with a stick last week for being late to my chamber for bedtime.

This was dangerous talk. If anyone heard Drefan, he would lose his position and quite possibly be thrown in prison. Being captain of the city guard—youngest with that title in the history of the city—awarded him some leniency with regard to tradition, but his position didn't shield him completely.

"I'm fine. How are the chickens?" I asked again, wishing to change the subject. The edges of my tiny ritual book dug into my fingers.

A reluctant grin softened his features. "Good. Feisty held off a hawk that came after the flock yesterday evening. The big girl flapped her wings, rose up, and tore at the hawk with her talons like she was a bird of prey rather than an egg-laying matron."

We laughed, and a pang of homesickness hit me. Drefan had kissed me once. He was a handsome one with his golden locks and sturdy ways, always holding open doors and offering me small gifts like a new pair of boot laces or a posy of flowers. The kiss had been...nice, but nothing like Gantu's embraces. I wish I would have fallen for Drefan. It would have been so much smarter. But the heart wasn't wise. Mine, at least, wasn't.

Drefan's gaze flicked to my face and remained there.

His lips tightened as he took in the runes painted on my cheeks. "I wish..."

"Don't say that, please, Drefan. I do too, but please..."

With a nod, he looked down at the wall separating us. He stepped back, gave me a shallow bow, then waved, and walked back into the city.

I wrapped my arms around myself and thanked the Old Ones for having at least one person who truly cared for me.

Determined to sleep in my bed that night, I studied and managed to learn the Sending ritual before House Mother came to test me. She dismissed me to my chamber, and I tried my best to sleep. Images of the cage ripped through any peace I could conjure.

THE NEXT DAY, I TRIED NOT TO THINK ABOUT MY upcoming punishment, but I didn't have enough mental discipline. During my allotted hour of Wandering, I went to the garden at the back of the temple grounds. Plots of herbs and spring vegetables sprouted green and filled the air with savory scents. I breathed them in and my fears dissipated.

The pebbles of the garden crunched pleasantly under my simple temple shoes, and I lifted my face to the setting sun. My patch of pixiebane was growing nicely, new buds showing their typical purple-black hue among the blue leaves. I ran a hand over their heads, the soft leaves tickling my freshly scrubbed hands.

Looking over the low stone wall, I stared again at the edges of the Gwerhune and the indigo lights. Technically, an acolyte could wander outside the walls during their daily hour as long as they stayed in the areas suggested by House Mother. But if someone saw me leave the temple walls and head into the Fae forest, there would be questions that would end in more punishment for me. Priestesses in training were not supposed to be curious about anything except the Old Ones and the Star Goddess. We were meant to protect ourselves from danger as well because we belonged to the temple and to the Goddess. Traipsing into a forest known for dangerous creatures and wild Fae would be what House Mother deemed a *poor choice*. When one made a poor choice, she made certain you had days on end in the cage to think about your mistake.

But no gardeners were working just now. Dinner had started in the main hall. I wasn't required to be there as fasting was a good choice, so I had a full hour to do as I pleased. I used to think that House Mother had people watching me and all the other acolytes, but I'd never seen evidence of that. Perhaps I could venture into the Gwerhune.

Just for a moment.

Just to smell the woods and feel the air beyond the Veil. It would only be a minute. I would turn right back around. My blood leapt in my veins. A smile tugged at my lips. The garden had no exterior gate, so I tied my long robes up on one side and climbed over the low wall.

2

BRONWYN

The ground was damp on this side and mud sucked off both my slippers. Chewing my lip, I peered back at the temple to see if anyone was watching. The windows were dark—the garden, empty.

I left my slippers and my bare, muddied feet carried me over the soft clover growing low to the earth until the line of oaks at the border were within reach. The treetops brushed the orange-hued sky, their new leaves waving to the first of the night's stars.

Wiggling my fingers, I stretched out an arm to pierce the Veil, and a sensation like sparks from a fire that were somehow cold instead of hot prickled across my skin. A laugh bubbled from me, and I covered my mouth to keep the sound from carrying.

I stepped through the Veil. That odd sensation of magic washed over me, head to toe, taking no heed of my headpiece or my robes. It traveled through all the garb to touch my skin.

The air smelled sweet and cool, and I wished I could somehow drink it in. The indigo lights bobbed over last year's leaves as I took another step. The last of the sun's light gleamed across the forest in ribbons of copper and gold. A large stone stood beside a pine, and something about it pinched at a memory of a story I'd once read. Oh, it was a drumstone, a portal to the world of the Unseelie. But the Seelie king had sealed them, so it was nothing to worry about.

"This is interesting," a deep, slow, sultry voice said from the shadows.

My heart seized up, then hung useless and afraid to beat. I pressed my fist against my chest, willing myself not to pathetically die from fear.

A figure strode from a cluster of maples and into the uneven golden light. He came forward and towered over me. The Fae lights blinked to life around him and cast an indigo glow over his pointed ears, silver and slitted eyes, and the intricate braids his black hair had been pulled into. Under leather armor, his skin was a dusky gray color that spoke of dark magic. A hood hung loosely down his back, below his braids, and along the tops of his broad shoulders. His arms were bare and his musculature made me wish I was a sculptor. My fears faded beneath the intensity of wonder I felt in his presence.

"You're so..." I put my hand to my stupid mouth before I could compliment his beauty.

A smile cut his soft-looking lips and a fang showed. I swallowed. He set a clawed finger under my chin and heat ran like a river of molten metal from the point of his touch, down my throat. "You think me beautiful?"

"I-I wasn't going to say that." Yes, I was. But what type of Fae was he? He couldn't be Unseelie, surely. This was the Seelie Fae's realm.

"Ah. Then what were you going to utter with that dirty human mouth of yours?"

"I'm not dirty." I pulled away, and my muddied toes showed under my hitched-up robes. "Well, all right. Maybe a little." My heart drummed against my wrists and pounded on my ribs. I needed to run. But I couldn't. He was just so lovely to look at. The most fascinating being I'd ever seen.

A laugh rumbled in his broad chest and made his silver eyes sparkle. "Congratulations. You're the most interesting thing I've found on this side of the stones."

This side of the stones. "Do you mean the drumstones?"

"Of course."

A chill rattled my body. "Right." No, he couldn't be one of them...

With a smirk, the Fae turned his back, picked up something glittering from the ground, then lifted it up to study it. It was a dark crown laced with gold and silver leaves. He set the crown atop his braids and grinned, showing both fangs this time. I was shivering now and couldn't do a thing to stop it. An Unseelie male—with a crown. He was right in front of me, but my mind couldn't believe this was happening. Maybe this was King Lysanael of the Seelie. Maybe the descriptions I'd heard and read were wrong...

"But I thought the Fae King was in Fjordbok with—"

"One Fae king is away currently. But he is not the only royal of pointed ear and dagger-sharp tooth."

"You're-you're Unseelie."

"Why yes, I am. The Unseelie King actually."

He bowed low, flicked his silver gaze to my face, and then a shimmering cloud of glittering dust burst around him. A growl issued from the magical haze and suddenly a gray dragon loomed in the Fae's place. The size of ten horses; the beast stretched its massive wings and lowered its head. Those same silver, slitted eyes stared at me.

Finally, my feet obeyed me and I ran.

❧ 3 ❧
TOREN

Toren shifted back into his high Fae form as the intriguing human female ran. She glanced at him over her shoulder as she fled, and the first grin of many, many days tugged at his mouth. With that spark of wild curiosity in her amber eyes and the way she'd been drawn to him despite his claws and gray skin, she had proved she was no ordinary human. Humans usually screamed at Unseelie and attempted to kill Unseelie immediately. But she had been genuinely attracted. She hadn't run. Not at the beginning.

Perhaps she could help him.

He had been trapped here in the land of the Seelie since King Lysanael sealed the drumstones. Toren had come through with a gang of trolls he'd been hunting.

The drumstones had been failing to hold back Toren and his kind for a while, and he'd had no warning that the Seelie King Lysanael was about to lock up the passageway. Keeping to the high branches of an age-old oak, Toren had watched Lysanael, the Seelie warriors, and the Seelie king's mate cut down the trolls and other Unseelie monsters after their joining ceremony. Heat rose in Toren's chest as he recalled the blood spilled. The Seelie king should have tried to herd Toren's monsters and contain them, killing only as many as was necessary to cull the herds and limit their violence.

Ever since that day, Toren had been seeking a way home.

He leaned forward, tracking the human female's rush back to the temple. Her lovely, long legs showed under her knotted robes, and the expanse of smooth skin shot fire through his blood.

Somewhere under the site of her temple, an ancient portal hid. If he could find it and get there without alerting the Seelie who lived so close to this human area, he could be home in moments. This place was painfully dull. Not a monster in sight. No good hunting. No source power to draw from. He looked down at his clawed fingers. The fine gray color of his flesh was going pale. This realm was slowly killing him.

But perhaps the human could assist him and save his life. She had access to the temple. She was intrigued by him. All he had to do was seduce her into doing his bidding. To get past the magical wards on the temple grounds, someone had to invite him in willingly.

Sounded like a pleasant plan, really, and far more interesting than dying.

❧ 4 ❧
BRONWYN

A s my heart attempted to break through my chest, I charged over the garden wall. Forget the slippers—I had to get inside immediately. I wasn't sure how far the magical wards extended past the actual temple and towers. Could the Unseelie pass into the garden?

My robes caught on the wall's stones, and I tripped, falling into my pixiebane and scattering their dark purple fluff into my face. Shoving to my feet, I hurried on. I glanced backward. The Unseelie king remained by the Veil, mostly hidden by the trees and the dark of the coming night.

It was unbelievable. The Unseelie king had spoken to me and shifted forms... Swallowing against my dry throat, I paused at the entrance to the first tower and looked for servants, or worse, House Mother, but the entry foyer was empty.

Everyone must still be at dinner. Good.

I skirted across the tumbled stone mosaic of the Star Goddess. Jade made up her long tresses, granite formed her lithe body and robes, and steel-gray hematite served as her eyes.

Eyes like his.

My muddy foot slipped on the stairs that led up to my chamber, but I caught myself on the railing and continued on, praying to that Goddess, to the one I didn't even believe in. I was lucky until I hit my chamber door.

"Oh, this is going to be a fabulous story." Seersha sat on the stool by the flickering hearth while a servant combed out her hair. Her beaded headpiece sat on the side table, and she'd exchanged her priestess robes for a gold-threaded white linen sleeping shift.

I gritted my teeth. "I was just in the garden."

Her gaze snapped to my bare and dirty feet. "And you were attacked by a bear? Or did the ground just grab you?"

"It was muddier than I expected."

"I'll call someone up for you," the servant said.

I knew her name was Poesin, but I wasn't permitted to say that out loud. House Mother forced us to maintain an emotional distance from the servants. She assigned new ones every week and rotated them endlessly through all the acolytes and priestesses.

"Off to solitary again tonight, I hear," Seersha drawled.

I ignored her and went into the bathing chamber. A hot bath steamed, waiting for me because we bathed every night. The words *Shining Purity Within and Without* were stretched across the walls in golden paint, a reminder that we had to remain chaste and without any stain on our bodies besides the ones we received in ceremony.

It would feel so good to scratch those words right off the plaster with my fingernails. It was insane how I'd judged this place as safe when I was fifteen, when Beanie ran the temple. If only I had known...

Penelope, an acolyte who had started the same summer as me, fell for the baker who delivered small pies to us—bread pockets filled with plain vegetables that were small enough to eat and keep our lip paint in place. Penelope was found to be unchaste and hung from the temple's central tower as a clear warning to outsiders —touch one of us and tragedy ensues.

I submerged myself in the bath and savored the feel of the hot water blocking out the world.

But one image smashed into my attempts at finding peace.

The Unseelie king shifting into a dragon. That fanged smile…

I sat up, splashing water over the lip of the copper tub.

"Sacred Sister, be careful!" An elderly servant in a white apron lunged forward with a bathing linen to mop up my mess.

I wiped water from my face. "So sorry."

She straightened, holding the wet linen and staring into my bathwater. "Why are you so muddy?"

"The garden," I said. "I was checking on my pixiebane. My slippers…"

The Unseelie king had spoken to me in the Fae woods. I shook my head, unbelieving. What was I supposed to do? Tell House Mother? Or maybe Drefan? The people of the city were far too superstitious to cause trouble here, so we didn't have anyone permanently stationed at our entrance or walls. No one, not even the worst of criminals, wanted to incur the Goddess' wrath. Pressing my eyes shut with the heels of my hands, I tried to think clearly— to plan around the fear. The temple was magically warded, but would it work against such a powerful monster?

The servant must have mistaken my behavior as worry over my slippers because she patted my shoulder gently. "I'll send someone out to find them. Don't worry," she said.

The servant dressed me in a sleeping shift similar to Seersha's and slid soft slippers onto my feet. She sat me on the stool by the mirror and began twisting my hair to knot it on top of my head.

"Like a waterfall of honey, your hair is," the servant said. Her hands weren't gentle, but they weren't as rough as House Mother's at least.

In the mirror's reflection, Seersha smirked from where she lay on her bed across the room. "Maybe the rats down there will leave your toes alone if you give them a lock of your hair."

I gripped the edges of the stool. I'd forgotten I was headed to solitary for being late to the herb ceremony.

The servant finished the knot and rubbed my shoulders. "I'll escort you down. House Mother gave me the key."

The key to the cage I would sleep in tonight. The floor of the cage was rusted and cold, and Seersha wasn't just joking about the rats. They always scuttled around as soon as everyone in the floors above the basement went quiet.

My mind flung itself back to the subject of the Unseelie king. If the wards didn't protect us from him, nothing would. I imagined the place ripped apart by dragon talons and dragon fire... A wicked grin tugged at my lips. I was an idiot because that dragon would destroy me too, and with it, any chance of living the life I wish I had.

Why hadn't the Unseelie killed me today? Everyone knew they were vicious, horrible demons. I'd have guessed he'd want to torture me, to drink my blood, and string my guts along the trees of his enemy Fae, the Seelie. But he had only been teasing and polite.

I hadn't imagined an Unseelie looking like him. I'd always thought their king would be just as grotesque as the gargoyles that roamed the city before Seelie Fae King Lysanael sealed the drumstones shut. The Unseelie king had been frightening with his claws, fangs, and dragon form, but he had pleased my eye rather than disgusting me.

What was he up to? Was he simply afraid the Seelie would come after him if he killed a human?

Drawing me up from the stool, the servant wrapped her steely fingers around my upper arm. She had been lecturing me, but I hadn't heard a word of it. There was no use fighting her, so I went along willingly. When we passed by the gathering hall, Mannix, the only male permitted in temple normally, was placing my name tablet into the absent box.

Two open-front boxes hung above the doorway and wooden tablets with every temple inhabitant's name—written in fine calligraphy—stood either in the green box or the black one. The tablets were arranged every night to show everyone's ranking as well. My tablet wasn't merely being shifted to a lower rank. When you went to solitary, you were marked as dead. Other tablets stood beside mine. Penelope's, Bora's, a scribe that had passed of old age, Ria's—her foreign aunt had snuck her out of the temple two years ago—and Beanie's.

My heart pinched, remembering the former House Mother who had been obsessed with the origins of the Star Goddess and the temple itself. Beanie used to drag us acolytes into the library to read the runes scratched into the corners and the shelves. She'd been convinced there was more to the temple than what was currently visible. I just loved the pudding she used to make with Cook on winter nights. Those times in the hall with her hadn't been like prison, like the temple was to me every other moment. They had been the only times I'd been at ease. Perhaps it was because Beanie had reminded me of the good parts of my mother.

I said a silent prayer to the Goddess for my parents' souls, even though I doubted the truth of the temple's teachings. It didn't hurt to throw a prayer up in case I was wrong.

We left the first tower and entered the library. The main areas gave way to the bare stone stairwell leading to the basement. Our soft footsteps echoed lightly off the walls, and my candle tossed our shadows to the vaulted ceiling. The scent of water and cold rock rose into the air as a shudder grabbed and shook me.

"If you'd only watch the time, Sacred Sister Bronwyn, then you wouldn't have to spend so many nights in this place."

I gritted my teeth, keeping myself from demanding an answer as to why being a minute late to a practice ceremony required such a rough punishment. It could be worse. I flexed the fingers of my writing hand, the hand House Mother had broken and then set the first and only time I had argued against the consequences of my behavior.

The cage door swung open with a creak, and the servant extended a hand to take the candle from me. I hated to give up my light, but once again, it could have been so much worse. I handed it over, and she locked me inside with only a bucket to keep me company.

Her form and the candle's light disappeared up the stairwell, and I was left in the dark to await the rats and my nightmares.

In them, I was always drowning. But I didn't drown in water. No, hands pressed me down, down, down, and suffocated me, blocking my mouth and nose. Countless hands. Sometimes, they wore House Mother's ring—all the hands at one time wearing the pearl adornment. Other nights, the hands of every servant who had taken care of me here at the temple drowned me. The hands never belonged to Seersha or the other priestesses or acolytes. Maybe because they were as trapped as I was, drowning in their own nightmares as we survived each day here, just steps away from an actual life, from the colorful world outside our rules and House Mother's expectations.

But my worst nightmares were always of myself. On those horrible nights, fifteen-year-old me floated above my sleeping present-day form. She still wore Gantu's ring even though in real life, I had thrown the ring at his bare back when I had caught him with another girl.

In the light of day, that nightmare seemed far less frightening than drowning in flesh, but when the dark dream came, it stripped me of my confidence, slashed my heart to ribbons, and left me sweating and shaking when I woke.

I don't know when I'd fallen asleep in the cage, but I woke to a tapping sound on the basement's single window. Moonlight bled into the cold room. I stood and gripped the cage's bars, trying to see what was making the sound.

The glass broke, and I couldn't believe what I was seeing.

5

TOREN

Toren set his hands on the dead leaves of the Seelie Fae forest floor and whispered to the creatures of the night. Magic tingled across his lips and his words sifted from his mouth as sapphire smoke that curled along the ground. The smoke slipped faster and faster along the roots of the massive oaks, maples, and pines.

"Take up her slippers and find her there. Return to her what is hers..." He whispered the command again, infusing it with his Unseelie will, his dark magic.

The leaves on the forest floor shuffled. Beetles with shiny backs and Fae mice with small horns and sparkling, black fur partially made of impossibly small mushrooms crawled out of the forest and headed toward the spot where the human female had lost her silken shoes.

Swarming around the slippers, the creatures picked and rubbed the fabric until it was as clean as muddied silk could be. Toren stood and leaned on an oak while they crawled over the temple's garden wall with their new treasure in tow. He let his arms fall as he stepped closer to the Veil, not quite piercing it, but coming close.

The silk caught the moonlight, and it seemed the beetles and the Fae mice were deliberating on which way to go to reach the female. Fae mice were the same in the Seelie realm as in Toren's Unseelie world, so they would be able to pick up her scent. Perhaps the wards did affect them after all? He'd thought the magical barrier would only hold and injure uninvited people...

The cluster of night creatures scurried along the temple's pathway until they reached a lower building—some sort of outbuilding, a chapel perhaps or a scriptorium? At least the creatures appeared unhurt and capable. Hopefully, their senses would remain healthy.

Though Toren's vision was exemplary, it was difficult to see how they were now disappearing into the structure. Perhaps under the front doors. Yes, that seemed to be it.

Why would the female sleep in an outbuilding? The cut on her pert chin flashed through his mind. Was she mistreated in this temple? And if so, why?

He crossed his arms and leaned against the tree again, wondering when the creatures would return.

If the humans mistreated the female he'd met, perhaps that would be helpful in luring her into spying for him. She would have far less loyalty to those in charge of the temple if they were hurting her in some way. He didn't know everything about humans, but he'd visited this realm often enough in his twenty-five years to know that.

He wondered about the runes she'd had painted onto her cheeks and over her collarbone. He was no rune expert, but the one on her cheeks concerned mating, or rather, the lack of. It was an odd thing to paint on oneself so he assumed the others there had applied the paint. Certainly no one would choose chastity, would they? Madness.

What would it be like to bed a human female? Her skin appeared incredibly soft, but her color was that of spoiled milk. She was still beautiful, but the tone of her flesh was off-putting. And she looked so fragile like he could pierce her chest and remove her heart with very little effort. He imagined that task and found he didn't like it. He wanted her to return and to see her wide eyes and her song-like voice. He'd smear her runes if he even touched her chest.

Ah, that was why they did it. To keep her accountable. If anyone placed a hand on her, they would know. How awful. So outrageously restrictive.

And humans thought the Unseelie were the monstrous demons.

The moon shifted in the sky and the night creatures still hadn't returned. He sat and shut his eyes to prepare to See. His stomach twisted as he released his awareness and sought the minds of those under his command. The magic of Seeing always made him dizzy. A cool brush of power swept over his shuttered eyelids, then the image of a moonlit chamber flickered to life in his mind's eye.

Through the eyes of the Fae mice, he saw the human female standing in a cage.

A cage.

Heat knifed his chest, and he fisted his hands so tightly that his claws pierced his flesh. He nearly lost the Seeing connection. Taking a breath, he focused again.

In the Seeing, the female's dark pink lips were moving as if she was saying something, but the words were garbled. Seeing wasn't Hearing, and he'd never been able to do that particular magic.

The night creatures dropped her slippers outside of the bars and she bent to retrieve them, her eyes wide like they'd been when he'd shifted to test her mettle. As the creatures turned away and scrambled out of a broken window, he opened his eyes and broke the Seeing. The chill of his Unseelie magic left him and only the breeze of the Fae forest touched him now.

They had her in a cage. Humans were horrid creatures. True, Unseelie Fae were violent at times, enjoyed a vicious hunt, and functioned on more of an instinctual level than Seelie and humans, but if this was what civilization wrought, well, Toren wanted nothing to do with it. Perhaps he would take this female with him if they did indeed find the lost portal inside the temple where the old stories claimed it sat. Could she survive there? If he willed it, none would dare to touch her. A smile warmed his mouth. He quite liked that idea.

The night creatures returned to him, brushed themselves along his bare feet, and went back to their evening hunts for food and mates. He shifted into his dragon form and rose into the canopy to do a bit of hunting of his own.

6

BRONWYN

Another servant, this one shorter than I was, retrieved me in the morning. As she let me out of the cage's door, I turned toward my slippers. I picked them up, wondering if anyone would believe me if I told them a bunch of Fae mice and beetles had brought them to me. Probably not. It was one thing to meet Seelie Fae and see the graceful way they walked and the power they could wield over animals, but humans had little experience with Unseelie outside of battling the ones that used to escape from the drumstones.

The rest of the day went as usual. Servants painted the temple runes along my freshly scrubbed face and over the top of my chest, just under my collarbone. I was wrapped in laundered robes and my hair was looped and tied beneath the beads of my acolyte headpiece. After practicing a set of our sacred dances, the other acolytes and I walked from the third tower to the main hall set into the first tower for a meal.

The potatoes were at least warm if not terribly bland. Sitting on my assigned stool at the table, I shut my eyes and imagined what kinds of foods the Unseelie king would have tasted in his lifetime. What did they eat? What did he eat when he shifted into a dragon? His silver eyes, the twist of his muscular arms, the way he'd ordered the tiny animals of the night to serve me… Flutters filled my stomach, and I opened my eyes to see Seersha and two other full priestesses standing on the far side of the table staring at me.

A sneer made Seersha ugly. "What foul thoughts are you cooking up in that odd head of yours?"

Heat flooded my cheeks, and I bit down on what I really wanted to say—bugger off. "I was only going over my steps for the exhibition this evening."

She snorted and left with the two others whispering beside her.

"…thinks she is better than anyone even though she fails promotion every time."

"She's the worst acolyte in history."

Once one joined, one couldn't leave the temple. I'd only come here to the Star Goddess temple to protect myself from Gantu's family and their perceived ownership of me. What a terrible mistake... I should have run away and escaped to the country or on a ship somewhere as a stowaway. Anything would have been better than life here. Old Beanie—who had been kind to me from the first day I'd arrived—had talked me into my official acceptance of temple life through the usual Blood Pact ritual, but she'd only done it to protect me. It was sad how someone could imprison another just by loving them.

I thought about running away many times. But I had no money now, and anyone that saw me would know my face. Everyone knew the faces of the priestesses and acolytes. House Mother would find me somehow. I just knew it. I was well and truly trapped.

IN THE CITRINE LIGHT OF SUNSET, I LINED UP IN THE garden behind the priestesses, alongside my fellow acolytes—all of whom were much younger than me. A crowd had gathered at the wall, blocking my view of the Gwerhune. Was the Unseelie king still out there? Would he be watching too?

"Move over." An acolyte named Yasha elbowed me in the ribs.

I shook my head at her. "You're the one in the wrong position." Pointing to the line House Mother had drawn in the tiny stones, I raised my eyebrows. The stones were nearly as small as grains of sand, and they picked up every one of our footsteps as we moved through the sacred dances. Yasha glared like the petulant child she still was, but she fell into step regardless.

House Mother clapped her hands three times, and we all went still, our hands folded over our hearts in the first position of this particular dance—the Winding. The servants rushed over to sweep the stones smooth. A lilting tune floated from the lute-man who played at the far end of our group. The music pulled at my heart, the minor key reminding me of the darkness of the Fae forest. I stepped forward, then drew my bare toe forward and around in a half circle to my right. Brushing my hand over an imaginary sword, I walked back two steps, then set my left heel down hard. We moved in unison, and the indigo lights of the Fae forest blinked in the distance, seemingly in synchronized movement as well though that had to be wishful thinking that our dances had any actual effect on the world.

Despite the way I hated this place, the dances warmed me, and I couldn't help but smile and tear up at various parts of the performance. The crowd beyond the wall clapped heartily at the dance's conclusion, some even wiping their eyes like I had to. I folded my hands in the ending position like my sacred sisters, and we bowed our heads as House Mother bid the onlookers a blessed month.

The crowd began to disperse, children tugging on their parents' clothing and friends chatting and laughing. They were probably on their way to walk the waterside with their loved ones or to the night market our city held on nights of the full moon. We weren't permitted to go to the night market, but I'd heard stories about the colorful cloaks set out for sale, the clove and cinnamon buns that always sold out before the moon was high, and the archery competition's flaming arrows. I had wished to go over and over again during my first three years here, but by the fourth year, I'd given up on wishing. House Mother didn't permit new and exciting experiences. I wondered if someday I'd dry up from lack of fun and become a husk of a person that simply went through the moves of temple life. Maybe deadening my desires was the best route, the less painful way to live...

But my mind threw out an image of the Unseelie king's dragon form. His wings had been wider than the library's reading room, and his teeth had been as long as my forearm. I smiled. After this dose of wonder, I only wanted more. I didn't want to become a shell of a person. I wanted life in full.

The Fae forest drew my gaze again, the lights shimmering and floating and the branches of the towering old trees swaying in the night's breeze.

The Unseelie king had returned my slippers. Why?

I would find out tomorrow during my wandering

time, and I didn't care if it meant another broken hand or another night in the damn cage. I'd risk it all to live, to see that magic, to be the person I was born to be.

Tomorrow, my life would begin and to the hells with the consequences.

❧ 7 ❧

TOREN

Toren couldn't stop staring. The human he had met outshone her fellow dancers. It wasn't even a competition. They were mere candles beside the brilliance of the sun. What was she thinking about as she moved? Her lips pouted and her eyebrows drew together a moment before her eyes were glistening with tears and her human teeth showed as she smiled again. Every emotion she appeared to feel hit him in the chest—sorrow, longing, joy... Desire welled inside him hot and demanding. His fingers wanted to draw a line from her knee to the inside of her thigh, to discover the curve of her long, lovely leg. His body ached to press against hers and to have her heart sound its drum against his chest.

How dare they put her in a cage. He longed to tear from the forest and destroy the warded wall with his bare hands.

But of course, in his high Fae form, the magic of the wards would kill him. The very taste of it told him about the bloody end he would face if he attempted to thwart its power. No, he had to be wise and measured with his actions. His younger self would have shifted and blown fire at the magic. It was doubtful the wards would hurt him in his dragon form. But he bore the scars of the recklessness of his youth. The Seelie would know of his presence if he shifted and was seen. So now, he would wait and try this plan of his.

The dance came to an end and the lute's music died away. A shimmer of...something washed over his vision—particularly over the area where the humans had been dancing. Blinking, he looked again, but couldn't see anything strange. He tilted his head and eyed his female. She stepped out of the dancing area and looked straight at him. The ground she had left flickered gold for a moment but the light was gone before he could be certain he'd seen anything magical.

How... What... What did her feet do to that space on the earth and why hadn't the spot where the other dancers moved glimmered like that? He'd never seen magic like this. None of the humans had reacted, so it must have been invisible to them. *Hmm.* Interesting. Here was yet another reason to draw the female closer. There was nothing like a mystery—especially when it was cloaked in such strange and eerie loveliness.

❧ 8 ❧
BRONWYN

In the hush of the mid-morning while everyone else was practicing dances in their private training areas throughout the towers, I stepped over the garden wall—this time wearing the gardener's boots.

I turned back to the gardener who was very reluctantly going along with my plan to visit the Fae forest again. "It'll be fine. Stop looking like I'm heading to my death."

She shook her head of pale yellow curls. "If she catches you, you'll wish the Fae beasts would have eaten you." The gardener shivered, and I knew well it wasn't from having stockinged feet instead of shoes on the garden's bordering flagstone path.

"But you have another pair, right?" I asked. "In case you need to leave before I return?"

"I do. Just take them. It's the least I can do for a Sacred Sister."

"Thank you." I gave her a smile then turned toward the forest, my heart jumping like a child at Yule.

I walked the short distance over the tall grasses that the crowd crushed during the full moon dancing. The Veil blanketed me in a shiver of cold and hot sparks as I passed through. I lifted my chin and inhaled the Gwerhune's special sweet aroma as an animal's path drew me toward a pool of water—a spring, it looked like. Around the pool's border, dark yellow blooms hung heavy on tall stalks and moss the hue of last night's sunset spread like a rich man's rug over the ground. It was soft on my feet, and the mushrooms sprouting here and there in its thick coverage reminded me of the Fae mice who had brought back my slippers.

"I know you're there," I said quietly, not wishing to alert any other Fae beasts. Funny that I was more frightened of them than I was the Unseelie king, the most dangerous beast of them all.

A voice shook my thoughts.

"You're such a rebel, aren't you?" The Unseelie king's voice threaded through the air and caressed my ears. I didn't realize I could be that attracted to a voice alone. "I like that about you. I like that very much."

He emerged from the forest's shade a bit farther

down the animal path. His braids were wet, and he held his vest in his right hand.

My throat tried to close as I studied his chiseled chest and stomach, the way his body narrowed to his hips and how his navel... I looked away quickly. Goddess save me. I'd been staring.

"Don't rush your examination on my behalf," he said, his voice a purr. "I never mind a lady's appreciation. Take your time."

He spun in a slow circle, and as I tried to form a sharp retort to defend my silly self, the angles and lines of his bare back stole every single word away. Taking a breath in an attempt to regain my wits, I set my jaw.

"Pride isn't attractive," I said. I was glad he wasn't bringing up the Fae mice, the beetles, or the cage. He had to know what they'd done to me, or he wouldn't have been able to send those creatures, right? Regardless, I didn't want to waste precious time with him in this beautiful place with talk of the cage.

With speed unlike anything I'd seen, he rushed up to me and pressed his body to mine. His hand splayed over the side of my head and shivers rode down my neck. He leaned close to my ear, drawing the fallen locks of my hair and the edges of my headpiece away. The movements sent another wave of shivers down my body.

"Isn't it?" he whispered.

A pounding heat roared to life inside me, low and

wanting. My mouth was dry, and I hated not knowing what to say or do. But I also loved it. This was so much more thrilling than reading, reciting, and practicing at the temple. This was life. Dangerous. Thrilling. Bright with unknown possibilities.

"My, but you are quiet today," he murmured. "Will you tell me your name so I can stop calling you human female?"

He chuckled and took a step back to look me in the eyes. His were the exact silver of a polished silver coin. Raising his eyebrows, he took my wrist in hand gently and flipped it over, exposing the tattoo every child received to ward off the power Fae had when they knew one's true name. The queen had ordered this new practice after her treaty with the Seelie Queen Revna and the Seelie King Lysanael.

"It's safe for you," he said. "I promise. And I cannot lie."

"I know that. I know." I cleared my throat. Why couldn't I speak clearly around him? "I'm Bronwyn Greensmith. You are?" I wanted to hear him say it.

His eyes pinched like my name meant something to him. "Toren of the Night Realm. Enchanted to meet you, Bronwyn Greensmith." He bowed dramatically, and I flinched just waiting for him to shift into a dragon again.

A dragon. I could hardly believe it.

Two thousand questions whirled around my mind. "Is that what you call the Unseelie Realm? The Night Realm?"

"Well, technically the Realm of Night makes up half of the Unseelie world. The good half. You don't want anything to do with the other half."

"Trolls?"

"Yes, and gargoyles and all sorts of rough creatures who have very little brains but brawn to spare."

"And you...fight them as we used to do here?"

"We have to hunt them on occasion to keep their numbers manageable. There is no kindness in them, only instinct."

I bit my lip. That's exactly what the Seelie said of the Unseelie like him.

"Oh, I know. Our Seelie *brethren*," he said, that last word barbed, "like to say we operate purely on instinct as well, but no, the high Fae of the Night Realm are perhaps more...to the point than the Seelie, but we reason and love just as they do. Of course, we aren't as soft as humans, but..."

He gave me a teasing smile. I raised my eyebrow in disapproval but felt a smile on my mouth. It was madness that I was here in the Fae forest chatting it up with the Unseelie king. Aside from the one male worker at the temple and Drefan, I hadn't even spoken to a man, or a Fae male, since before I joined.

"My father's apprentice used to talk about your kind."

"Oh yes? What does your father do for a living?"

"My parents died from an illness just before I joined the temple, but when they were alive, they ran a sheep farm."

"What could a human sheep farmer know of the Unseelie?" Toren's tone wasn't as arrogant as his words seemed to be. His open gaze showed curiosity.

"I'm not sure, honestly. He liked to talk and acted like an expert on all things."

Toren waved a hand. "I know the type."

I grinned.

"Is that why you joined the temple?" he asked.

"Oh, well, partially, but really it was because of a broken betrothal."

"At fifteen?"

"It's not unheard of. Especially in the area where I grew up."

The muscles in Toren's jaw worked under his smooth skin, and his gaze focused on a spot in the distance. "I'll try to remain polite with you, but human behavior makes it very hard for me to keep my arguments to myself."

"Why are you being polite?"

His lips parted, and his eyes softened like I'd wounded him. I held up my hands.

"I didn't mean to offend you, but as you said, the Unseelie are more to the point. More brazen, perhaps. Politeness doesn't seem to play a role in such a society."

"You are a clever woman, Bronwyn. I want something from you."

A chill swept down my back. "What?"

"I won't take anything from you that you don't wish to give."

A fluttering sensation danced down my chest at his tone, but I held my tongue, wanting him to explain.

He crossed his arms and lowered his chin, his eyes going deadly serious. "Under your temple, there lies an ancient portal."

"A portal you could use to get home?" I chewed my lip.

"Yes. I can't alert the Seelie that I'm here or they'll attack me at best and string me up at worst. I can fight many, but I can't beat an entire army of my fellow Fae."

He wanted to enter the temple to see this portal. "Do you know if it works?"

"I don't. I don't even know if it's in there, in fact. That's where you come in. Can you look around the oldest parts of the temple and tell me if you see any runes or engravings? Perhaps write them down. But keep them in disjointed lines so the magic in your blood doesn't activate them."

I froze. Magic?

❧ 9 ❧
BRONWYN

A flashback of my mother whispering in my ear hit me like a punch to the gut. *Don't do that anymore, cabbage.* I had been playing, moving in circles and watching a hawk soar through the sky. The ground had rumbled softly under my feet. All these years, I'd thought I'd dreamed up that moment or at least exaggerated it. But could it have been more than a child's imagination?

"I have no magic. I'm human."

"So is the Witch."

"Truly?" The powerful lady who worked for kings and queens was the only magic-worker in all the realms not of Fae blood, but I thought she was some other type of person and not human at all.

Toren shrugged and hooked a thumb in the waistband of his trousers. Goddess save me but he was gorgeous. And frightening. I cleared my throat and ignored the smirk blooming to life on his face.

"I'll prove you have power," Toren said. "Dance here. For me."

"Here?" In the middle of the forest? "It's forbidden." I had no idea why, but that fact had been drilled into my head year after year.

His eyes became slits of moonlight, and he pursed his full lips. "Of course, it is. Those who imprison you in that temple are afraid of losing control. If they permit the common folk to have unheeded access to the rituals, they lose their mysterious allure. This mystery of holiness is how superstitions are often created and held over a people. Not all, but many religions are like this. I've even seen it happen in my own realm."

"If anyone finds out, they'll hang me for breaking this rule."

"How would anyone find out? You're cloaked from prying eyes by the forest and..." He raised his nose to the air and sniffed. A chill slipped down my spine. He looked more animal than person. "No more humans present at the moment and only a couple of Seelie Fae."

"Where?" I stepped closer to him and realized I'd taken his wrist in my fingers. I released him, blushing.

He smiled, and his gaze glowed like a banked fire. "They are at least a mile away. They won't be trouble.

Remember, I can hear sounds you cannot. I scent better than any human could dream of."

"We don't dream about improving our sense of smell."

Running a hand over his face, he chuckled. The charcoal-colored claws at the ends of his fingers sent another chill down my back, but this time the sensation accompanied thoughts of those claws lightly dragging across my stomach. I gasped and swallowed. I was an idiot.

He was studying my face. "Don't be ashamed of your desire for me. It's unusual for a human to long for an Unseelie Fae, but it's not unheard of."

"It isn't?"

"I've never experienced it, but then again, I rarely interact with anyone outside of my realm. I've heard stories though."

Interesting. I forced the shame over wanting him into the back of my mind to deal with later. For now, I wanted to know how he could prove I had magic. There was no way I had power like the Witch or the Fae.

"What type of dance should I do?"

"Are there themes to your performances?"

"Yes. Melancholy. Courage. Leaving a loved one. Joy in community. There are thousands of dances."

"How many do you know?"

"I am fully trained in eighty-one dances, but I could

pick up the others easily because the movements are similar with small tweaks."

He rubbed his chin, then pulled his vest over his head, lacing it at the sides. I was glad because it would be easier to focus on dancing without a half-naked monster standing beside me.

"Dance the one for creating joy and let's see how the Gwerhune reacts," he said.

"I think you're crazy, but fine. I'll try it."

I walked a few steps away from the spring's lovely pond and shut my eyes. Inhaling deeply of the forest's delightful scent, my nose caught another aroma—leather and vetiver. Ah. It was Toren's scent. Heat swirled low in my belly and my heart raced. He thought I had magical power. Never in a million years could I have dreamed up something as thrilling as this.

I stretched out my hands in a welcoming gesture and began to dance. Each step and circle of my feet crunched old leaves and whispered through clusters of golden flowers. Spinning twice with my arms wrapped around myself, I imagined my parents returning to see me and demanding my release from the temple. I stomped a foot and the wispy seeds of a knee-high plant lifted into the breeze to swirl in a column of sunshine. Three steps right, then one heel planted. I drew a half-circle in the forest floor with my right toe, but since there were no tiny pebbles here like I was used to my toe made no visual mark.

"Look, Bronwyn Greensmith. Look what your magic has brought."

I lifted my chin to see thousands of the indigo Fae lights whirling in the branches above my head. A laugh fell from my lips, and Toren's subtle smile stole my attention.

"Why? What is happening? Do you know? What are these lights anyway?"

"They are creatures just like a deer or a beetle. Creatures of the Fae Realms, both Seelie and Unseelie, are drawn to magic that relates to something in them. The Unseelie call these creatures pastlights."

"What an interesting name."

"They are said to make people wistful for times in the past. Sounds a bit over the top to me, but..." He shrugged, then crouched and began running his claws lightly over the area where I had danced. "When you dance, the ground shimmers with power."

"I have never seen anything like that."

"No, I don't think humans eyes are capable of seeing all forms of magic." Pointing to a pressed place in the grasses, he looked up at me and his eyebrows lifted. "See here? I think your dances press runic magic into the earth."

I knelt beside him, enjoying the scent of him and the

idea that if anything did come out of the forest at me, he would most likely be able to handle it. I surveyed the surroundings, but nothing looked out of the ordinary to me, well, nothing beyond the Fae plants that I had only recently seen for the first time.

"I don't understand the purpose of this magic."

"You never know," he said cryptically.

We stood and a flock of black and green birds flew overhead, high above in the canopy. Toren's eyes darted, watching them as an animal would rather than a person. He was just so...different.

"Have you decided if you're willing to help me?"

"You want me to explore the oldest sections of the temple and write down any carvings I find?"

"Yes. There should be a set of runes that lead to the portal and that serve to activate its power."

"The oldest section of the library is the lowest level. Two chambers branch on the second set of steps. The eastern chamber has shelving for storage of some ritual scrolls as well as that cage where your Fae beasts found me."

Murder glowed in Toren's eyes—anger on my behalf. I gave him a smile, appreciating that he cared.

"The other chamber houses the oldest scrolls, and only the archivist goes down there. I suppose I could make an excuse to visit. I am known for sticking my nose into old books."

"What do you like to read about?"

"Ancient sacred sites, actually."

"Are you looking for a portal too?" His tone held a joke, and I smiled.

"I thought maybe I could talk House Mother into allowing me to travel to see some of the Old Ones' and the Goddess's wells and temple ruins. I want to see more than this temple and the land immediately around it. My childhood was spent on the farm, seeing only our fields and occasionally going into town to set up a table at the market. My parents were very protective and never allowed me to venture around the other tables though. I have seen so little of the world."

"Such a waste of a life."

"Agreed."

"Well, if you find that portal, I could take you on the grandest adventure." The wicked grin that spread over his handsome face turned my heart over twice.

"I'd like that." I would? I'd like to visit the Unseelie realm just for some fun? I'd lost my mind. "Am I going mad?" A slightly off-kilter laugh bubbled out of me.

Toren took my hand and kissed my knuckles. I held my breath as he paused, his lips warm against my skin. A feeling like a lutestring about to break stretched between us. He met my gaze and heat shot directly to my heart, traveled down my torso, and gathered between my legs.

"The adventure would be worth the risk. I can promise you that, Dancer."

What was this wild sensation inside of me? It was desire; I knew that much. But it was so much more than that. So much stronger than anything I'd felt at fifteen when I'd been head over heels for Gantu. Had I not been fully in love with Gantu? Yes, of course I had been. At least, that's what I'd always said to my parents and to Drefan. I had been in love.

I shook my head and pulled away. "I'll do as you ask and meet you here tomorrow."

"Thank you, Bronwyn Greensmith."

"Why do you keep saying my family name? Is that a good manners habit of the Unseelie or something else?"

"I like how you don't tiptoe around questions. It's because your family name demands respect of me as the Unseelie king."

"Why?"

"You should go. I will answer you when next we meet."

I glanced over my shoulder to see a servant and Seersha walking through the garden. It looked like their heads were on swivels. They had to be looking for me. My hour was up.

"Goodbye, King Toren." I gave him a nod then hurried away.

Keeping to the shadows, I waited until Seersha and

the servant disappeared inside the library. I dashed from the forest, holding my breath and praying no one would see me leaving the Gwerhune.

I jogged through the garden area, cracked the tower's door open, and hurried toward my chamber. The hallway was silent except for the sound of everyone practicing their dances in their own rooms. I'd have to come up with some reason Seersha had missed me. Maybe I'd used the main hall's water closet. Yes, that might work.

The wood of the corridor outside my chamber creaked, and I turned to see House Mother standing there, a flash of anger in her cold, cold eyes.

10

TOREN

Toren rubbed a knuckle over his lips as he pondered the last few days. Bronwyn was the kindest person he'd ever met. Granted, he didn't know her well, but he felt as though he could see straight through her beautiful body into her soul to see it shine with goodness. There was dark in her too, as there was in all, but she was so open-minded about him and so incredibly brave to visit him here. She was naive due to her sheltered life, but it wasn't as if she didn't know there were inherent dangers in knowing him. And yet she came.

His chest tightened, and he pressed a fist against his knocking heart. Seeing the forest through her eyes was like being born a child once more, full of wonder and joy. She wasn't a fool. She was simply...youthful in her appreciation of the world. And he didn't think that was due to anything she'd been through. That was just how she was —delighted with life. Trapping her in that tomb of a temple was a crime.

Stars peered through the forest's canopy and revealed constellations over Bronwyn's prison. It was time to hunt. Toren shifted into his dragon form, relaxing into the familiar prickle of his magic and the pleasant sensation of his wings spreading wide. He took off and headed northwest. The wind lifted him, and he barely had to move his wings as he soared just below the canopy.

Keeping his nose alert for any Seelie, he searched the forest for movement. Moss deer were plentiful in this area, and so far he'd been able to evade the wild Seelie's notice by keeping to the untraveled areas of the forest. He sniffed the wind and caught the scent of a stag he'd missed out on last night. This time, he would take that prize and eat his fill. Sweeping down through the branches of the cedars that dominated this area of the western forest, he extended his talons and latched onto the stag. He landed and a gasp sounded behind him. Keeping hold of the stag, he rotated to see what unfortunate soul had found him here.

It was a wild Seelie, clothes ragged and hair tangled above a pale face. "An Unseelie dragon," the Seelie whispered.

A second wild Seelie strode out of the brush, holding

a bow with a nocked arrow. "This tip is pure bloodiron, Unseelie. You're about to die a painful death."

Both Seelie laughed, and the armed one let his arrow fly. Toren had no doubt it was true. They were like him and couldn't lie. He had no time to leap into the air to escape or to fight, so he unleashed his dragon fire.

A rippling, blazing stream leapt from Toren's throat and into the air, the fire directed at the Seelie and their arrow. The heat of the white flame melted the arrow into nothing and burned through the two Seelie before they could shout for help. They were dead and he had killed them. He shook his head, wishing for the thousandth time that he was back home.

Toren turned away from the scorched earth and set his mind to feasting on the stag.

Once he finished and cleaned his snout in the river's cold water, he flew back to the place where he met with Bronwyn. Shifting into his high Fae form, he prepared to sleep. Hopefully, no one would miss those two Seelie. The last thing he needed was a group of them coming after him. If he killed too many, word would get out that something was amiss in the Gwerhune. Even if King Lysanael wasn't currently in his kingdom, his generals would be and they would march on the threat in the Gwerhune with all their usual efficiency. They wouldn't wait to listen to Toren's explanations about why he was there or why he'd been forced to kill Seelie. No, they would fire on him with the rare bloodiron they hoarded and he would die screaming at their feet. His people would be left leaderless. He should have named an heir ages ago. His friend Flok was right about that, and he regretted pushing off the responsibility.

Sleep evaded him, and he decided it was time to irritate those temple leaders who were unkind to his dancer.

He grinned, crooked a finger of his right hand, and pressed his left palm against the earth. "Grow and pinch and sting the evil ones. Leave the goldhearted alone."

His grandfather had taught him this magic, and it had been Toren's favorite trick as a naughty youth.

"But you don't hurt the good ones," Grandfather had said.

"How does it know who is good?"

"All are good and bad, but some are goldhearted and even their bad isn't so bad."

The old Fae had always spoken in riddles, but Toren had loved spending winter nights with him. They'd practiced Unseelie magic by the warmth of the hearth fire. So many stories...

The ground under Toren's palm rumbled and erupted with thorns peaked in silver. Crawling toward the wall, the thorns moved swiftly toward their target. Once they disappeared over the wall, Toren could no longer track their movements, but he knew the process. The magical plant would bury itself in the soil around the temple and prick those who had dark hearts. He was glad the spell wasn't directed at him because he knew well he was no goldheart.

Once the magic was complete and the sizzle and spark of power faded from his hands, he tucked himself into the roots of an oak and shut his eyes.

A scream of pain woke him, a scream too sharp and too full of pain to be the result of his small thorns. He stood, heart pounding. The fine hairs on his arms stood on end. That was the sound of someone being broken. And he knew that voice. Rage boiled through his blood.

"Bronwyn."

His body rippled with power. Scales layered their way down his limbs. Magic sparked along his jaw and over his eyes, altering his vision so he could see every blade of grass, every beating heart inside that temple. He lifted his dragon head and roared as he took flight and aimed for the ones who dared to hurt his dancer.

BRONWYN

"You will tell me where you wandered." House Mother paced as I knelt before her. My knees were chilled by the wooden floorboards outside Seersha's and my bedchamber.

She wouldn't believe a lie that had me wandering in a normal place. No, when her vein throbbed at the side of her head like that, I had to admit to something even if I hadn't done anything wrong. Pretending innocence here would only worsen her reaction.

I bowed my head. "I went to the market." Her pacing halted, and I stared at the toes of her silken slippers that peeked out from under her black and red robes. "I just wanted to see the wares and the people."

Slowly, she approached me. She grasped my chin and

roughly raised my head. I met her gaze, forcing any fear or deception from my face.

"You are not a person. You are an acolyte. The market is filthy, and though many respect us, there are people who would steal you and sell you."

"Life can't be lived without some risk," I blurted, snapping my mouth shut the moment the words were out. I just couldn't hold my tongue even when I knew better. It's not as if I could win her over and persuade her to relax the rules.

Her fingers left my chin to lace themselves around my throat. Pressure built and made my eyes water. I coughed against her hold, spots dancing in front of my face. The scent of her soap burned my eyes.

"You deserve to die for throwing your blessed self into the dirty crowd. A place where coins are traded and animals are slaughtered. I can already see the rope around this throat. Do you not remember your oath?"

The fact that she smeared my runes was more frightening than the choking. She didn't want answers. I couldn't speak anyway. Darkness swarmed at the edges of my vision.

"You promised," she hissed, "to remain pure. Chaste."

If she only knew about everything I'd done with Gantu...

"Unblemished by marketplaces and crowds," she

continued, "as well as the hands of lovers. And yet, you break this oath like the Goddess means nothing to you. What am I to do with you?"

With what I could only describe as a snarl, she released me and I fell back gasping for air. She grabbed me by the hair and dragged me down the corridor away from my bedchamber. I scrambled to keep my feet under me, but it was impossible. Pain lanced through my scalp. My foot turned as she pulled me and my knee bashed against the floor, sending agony echoing up my leg. At the stairs, she paused. Would she throw me down?

Two servants had stopped their sweeping on the landing below, but at a look from her, they went back to their work.

I wanted to stand. To shove her down the stairs. Rage simmered inside me like bees trapped in a fallen tree.

She eyed me once more, then shouted, "Mannix!"

Mannix came running. His shirt was damp under the arms from his efforts cleaning the gutters around the library's roof.

"Take her to the library basement and chain her to the wall."

Chain me? I'd thought those chains were ancient, and I'd never seen them used. Maybe this time, I really would die by her hands.

Mannix paled. "House Mother..." His gaze went to me and melted. He'd always had a soft spot for me.

"Do it, or I will and that will be worse for her," House Mother said.

I didn't doubt that, so I didn't fight as Mannix took my arm and led me out of the first tower and into the garden courtyard. I squinted, trying to see into the Gwerhune. The urge to call for Toren pushed against my closed mouth. I couldn't ask him to save me; he'd lose his life if the Seelie caught him. Mannix threw the library door open like he was trying to get this awful chore over with quickly.

We passed a servant and a small crowd of acolytes and priestesses who gathered in the main room of the library. Their accusatory glares didn't burn me like they had when I was younger. They were just products of House Mother's cruelty and of the cult of this place. For the thousandth time, I wondered if the temple had been lovely and good when Beanie had been fully capable in her former role as House Mother—before she'd handed over the reins.

We hurried down the stairs, the light dimming as the chill of the partially underground chamber wafted over my skin.

There, behind the cage, were the dusty shackles and chains hanging on the back wall. I swallowed bile, and my legs shook. I fisted my hands. The idea of revenge kept me from vomiting from utter fear.

"I'm sorry for this." Mannix lifted one of my hands and shackled my wrist to the wall. "I don't agree with how she runs the temple."

My mouth fell open. He'd never spoken more than three words to me, to anyone. "It was different when Beanie, I mean, House Mother Beatrice was fully in charge. Wasn't it? That's what I remember anyway."

"Very different." He secured my other wrist, then looked me in the eye. "I will come down here and release you if House Mother decides to... Well, if things get worse. You should know that I have an illegitimate child, and one of House Mother's sisters keeps her in town. If I go against House Mother, I will have to grab my daughter and run. She is too powerful in this city."

"I had no idea." A daughter? "How is keeping a child to control her father a blessed way to live?" I practically snarled my rhetorical question.

"Exactly. House Mother is no blessed sacrifice to the Star Goddess. She is a demon," he whispered, his words like knives cutting away what little faith I had left in this place, but igniting the rebel inside me even further. Toren had called me a rebel, and the name felt right. Could I find a way out of this? If I did, how could I rebel?

The best way would be to escape this place as Toren

had mentioned. But a portal? It seemed like a fever dream. Nothing magical sat in this dank, cold place.

Mannix left without another word, and I stood against the wall, my arms pulled high above my head as the sunlight turned bloody through the cracked window set into the stone wall. Toren's creatures had broken open the bottom corner though no one had yet noticed. How I wished I could grow small and escape like the Fae mice had.

What felt like a month passed as I waited for the inevitable.

At last, House Mother arrived.

And she had a knife.

"I'm going to cut the darkness out of you."

The heat simmering inside me boiled over, flushing out all fear. "Why don't you just kill me like you did Penelope?"

Her cold, calculating gaze darted sideways at me as she set the knife on the floor and began rolling up her robe's sleeves.

I wanted to poke her until she seemed rattled. I couldn't stand that emotionless face of hers. Toren's words filtered through my memory. Magic.

"Is it because I have magic in my blood?"

Eyes wide, she gripped her rolled sleeve with shaking fingers. "Madness. No humans have magic, except for the crown's Witch."

The confidence in her tone was convincing, but the narrowing of her eyes said she was lying. *She knew I had magic.*

My blood rushed with the knowledge and the desperation of how I could use it to survive this. Toren had been right, and what had happened in the forest hadn't been an odd coincidence. I had power. But I also had no idea how to use it.

Retrieving the knife, she straightened and looked at me with those dead eyes. When she set the blade against the runes painted across my chest, just below my collar-bone, I locked my jaw, refusing to cry out or beg for mercy.

I held out as long as I could before a scream took flight from my throat.

12

TOREN

As a dragon, Toren launched into the night sky. Though the scream hadn't happened but once, the raw sound echoed over and over in his mind. He pictured Bronwyn's eyes squeezed shut, a tear blurring the runes on her cheek, and her chest rising and falling in her distress. He roared out his anger into the night, no longer caring if the Seelie saw him. Rage against Bronwyn's enemies burned through any fears for himself. They were hurting her, the kindest soul he'd ever met. The dancer was a rare gem, priceless in heart and in body. Her enemies were about to feel his wrath.

Diving toward the third tower, he built speed and coaxed fire into his throat. Bronwyn's muffled scream had come from the library. He could destroy this tower without injuring her.

His Unseelie magic sparked across his chest and over his partially tucked wings. A jolt of negative energy hit him like a fist to the throat as he crossed the wards, but the sensation faded quickly enough. The wards couldn't stop him in his dragon form. At the last moment before he hit the tower, he turned and stretched out his back talons. He grasped the conical roof and tore the tiles and supporting wood away. New screams erupted from the structure but none came from Bronwyn. He could hear the differences in the voices quite easily.

Wheeling around, he aimed at the tower entrance and blew dragon fire. Flames billowed from his mouth, not nearly as hot as his rage. Flying high again, he rammed a foot into the tower and stones fell, leaving a gaping hole. Two beds sat in the exposed chamber, and humans ran in every direction.

He soared low over the library, scenting the air for her. Many inhabitants fled the structures and ran away from the temple and into the town, but still, Bronwyn didn't appear. Turning back with the flames of rage burning him, he drove his whole body into the third tower and shook it on its foundation.

13

BRONWYN

Dust filled the basement, blocking my view of House Mother and her knife. She coughed and from the sound it seemed as though she was at the window, probably trying to figure what was happening.

"Goddess, save us," she said, her voice tight. I'd never heard her panicked. "It's an Unseelie monster. A gray dragon."

I sucked in a breath. Toren. He'd heard me and come to save me. This was bad. Very bad. Granted, House Mother wasn't hurting me any longer, but now Toren's presence was revealed—his dragon form, at least.

The wall behind me shuddered, and the rumble of falling stone sounded in the ceiling. He was tearing the temple apart.

"Unshackle me. You want me alive for some reason so let me go. I'll die in the rubble if you don't."

Why she wanted me alive, I had no idea, but if anyone else had been caught in the Gwerhune especially when they weren't supposed to be Wandering, they would have been dead already.

Her silhouette showed in the candlelit dust as she hurried back to me. She took out a key and unlocked the shackles. "Do not try to flee." Her eyelashes were thick with fine debris, and her hair was covered in pale specks.

She ran toward the stairs and I followed her, warm blood running down my chest. I had no idea what I was going to do once I saw Toren. How aware was he in his dragon form? Would he know me? Would the others know he was a high Fae in his animal form or would they simply think he was a regular Unseelie dragon? I didn't know how to tell the difference between shifting Fae and creatures who were simply what they were.

Outside the library, the courtyard was a disaster.

Where was Toren? The sky was empty of all but the smoke of a fire blazing from the wooden roof beams of the third tower. Toren had nearly ripped the structure in half and most of the roof tiles lay smashed in the court-yard. I could see right into the main floor. Broken walls slumped and dropped more stone, Yasha and Poesin shouted orders, Mannix called for help, and smoke billowed thicker and thicker from the roof.

A shriek from another acolyte had me eyeing the sky again. Sure enough, Toren circled above. Smoke his fire had wrought cloaked his wings. He looked down on me and roared so loudly that my chest and feet vibrated, and then he shot across the night and returned to the Gwerhune. Goddess, but he was magnificent.

"House Mother!" a man's shout carried from the front gate beyond the tower closest to the road.

I recognized that voice. It was Drefan. At least a dozen city guards stood behind him as well as other warriors. The guards wore the gold and black livery of our city mayor and the additional warriors were in the scarlet of the royal House of Saxonion.

Drefan's burnished gold hair stood out in the darkness and the torches his men carried shining off the metal studs in his leather armor. "House Mother! Invite me in. We are here to help. Please tell me I'm wrong, but was that a dragon?"

"Yes, and it was no forest dragon either," she said, her face pinched. She hesitated with her hand on the front gate and her gaze traveling over Drefan's face. "No interfering aside from defense and repair?"

Drefan's lips parted, then he noticed me behind her. His gaze snapped to the blood running down the front of my robes. His throat moved in a swallow, then he set his gaze on House Mother, wariness replacing the concern that had been there. "Agreed."

"You are welcome to enter this Star Goddess temple." House Mother swung the gate wide and the warriors hurried in.

Immediately, they went to work with buckets they'd brought, drawing water from our well and handing the buckets across a line of men so they could put out the last of Toren's flames. At least, I hoped it was the last of the flames. Most of the tower was stone so it wouldn't have as much fuel as it would have had in town where people built their homes of wood and plaster.

After Poesin cleaned and bandaged the wound given to me by House Mother, I helped her tend to Yasha who'd cut her arm deeply on a piece of cracked timber that had fallen through the stairwell. I went to fetch more bandages from the library's basement, but before I finished crossing the courtyard, Drefan found me.

"Tell me what you saw." His gaze shot back and forth across my face as he examined my wound and the ruined runes on my cheeks. He wiped a bit of ash from his upper lip and whispered, "Do you need help here? Cross your arms if you do."

What would he do if I told him I knew the dragon personally, and with the Unseelie king on my side, I was going to be just fine? I nearly laughed, my head feeling far too light to be healthy.

He frowned and offered a skin of water. I took it and drank as much as I dared. My stomach turned as I handed the skin back to Drefan. I was pretty sure I was about to be sick.

"We'll call in the Fae border guard," Drefan said.

My limbs went cold.

"They know how to handle the monsters from their cousin realm," he said.

I fisted my hands and tried not to be sick. This was awful. I wasn't fine. I was stuck here still, and Toren wouldn't be able to help me. He would be killed by the Seelie. Even if he regained his reason and stayed away, they would hunt him down. I couldn't let that happen.

"The creature is gone now," I said shakily. "Perhaps the wards scared him off. Maybe they hurt him somehow."

"The wards have only ever held back humans and Fae. Animals aren't affected. You see birds here in your gardens, don't you?"

The man thought I was daft. "I do. I'm sure you're right," I said, trying to placate him. "But he's gone." I gripped my robes. "I mean, the dragon is gone. It'll be fine."

"And this?" He nodded at my wounds.

It was kind of him to care, especially since he was going against everything we, as a city, had been taught. Parents raised their children to have full faith in the temple and upheld the idea that the temple leaders were always right. I couldn't throw his brave kindness in his face. Plus, maybe a swordsman's presence would curb House Mother's violent ways.

"Maybe if you station one soldier here…"

"Oh, we'll have more than that present." He looked toward the stars, surely watching for the dragon. "As I said, I want some Fae border guards to keep watch. If House Mother will allow it, we'll ask them to remain awhile too. I always wondered when trouble would come from being this close to the Realm of Lights."

"Being close to the Fae Realm might have nothing to do with it. There are drumstones everywhere."

"Far more of them in the Gwerhune," he said.

"True." I couldn't argue that.

"I wonder how that dragon slipped through the sealed stones. It's a mystery." Drefan shook his head, then nodded in respect. "Please, find a place to rest and I'll send our healer over."

"Thank you, but the servants set it to rights. I have to fetch more bandages for the others."

Drefan bowed and left quickly to join his men by the ruined tower.

I had to get to Toren to warn him that an entire unit would be headed for him soon, but I couldn't leave yet. These people needed help.

Exhaling, I began bringing water to those affected by the smoke and checking on various acolytes and priestesses to see if everyone was accounted for. I had to be careful with my wound though. The cut pinched as I moved and I was afraid of it beginning to bleed once more. The fire in the tower blazed up again, and we all joined in the effort to douse the top floor with well water for a second time. I had to redo my bandage three times.

The Seelie Fae unit arrived. They stood a head taller than the rest and the quivers on their backs held arrows fletched in gold and green. One pointed toward the garden wall near where I had crawled over. The Fae male next to him went to the wall, pulled out an arrow, and nocked it. As the archer turned slightly, the flames Toren had left in his wake flickered off the blood red tip of the arrowhead.

Bloodiron. If that arrow hit Toren, he would die. It was poison to the Unseelie.

I took another bucket from Seersha, who was actually very focused on our duty, and handed it to the next person in line, Mannix.

Once the flames were doused, House Mother called all the priestesses to the ceremony room for a meeting. In my undamaged chamber in the first tower, I changed into clean robes by myself and reapplied my runes as best I could. All the servants were at work elsewhere.

By the time I returned to the garden area, the city guardsmen, the Fae unit, and everyone still awake were erecting temporary wooden structures to house those without a room. It was managed chaos—the usual rules and procedures completely thrown out the window. I could have stood on my head naked and no one would have noticed for how hard they were working.

Two city guards manned the front temple entrance. As they spoke to one another about the Fae unit, I walked right past them and through the gate like I was doing exactly as I was meant to, and they didn't say a word. *I should have had a dragon attack the temple earlier,* I thought, snorting at myself. I hurried down the dark street until I could slip behind the cooper's workshop, then doubled back toward the edge of the city and to the Gwerhune. So far, no one had followed me. Even if House Mother had someone trailing me, I had to risk discovery to warn Toren.

"Please just stay away, you beautiful beast, you," I whispered into the night.

❧ 14 ❧

BRONWYN

In the Gwerhune, I cupped my mouth and quietly called out Toren's name, aiming my voice toward the canopy of leaves lit by the pastlights. "Where are you?" I said, a bit louder now.

Insects chirruped high above and small creatures ran this way and that as I walked along the animal path.

"Toren?"

Still no answer.

He hadn't been injured, had he? It was a possibility. Perhaps one of the guards had spotted the dark shape in the sky before even reaching the temple's gate and taken aim. What if Toren was out here, broken and bleeding? If any Seelie came upon him like that, they'd kill him. Or any number of Fae beasts could attack while he was vulnerable.

The brushy growth beyond the animal path shuffled, and I froze. A sapling bent almost in half and a snuffling came from the shadows.

Shaking, I gripped my robes, ready to run. I should have brought a weapon. But of course, I had never been trained to use a blade or bow so would it have been of any help? My heart tapped insistently on my ribs, urging me to run back to the temple, to the threats that I was at least familiar with.

My only power was the one that Toren claimed I possessed—my dance, my movements and the shapes they drew into the earth. Perhaps a show of power would keep any Fae predators at bay? I released my robes and stood in the starting position for the dance of Bravery. But would it give me courage or embolden the monster stalking me?

Cold with fear, I stepped carefully in a westerly direction, then turned a slow circle, stopping to stamp my other foot in rhythmic patterns of three as the cut hiding under my bandage thumped with pain. The indigo pastlights gathered around me, their glow growing brighter.

A growl vibrated through the forest, humming along my bones, and I began shaking harder, but I didn't miss a step. I kept shifting my weight, drawing lines in the air with my fingers and on the ground with my slippered feet. The pastlights swirled above me like flying sparks from an invisible bonfire.

A bear with a coat that began as dark fur then grew as ivy past his shoulders ambled out of the woods. I paused, my feet longing to take off running. His eyes glowed with the hue of the pastlights. My blood slowed, icing me to the core, but I started moving again, my body remembering the steps while my mind twisted with imaginings of every way this could go.

The dance called for a wide circle made with small sideways movements made with the balls of my feet. Careful, tiny steps that created a large ring. With my arms outstretched and my chin lifted as if I didn't have a worry in the world, I created the circle.

The bear didn't move.

Forcing myself to breathe, I bent my knees and tilted my head as I took the final position of the dance.

With a grunt, the bear pawed the earth and threw dirt and leaves toward the invisible circle. My limbs trembled. I was going to pass out. Then the bear of fur and ivy turned and lumbered back into the darkness.

I breathed out and nearly collapsed.

"Very well done, Dancer."

My heart leapt. I spun to see Toren's silver eyes flashing. He rushed to me, his movements too fast to see. With one clawed fingertip, he gently touched the area around my bandaged cut. I shivered, the touch frightening but also...delightfully thrilling.

I took hold of his hand. "Careful," I said, wary of the runes that crossed my cheeks and ran around my bandage.

"I can't believe they did this to you," he said, his voice built of ice and steel.

A cut marred his smooth forehead. The blood there was clotted now beside a mottled bruise. His upper arm was swollen.

"You've been hurt too."

He made a sound in his throat that seemed like a dismissal of his injuries. As he studied my bandages, then examined me for more wounds, lifting my hands and examining the flesh that peered from the depths of my robes. But there was no leering gaze or blatant desire —only concern shone in his otherworldly eyes. The muscles around his jawline worked beneath his gray skin and his nostrils flared. His lips lifted to bare his Fae fangs. A chill ran down my back.

"Give me the description of who cut you," he said. "They will die slowly the next time I shift."

"No, no, no, Toren. You can't go after anyone. You shouldn't have come for me."

"Why in the hells not?"

He pressed closer until my back was against a tree. His hands gripped my waist, claws almost digging in but not yet painful. His thick eyebrows knotted, and his sharp cheekbones reflected the pastlights floating above us. He was anger incarnate. I had to remind myself his rage was on my behalf instead of aimed at me as the anger I'd seen in my life thus far.

I set a hand on his bare arm to soften my words, to let him know I was aware of his concern and grateful for the regard behind it. "Because of your attack, the temple now has a Seelie Fae unit stationed there. Maybe permanently. They have bloodiron."

His gaze snapped to a break in the trees in the direction of the temple.

"I saw them myself," I said. "Their arrows are tipped in bloodiron."

His gaze bore into mine. "Red as blood?"

I nodded. "They will hunt you here now. You can't expose yourself."

He set his forehead against mine. "Can you get me inside the temple tonight? I'll seek the runes myself, and we can escape before dawn."

Escape. He said the word like it was truly possible. Was it? "Will we find the runes that easily?"

Pulling away, he lifted one shoulder in a type of shrug. "If not, we will try again the following night. There's no way they can know if you invited someone in, correct? I've seen such warding magic before, but I don't know the details of the specific spell set on your temple."

"No, they won't know unless they witness it themselves. I have to be on temple grounds though. At least, I'm fairly certain that's how it works. But if we don't find a way out tonight, where can I hide you? The guards will be everywhere."

"They won't be in the lower levels. It's not a threat from the inside. They will focus on the sky stretching between the temple and the Gwerhune."

That made sense. "All right. Then I can get you to the two basement chambers. I know that path well enough." Bitterness colored my words.

Toren set his forehead against mine. It was such a tender gesture. My stomach tightened, and I relaxed into him a fraction.

"The basement chambers are the lowest level that your folk use this day and age?" His breath stirred the loose strands of my hair.

"Yes," I said.

"I'm not certain the portal will be accessible through the basement, but it's the best place to start looking."

My head pounded, and I shut my eyes. "If they catch you..."

His hips pressed close to me, and the beat of his heart touched my chest. "I'll take down as many as I can before they end me. Describe your tormentor. I will take that human out first."

A fluttering sensation filled me. "No, you can't attack House Mother."

"The female who was standing beside you? She is as good as dead."

I shouldn't have liked his murderous rage as much as I did. "Toren, no. You must be cautious."

He slid his hands up my back and pulled me against his muscled chest and flat stomach.

"Careful of my runes." My voice was husky and strange.

He pulled away a fraction, and his silver eyes flashed with some emotion I didn't recognize. What did it say about me that his mention of killing someone put butterflies in my stomach? Honestly, I didn't care. House Mother deserved whatever he doled out. I just didn't want him to end up dead or injured for me.

"What happens if we do get through the portal and into your realm? Do I stay? I don't want to come back. I have nothing to return to."

His fingers tangled in my hair and he tilted his head, his eyes half-lidded. "You are welcome to stay in my castle until the end of your days, Dancer. You will live as you see fit and I will end anyone who gets in your way."

I took a slow, shaky breath and looked at his chest and the way it rose and fell. This was all too good to be true. Granted, the Unseelie realm was filled with dangerous beasts, but it wasn't as if my world had proved kind. Raising my chin, I met his gaze. "Thank you." A smile ghosted over my lips. "I think I'd like that."

He set his lips gently on my forehead and his warm breath brushed my temple. I breathed deeply of his scent and leaned into him as much as I dared.

"This is madness," I said, "but we should go now while everyone is distracted. Follow me."

"As you order, Lady Dancer. I am yours to command."

15

TOREN

Drawing his hood low over his head, Toren followed Bronwyn through the Veil, out of the Gwerhune, and into the human city. He'd been this deep into human lands once, on a dare.

Bronwyn turned a corner at a roughly plastered smith's forge and looked back at him. "What are you snickering about?"

"I was fondly recalling the last time I was loosed upon a human city."

"What did you do?"

"*What didn't I do* would be the better question." He aimed a wicked grin at her and was pleased to see a blush fill her cheeks. His body pulsed with want. Once they were out of danger, he would make her do so much more than blush if she permitted it.

Graceful as usual, she hurried from shadow to shadow as they passed the city fountain. Fresh-smelling water gurgled from what appeared to be a gargoyle's mouth. Humans were so odd.

"Tell me about that night. It will keep my mind off the madness of our little plan here," Bronwyn said.

"All right. But remember, you asked to know."

"Consider me warned."

His heart lifted at her joking tone. For one who had lived the last several years of her life in such a suffocating style, she was certainly flirtatious and daring. Perhaps it was due to that naiveté. She didn't know better than to ask him, the King of the Unseelie, about his youthful mischievous activities.

He sidestepped a puddle of mucky water—humans were disgusting—and sidled past a row of shuttered windows. Just in front of him, Bronwyn's robes fluttered in the night breeze, making her look like a spirit.

"It began with stealing a barrel of a spirit you humans call pine wine."

Bronwyn's head swiveled, her all-too-innocent eyes wide. "Isn't that drink horribly strong?"

Toren smiled. "It is."

The corner of Bronwyn's lips lifted, and Toren's stomach lifted like he'd jumped from a high tree. Damn female was twisting him up. Like some sweet doe that was on the verge of turning into a barrow demon. Fascinating.

"Once we had our fill of the pine wine——"

"Who was with you?"

"My friend, Flok, a whip-thin maniac who thrives on violence, and my brother, Thor, who died at the hands of a gargoyle the very next moon." An invisible hand pressed on Toren's chest, and he silently whispered a blessing for his lost brother.

"I'm sorry for your loss."

"Abide in starlight."

She blinked at him. Of course she didn't know Unseelie tradition.

"When one wishes another something kind, we respond with that phrase. It's meant to be a blessing."

"Oh, that's lovely. Thank you."

She was definitely going to need him by her side at all times in the Realm of Night if she was going to survive. She was far too soft.

"Flok had a map of this city...how do you pronounce it?"

"Veilbury."

"Yes, and he led my brother and I to a storage building where the humans, where your kind, kept firestars."

"When was this?"

"It's hard to say because time moves differently for

Fae in this realm versus my own domain. So of course, we took up every firestar we could carry and tucked them into the finest ship in the bay."

"I wonder if it belonged to the pirate king. I heard something about his ship a long time ago."

"I couldn't tell you, but the display it provided was outstanding."

Bronwyn led him around a corner as she chuckled and shook her head. "We're nearly there."

"While the human males ran to fight the fire that jumped from the ship to the dock, we slipped into their beds and tempted their females."

"You didn't..." Her voice blazed with righteous anger.

It hurt that she would think such a thing of him. "No, I would never force a female. I have no need." He waited until she glanced his way to slowly lower his gaze. "I simply offered them what they were afraid to admit they wanted." He slid his focus down the pale column of her throat as the pulse just under her skin leapt.

"Females, I mean, women aren't always afraid to speak their needs," she said.

He stepped closer to her. The warmth of her body radiated through the cool night air to touch his bare arm. "True. Are you one who does or does not?" Gently, he drew one claw over the inside of her wrist, then dragged it to the crook of her elbow. Her skin pebbled and heat shot through him. A very insistent part of him wanted her on the ground beneath him. Now.

"You'll just have to find out." The admonishment in her doe eyes only made the heat in him increase. "And so will I," she whispered more to herself as she faced the road.

His heart hammered and his hands grew slick. Hells, but she made him sweat. Never once had a female made him so desirous and nervous at the same moment.

"I'll go in through the front," she said. "Do you see that pine near the first tower's roof?"

"You want me to climb the tree and enter the temple through the first tower's roof."

She nodded. "But wait until I have whispered the invitation from that front courtyard there. I think your Fae ears will hear a whisper from here, yes?"

"I can hear your heart beating as well as the jokes between the guards stationed in the garden."

She spun, her mouth open. "On the other side of the temple grounds?"

"Yes."

"Impressive. All right. I'm going." She reached back and squeezed his hand briefly before hurrying to the front gate with her head held high.

Toren flexed the hand she'd squeezed, his heart thudding in his ears. He was doomed. Exhaling, he pushed everything from his mind and listened to her approach the guards.

"...and I had to get something for the healer."

"Of course, Sacred Sister," the first guard said as the second opened the gate for her.

She disappeared behind a row of shrubbery, so Toren leaned against the building serving as his hiding place and prepared himself to wait for the sound of her whisper. He would wait for any amount of time she demanded. Eons. Ages. Until the end of all realms.

His dancer had him by the heartstrings.

❧ 16 ❧

BRONWYN

Three guards stood at the garden wall. Drefan and two Fae. The rest must have gone home for the night or were resting in the makeshift shelter they'd put up in the corner of the garden. If anyone was watching—House Mother or the servants—they needed to see me head to bed. Even though the day had been wildly unusual for the temple way of life, the excitement was over and I was expected to get my rest so I could serve the Goddess properly. I entered the tower and started up the winding stairs.

"Where are you scuttling in from?" Seersha's voice stopped me.

I looked down at her. Standing on the main floor, she held a cup and a cloth.

"I should ask you the same," I said.

The sounds of men talking rose, and it was so odd to hear in this place.

"Never mind," Seersha said, joining me on the stairs. "Everything is out of place right now, and I don't have the energy to give you trouble."

"I'm glad of that." I feigned a yawn. Truly, I was wide awake. "Have you heard anything else about the dragon?"

She walked with me to our room, sipping from her cup. "No, House Mother is nowhere to be seen, so I assume she is meeting with the town council. She'll have to be in cleansing all day tomorrow."

Only House Mother could do such a thing as attend an outsiders' meeting.

I had to invent a reason to leave our room again so I could go back outside and invite Toren in. "Oh, I forgot my ritual book."

Seersha only rolled her eyes and began readying herself for bed. "I suppose we'll have to do without servants tonight. They're all with the injured. Did you see that Mannix has a broken arm?"

"No, he was fine earlier."

"He fell trying to right a roof beam."

"That's awful."

"I guess the Fae and the city guards will have to do our labor until he is healed?" A spark of mischief lit her eyes.

I wanted to trust her and joke along, but I had done that before and watched as she reported my every word to House Mother. Seersha delighted in luring me in and then getting me in trouble. So instead of playing along, I shrugged and left the room before she could go on.

I SNUCK OUT THE SERVANTS' DOOR OF THE TOWER AND crept into the dark front courtyard. Curling my hands around the cold stone of the temple wall, I whispered into the dark, "I invite you in, King Toren."

He was there in a heartbeat, silver gaze on my cheek like a kiss and his clawed fingers taking hold of the wall before he leapt over with the agility of a stag.

"Lead me, Bronwyn Greensmith."

"Someday, you'll have to tell me why you like my family name so much."

"Someday."

I brought him to the side of the tower where the dark was like ink. Everyone had to be asleep by now, and even the guards stationed at the garden wall facing the Gwerhune had gone quiet, fatigue silencing their jokes and ruminations. Drefan and the two Fae warriors stood under the torch's flickering light.

Would Drefan help me if he knew what I was doing? No, definitely not. He would see this whole endeavor as ludicrous. He would want to kill Toren without asking questions. Drefan was a good man, but he didn't dance outside the stones as the saying here went.

"The Fae will hear your footsteps."

I nodded and held up a finger. I had a plan. I pressed a hand against Toren's chest, his leather armor warm against the musculature of his body. *Stay here*, I mouthed, knowing his Fae eyes could see my lips. His eyes glowed in the dark like an animal's.

Walking like it was normal to stroll at midnight, I made my way to the temple's library.

"Everything well, Sacred Sister?" Drefan's voice stopped my feet.

"Very well, thank you." I gave him a genuine smile.

He tilted his head, his lips parted as if he wanted to say more, but then he turned around again, ever the dutiful soldier.

I opened the library door, taking my time to signal to Toren that it was now or never.

A rush of cool air told me he had entered the library behind me. The place was as dark as a tomb and the cavernous vaulted ceilings swallowed the echo of our feet on the stone floors. I rushed toward the narrow steps that led down to the lower levels.

Feeling my way with my hands against the walls, I moved carefully and tried not to think about the shackles and the cage that we were about to see. We walked through one more level of stored scrolls, then down another flight of steps.

"Remember I told you there are two chambers on the lowest level. But I just now recalled that the first chamber was added during a tunneling project. Beanie, the former House Mother, told me about it. So I'm going straight to the other one."

At last, we made it. Fumbling for the flint and striker House Mother kept on the table beside the base of the stairs, I took comfort from Toren's presence behind me. He wouldn't let anyone put me in that cage. He'd help me fight if we were caught. Why did I trust him? Well, he'd shifted into a dragon at the sound of my scream and interrupted my torture once already.

I lit the wide beeswax candle and filled the room with a golden glow that seemed wrong considering what it housed.

"That's where she kept you." He threw the words like daggers into the dusty chamber.

I didn't answer. He'd sent the night creatures to me. He knew.

"I saw through their eyes, you know," he said quietly, his voice still deadly. I had no doubt that if House Mother showed up right now, he would kill her. "Don't you want revenge?"

"You say that like it's over. I haven't escaped yet."

"You're through with her and her kind."

A stillness came over me. He was right. I was through with her. Even if this portal plan went all wrong, I couldn't stay here. I would risk my life to leave this horrible place.

My hand went to Toren's back, and I hadn't even realized I was reaching for him. He spun, and I was in his arms before I could decide if this was a very bad idea or a very, very bad idea.

His mouth met mine with an intensity that set me on fire.

"Be careful of the runes," I rasped out.

Fingers clasping my hipbones, he pulled me roughly against him, and I gasped as his tongue found mine. Keeping my head angled so that his cheek didn't smear my runes, I nipped at his lip. Our teeth clashed for a moment, but it was only further evidence of our wild desire. I wanted to be closer to him, to devour him, and it seemed he longed for the same because his kisses intensified as he drove his tongue into my mouth.

His hand slid to my thigh and he grasped my leg and drew it up and over his hip. He set his thigh against me, and the pressure threw spirals of pleasure up and down my body. I leaned into his leg and moaned as he pulled his lips along my throat.

"The runes," I choked out, "on my chest."

He halted his caress of my throat before coming to my collarbone, then pulled away. His eyes shimmered in the candlelight. I reached for him, to yank him against me, but he held back.

"We must hurry."

I took a shuddering breath, marveling at the liquid feel of my knees and the intense humming between my thighs. "Yes. You're right."

Shaking myself, I took up the candle and led him toward the back wall of the chamber. I kept my gaze away from the cage. "This wall is newer than the rest of this chamber."

Toren ran a hand over the smooth stones. "But no runes? You don't see any over there, closer to the window?"

"No. It's all smooth except for the plaster between the stone."

"They had to keep the sealing runes here if the portal remains intact. Though this is newer, it is still quite old. The smell of it tells me that."

"I've read about the reconstruction that occurred after an earthquake."

"Hmm."

"They rebuilt the foundation of the temple over one thousand years ago."

He fisted his hand. "Ah, maybe the runes were set into the plaster."

We both studied the plaster, scraping some away

here and there. The candle was reduced to a nub as we searched.

"I must return before Seersha wakes. At least she sleeps like the dead."

"A blessing."

"Maybe you can hide behind the shelves there?" I pointed to the collection of scrolls housed in wooden tubes along the wall beyond the cage.

He pressed a kiss to my forehead. "I'll keep searching and hide myself when anyone approaches."

"You won't leave if you find it, will you?"

"Still longing for the most dangerous adventure a human could experience?"

"To visit an entirely different world with that realm's king on my arm? Definitely."

He chuckled and watched me leave. It was incredibly satisfying to imagine how horrified House Mother would be if she knew I'd invited the King of the Unseelie to spend the night under our temple.

When I opened the library's outer door, Drefan surprised me. His light blue gaze roamed my face, and I hoped my runes weren't smeared.

"I won't pretend to know the inner workings of the temple," he said, "but I'm assuming you should be in bed. Doing research on the dragon? That's wise. Did you find out anything?"

"Nothing. The temple only has a few books and

fewer scrolls that contain information about Unseelie monsters. Has anyone seen anything out here?"

"No. Hopefully, it is gone and won't return. The Fae here said they will take the concern to their king if the dragon is spotted again. Do you need me to make an excuse for your late return to your chamber?"

"House Mother tolerates you here because of the attack, but she wouldn't accept any interference from outsiders."

Drefan nodded. "I understand."

I turned to leave, but he reached for me. I pulled away just in time. "Remember. You can't touch me." I lowered my voice. "Someone could be watching."

The skin around his eyes tightened, and he spoke just an inch from my face. "Are you sure you don't want me to help you out of this place? I would go with you wherever you wish to run. This place is awful. I don't for one minute believe any god would be honored by the way House Mother runs the temple."

"I agree with you, but no. You can't help me." An Unseelie king and a portal might, but anything less would just be a recipe for death.

I eyed the Fae still standing guard several feet away. Would they eventually catch Toren's scent? Would they guess it was related to the dragon's earlier appearance?

There were so many ways this plan could go awry.

"Thank you, Drefan. Truly," I whispered.

I hurried away and didn't turn back to see if he had returned to his position. He had to stay out of this. I didn't want him getting hurt or being blamed for what I was up to with Toren.

Now, I had to get through the last hours of the night and pray the Seelie didn't sniff out Toren.

✨ 17 ✨

TOREN

Toren set his palms against the cold floor of the temple library's basement and called for motyxia millipedes. Not an army of them which would be noticed by the guards outside, but a small cluster—a family unit—of the beautiful creatures. Unseelie magic coursed over Toren's head and down his back, then through his arms and out his fingers. The pulsing power echoed through the earth. Hopefully, the Seelie outside wouldn't notice that either. Seelie tended to be rather thick-headed about Unseelie magic, preferring to see Toren's type of Fae as mere beasts with very little power at all.

It was true that the Unseelie monsters had little to no magic, but Unseelie high Fae could work low level runic magic while Seelie could not. Toren's ability to work with the forest's night creatures was an effect of being crowned King of the Unseelie. He gained the power at his coronation, and even if he gave up his rule, he'd keep this type of magic. Once it was awakened, it remained active.

With the call sent, Toren sat back against the stone wall and eyed the cage. He imagined Bronwyn inside shivering. Claws pierced his heart and threatened to spill his rage and overwhelm any rational thought. The way that human treated the sweet Bronwyn was absolutely untenable. He would see that female suffer. Fae lived long, and he would make time for the pain that monster deserved. Or he would hold her and delight in Bronwyn's revenge. Either way, that human's life would not end in a peaceful death. He drew a claw across his palm and blood beaded along the cut.

"I swear it," he whispered. He set his bloody palm against his throat and then his third eye—the spot between and slightly above his eyebrows. The magic of the oath shivered its way over his temples and into his chest.

A clicking sounded at the window, and soon a line of green glowing insects flowed down the wall. He stood to greet them.

"Light my search," he ordered.

Like all night creatures, they seemed to know his mind even when he wasn't specific. They spread into a half circle and he leaned close to the wall, using their light to see any shallow indentations in the stone that he and Bronwyn might have missed. The millipedes moved along with his progress, but soon he felt that they were fatigued and needed to hunt to sustain themselves.

"Go with my gratitude," he whispered to them, urging them back to the Gwerhune.

As the first light of dawn washed the window in shades of bone and shell, he sat down behind the shelves and did his best to sleep. He knew his body needed rest, but his mind refused it. He had to smile, thinking of what Flok would say about him hiding in a human temple. Toren didn't care much about being properly kingly, and it amused his friend to no end.

You're going to love her, Flok, he thought, knowing it was silly to imagine speaking to him, but he was homesick so he did it anyway. In his mind, he told Flok all about Bronwyn until sleep finally stole him away.

Though his dreams began beautifully with Bronwyn's hands sliding over his bare back and her tongue touching the tip of his ear, soon enough nightmares of Seelie Fae rushing the chamber hounded his sleep. In the horrible scene his mind created, their swords were tipped like their arrows—in scarlet bloodiron.

The next day, I went about my duties like a good Sacred Sister. That in and of itself should have been a warning to everyone that I was up to no good. I did my best to hide my smile— the grin that bloomed every time I thought of the dark king I had hidden in the library. The powerful monster that had kissed me. Maybe I'd lost my mind, but I didn't care. He was gloriously beastly and saw the real me unlike anyone ever had. Plus, he was going to take me on an adventure that hardly any humans—maybe none— had experienced. If we could find the portal before the Seelie found him and ended him with their foul bloodiron.

I sat at dinner, calmly eating the bland, small bites of

potato and fish. What foods would I try in the Realm of Night?

"Really like that potato, hmm?" Seersha took a bite and raised her eyebrows. Behind her hand she whispered, "I think it's a certain city guard that has you grinning like an outsider."

Drefan. I'd avoided him today, keeping to the towers. But I'd heard his voice through the windows as he'd met with the Seelie who had been searching the Gwerhune for the dragon. It seemed they didn't realize it was a high Fae that had shifted into a dragon.

Seersha poured herself more water. "Don't look so worried. They're going to stay for the rest of the moon, House Mother says. We're going to have a group meeting with them in the garden tonight."

"Tonight?"

"Yes. We're dancing for them. How do you not know this?"

I'd been so lost in thought that I guess I'd missed the news. "Which dance?" I pretended that was my new worry.

"Intuition."

I swallowed. If my dancing truly did create magic, what would that do in this situation? Would I be guilty of aiding the city guard in finding Toren?

"If you grip that spoon any harder, you're going to snap it in two," Seersha said.

I loosened my hold on the wooden utensil and took a breath. "I need to practice my steps."

Seersha stood to leave as servants cleared our plates. "I wouldn't fret too much."

"But we haven't practiced that one in ages."

"There is an illustrated diagram of the dance that House Mother is going over with us before we perform."

A chill swept down my back. The illustrated diagram scrolls were kept in the basement—in the shelves where Toren was hiding.

"Are you unwell?" a servant asked, a soft hand on my back.

Sweat beaded along my hairline. "No. I'm fine. Thank you." I looked up at Seersha who was frowning at me. "If you see House Mother, tell her I went to fetch the illustration. After all the trouble I've been..." I shrugged, trying to stay calm and act lackadaisical.

"Oh, yes, that's not a bad idea. I'll tell her. But she might have already gone down." Seersha turned toward the end of the table where the temple leaders sat.

House Mother had left the hall.

❧ 19 ❧

TOREN

Toren woke to the scent of a human and the sound of soft footsteps. Candlelight illuminated the chamber, and he stood up silently as only Fae could. He peered around the shelves to see the wicked female who had mistreated Bronwyn. Perhaps he would fulfill his oath right this minute.

Grinning, he flexed his clawed fingers and prepared for bloodshed. What he'd told Bronwyn was true. This world was killing him. His strength wasn't near its normal level, and he'd slept far longer than he'd ever needed to before becoming trapped here. But he had strength enough to destroy this human.

But as the female sorted through the scrolls set into the shelves farthest from him, Bronwyn's voice seemed to echo in his head, words she'd never spoken but she probably would in this situation.

If you kill her, they will look here for her and find both you and her body.

Then the Seelie would come for him.

Gritting his teeth, he forced himself to remain in the shadows. This foul female's death would have to wait until they found the portal and their escape was clear.

The female stepped closer and made a humming sound of frustration as she searched the scrolls. Keys looped into her belt clinked as she shifted her weight. What had happened to this soul that had made her so evil?

Granted, some were simply born evil. Flok didn't agree with him on that point—they'd discussed it at length one night while deep in their cups. But there was no reason why Toren's father had been evil. He'd had a good family life from what Toren knew, and he had all the advantages of rank and bloodline and health. No one had betrayed him. No, Father had just been evil from birth. Toren was convinced of it and hadn't mourned for longer than a day when the old Fae finally died. He had lain with Seelie outside of his marriage to Mother too. Filthy. She had deserved better, and Toren had told her so before she too passed on.

Perhaps this female was like Father. Well, until he or Bronwyn could end her in a delightfully horrible fashion,

Toren's thorns would trouble her. He lifted his hand, palm up, and shook awake the magic of the thorns he'd sent here days ago. *Follow her,* he said in his mind as magic simmered over his scalp and over his open palm.

"Ah!" The female grabbed a scroll and smiled triumphantly, her pretty face framed by the wooden slats of the shelving. She turned, took up her candle, and left.

He wished he could watch the thorns' subtle stalking, but he'd have to placate himself with imagining. Voices carried down the stairs.

"What are you doing here?" the female asked.

"I was going to fetch the illustration for you."

Toren's chest tightened. It was Bronwyn.

"Seersha said you wanted to show it to us before tonight's dance," Bronwyn said. "But I see you already retrieved it."

"I did," the evil human said. "Go to the garden."

"Yes, House Mother."

"Well, go!"

He could almost feel Bronwyn's desire to check on him, the pull between them. Unseelie didn't have fated mates. Most Seelie didn't either. But this sensation seemed quite close to what those tales of fated mates explained.

The females' steps faded as they left the stairwell. He was alone once more.

A shudder traveled through him. Soon, his magic

would be entirely gone. His power had been away from the Unseelie earth for too long. Once his magic went, he'd quickly wither away.

It was time to do some more searching for the portal. He called up a few more millipedes this time, and he spread his hands over the stone wall's surface. It had to be here. The tales of the portal were old, certainly, but that didn't mean they were wrong. This temple had been built over a spring drawn up from the center of this world by the female that the humans called the Star Goddess. Really, she was simply a very powerful Unseelie from the days of old. He chuckled, thinking of how the humans would react if they learned their precious deity was actually Unseelie. They called his kind demons.

"Fools," he muttered.

The claw on his thumb caught a dip in the stone near the floor under the window. His pulse increased and his stomach twisted. Could this be it?

On his urging, the millipedes circled the area, and he knelt to examine the age-worn scratches. Outlining the three uneven lines, his finger traced the rune for travel. He ran his fingers over the floor near the rune, but it was smooth and unmarked.

"It has to be here."

So far, he'd been able to push away worries of leaving his kingdom without a king. There weren't as many Unseelie high Fae as there were Seelie, so in some ways it was easier to run than Seelie King Lysanael's kingdom. But in other ways, reigning over the Realm of Night was far more difficult. Monsters roamed and created havoc if they weren't maintained through hunting. The council leaned heavily on Toren for the hunting schedules. His gut told him when to do what needed to be done before tragedies occurred. He hated to think that the council was struggling without him, and the villages on the border with the wilderness would be suffering losses.

The other threat was Hanina, his disgraced general. She was an amazing fighter and strategist, but she'd grown too ambitious. Toren had never been able to prove she'd been behind the attempted coup last year, but he knew she had her hands in it. He'd sent her to the borderlands, so she'd be too busy to organize any type of rebellions. But who knew what was happening now? And Flok had to guess that he was dead. They all probably thought he was dead.

His palm smoothed across the floor, brushing debris from his attack into uneven piles. A sizzle of power sparked across his hand. Getting into a crouch, he cleared the area completely.

"Please be here. It has to be here somewhere."

The rune for direction or intent or something like that would most likely mark the spot. But there were no more runes. Or they were under the new wall. Time to tear some more human shite down.

He stood, gathered himself, then launched a foot into the stone. The wall shivered and cracked under his Fae strength. He kicked it again and again, and the plaster gave way and the wall tumbled backward into a void.

Of course, he worried the Fae—with ears almost as capable as his—would hear the destruction, but he didn't have all the time in the world.

Maneuvering over the broken wall, he peered into the darkness.

❦ 20 ❧

BRONWYN

Wiping my sweating hands on the black and white leaves embroidered on the sides of my robes, I took up my regular position for the dance of Intuition. I couldn't believe House Mother hadn't seen Toren. He'd been right there, only steps away. I took a deep breath and tried to focus on the dance.

The servants and the librarian began humming because the lute had been broken during Toren's attack. Minor notes lifted into the stars, and my feet shifted this way and that. I raised my palms to the night sky, closed my eyes, and walked in a rhythmic fashion in the shape of a figure eight, weaving through my fellow Sacred Sisters.

My forehead warmed, and I glanced at my feet to see

if I could witness the magic that Toren saw when I danced. But it was invisible to me, if it was even there. I didn't necessarily believe Toren had been lying because Fae couldn't, but perhaps the magic only occurred once in a while or maybe Toren had been mistaken. I thought back to the bear and the indigo pastlights... Maybe I did have power. House Mother seemed to think so too. But how?

The Seelie tilted their heads and whispered, their gazes interested and curious. The city guards, Drefan included, kept glancing from the woods back to the dance. Were the Seelie noticing my magic?

A childhood memory surfaced.

I grasped my father's finger with my little hand as we walked the fields around our cottage. A group of green-yellow fireflies surrounded us suddenly, and Father began praying.

That was the entirety of the memory. Was that related to whatever power hid inside me?

As I danced, I mentally arranged the information. The Unseelie King could see my magic as light when I danced. Our steps created runes or glyphs in the earth. I was the only Sacred Sister that produced the magic—at least that was the theory based on what Toren witnessed. I had stopped a Fae bear from attacking me. My dancing lured the indigo pastlights and perhaps drew fireflies as well. If I did have a power, where did it originate? No one in my family had magic. Did they?

I thought back to the few memories I had with Grandmother. Grandfather had died before I was born. I only recalled Grandmother singing and rocking me when I was still a thumb-sucking toddler. What had she sang to me? It was the same song every time. The notes had been eerie but also somehow comforting. And the lyrics... I couldn't recall a word of them.

The dance concluded and the compliments from the guards broke my line of thought. The Seelie remained at their stations, so at least the dance hadn't urged them to search the library or the basement below.

We were incredibly lucky that House Mother hadn't found Toren. He had to have been standing in the shadows just a few feet from her when she'd gone to fetch the illustration of the dance. It was a wonder he hadn't killed her. The rage that had flickered in his silver eyes when he discovered more about my treatment here...

While everyone was talking and taking refreshment offered by the kitchen staff, I snagged a candle from the stand by the first tower door, walked casually across the back of the garden courtyard, slipped into the library, and hurried down the stairs.

"Toren?" I whispered.

The newer wall had been torn down in the middle, and I heard movement. A strange prickling traveled over my skin, pebbling my skin as I walked forward.

"I found it," Toren said from behind a portion of the wall.

I leaned over the debris and held out my candle. The fire's light burnished his sharp, dark features, making him look like a creature formed of old gold. He held out a hand to me, and I took it. His fingers were warm and large, and I wanted to keep holding them even after I'd climbed over the fallen stone and into the space behind.

"Watch," Toren said, releasing my hand.

I tried not to frown at the loss of his warmth.

He crouched and pressed his palms into the stone floor. It was then I noticed the flooring here wasn't the plain, smooth stone of the rest of the chamber. A mosaic in an array of jewel-hued rocks decorated the space. Toren was touching a spot marked with two blue-green spirals.

The prickling sensation increased as he whispered words at the empty wall at the back of the space. An archway shimmered into existence.

Toren stood with his palms out as if he was directing the portal in some way with his Unseelie power. A flash of blue and green, then black and gold, washed over the archway's center then began to spread. Crackling and snapping, Toren and I winced against the brightness. The Unseelie realm appeared slowly.

Stars glittered green in a dark blue sky. Candles flickered at wooden market tables and Fae in all shapes, colors, and sizes hawked red beads, black melons dotted with what looked like cloves, and glittering knives. Fae children ran down the winding path between stalls, their laughter carrying through the portal.

The smile on Toren's face lifted my heart and sent a fluttering sensation into my stomach. This was his home and it was beautiful. An ache suddenly filled me up, and I reached out and squeezed his forearm.

A bump and a scrape sounded behind us.

I spun to see House Mother, Drefan, all the Seelie Fae, and a few of Drefan's men. My heart plummeted into my knees. Toren growled, pulled me behind him, and the portal shifted to a forested scene.

"Shoot him," said one of the Seelie Fae.

Everything happened in a whirlwind of noise and movement. Shouting, Drefan and his men rushed to our right and through the broken wall as one of the Fae loosed a bloodiron arrow. House Mother called out my name. Toren grabbed my arm, and suddenly, I was falling into nothingness with the feel of blood droplets hot on my cheek.

II

THE REALM OF NIGHT

21

TOREN

The darkness whirled around Toren, and he fought to keep a hold on Bronwyn. The portal was working. They were headed to his realm.

But he had been shot by bloodiron.

Already the poison was lacing through his blood, making him shudder. The pain would come soon, and after that the delirium, then death. He refused to die before he saw Bronwyn to safety. She wouldn't survive the Unseelie realm without him or another helpful soul. Though she was brave and smart, she didn't have any fighting skills.

The portal spat them onto a pine-scented ground, and the black of his vision cleared to show a moonlit forest in his kingdom, the Realm of Night.

Bronwyn lay beside him, her eyes closed and her lips parted. Pastlights floated high above them, and the moon cast a shadow of a birch's branch across Bronwyn's heart-shaped face. She was too still. Claws gripped Toren's heart.

"Bronwyn?"

She couldn't be... The portal wasn't that bad. But maybe that's why only a few humans had ever visited this realm, and those visits had been purely accidental. They had also ended in less than delightful ways.

No, the color on her cheeks was still pink, and her lips were rose red—soft-looking. He knew they tasted like salt and sugar.

Her eyes fluttered open, her dark gold eyelashes stuck together with tears. Then her eyes went wide. "You're bleeding! I forgot."

She sat up, nearly knocking her forehead into his jaw, and he dropped back. Now she loomed over him, her hands patting his body like mere touch could will away the poison.

"Where exactly is the wound?" she asked. "The blood is all over the place." She sounded so horrified. She definitely needed help to survive in his kingdom.

He gestured toward his upper chest. "The arrow grazed me. It would be nothing if it weren't tipped in bloodiron." His gaze fell to the forest, and the monsters that would come at the scent of his blood.

Her fingers gently prodded the ripped leather of his vest. "We need to clean this. And..."

Taking her hand, he locked her down with his gaze. "The only thing we are doing right now is getting you to Flok's cottage."

He got to his feet, vision going a little wrong, then aided her in rising too. She swayed a bit, but seemed to be well enough despite the portal's effect.

"If I'm right," he said, "we are about a day's walk from his place. I meant to land us in my castle, but the Seelie's and humans' appearance at the portal distracted me."

"But you're hurt. You said the bloodiron would kill you."

She wasn't even looking around, enjoying the beauty of his realm. Her stare went from his wound to his face and back again. His chest pinched. She truly cared. He took her face in his hands, marveling at the velvet feel of her skin and the amber color of her beautiful eyes. His mind whirled like he was back inside the portal's magic...

"How did I manage to charm a goldheart? You are breathtaking."

He pressed a simple kiss to her lips and felt her weight drop as she let out a soft moan that undid every thought in his head. Lacing an arm around her waist, he let her guide the kiss. She opened her mouth to him, and he licked her upper lip, then drew his tongue slowly over hers. His body hummed with desire, his muscles tightening and his blood rushing south.

Then his legs gave out, and he fell. She gasped and followed him, kneeling beside him near a cluster of white-barked birch trees.

"What can I do?" she asked. "What do we do? How do we fix this?"

"We don't." He coughed and sat up, heat rising in his chest and cheeks. He hated looking weak, especially in front of her. "There is no cure for bloodiron poisoning. Well, except the Destroying Spirit."

He braced himself on one of the birches, got to his feet, and began to walk. Bronwyn leapt up and grabbed his arm and made him stop and face her. The lines of her features blurred. He swallowed the bitter taste of death at the back of his tongue. It was truly happening. Death approached.

But he had so much more to do...

She was shaking him, holding him by his vest. "Toren! Snap out of it! What is the Destroying Spirit?"

"What? Oh, it's a very rare mushroom. We will never find one."

"With that attitude, we won't."

"Before I lose my head, listen to me, Bronwyn."

She nodded. "I'm listening."

"Head northeast until you find a wide river. Cross at

a bridge marked with green banners. Do not cross the bridge with black banners. Wait until you find the green bridge."

"All right."

"Then go through the purple aspens there."

"Purple?"

"Yes, our trees grow in colors that one doesn't see in the Seelie and human realm. Go through those and find a path lined in rowan trees. The rowans will lead you to Flok's cottage."

"Fine. I know the way. Now, tell me how to seek out a Destroyer whatever it is mushroom. We are in a forest. It looks like the largest forest I've ever seen, not that I've seen many. There has to be one of these mushrooms somewhere around here." Her voice had thinned, and he noted that was what she sounded like when she was panicked.

A flash of movement caught Toren's eye, but his body didn't respond how it should have by putting himself between the possible threat and Bronwyn. Instead, his feet continued walking. When had they started walking again? Bronwyn was speaking, but he couldn't grasp the meaning. He squinted into the shadows of the forest and studied the shapes painted white by the beams of moonlight cascading through the trees.

What had he seen? A monster?

"If a gargoyle or a troll comes at us," he said, "try your dancing to enchant it. If it's anything else, climb a tree."

"Climb a tree? Yes, that will be easy." She lifted her robes and huffed. "The mushroom. Focus, Toren. We were looking for the mushroom."

They crossed a damp expanse of low-lying ground where moss grew like Bronwyn's hair, dark gold and thick, across round boulders.

"Destroying Spirit mushrooms grow near Fae oaks."

"How do I tell the difference between a Fae oak and a regular oak? Do you even have regular oaks?"

Her question trailed off, and her gaze went to the trees. She stopped walking as a Dreamfeather soared overhead. She reached for the bird, and its luminescent leaf-like wings spread a pale blue glow over her upturned face. He wanted to wipe those runes off of her cheeks and free her completely, but that was her decision.

Turning to him, she smiled and it lit him up inside. "Your world is beautiful." But then her eyes narrowed. "Now, keep moving and talking."

"Fae oaks…" His thoughts tumbled over one another, and he fisted his hands, pricking his palms with his claws to keep himself alert. "Fae oaks have leaves that change color frequently. Not according to season."

"Is this something I can witness in a short span of time? Can I use the changing colors to seek them out?"

"Yes. They sense the...aura of the creatures nearby and switch to match it."

"Aura?"

"It's a light that one's soul gives off. I can't see them, but that's what the scrolls claim. My kind, the Unseelie high Fae, have lost magicks that we used to wield with ease. At one time, we were all like your Star Goddess."

She frowned. "I have questions, but now isn't the time. All right. We watch for a tree that is changing color. Got it. Now, what does the mushroom look like?"

"It's pure white with gills under the cap that don't quite reach the stem. You can touch it and not suffer any ill effects, but if you eat it, you die within five days."

"How do we use it to heal you of the bloodiron's poison?"

"I must eat it."

"I consider myself a smart person, but I have to admit I'm lost."

"The mushroom's magical properties will flush my blood of the bloodiron. Supposedly. I have to survive it though."

"So you must ingest a deadly poison to get rid of another deadly poison."

"Yes."

"Sounds like we have a lovely evening ahead of us."

A chuckle left Toren's mouth, surprising him. The forest and Bronwyn grew hazy and began to spin.

The pain began.

"Toren..." Bronwyn snagged his arm as he fell.

❧ 22 ❧
BRONWYN

I snaked an arm under Toren's and tried to lift him. Not happening. He was such a big male. "Toren, please. We are almost to Flok's cottage, right? You can go a little further."

I was lying through my teeth. We'd only walked a short way. But I had to motivate him to try, to keep fighting.

Stones, but he looked awful. His gray color had faded to a dusky charcoal hue and the veins in his neck and forehead stood out as he gritted his teeth against what had to be terrible pain. He coughed and his eyes opened. They were bloodshot like he'd been staring into the sun.

"Go on without me," he said, his voice rasping. "Tell Flok what happened. He can..."

"Ah, you're trying to get rid of me. Being selfless and

all of that, but you can't lie. I'm going to find that mushroom, and you'll have to suffer my presence for years to come."

I didn't want to leave him lying there, all helpless and alone. He'd be a nice, big snack for whatever monsters were roaming this kingdom. But I couldn't drag him along while I sought out Fae oaks. I ripped the embroidered hems of my robes free, then began unraveling and tearing them as best I could.

"I'll be right back, King Toren." Maybe using his name would remind him of how his people surely needed him.

While searching, I stopped every once in a while and tied a strip of cloth on a bush or tree branch. I could not afford to get lost out here. For one, Toren would die alone. And, I was pretty sure nothing in my nineteen years had prepared me for surviving the Unseelie realm. I would be lucky enough if I could live through this search.

"Goddess," I whispered into the moonlit trees, "if you're real and if you care about little old me, then perhaps keep all those monsters away, all right? I know I was the absolute worst Sacred Sister, but maybe you appreciate my honesty and humility?"

I shook my head at myself. Not even Beanie would have said the Goddess was known for mercy.

The moon shifted in the sky as I examined tree after

tree, watching to see any alterations in color. The closest I came was an aspen that had glittering bark. A host of glowing insects surrounded it, so I kept my distance. Toren had said the leaves changed. He'd said nothing about bark.

I was down to my last strip of cloth. I had to go back empty-handed and watch Toren die. A chill wrapped my ribs, and I began to shiver, feeling colder than I'd ever been.

Toren was the only person who had taken the time to see the true me. Granted, he'd wanted something from me, but still... I might have been sheltered these last years, but I knew real emotion when I saw it. Toren cared for me and I for him. I refused to lose him without at least trying to undo what my realm had done to him.

I left the last strip of cloth in the distance and memorized the bend of the next tree's largest limb. A small stream greeted me, and I took up a few smooth stones from the cold water to make an arrow shape, pointing toward Toren.

Just a little farther...

The oak and its mushroom could be around the next pine...

23

TOREN

Toren didn't know how long he'd been on the forest floor, writhing in agony. An invisible flame burned its way from the place where the bloodiron had cut through his leather vest and across his chest all the way down his torso and into his legs. He felt as though someone had stuffed him with glowing coals. How was his skin staying on? He should have been melting at this level of heat.

The moon's glow blurred the leaves and branches above. The scent of a deer whisked over him as he got to his knees. He tried to stand, but his legs trembled and his vision swam so he remained where he was, his face aching from clenching his jaw to keep from screaming. A crash sounded in the trees behind him.

"Bronwyn?"

The ground shook with the footsteps of a creature far larger than many Bronwyns.

"This is unfortunate," he rasped out, clenching and unclenching his jaw and trying to stand.

A gargoyle spread its thin, ragged wings, breaking branches from the birch trees and sending them snapping to the earth. The beast threw its head back and shrieked. Night creatures fled in scurrying bursts, some scampering over Toren's foot and the hand he had braced on a small boulder. He'd made it to his feet only to be greeted with the strongest monster his realm had to offer.

"Greetings," he said, his vision clearing then blurring. Needles jammed into his flesh again and again, the pain taking on a new angle. Creative poison shouldn't exist. It was just over the top. He shook his head. He had to focus.

The gargoyle swung its fist at him. It was easy enough to fall back onto the ground so the monster missed its target.

"Thought you had me there, didn't you?" Toren croaked. He set his hands on the earth, sending his will into the earth in an attempt to influence the monster through his Unseelie King power. But the magic fizzled away and left him even dizzier.

Taking another step forward, the gargoyle reached for him. Fingers the length of two Fae laced around his body and lifted him into the air.

"I am your king. I realize you don't recognize me as such, but when you venture from the wilds and into the civilized realm, well, I'm the one you must answer to, dear beastie."

The gargoyle drew Toren toward its bedchamber-sized face. Its pale eyes blinked slowly, and Toren's reflection showed faintly in the milky depths. Toren's mind tried to think around the pain, but his thoughts slid around like snakes in a flooding garden.

Magic. He had power—maybe.

He set his palms against the gargoyle's finger as the monster opened its great maw to show off sword-length teeth. Magic stuttered and sparked from Toren's head and through his chest, eking its way too slowly, too weakly, toward his palms and the physical connection he had with the gargoyle.

"I am your king," he whispered, pushing his intent and his magic into the words and into the point of contact between him and his subject. "I am your king. Submit to my will."

Mouth opening wide, the gargoyle lifted Toren higher and readied to drop him into the death that Toren hadn't thought he'd experience.

"I am your king, gargoyle." Toren shut his eyes and threw his full belief into the magic. "You will set me down. You will bend to my will. I rule you and your kin.

I am the Unseelie King, Ruler of the Realm of Night, Star-Caster, Moonbleeder, Breaker of Bones."

The monster gripped him tighter, and Toren sucked in a breath, his ribs near to popping. He could no longer speak or draw a full breath. The bloodiron didn't care. It racked his body with bright agony like a foul human with a whip to his slaves. Toren's view of the gargoyle hazed and black spots danced in front of him like large flies.

The wind increased. Toren opened his eyes.

The gargoyle was placing him on the ground.

Released, Toren stumbled but managed to remain standing. He stared up at the gargoyle.

"Wise choice, monster. Now, return to the wilds and to your kin. If I see you again," Toren winced as a dagger of heat pierced his chest, "I will have to end your life."

The gargoyle turned and tromped through the forest. The trees cracked and swayed in the wake of his retreat.

"I can't believe I managed that." Toren promptly fell face-first into the moss and wild grass. Darkness swamped his senses and he knew no more.

❧ 24 ❧
BRONWYN

I 'd left him too long. He was going to be dead when I returned. Pressing my eyes shut, I swallowed and tried to push down the panic thrashing in my chest.

I stood in the center of five Fae oaks.

But not a single mushroom grew anywhere nearby.

On my knees, I lifted my cold hands and dirt fell from my fingers. I couldn't see well enough to look properly among the roots of the amazing trees. I looked up at the ruby-hued leaves. They shook and shimmered, then turned a bright pink with gold striations.

"Does that mean something?" I fought the burn of tears and the ache of a sob desperate to crawl from my mouth.

And I kept on searching.

Wait. What if a dance could help me find the mushroom? I got to my feet. The name of every dance I knew whirled in their own patterns through my head.

Courage? Determination? No. I had those right now in spades. I was set on saving Toren. Intuition? It didn't feel right, which was ironic. A dark laugh huffed out of me. I smoothed my hands over my face and froze. Pulling my hands away, I watched the moonlight illuminate my palms. I'd smeared my runes. And it didn't matter.

I was free of the temple, of House Mother, of beatings, and the cage. I could wander this new world with no boundaries. It was all due to Toren.

How had we happened to meet? I must be the luckiest person alive, to run into the one soul who could help me escape my life completely. Luck. That was it. I positioned myself to start the dance of Luck.

The steps were faster than most, and I had to be careful of the leaves and hidden roots as I moved to my right in a half circle. The pattern had me shifting backward, bowing so low that my nose brushed a cluster of damp, glowing moss before I swept my left arm high and drew an invisible slash across my view of the canopy, the stars, and the moon.

My chest lightened, and my worry for Toren melted away as I spun like a top three times, spotting by locking my eyes onto one of the Fae oaks' trunks each time I turned, a skill that had taken me two years to perfect under House Mother's cruel hands. I dipped low, then leapt like a doe over the circle my spinning had created on the earth. I dragged a foot over the ground, adding a line to the circle and connecting it to the half circle from the start of the dance. Humming, I let my mind drift to a version of today in which I found the mushroom and ran smiling back to Toren who was suffering but still fighting to live.

Concluding the dance, I stopped and noticed the forest had hushed. All the night insects had gone quiet and nothing small shuffled in the brush. The only sound was my breath, as if the very air had stilled.

I looked down, and between my feet, a mushroom stuck up from the surrounding leaf litter and thick clover like a poorly buried bone. I plucked it up. It seemed so small and unremarkable. But it fit Toren's description perfectly with the gills that didn't quite touch the stem. It was time to save Toren with a deadly fungus.

Shaking my head, I hurried back to the stream and the arrow of stones I'd set up. The last piece of cloth I'd tied onto a tree almost seemed to glow. I untied it and tucked it into my pocket next to the mushroom as I walked through a small clearing full of silver moss and red-and-blue-speckled mushrooms that stood elbow high.

Hmm. I didn't remember passing these...

I walked on, looking for another pale piece of cloth, but there weren't any. Sweat pearled on my forehead, and I wiped it away. I retraced my steps back to my stone arrow and tried again to follow the way I had come originally.

A rough meow echoed from the moonshadow of a tall boulder, and a cat the size of three cats at home sauntered toward me, tail held high. It was the ugliest cat I'd ever seen with matted orange fur and a scar across the place where its right eye had been. I reached down and ran a hand over another hairless scar, one that zigzagged across his back.

"Well, hello."

The cat's purrs were loud enough to wake the dead. He leapt away from me, and I followed him to where he sat beneath a tree beyond the boulder. Beyond the cat's chosen tree, in a spindly pine, a slip of white practically glowed in the moonlight. I shouted with joy, running to the strip. The cat meowed sharply as if reprimanding me.

"All right, Sir Cat. Perhaps I should keep quiet in the middle of a dark Unseelie forest."

After that I found the rest of the cloth strips quickly, and soon, the birch grove where I'd left Toren was reaching its white arms into the dark canopy.

Toren lay still, stomach down, with one cheek pressed to the earth and his eyes shut.

A chill rattled my spine, and Sir Cat let out a quiet, stuttered meow.

"Toren? You had better not be dead because I found the mushroom and I deserve to say *I told you so* to your face."

I knelt beside him, touched his forehead, then smoothed a lock of black hair from his face. Sir Cat walked on the moss around Toren. The growth had been roughly torn from the ground and pushed into bunches. Something large had been here.

Was Toren wounded in more places than the arrow's cut on his upper chest?

I hurriedly unlaced the leather ties at the side of his vest and loosened it enough to glimpse his torso while Sir Cat licked Toren's pointed ear. The moonlight only slightly illuminated Toren's skin, but from what I could see, he wasn't additionally wounded. Maybe he'd been hit on the head by whatever monster had been here. I moved my fingers through his mussed braids as gently as I could. No spots of dampness that would indicate bleeding or bumps.

"Toren." I shook him a bit. "Wake. I have the mushroom. Should I just shove it into your mouth? I don't know what to do with it. Wake up, Toren."

Sir Cat yowled.

Suddenly, I was pulled to my feet and something sharp was pricking my throat. The cat hissed. A low voice rumbled in my ear as I grasped at the attacker's hand.

"What did you do to my king, human?"

My pulse was a fish on land flapping like mad and accomplishing nothing. I took a breath and felt the tips of what must have been the attacker's claws. Sir Cat yowled at the attacker as if his noise could drive the male away.

"I am trying to save him," I said.

A harsh laugh made my ears ring. "Humans lie."

𝔰𝔢 25 𝔰𝔢
BRONWYN

"Yes, we do sometimes," I said to the attacker, "but this isn't one of those moments. A Seelie's bloodiron arrow cut the king's chest, and he sent me to find a Destroying Spirit mushroom to flush the toxins from his body."

The hand at my throat disappeared. The attacker spun me around and held tightly to my upper arms. He was a wiry-bodied, tall Fae male with dark eyes that were slitted like all Fae's and a head of short, tousled flaxen hair. He wore a tunic and trousers, and he had several knives on his belt but no sword and no shoes, just like Toren. Toren had said Flok was thin, and we were near his cottage.

"Are you his friend, Flok?"

Surprise flickered through the male's eyes. "That is what I'm called, yes."

"Then help me." I took the mushroom from my pocket, spilling a few of my white strips of cloth in the process. Sir Cat wound his way through my legs.

Flok shook his head and went to Toren's side. "My king, please wake up." He unlaced the shoulders of Toren's vest as he talked. Panic sharpened his words. "There is a human here who claims you need a highly poisonous mushroom for a midnight snack."

Pulling the vest free, Flok gasped at the sight of the bloodiron wound. The cut had darkened at the edges and white lines stretched from the dried blood across his collarbone. Keeping his gaze on Toren, Flok extended a clawed hand toward where I stood behind him.

"Give me the mushroom."

I did so and knelt beside him with Sir Cat taking a spot on the far side of Flok.

"Do you know what to do?" I asked Flok. "Can he handle this type of healing right now?"

"Considering I'm not sure he's even properly alive, I don't know."

I felt for the pulse at his neck in the way Drefan's mother had done with our childhood neighbor when he'd fallen off his horse after negotiating with my father at our farm. A light hammering touched my fingertip, and I remembered how to breathe.

"His heart beats."

Flok nodded once. He plucked the stem from the mushroom and tossed it into the brush. Placing the cap between his palms he began to smash the mushroom. A scent like tar filled the air and made me cough.

"How many times have you given this cure?"

Turning, Flok gave me an incredulous look with wide eyes and his jaw jutting out. "Never. I have never once given a highly poisonous mushroom to anyone. This is an old wives' tale. I have no idea if it will work."

I seized his arm and stopped him from placing the smashed mushroom cap into Toren's mouth. "Then why risk it?"

"The white lines there." Flok jerked his chin at Toren's wound. "Those mean he has approximately one hour to live. I have seen many die from bloodiron. I'm a damned expert on that," he muttered, his voice almost breaking.

He might have called him king, but it was clear Flok considered Toren a close friend just as Toren had said. My heart clenched at the sight of him placing the bits of mushroom into Toren's mouth.

I was lifting my hands and moving my feet before I even thought about it. Sir Cat backed away and watched me, his ears and tail twitching. Flok glanced at me, then back at Toren whose lips moved slightly. Flok leaned close to Toren who chewed.

"What was that, my king? I'm listening," Flok said.

"Dance for me, Bronwyn Greensmith," Toren croaked.

I gasped, tears searing my eyes. His words made my feet move with more confidence as if he'd somehow pushed his magic into mine. I danced a new pattern, one that no one had taught me but came instead from my own mind and soul. I stepped in arching lines that branched from a crescent before spinning back to the starting place.

"The ground..." Flok's wide-eyed gaze locked onto my feet. "What magic is this?" He turned back to Toren who had gone even more pale than he was when he'd been unconscious. "This human you brought...she is a rune dancer? I didn't know they were real."

Toren coughed, blood speckling his lips.

I forced myself to concentrate on the gratitude I felt for how he had helped me, and the heat of that feeling rose and grew inside me. My thankfulness spun down my body and into my feet. The feeling uncurled in my fingers too as I smoothed them along an imaginary burst of starlight. What was this dance and how could it help Toren?

Flok positioned himself behind Toren, thrust his arms under Toren, and dragged him to standing. Flok tucked Toren's arm over his neck, then eyed me reverently.

"We must get him back to my cottage before the mushroom takes hold." Distrust still flickered in the pinch of his eyes, but his tone had lost its aggression.

I closed the mysterious dance with my feet side by side and my hands over my heart. Strength poured through me. "He will live. I can feel it."

"Perhaps." Flok started in the direction Toren and I had been traveling before he'd fallen. "But he might wish he didn't by the time we get home."

I took Toren's other arm around my neck, and we began the journey with Sir Cat leading the way as if he knew every route to every location in this Unseelie forest.

A river rumbled beside the path and two bridges appeared just as Toren had said. The bridge with the green banners was too narrow for all of us, so Flok walked the thin slats, holding Toren. A rope snapped on the far end and the bridge dropped a foot and shook. Flok froze, Toren's head on his shoulder. Once the bridge stilled, Flok continued and I followed as soon as they were across. Sir Cat padded behind me. The bridge creaked as I stepped delicately across the ramshackle structure, and the river rushed and growled beneath us.

Once across, I resumed my position under Toren's right arm, and we traveled for miles in the dark forest. Every time Toren began to fall, we paused and let him gather himself. He stepped unevenly, his weight heavy on my shoulders. My slippers kept coming off and finally I shucked them free as we strode on slowly. The earth was cold on my feet, but it was better than tripping over shoes.

Toren's breathing had become no more than shallow panting.

"I think we need to fully carry him," I said.

Flok nodded and set Toren gently on the ground near a puddle of water as silver as Toren's eyes.

"Will you get some of those vines?" He pointed to the spindly growth spiraling down from a maple. "I'll get two limbs so we can make a litter."

I yanked the vines, and they pulled back like they were sentient. Sir Cat had disappeared, and I hoped he was all right. Swallowing, I grabbed the bulk of the vines at a higher spot and tried again. This time they cracked and snapped so quickly that I fell backward, landing beside Toren. He didn't even flinch at the sound or movement. His eyes remained shut and the blood on his lips and chest made me hurry to my feet to untangle the vines so they'd be usable.

Flok returned with two limbs. "I wish I could just toss him over my shoulder, but my king is a large fellow and I'm not as strong as some Fae are."

"This will work well," I said, trying to believe my own words.

We braided the ivy quickly and looped it around the

thick branches. Once Flok tested its strength with a push of his clawed hand and the litter proved itself, we dragged Toren into place and set off once more.

Flok held both handles at the front and I walked in front of him, moving logs and steering him around boulders as best I could in the moonlit forest. We walked for hours. I was glad that dancing on stones had toughened my feet for this, but even my strong soles were not much of a match to the rocks and sticks and uneven ground. Pain lit up my toes and arch, but I bit down on any complaints because it was all so much worse for Toren. I walked beside him through a wider pathway in the forest. He coughed and blood trickled down his chin.

"Would he have done this for you, do you think?" Gasping from the effort, Flok had to work hard to speak.

"Definitely. He shifted into his dragon form and attacked a temple when he knew House Mother was mistreating me. He risked the bloodiron for me."

Flok turned to look at me. "Why was he in the Seelie realm anyway?"

"He was trapped when Seelie King Lysanael sealed the drumstones."

"That was the general's guess. But she believes him dead or at least that's what she has been telling everyone as she sits on Toren's throne."

"Someone stole his throne?"

"Yes. General Hanina. There will be a fight if Toren lives through this."

✿ 26 ✿
BRONWYN

Someone had taken power while Toren had been trapped in my world? "We have to help him get it back."

"Agreed. The one who did this is about as kindly as a basket of vipers. But before all of that, let's see if we can keep Toren alive."

The forest thinned, and a meadow spread between a stand of firs and aspen. A two-story cottage with green shutters and window boxes bursting with bright green, white, and purple herbs sat in the moonlight.

"Welcome to my home."

"You've changed your tune with me."

The side of Flok's mouth lifted a fraction as we helped Toren from the litter. "I can't imagine any devious scenario in which a human would willingly come to our realm and then wander the dark for a deadly mushroom. You must care for him or you would have left him to die and gone about whatever business you have. Plus, you're a rune dancer."

We shuffled Toren through the front door, his feet dragging over the raised threshold, then set him on the long, feather-stuffed cushion of a wood-backed chaise. Flok disappeared up the stairs at the back wall of the room then reappeared quickly with linens. I found a bowl at the sink and poured water from a pitcher and helped Flok clean and bandage Toren's wound. I smoothed a damp cloth across Toren's chin to clean the blood away.

Toren went very still. I set a hand on his chest and held my breath. "He isn't breathing."

Flok stepped back and a hissing sound came from his lips, a very Fae sound that was more animal than person. "The mushroom's death has arrived. We can do nothing except pray that he rises from it by dawn."

I fisted the hand on Toren's chest and gripped the cloth so tightly that my knuckle popped. "He is dead right now?"

"It is a shallow death, or so the scrolls say. The poison takes him to see death and then he is born anew if he wakes."

"What chance does he have?"

Flok shrugged. "I've only read a few instances of

using the Destroying Spirit's power to flush bloodiron. Of those three, only one made it through."

I stared at Toren's pale gray eyelids. Would I never see his silver eyes again? Unshed tears burned my own eyes, but I refused to let them fall and instead kept wiping his face and hoping he knew we were here for him.

"Was there anyone following you?" Flok's gaze had gone to the window over the sink.

My pulse ticked up a notch. "No, why?"

"It's probably just an animal. I saw something pass by." Flok went to the kitchen area and pulled a large, flat-headed butchering knife from the top of a tall chest of drawers. "I'll check." He opened the door. "Keep this shut no matter what. We must protect the king."

I nodded as my stomach swam with worry. Straining to hear, I held my breath again, but no sound came from outside beyond the usual chirp of night insects and the occasional pop of the old cottage's walls.

Toren remained painfully still and silent. I dipped the cloth in the water bowl then ran it over his forehead.

"Come back to us, Toren. Someone stole your place, and you need to get it back. I'll help you. We are at Flok's cottage. You'll be fine. Turn away from death. You have to live to show me around your kingdom. It's so beautiful, and I can't even image how amazing your castle is. We can research the magic you discovered in me, dance the days away, and eat everything in sight. It will be so grand. So just return, all right?"

At some point, the tears I'd been holding fast to had streamed down my cheeks. I wiped my jaw with the back of my hand only to see rune paint. I wetted the cloth again and cleaned every rune from my face and upper chest, being careful not to disturb my bandage.

"See?" I said to Toren. "I'm finished with that place and that world. I want to be here, free with you."

Hopefully that was what he wanted too.

The door opened, and Flok nodded in greeting. He put his large knife back in its place and came close to stand over Toren.

"Did you find anything?"

"No, and I can't scent a thing out there with your human odor fouling up the air."

"Nice to know you too, Flok."

He side-eyed me, then crouched taking up Toren's hand. Examining Toren's claws, he said, "He's lost his color here too. Not a good sign."

"Try to be hopeful."

"I'm not the best at that particular activity."

"More of a doom and gloom sort, hmm?"

Flok seemed to realize I was attempting to keep myself together because he sat cross-legged beside me and cleared the storm clouds from his gaze. "Yes. But I consider myself a realist."

"Right. When did you meet Toren?"

"We've known one another since childhood."

"He told me about the time you visited Veilbury."

Flok's eyebrows lifted. "He did? I'm surprised you're by his side after all of those tales."

"Why?"

"Most females would be jealous of his past lovers."

"How many females do you know well enough to hear that from them?"

"Well... You make a good point. I have only known the females at court who are just as grasping as the males. And my mother, who was wonderful."

"Most females I've met are confident and wouldn't let the past ruin the possibility of a future."

"All right, Tutor Bronwyn. Lesson learned." His smile eased the snark in his words.

"Toren used to hunt near here when he was very young. My father was the court's long distance messenger, so the former king and queen permitted their son the prince to visit on occasion."

"Is he much like his parents?"

"Oh no. Definitely not. He isn't a goldheart, but he is damn near close. His parents—may they rot, unremembered—were the worst sort of monsters. I would have preferred the company of a gargoyle or a troll over them any day."

I almost laughed, but my heart wasn't in it.

A cough rumbled from Toren's chest and a sheen of sapphire light rose from his body, expanding in all directions and lighting the cottage like a thousand candles.

Flok stood in a blur of movement, his features tight. "It's happening."

"Death or life?" Sweat rolled down my back, and I held onto Toren's arm despite the blue magic coursing and prickling over the place of contact.

❧ 27 ❧
TOREN

The world around Toren blurred like he was looking through a waterfall. He was shivering from a cold so deep it felt as though his very bones were made of ice. What was that shape there? A person. No, two people. One pale and one darker.

Realization washed over him and sent a bolt of lightning straight through his heart. He sat up.

"Bronwyn. Flok." His vision cleared, and their smiles chased the cold away.

Bronwyn threw herself against him, hugging him tightly.

Her care made him feel as though his soul had taken flight. "Careful, love. I'm not prepared for ravaging just yet."

She laughed into his neck, and her salt-scented, wet

cheeks told him she'd been weeping. Over him. He couldn't stop grinning.

Flok clapped a hand on his leg. "Such a dramatic entrance, my king. I shouldn't be surprised, I suppose. You've always been a mummer at heart."

"Friend, it is absolutely divine to see you."

Bronwyn moved back, still laughing with joy, and Flok hugged Toren and slapped his back sharply.

"Was death as dull as I guessed it will be?"

"I wish I could tell you. I wasn't paying enough attention. Too busy fighting to get back." There had only been colors in red, yellow, and green, and the pain... Toren didn't think he'd actually died. "You gave me the Destroying Spirit, didn't you?"

He pressed a hand to the bloodiron wound only to find it completely faded into nothing like it had never happened.

"Thank you, both, for the worst night of my life."

Bronwyn curtseyed. "You're welcome."

Flok chuckled along with Toren.

Still hazy, Toren let them talk over his head. At some point, he moved to a different chair by the fire but didn't quite remember it. Flok was cooking stew over the hearth fire. The scent of meat and cabbage filled the cottage. Dawn passed in a pleasant haze of comforting foods and quiet conversation that he couldn't quite yet participate in.

Flok told Bronwyn about the first time he'd seen Toren shift into a dragon and how he'd literally pissed himself.

"You would have too if you'd been but a child seeing that happen to your best friend," Flok said, scowling.

"But you all shift don't you?" Bronwyn asked.

"Not me," Flok said.

"Only some have that magic," Toren said, eating a slightly stale sweet bun Flok had procured from his storage shelves.

Bronwyn shared the story of the time she'd accidentally bought five mules at market instead of the single one the family required. "I was only twelve. I thought more was always better."

Toren laughed and brushed crumbs from his knee. The firelight on Bronwyn's face was more lovely than the morning sun cascading through the cottage windows.

"What did your parents say?" he asked.

She finished chewing her sweet bun and shook her head. "No more mules."

Flok snorted a laugh, stood, and poured watered wine into all of their crockery mugs. "We must get serious now, though, my king."

"Oof. I know things are bad when you call me by my title."

"General Hanina has claimed your throne."

A stab of rage cut through his gut. "What possible reason is she giving? She isn't even in the line of reign."

"She says you left her in charge in your absence. Says you are obviously dead because you haven't returned. And she says that she will hold the throne until Harold is of age."

Harold was Toren's fifteen-year-old cousin. He was already of age. Toren fought the urge to throw his goblet into the fire.

"Unfortunate for Hanina that I'm alive."

"Such an inconvenience," Bronwyn said sourly. "What do we do about it?"

"I toss her out on her arse." Toren finished the spicy, cool wine and stood. He began pacing, thoughts and plans battling inside his head. His head was at last clearing.

"What about the castle guard?" Bronwyn asked. "Are they on your side or hers? Did she change them out once she had power?" She looked up at him, her doe eyes wide. The innocence in them somewhat hid the wisdom there.

"Where did you learn the tactics of power in a human Star Goddess temple?" Toren asked.

Flok stared, his free hand fisting.

"Easy, Flok. I trust her."

"Are you certain that is wise?"

"I thought you trusted me after seeing me dance."

"You used your power?" Toren asked.

"I did. To help me find the mushroom and then again to make it work on you."

"She did," Flok said, though he sounded resistant. "But why do you have such interest in my king's power at court?"

"He is the only person besides you that I know here. Of course, I'm invested in his power here. The rest of the Unseelie might very well decide my head would look nice on a pike."

Flok let out a reluctant huff of laughter.

"I trust Bronwyn." Toren threaded an unspoken command into his tone. "She is my friend, and you will aid her as needed as you do me."

Still holding the wine pitcher in one hand, Flok bowed. "I am your servant, my king."

Toren nodded and looked at Bronwyn whose gaze flitted over Toren's face before landing on his lips. Her throat moved in a swallow. She was attracted to his power. Well, one couldn't blame her. That didn't make her an enemy.

What did Bronwyn think of this whole situation? Did she trust Flok? Did she trust Toren fully? She'd been cooped up in that temple since she was a child, so she certainly had a limited experience with people, but she was no fool. She hadn't trusted House Mother or Seersha from what she'd said, and she had found a friend in the old woman who had once run the temple. The woman's name escaped him. Greenie or something.

"Did either of you notice anyone following us?" Flok asked.

Bronwyn shook her head and turned her eyes to the fire. Her delicate hands were wrapped around her mug, and her feet were tucked under her in Flok's favorite chair.

Flok's gaze touched on the window that looked toward the path home. "I thought I saw someone outside, but it must have been an animal."

Toren was fairly certain... But that could wait. It would be best to let that situation play out if it was what he thought it was.

"Would you like to bathe and sleep, my king?"

"Ah, yes. But I'll get the water."

"No, you won't." Flok was already walking toward the bathing chamber. He came back with two buckets. "I'll fetch the water if you start that abominable contraption in there. I swear the thing has a soul, and it lives to taunt me."

"What's he talking about?" Bronwyn set down her mug on the small circular table by the hearth as Flok shut the door behind him.

"Come. I'll show you." Toren led her into the tiny chamber off the side of the living area.

The bathing chamber looked the same as it had the

last time Toren had visited. A tub—an intricately carved wooden cabinet lined with copper—sat atop the metal shelf Toren had ordered built for this exact purpose.

Bronwyn bent to look into the space under the shelf. "What is this?"

"I dreamed a contraption that could heat water under a tub and had my craftsfae develop this. We build a small fire there." He pointed to the closed-off, custom hearth in the wall. "Then the hot air feeds into this tubing here." He clicked his claws along the copper that ran over the floorboards like a strange, wide snake. "The hot air releases under the shelf and heats the copper lining of the tub, thereby heating the water inside."

Using the flint, striker, and tinder left for the job, he lit the fire. Flok came in with water and poured the buckets into the tub. He left with a quick bow.

"Thank you," Toren said to Flok's retreating shadow on the wall.

Bronwyn examined the piping. She straightened and blinked, her muddied fingers gripping her robes. "This is wonderful!"

"You will be its next victim."

She laughed and held out a hand. "No, King Toren. I think you have more than earned a soak after dying and all."

He cocked his head and went to her side, taking her

hand and setting it against the place where the blood-iron had cut him. "You saved my life."

"With Flok's help. And the cat's."

A chuckle bubbled out of him. "I do remember the foul-furred demon. Where did he run off to?"

"I don't know, but I think my magic brought him to me. He helped me find my way back from where I picked the mushroom."

Toren smoothed a fallen lock of her hair away from her face and tucked it behind her ear. Her eyes lowered slightly, and a she took a small, stuttered breath. She definitely desired him. He pulled her close, urging her to set her head against his chest. Her skin was the softest thing he'd ever touched.

"Thank you, Bronwyn Greensmith."

She pressed closer and desire surged through him. "Tell me what my family name means."

"Well, you know what a smith is."

He pulled away, then gently removed her bandage. Rage stabbed his chest. He wished for vengeance, for fire and blood and retribution. He took a square of linen from the stool beside the tub and walked to a bowl sitting on a high table near the back wall. Once he had the cloth damp, he returned to her and cleaned her wound.

"Yes. A blacksmith," she said.

"The Greensmith was the one who first made

weapons for the Fae before the times of separation between Seelie and Unseelie. At that time, we had no knowledge of metallurgy. The humans taught our forebears the art." He tossed the dirtied square of linen into a basket by the door.

"I wonder how my family ended up on a farm rather than in a forge."

"It was a long, long time ago."

"In the time of the Star Goddess?" she asked.

"Could be. It's hard to define the time that has passed since then."

"Because of how time moves here?"

"Yes, and simply because the ancients didn't care much for recording the passage of moons and years."

"I've noticed that in my readings."

He took her by the arms and held her away from him. "You need a bath and some rest. Would you like help or would you prefer to be alone? We have no servants here."

"I...I wouldn't mind your assistance."

She looked up at him through her dark gold lashes and longing shot through him root to crown.

"You're certain?" He left her side and shut the bathing chamber door firmly. Flok would get the hint and take a walk in the forest.

Nodding, she began to shed her robes. The first layer was a wrap with a double laced tie. Though the hems and collar were embellished with black and white embroidery, it was a simple frock. She let it fall to the floor. Underneath that, she wore a type of black-dyed shift, its neckline low and wide. More embroidery ran from neck to ankle. The stitching was sewn to mimic thousands of stars in every jewel shade—ruby, emerald, sapphire, diamond, and ones he didn't know the names of. The shift sat tightly against her willowy body and the curves of her hips threw dangerous imaginings into his head. His heart beat more quickly.

She held out her arms and nodded at him, so he untied the knot at her waist and removed the fine shift. Yet more layers remained between his gaze and her body. He hung the shift over the wicker chair by the tub, then folded the outer robe and laid it on top. He hoped she wouldn't be annoyed by his desire to keep her garments from damage.

"If you wish to set these garments on fire and dance on their ashes, I will light the bonfire at your command. But if not...they are beautifully crafted."

"I'll think on it. Thank you." She grinned, her pink lips drawing up toward the dimples in her cheeks. "Can you get this?" Giving him her back, she pointed over her shoulder at an intricate set of knots holding two more layers of clothing in place.

He ran a knuckle down her back, beside the knots, and felt her body move as her breath caught. Smiling, he slowly undid the first of the ties. "Just how frightened of your body were those at the temple? They have locked you up like the most fearsome beast."

She laughed, and the sound wasn't shy or coy, but laced with wickedness.

"Laugh like that every time you can." He slipped the final knot free and slid his fingers under the edge of the plain white cloth. "I like it very much."

"And you think I long to please you, King Toren?" She extended one smooth arm, spun, and then the two last layers of clothing rippled down to her feet. Her eyes burned into his.

He couldn't breathe. Her beauty stole every thought, memory, and piece of knowledge from his mind. The shapes of her... The shadowed angles and inviting curves...

She laughed that laugh again.

He coughed and tried to find his voice. "I've never seen a more lovely creature in my life, and I've seen more than my fair share."

Her cheeks blushed, and she climbed the short steps at the base of the tall tub. Lifting one leg at a time, she entered the bath. Steam rose around her like an echo of her power, circling and ringing her, shielding the full view of her glory from him.

Taking a cup from the table near the door, he cleared his throat once more and adjusted his trousers. He knew she realized his desire for her, but he didn't want to be too aggressive. If she'd ever been down this road, it had been years. That much was obvious. They would take their time.

"Would you like me to wash your hair?"

❧ 28 ❧

BRONWYN

W as I dreaming? Yes. I had to be.

Toren, King of the Unseelie, was pouring hot water over my hair and humming softly to me. Yep. Had to be a dream.

The cup clicked on the stone floor as he set it down and finished wetting my hair. I heard him shuffling around then he was stroking the crown of my head and the nape of my neck with a bar of scented soap. It smelled divine, but wasn't nearly as divine as the feel of his other hand in my hair. His knuckles rolled gently over my scalp, and he drew my tresses over my shoulder. Shivers of pleasure danced down my body, and I tried to stifle my sighs so I didn't seem so ridiculously green and desperate for his touch.

He handed me the bar of soap, then set to drawing

his claws carefully from my hairline at my forehead down the length of my hair. My thighs clenched, and I smoothed the soap over my neck and down avoiding my wound. He poured water over me again. The heat and the sound of his humming made my head swim as if I were fully under the water. I was delighted to drown in the feel of this moment.

With soft movements, he rung out my hair, twisted it, and tucked the ends so it stayed in place. He had long hair too so I supposed he had experience. This had to be a Fae sort of thing to do. I couldn't imagine a human male being this considerate and tender. But maybe they were. I didn't know anything about it. Gantu hadn't been this kind certainly.

Toren ran a hand over my shoulder. His hand was warmer than the water and though he had callouses from sword fighting and life in general, his palm was smooth and pleasant. I lifted his hand and studied his gray-black claws. They were more like talons, really. Like small versions of the ones he had in his dragon form.

His breath tickled my ear. "Do you find me interesting?"

"I do."

"Would you like to see how the Unseelie tempt their females?"

"If all of that hair washing and humming isn't a part of the repertoire, I highly suggest you add it."

His chuckle warmed my cheek. "I'll remember that."

"Show me." Avoiding my cut, I set his hand above my breast, curiosity whirling around the desire that pooled low in my body.

He drew one talon up the column of my throat, then set it against my pulse beneath my jaw. My heart raced. He could kill me with one rip of that finger.

"Are you afraid?"

"A little. I am trying to trust you. I mean, I do, but I don't."

He huffed a quiet laugh that dusted over the nape of my exposed neck. "The fear heightens your senses, and because I've proven I won't actually hurt you..."

His pause urged me to speak.

"You have proven so," I said.

"Then the fear is a gentle one. A pleasant one, if you will."

His other hand drew a delicate line from my shoulder, between my breasts, along my stomach to where it stopped at my navel. He dragged his talons softly back up that same path and my body shivered with desire.

"It's..." My tongue tripped over my words as the heat inside me intensified. I wanted so much for him to touch me everywhere. "It's odd that you avoid the... more common areas of...interest."

"Areas of interest?" A jovial tone hid in his words. "Do tell me what those are in your world. Although I have spent time with the humans now and again, I'm not sure I know your ways."

"You're teasing me."

His lips touched the back of my neck, and I swallowed. "Do you want me to stop?" he asked.

"Teasing or touching?"

"Either or both. You tell me, Darling Dancer."

"Neither. Thank you."

He chuckled, then made a noise in the back of his throat, something close to a purr. "Now, what about those areas of interest?"

I took his hand and brought it just under my breast. His fingers curled slightly, cupping me. His talon left the pulse point under my chin, but he set his teeth against the tip of my ear and began moving his thumb slowly back and forth.

"Such exotic, round ears you have, Dancer."

Pleasure fluttered down my torso and into my thighs, and my head fell back against his chest as his other hand traveled lower. He flicked a talon over my hip, splashing the water lightly. Curling that hand, he poised his talons around my hip, the slight prick of their sharp points drawing a shuddering breath from me.

His tongue touched my ear lobe, then his teeth bit lightly.

I gasped, then he licked the spot as his hand left my hip to grip my jaw firmly.

A knock made me jump, and Toren growled like the Unseelie monster he was.

"What is it?" he snarled.

"I think you need to see this. Now. I apologize, my king." Flok's voice was higher pitched than normal.

Toren grumbled in my ear. "We will continue this at the soonest possible moment, Bronwyn." He set a dark blue, folded bathing sheet on the side of the tub and met my gaze. His silver eyes seemed darker somehow, the slit narrow as an assassin's blade. He bowed his head, then left the room.

I finished scrubbing the mud from my body with shaking hands. I had almost made love to the King of the Unseelie. Could I just do that? What would the repercussions be? Weren't all kings betrothed by his age? Would a Fae female attack me for my relationship with Toren? And what about his council and his people? Were they like the Seelie who were heavily ruled by a small council until King Lysanael's recent overhaul of their government?

Drying myself with the sheet, I eyed the shelves on the wall for any guest clothing. I had no idea what Unseelie customs were in this situation. When guests stayed at our farm when I was younger, Mother always provided them with blankets and a washbasin, but we never had enough gladecoin to provide additional clothing. But Flok's house screamed wealth, so maybe he would have something stashed away.

Wrapped in my sheet with my hair braided over my shoulder, I went to the armoire in the corner. Blankets woven in shades of night sat next to a collection of lovely-smelling beeswax candles. The chandler had pressed bird designs into the wax and I ran a finger over the tiny wings. Above that, a reed basket held another bathing sheet and a clean shirt. I took it and shook it out. It was a man's shirt—I mean, a Fae male's—but it came to my knees so it would serve well enough until I washed the mud from my Sacred Sister robes. I found some bandages too, so I wrapped my wound to help it heal without getting dirty.

A shout outside the cottage had me dressing as quickly as someone very damp can manage. Barefoot, I ran into the main room only to find it empty. I swung the front door open, hoping to see Flok and Toren.

But the area around the house was quiet.

Who had been shouting? And why?

A pair of strange shoes sat beside the door. They were made of wood and leather and had pointed toes. There were no laces to loosen and tie, so I just slid them on and headed into the forest.

I stopped when I felt eyes on me.

"Who is there?" Was this the one who had been following us?

A meow startled me and Sir Cat loped out of the woods. I bent low and he jumped into my arms. "You weigh a lot for a cat."

He made a disjointed growling noise like he wasn't happy with my judgement.

I rubbed his head and walked a little farther into the forest. "Where did you run off to earlier? Did you see Toren and Flok out here just now?

A crack sounded behind me, and I whirled.

"Uh oh."

🎐 29 🎐

TOREN

"What exactly did you see?" Toren asked Flok as they climbed a small rise near the cottage and looked down from the canopy and into the area beside the river.

"Only movement in the shadows. And it smells human. At first, I thought I was only scenting Bronwyn, but now..."

Toren chewed the inside of his cheek and lifted his nose to the air. "Definitely human."

A quiet growl issued from the back of Flok's throat. "Do you think there are any Seelie with this human?"

A family of fern foxes' leafy tails fluttered as they scurried past the bridge and into their hole in a fallen log. The sun had gone orange and was drifting down, turning the sky to shades of gold. They needed to rest, eat more, and then get on the road to home. General Hanina's days were numbered...

"I don't smell any Seelie, but I have always thought they can perhaps mask their scents."

"Wily ones."

"Yes. I had hoped to be finished evading their blood-iron now that I am home, but I guess this is to go on for a while."

Flok clapped a hand on his shoulder and smiled grimly. "But you have me at your back again, so this time, they will be the ones who must hide themselves." His grin was death, and Toren knew his own smile echoed the sentiment.

They started back toward the cottage when a scream pealed through the trees.

"Bronwyn." Toren was running before he finished saying her name.

Flok almost kept pace with him, but Toren shifted and then he was flying. To the southwest of the cottage, Bronwyn held that hideous cat against her chest and in front of her a gargoyle swung its meaty fist.

He shot toward the gargoyle's head, gathered fire in his belly, then let it ripple out as he flew past the monster. The gargoyle shrieked and fell backward as Toren rose higher into the forest canopy. Flok stood in front of Bronwyn, his sword out and his dagger flipping from his skilled hand. The dagger stuck in the gargoyle's gut and the creature roared. Blisters from Toren's blaze rose on its head and chest, and blood oozed from the wound Flok had inflicted.

Arrows zipped from the forest and peppered the gargoyle's throat. Toren summoned fire again and blasted the gargoyle until it dropped, smoking, to the earth. The stench of its burning flesh seared his nostrils and blocked out his ability to scent out who might have fired those arrows. They weren't bloodiron tips though. He'd seen their plain steel tips as they'd flown to their mark.

Remaining in his dragon form, he landed beside Flok and Bronwyn. The cat yowled once as if in thanks.

He lifted his head and roared. Only he could take dragon form. Those in the forest would know who he was. He shifted back into his high Fae form and drew his sword.

"Your king orders you from your hiding place to thank you for your assistance." He turned to Bronwyn, checking her for wounds with his gaze. "Are you all right?"

"I am. Thank you. I thought I saw you two over here, so I came to see what was happening."

"Understandable. We will talk as soon as I figure out what is going on here exactly."

She nodded, and he eyed the place from where the arrows had been shot. All was silent.

"Don't be foolish. Come out or I'll come after you, and I promise you won't enjoy that."

If he had to enter that area, would he be ambushed? Perhaps he should send Flok back with Bronwyn.

At last, a male rode forward on a black stallion and cleared his throat. "King Toren?"

It was Norinal, a warrior known for his work during the plague that had turned all the beasts against anything that moved. Norinal dismounted, took a knee, and bowed his head. He wore a bow on his back and the quiver at his side was empty.

"Thank you for your help. Who is with you?" Toren eyed the space behind Norinal. "Reveal yourselves."

Norinal wasn't a bad sort, but he had been enamored with General Hanina so it was impossible to know on what side he stood with Toren being gone for so long.

Finally, Norinal's companions rode into the small glen. They were all warriors who had worked special missions for Toren through the years. Not his top warriors, but the ones who had worked under those chosen males and females. Mimicking Norinal, they dismounted, went to their knees, and dipped their heads in respect.

"A bit tardy on the show of submission, aren't we?" Toren raised an eyebrow and kept his sword out, lowering it. "Tell me. Are you shocked to see me here? How is everything in my kingdom?"

Glancing at one another, they rose. Three kept swords unsheathed—a crime in the presence of Toren while at court. In the forest—well, rules were more of suggestions while out in the wilds. Toren wasn't one to stand on ceremony or inflict rule for no purpose. But if they did this as a show of rebellion, they would soon be greeting their ancestors in the afterlife.

"Everything is well, my king," Norinal said stiffly. "We're shocked and glad to see you. We were told you had died."

Flok traded a glance with Toren.

"Who told you this lie?" Toren took another step forward and sheathed his sword. He wasn't afraid of them. If he shifted, he could end them with one breath. "Come now. You must recall where this sad rumor originated."

"General Hanina believed you had been trapped when the drumstones were sealed, and that King Lysanael of the Seelie had murdered you after his wedding. We felt the death of many Unseelie monsters that day."

"But no high Unseelie Fae were there except for me. Only monsters. No one saw the crown go black here so why would you believe her?"

"She said the spell on the crown was old magic and couldn't be relied on."

Bronwyn came forward, and many of the warriors' gazes dusted over her bare legs. Toren let out a low warning growl and all gazes returned to his face.

"Why would the crown go black?" she asked.

The warriors and Flok murmured and made small sounds of shock and disbelief.

She dropped back a step. "I'm sorry. Did I do something wrong? I was only curious."

"It is customary here to request permission to speak when the king is present unless you are asked a direct question." Toren pursed his lips, hoping she would understand that in order to rule, one had to retain certain behaviors that separated king from subject.

"Forgive me." She bowed her head.

He lifted her chin with a finger. "You don't bow to anyone anymore, Bronwyn Greensmith. Besides, you don't know our customs. There is nothing to forgive. As for the crown, it is the ancient crown of the Unseelie throne and the gold and silver leaves that decorate the adamant go dark when the ruler dies."

Her cheeks colored, and her eyes softened. Oh how he longed to take her home and spoil her, to protect her within the walls of his castle. He wanted to show her off and watch as others fell for her as he had. It would take time, of course, and there would be trouble at first, but surely they would all see the beauty of her heart and soul.

Releasing her, he faced Norinal and the rest. "We will sleep for a few hours here. You keep watch outside the cottage."

"Aye, Your Majesty," they said in unison.

Norinal began ordering them to various positions around Flok's home as Toren led Flok and Bronwyn back inside.

Flok set his bow and quiver by the door. "You don't actually trust them to watch over us, do you?"

Toren removed his weapons and belt and set them on the chest beside Flok's bow. He ran a hand through his hair. He was exhausted and frustrated that he and Bronwyn had been interrupted.

"No. We will have to take turns keeping an eye on them."

"I'll take first watch," Bronwyn said.

Toren shook his head. "Absolutely not. You're sleeping the entire time. I'll take you to the guest bedchamber. Is that all right, Flok?"

A smile crossed Flok's mouth. "Thank you for asking."

"It's your home."

"I would be honored to house your guest, my king." His gaze flicked to Bronwyn who was setting the cat on the sling-seat by the hearth. Flok still didn't trust Bronwyn completely. They'd have to change that.

Bronwyn followed Toren up the stairs to the door of the guest chamber. He swung the green wooden door open, and she went inside.

"This bed is lovely." She sat on the edge of the fluffy madness that served as a bed.

"I'm glad you like it. That thing swallows me when I lie down. I prefer the floor by the fire downstairs."

"Really? A king who chooses the floor?"

"Flok has furs enough to make it comfortable, and I don't risk suffocating in luxury."

She chuckled and crossed her bare legs. The sun reached through the three-paned window and painted her thigh in shades of pearly light. His lips longed to kiss her there and to feel the velvet softness of her skin.

"You...you could stay," she said, her voice almost too quiet to hear.

Oh, how he wanted to. But dark circles ringed her eyes, and he felt bad for even desiring her when she so clearly required rest.

"No, you need sleep. I know how weak humans are without proper rest. I shouldn't have bothered you during your bath."

He bowed his head—something he hadn't done since his mother and father died—then left quickly before his body could demand that he take her up on the invitation and spend their entire rest time in the throes of passion.

Besides that, Flok needed a turn to rest as well so Toren had to watch the warriors for a spell.

Soon, it would be time to fly to the castle and confront whatever treachery awaited him. Blood would be shed.

❧ 30 ❧

BRONWYN

hy was he leaving? Did he regret the way he'd touched me in the bath? I went to the window and set a hand on the cold glass. The warriors stood in a half circle around the cottage, their shapes warped by the imperfections in the window glass.

I crawled into bed, my mind whirling. Gargoyles. Toren dying and coming back to life. Potentially disloyal and armed warriors right outside. What had Flok seen outside? Had it been something other than the gargoyle?

My body thrummed with the memory of Toren's hands skating down my chest and stomach. I couldn't believe he'd rejected my invitation to stay. He must have decided it was time to stop playing around with the human since we were back in his kingdom and there were problems to deal with. But the way he'd said I would never again bow to anyone—what did he mean by that?

With so many worries, it all began to blur in my head. I shoved it to the back of my mind and closed my eyes.

I dreamed of a dragon with silver eyes and of flames that circled me. The fire burned so brightly that I was blinded...

A quiet knock woke me. The sun shone brightly through the window and cast shadows across the wooden floorboards.

"I have some food to break your fast if you're hungry." It was Flok's voice. He didn't sound happy.

I took a summer weight throw blanket from a chest in the corner and wrapped it around me before going to the door and cracking it open. Flok's features gave away no emotion.

"My king isn't awake yet, so keep your tromping to a minimum please." He spun and started down the stairs, his graceful Fae feet making no sound.

I trailed him and slipped through the living area. Toren snored lightly in front of the hearth, his features serious, and a fur was draped over his body. He wore no shirt, and I wondered if he was naked.

Flok clicked his tongue at me, and I joined him, heading through the arched doorway into the kitchen area. He had set up a round table and put out plates and mugs. Platters of varying foods steamed. I didn't recognize a single item. And I couldn't stop smiling.

This was freedom.

Rubbing my hands together, I tried to decide what to try first. Should I ask what customs they had with regard to mealtimes? Though I was thrilled to be emancipated from House Mother and her rules, I didn't want to be rude toward Flok or Toren and his people. I planned to stay here if they would let me, and it would be good to learn their ways. Any rules I followed here would be done by my choice unlike the ones I'd been beaten into following at the temple.

Flok was ignoring me as he poured himself something orange. He wore simple trousers and a plain blue tunic belted low on his waist. He wore two daggers and the hilt of a small knife stuck out from a pocket in the leather vest that he'd tied on over his tunic. His pinched mouth and furrowed eyebrows told me to leave him alone.

"Not a morning person, eh?" I scooted my chair closer and one leg caught for a moment and squeaked against the floor. Grimacing, I looked through the archway for Toren, but he was gone.

"Looking for something?" Toren's voice from across the kitchen made my heart leap.

He was pouring himself a cup of whatever stuff Flok had been doling out a moment ago.

"How did you get...ah, never mind. What is our plan now that these warriors are here?"

"We'll travel with them to my castle. Of course, we'll arrive first. Even if they shift, none of their animal forms possess the ability to move as quickly as I do as a dragon."

"Oh, what type of creatures do they shift into?" I leaned forward in my chair to look out the window.

"A wolf, two stags, and a vulture. The rest don't shift."

"So that ability is simply inherited or not?"

Toren nodded and pulled out a chair. "You two will ride on my back." He sat and lifted his drink to his lips.

"I..." On his back while he was in his dragon form, he meant. I was going to ride a dragon today.

Flok chuckled and wiped his mouth on a square of linen.

"What?" I asked.

"Your eyes were as big as Darius' boulders," Flok said.

"Who is Darius?" I asked and set my three-pronged fork down, worried I'd done something against their customs. I hadn't even touched any food yet because I didn't know what was what and how to eat any of it properly.

Toren waved my question off. "Just the name of a spot beside the castle's moat. Stop teasing her, Flok. It would be odd if she wasn't shocked about our life here."

"Do you often ride your king, Flok?" I gave him a salty look.

Flok spit his bite of some yellow fruit onto his plate and coughed. Toren patted his back and laughed.

"She can dish it back, can't she?" Toren gave me an appreciative glance, and the spark in his eye warmed my insides more than it should have.

He had rejected my offer last night. I would leave off tempting him or being tempted by him from now on. I was happy enough being free of the temple. I didn't need love too.

"Can we bring Sir Cat?"

Toren's smile fell flat.

"Come on. He's adorable." I clicked my tongue and the big, furry beast shot from the living area and into my lap. His purr rumbled against my body. "What type of cat is he? Our barn cats were never this large."

"He's a mountain cat," Toren said. "They are three times the size of cats in your realm, and they live, well, no one knows for certain. They don't usually spend much of their lives around people."

His fur was incredibly thick and soft. I wondered where the scar along his spine had come from. Maybe a monster attack.

"Allow me to tell you about the foods here," Toren said, eyeing my empty plate. "Since my friend seems to have been a little grumpy and reticent this morning." He threw a glare at Flok who shrugged.

"She didn't ask."

Toren raised a black eyebrow. "You sound like a youngling."

"Apologies, my king."

Pointing to a tray of pink-tinged slices, Toren said, "This is fire fish. It's smoked, and it has a spiciness to it that doesn't hit your mouth until your finished chewing. Those there are star buns."

I picked one of the iced bread items. "They look a little like our scones." I bit off one of the six arms of the shaped bun and flavors exploded over my tongue. Ginger, sugar, and lemon. "Oooooo. This is my favorite."

My dream had been to be free, to eat what I wanted, and go where I chose. And Toren's world provided all of that and more. But then I remembered what had drawn them out of the cottage before my run-in with the gargoyle.

"What did you follow in the forest? Before we met the monster and the other warriors?"

Flok eyed Toren, who took a slow breath. "Someone is definitely trailing us," Toren said.

❧ 31 ❧
BRONWYN

I paused in choosing something to eat. "I guess you
don't know who."

Toren shrugged. "I have my theories, but I
haven't seen them clearly. Now, this here," he said, obviously changing the subject, "is brunhost, a sweet
cheese."

"It's brown." I fought a shudder.

Flok set a slice of bread on my plate, then placed a
sliver of the brunhost on top. He motioned for me to
try it.

Toren's eyes were sparkling with mirth again. "The
cheese won't bite you. It's very good. I dare you to
try it."

I took a bite. The bread was hearty, and the cheese
was soft and sugary.

"See? You like it, don't you?" Toren leaned forward on the table.

"I do, actually."

Sir Cat raised himself up and sniffed at the brown cheese. I smeared my fingertip in the brunhost and let him lick it off. Flok and Toren traded a wearied look.

"She'll have the whole forest coming with us to be spoiled at your castle keep, my king."

Toren shook his head and served himself some of the fire fish. I wasn't too keen on eating something that smelled so strongly in the morning, so I kept to my sweets.

ONCE WE HAD CLEANED UP AND DRESSED, TOREN AND I went out the front door. I wore my robes once more though they were still stained with mud along the hem, and some specks of blood remained along the sleeve and front. Hopefully, I could find new clothing somewhere in the castle town. A lightness bloomed in my chest at the thought of perusing the market for whatever clothing I wanted. Of course, I had no money so perhaps that was presumptuous. Sir Cat meowed up at me, and I bent to run a hand over his pelt.

Outside, the warriors had mounted their horses and seemed ready to do as Toren ordered. Their faces gave away no emotion as they awaited his commands.

Flok joined us and handed me a satchel with a long strap. "For your cat." He made a face like the words tasted bad.

Delight wove through me, and I squeezed Flok's arm. "Thank you."

He stiffened at my touch, but seemed to relax after a moment. "You're welcome."

As Toren spoke to the knights, I crouched and opened the satchel. "Come on, then. If you want to join us, you'll be safer in here."

The cat made a sort of low growling noise, but he snuggled into the bag anyway. I hefted him up and set him against my chest like I had seen women do with their babies.

The warriors galloped into the forest, and I trailed Flok and Toren a little ways from the cottage. Toren faced me and tilted his head. "Prepared to ride?"

He extended his arms, and in a flash, he was not a Fae king but a towering dark gray dragon. But his eyes were the same silver. His wings stretched wide like the ceiling of the temple library, the bones and sinew a work of art. He lowered his head and neck, and his belly brushed the clearing's mosses and clover.

Flok took a long rope, flung one end over Toren's neck, then proceeded to knot and loop it until a length ran over Toren's back. Then he stood beside Toren and held out a hand to me. I took the offered help and stepped up onto Toren's wingtip. Toren held his wing completely still for me, then once I was steady on my feet, he raised me to his back.

I settled myself—with Sir Cat in front of me in his satchel—just behind the bend of Toren's dragon neck and held onto the rope. Toren's scales were subtly iridescent, and I rubbed a hand over them, marveling at the magic that could turn a Fae male with smooth skin and pointed ears into a miraculous monster with scales like precious stones and wings the size of a building.

Gracefully climbing up behind me, Flok cleared his throat. "You are the second person to experience this. I myself have only been permitted such favor once, and that was a dire emergency."

Toren ran toward the clearing at the side of the cottage, leapt into the air, and beat his wings against the gusty wind rising from the west. We lifted into the sky above the forest canopy, and the sun dusted gold over the view of countless dark green trees and a distant rocky ridge ringed in a sparkling mist.

"It's stunning."

Flok was being careful not to touch me overmuch. He sat a hands-width behind me and kept from pitching off Toren's back with just the strength of his legs, which was a wonder in and of itself.

The wind blew through my hair, and I was glad I'd secured it into two low, braided knots on the back of my head. Hopefully, the leather ties Flok had given me would hold. I wanted to ask Flok a million questions, but the wind was loud in my ears and it stole the breath from my mouth. The cat had burrowed its way to the very bottom of the satchel, curling into a ball that seemed too small to be possible for an animal of his size.

Toren's wings tipped slightly, and I adjusted my weight as we veered toward the sun. The daytime sky looked different here. Instead of the blue of the Seelie and human realms, a golden hue stretched from horizon to horizon. The day also didn't seem as bright, like even though the sun climbed as it did in the other world, it glowed with a softer light.

We flew for hours, and my legs itched to get back to walking. I wasn't used to sitting in one place for long periods of time. Nor was I used to riding an Unseelie dragon. A laugh bubbled up, and I shook my head. I couldn't believe this was my life.

My mind wandered back to the person Toren believed was following us. At least this shadowy person would be left far behind. There was no way they'd keep up. Even if they had a horse, they'd be behind the knights and be forced to draw away if they wished to remain hidden. Pushing that worry away, I adjusted my grip on the rough rope and let myself relax and enjoy the ride.

With my free hand, I reached out and smoothed

Toren's shoulder. Did dragons have shoulders? His scales were wildly beautiful. I looked beyond to his head where large black horns curled toward his back. Raised plates grew along the back of his skull and extended a bit down his neck.

The strange mist I'd seen far off came closer, and through it, a castle and its double set of walls appeared. From a distance, I'd thought this was a ridge of rocks, but it was Toren's home. The walls and the buildings in the inner bailey—including the keep—were the color of the darkest emerald. Made of a smooth stone, they should have reflected the light, but they did the opposite, drinking it in and drawing me in. I wanted to know how Toren lived inside these walls, who he cared about and why, and how the Unseelie high Fae lived. But the most key question was...

Would they accept me?

32

BRONWYN

We soared over the glistening moat and the outer bailey with its massive labyrinth of turf-topped and dark wood buildings. Unseelie folk halted in the streets and pointed upward, their eyes wide. They'd thought their king was dead, and here he was flying right over them. It had to be a shock.

Toren flew toward the keep, his shadow blackening several rectangular structures, a massive garden, what might have been stables with all the horses going in and out, and a series of buildings that were probably kitchens and storage areas. Archers on the walls aimed at us, but lowered their bows as they shouted a welcome to their king.

We landed behind the keep in a large courtyard surrounded by peaked archways. Lanterns sparkling with a strange green light hung from each passageway and tall men stood underneath them. Not men, I silently corrected myself. Unseelie Fae. Battle axes hung from their belts, and they wore livery that was gold and a green just a shade lighter than the walls. Some started to pull out their weapons and step toward us, but of course, they must have recognized Toren's dragon form. They were simply surprised.

Flok helped me maneuver onto Toren's wing tip, and then Toren lowered me to the courtyard. Flok hopped down beside me.

With servants and knights bowing all around, Toren shifted into his Fae form and held out his arm to me. I bent to free Sir Cat before accepting Toren's arm. He looked down at me, his eyes sparkling with mischief and one corner of his mouth lifting to show a Fae fang.

"Did you enjoy the journey, my dancer?"

Perhaps Toren did want to explore a relationship with me. That look in his eyes was more than friendly.

"I did. You're very fast."

Flok came up behind us and grinned, obviously entertained at our exchange for a reason I didn't grasp. Toren popped Flok's stomach with the back of his hand. "Go on, Flok. Mind your own business."

Chuckling, Flok dropped back to give us privacy.

Toren stopped to speak to a Fae male with dark red

hair who had emerged from the keep's back door at our arrival. He wore a deep blue tunic with a silver dragon symbol over his slight frame. Perhaps he was the castle steward. He didn't seem to have the right body type to be another guard or a knight. Once Toren finished speaking to him, the steward hurried inside the keep through a small door I hadn't noticed set cleverly into the wall.

With Flok a few steps behind, Toren and I entered the keep through another door, this one larger and guarded by two Fae that had to be twins. Both had slender tails and orange-hued eyes. I turned as Toren led us onward, and the guards were staring at Toren's back. Flok followed my gaze, then met my eyes with a look of concern. He seemed worried about whose side the castle guards were on, but Toren didn't appear tense at all. Smiling, he brought us down a narrow corridor that turned into a stairwell. Green-and-blue-flamed torches flickered on the walls as we climbed up with Flok on our heels. A servant popped out of a side door, dipped a curtsey, and listened as Flok asked her a question I couldn't hear.

"I'm very glad you didn't fall off my back," Toren whispered to me as we continued onward. "Of course, if you had toppled, I would have been able to rescue you and delight in your gratitude."

I leaned closer. "And how would you prefer me to

display gratitude if I find the need to do so?" I whispered.

Flok's steps sounded farther back on the stairs.

Toren rubbed his sharp chin with a talon. I really did think of them as talons now that I'd compared them to the cat's claws and his dragon talons. They were more solid and larger than claws.

"I wouldn't be against the reward of your undivided attention at the upcoming ball," Toren said.

"You're hosting a ball?"

"It's nearly time for the Star Festival. A party is required. It's tradition."

"How are Unseelie events such as this different from Seelie? I know the Seelie tend to dance like humans, in lines or in groups, with measured and practiced steps. They are known to lay out massive feasts and pour wine until dawn."

"Doesn't sound too bad, but we are far more fun than the Seelie. I assure you. For starters, we don't stick to rules when it comes to dancing. We embrace our wild side." His glance slid my way, and the half-lidded, beastly look made my heart flip.

We came to a door embellished with painted gold dragons.

"This will be your bedchamber for now," he said, glancing at the door. "Let me know if you wish to move when I return. We will have games today after I take care of some business."

"Games?"

"Archery. Axe-throwing. Tafl."

"What is Tafl?"

He faced me, took my hand, and set his talon in the center of my palm. Looking up at me through his thick, black eyelashes, he began to explain the strategy. "...and the king and his knights are in the center of the board. To win, the king must reach one of the corner spaces."

I shivered slightly as he moved his talon along my palm, and he grinned. I rolled my eyes. He was so full of himself. Why did I have to react to his every touch?

"But it's not easy," he said. "The soldiers are always attempting to squeeze the king with their positioning."

After giving my palm a quick kiss, he released me and opened the bedchamber door. Two servants curtseyed as we entered the large room. The older of the servants, a white-haired female with lighter gray skin than Toren's and bright pink eyes stood beside another female. She had a knot of teal-colored hair and a scar running over her nose. Both of their stares went from me to Toren and back again—a human and a male they had been told was dead. The older Fae moved her claw across her opposite wrist in a behavior I didn't recognize. Toren didn't seem to notice.

"Please care for my guest as if she was me," Toren

ordered with a firm but polite tone. "Do not permit anyone else to enter this chamber. I will set a guard at the door." He faced me. "I asked my steward to bring several sets of clothing so you can choose what to wear today. It is a casual affair, but I encourage you to wear whatever you want. You have freedom here, and I will defend every choice of yours to the death."

Warmth encircled my heart, and I touched his arm. "You don't have to do that. I'm incredibly grateful just to be away from the temple."

"I know I don't have to. I want to." His eyes simmered, and he covered my hand with his, sending a tingling sensation down the length of my body. "I will come back for you after a few hours. For now, you need to rest."

He left me with the servants, and I turned to greet them properly even though my mind stayed with Toren. What would his first step be in removing General Hanina from power? Was he worried for his safety here?

"What can I call you?" I asked the older Fae.

"Maja. And this," she said gesturing to the other servant, "is Sofie."

"Nice to meet you."

I sat on a stool by a long mirror, and Maja removed my bandage while Sofie stoked the fire. With a linen dipped in steaming, sandalwood-scented water, Maja washed my wound. I was glad to see it had scabbed over and was healing well. Maja then cleaned my face and hands.

"Did you truly believe King Toren was dead?" I asked, hoping they wouldn't be too afraid to answer.

Sofie spun. "Is he not an *onde vardoger*?"

"Sofie! Silence." Maja's voice was a slap, and the other servant returned to the fire without another word.

I wanted to ask them to repeat what she'd called Toren, but I didn't wish to start trouble for them. My curiosity could wait. This was Toren's kingdom, and he knew what he was doing.

A knock sounded, and Sofie opened the door. Another servant brought in an armful of clothing, bowed, then left. Sofie began sorting the clothes and laying them out on the bed. Maja braided my hair as I studied the dresses, tunics, and leggings.

"What would a lady usually wear to participate in games with the king?"

Maja's hands stopped moving on my head, and she gently turned my shoulders so that I faced the mirror again. She'd braided my long hair into three sections and set them on the crown of my head. It was an unusual style for me, but I liked it.

"I love it. Thank you."

"You're welcome. To answer your question," Maja said, going to the bed and eyeing the fabrics. "A court lady would wear this dress to play strategy past-time games with the others ." She held it up for me.

The design was simple—a wide neckline that would show the tops of my breasts, a form-fitting waist, and a slight flare at the bottom. Most of the dress was dark blue and embroidered silver and black showed at the hem and neckline.

Sofie went to a small chest sitting on a table near the bed. She rummaged around and came up with a necklace that mimicked the colors of the embroidery. The stones were shiny and seemed black at one angle and then silver when you tipped them toward the light. They were like river stones sitting under the water with the sunlight rippling over their smooth surfaces. It brought my mind back to the forest and to the mysterious person who had followed us. Why wouldn't Toren reveal who he thought it might be? I wouldn't know the person of course because I knew no one here, but Flok would have surely. Why was Toren keeping information from his closest friend?

"So you like it? Are you ready to dress now?" Maja's voice shook me out of my wonderings.

"Oh, sorry. I'm just...tired. It's perfect. Thank you. Yes."

They dressed me with quick and capable hands, then I sat in the chair by the fire to await Toren. A tray of food was brought, and I was so hungry that I ate every single item without asking even one question about any of it. I drank down a goblet of a light, sweet wine and felt delightfully relaxed. I fell into a dream of clever, dangerous hands, and the low whisper of "Dancer" in my ear...

33

TOREN

Toren lounged in the bath, steam rising from the water and thoughts of Bronwyn drifting through his mind. He wished she was here with her sweet laugh, long limbs, and soft skin...

"My liege," Crommie said, his voice as familiar as Toren's own. "Sir Hollan is at your door."

Hollan, a powerfully built brute of a male who'd been in the military for over a decade, was basically General Hanina's right hand. Rage prickled along the back of Toren's neck, and he bared his teeth. "Thank you, Crommie. Please tell him I am indisposed."

"He has been told and will not leave."

"Then have him arrested."

"As you say, my king."

"Actually." Toren stood up and climbed out of the tub. "I'll handle this."

Soaking wet and infuriated, he walked to the door and yanked it open.

Hollan bowed low, and the low knot of his black hair came loose. "Apologies."

"Apologies, what?"

He shoved his hair away from his face and began to rise. "My...king."

Toren gripped the male's hair and yanked him close so he could look down into Hollan's traitorous blue eyes. "Why did it take you a moment to decide to call me your king? Be careful how you answer."

Sweat beaded on Hollan's wide forehead and square chin. "The general said you might be an onde vardoger."

Toren nearly released him.

Ice crackled in Toren's veins. An onde vardoger? They were incredibly rare spirits that could mimic the recently deceased and take their place in the world. The spirits' main goal was to bleed a person dry of energy. It was a horrifying thing, and he'd only seen one in his entire life. He couldn't believe his people would swallow that story from Hanina. It was so outlandish.

Fury burned Toren's shock away, and he brought the thick-necked Hollan to his knees. "Would a demon with my face be capable of this?" He drew his hand back and smashed the vile male across the cheek, aiming so that his signet ring cut the skin. Hollan spit blood and coughed. "I'll save you the trouble of answering. A vardoger wouldn't be wearing my signet ring, would it?"

"No, my king."

Toren threw the male across the corridor. He fell against the wall. His arms spread wide and blood poured down his face from the cut. "Go to your traitor, to your false queen, and tell her what I said. Tell her to expect a visit."

"Wh-where, my liege?"

"She'll have to figure that one out herself." He snarled and Hollan hurried off, scattering a small group of courtiers that had gathered to watch. "Be gone, vultures!"

The group scattered like mice. Toren went back inside and slammed his door shut.

"May I be of assistance, my liege?" Crommie held out a linen sheet.

"Thank you." Toren took the sheet, dried himself quickly, then began pacing in front of the fire. "My second set of leathers, Crommie. I won't be meeting this serpent in my court clothes. This is war, and I plan to make her pay."

DRESSED AND ARMED, TOREN STORMED FROM HIS bedchamber to the council's readying room, a small but finely appointed chamber where council members took breaks between long meetings.

Hanina was there. He wasn't sure if he hated or appreciated the fact that she had known he'd want to meet her there—the place where he had raised her to her high rank and praised her to everyone. It was also the place where Sir Brighan, a low-level courtier, had informed him of her skimming off the tax money gathered from the southern towns under her control.

She didn't look at all penitent. As he entered, she uncrossed her arms and curtseyed low.

"King Toren."

He let her stay there, waiting on his word that she could rise. He wouldn't be giving her that word.

"Just what in the name of all the Old Ones did you think would happen when I returned?"

She began to rise, but Toren clicked his tongue and shook his head as she glanced at him. Her head bowed once more, and she resumed her bent knee position.

"I can explain."

"I should hope so. I'd like a minute to think on how I'm going to kill you."

From the side, he saw her throat move in a swallow, but the female didn't shake. She had nerves of adamant. He would at least give her that.

"You were gone with no words for months on end, Your Majesty."

"Yes. And I have an heir in place even if I haven't officially named him. Why didn't you support my cousin's elevation?"

"I never spoke against him. I only took control until we could decide how to proceed."

"So the council agreed to put you on my throne instead of my cousin who is of age?"

"He is fifteen."

"And wiser than the both of us combined. You didn't answer my question."

"No, the council didn't agree with my elevation."

"You had yourself crowned." When Crommie had told him that, he'd been stunned. "How exactly did that play out? I'm curious. Did you snatch the crown and mutter excuses about it not turning black? The crown told the truth of it. That I lived. That I would return when I was able."

Her legs shook as she remained in her curtsey. "I thought that was an old story, created by younglings."

"It isn't. Did any of the council crown you?"

"Yes."

"Who?"

She took a breath.

"I will find out regardless and you know that. You might as well expose your supporters in hopes that I show you mercy instead of what it looks like inside a dragon's rippling flame."

"Sir Hollan and Lady Starssen."

Starssen. She'd didn't seem the type to risk her neck. Hollan did, but not her. Starssen had been quiet, compliant. But sometimes those were the type one truly had to keep an eye on.

"They crowned me in the hilltop chapel in front of a small audience."

Coronations were always carried out in the great hall of the keep. The hilltop chapel was for secret weddings of rebellious nobles and desperate prayers made before one met death. It was disgusting that she had taken his crown, two of his council, and named herself ruler in that dank ruin.

"Who was in this small audience of yours? Did they come willingly?"

A drop of sweat fell from her face to the floor. "Hollan did. Starssen was... prompted at sword point."

"Ah. I'd guessed as much. Now, how do you see this going forward?"

"I accept any punishment you order, my king."

"It's adorable that you think I need your acceptance. What did you accomplish for the kingdom in my absence?"

"I drove a group of trolls from the western woods and secured the southern towns' trade with the north."

"I'm glad you brought that up. I have heard some

disturbing things about your rule on the southern lands your family was given by my grandfather."

"I no longer take a percentage of the crown's tax. I swear it. I paid back every coin that I had taken. It was only a mistake, and I owned up to it. You know that, my king."

"Hmm." Toren stopped pacing in front of her, anger boiling in his blood and the dragon in him pushing to be free.

The general threw herself onto the floor. "Please spare my life, King Toren. I will serve you in any way you choose. You have only to name my task, and I will do it with joy and professionalism."

"As if I could ever trust you again to do anything besides empty my chamber pot."

"Please. Have mercy. Remember our grandmothers."

Hers and his had been great friends. The stories of their adventures were legendary. Toren's grandmother had been the only adult in his family that treated him with a gentle hand. She alone had sensed the nature of him and helped him escape castle life with his terrifying mother and father to climb trees, chase pixies, and sleep out under the stars.

"For my grandmother, I will not sentence you to death. This is your only chance. You will serve me here at the keep by organizing security for special occasions.

You will report to me every three days, and I will have a trusted servant following you at all times. All. Times."

"Thank you, my king. Thank you so much."

Her tears were false, and they did nothing to move his heart. "If you so much as sneeze in a way that displeases me, I will rise in my dragon form and burn you to the ground. Now, get out and don't let me see you again until our meeting. We are to have the Star Festival ball as is customary." He'd already sent messages to the castle staff about the event and his expectations. "See to it that my guest of honor, the human Lady Greensmith, is treated like you wish you could be. I will be watching."

With more stammered apologies and bowing, she left the room. He would have Sven follow her.

He still wanted to kill her. She deserved that and more. But the people needed to see that the crown had value. He would act as though he'd permitted the takeover to retain the crown's dignity.

It was interesting that she hadn't brought up her rumor that he was an onde vardoger. Perhaps she knew how ridiculous it sounded and didn't want to further irritate Toren. He would dispel that rumor quickly enough at the ball tomorrow night. How, well, he wasn't sure yet. Perhaps it would be enough to be in attendance and acting as his usual self. He shook his head. What a far-fetched rumor.

His mind also twisted around the person who had

followed Bronwyn, Flok, and him. Was the stalker in town? Past the gates?

Tonight—after a day of strategy games like Tafl—he'd take Bronwyn to the night market and give the stalker a chance to expose themselves. The night out would also permit the individual to watch how Toren acted. Either or both would move this situation forward.

❧ 34 ❧

BRONWYN

Toren escorted me to a hall with a high ceiling of rough-hewn beams. "Soon, all the nobles in the vicinity as well as those who traveled here for the event will show up to join in the games. Most of the council will likely arrive as well. It's a casual affair, though I think today will be a little less light-hearted."

Because they thought he was a monster. Hmm. This was going to be interesting.

The Unseelie had set up tables all around. Some surfaces held boards marked in circles while black and white gaming pieces littered others. Stacks of leather rectangles painted with red flowers and blue knights stood in the center of a larger table not far from a tall window that let in the light. It was chilly in the large room but Toren led me to a small square table near a massive, crackling hearth fire, and the heat warmed me pleasantly. A blue and white painted board sat in the center of the polished wood surface.

He held out a chair for me. "Lady Greensmith, this is the game of Hnefatafl, the King's Table."

"Ooo, I'm excited to try it. I was pretty good at chess."

Once we were seated, two side doors opened and a dozen or so Unseelie high Fae streamed in. I was glad that Maja and Sofie had dressed me nicely because all the females were attired similarly. The incoming crowd eyed Toren warily, but no one spoke out against him or called him that odd name as they took seats at the various gaming tables. What was it again? Sofie had said it again when helping me dress. An onde vardoger.

"I wondered if the council would attack me straight-away," Toren whispered as he organized carved wooden knights onto the board at our table. "But the three members present are only casting disparaging glances my way."

I took up the group of white-painted wooden knights and waited for instructions on how to place them. "Do you think they all believe this wild rumor?"

The door Toren and I had come through opened and an orange shape lumbered through. I gave Sir Cat a wave of my fingers.

"We have at least one supporter here now," I whispered to Toren.

Sir Cat looked up at Toren, yowled, then curled up under the table.

Shaking his head, Toren reached under to scratch the cat's head.

"Surely not all the nobles believe the general." I kept my voice as low as I could manage.

Toren shrugged and eyed the game board. "We will see. They might just be angry with me for being so foolish as to be stuck in the Seelie realm as I was. I don't blame them for that." He nodded toward my handful of little knights. "You hold the king in your hand, my lady." Mischief gleamed in his silver eyes.

"Oh, do I?" I smiled then studied the pieces. They had small circles for eyes and nicks that lined up to mimic swords and shields. One did wear a crown. "He's here!"

I held up the carved king and ignored the narrowed eyes of the courtiers who were, of course, far more interested in trying to figure out if Toren was a monster or not than in any board game.

"Yes," Toren said, bringing my focus back to our pieces. "He goes right in the center there and his knights surround him."

We put the pieces in place and Toren explained that his knights were those of four invading clans, set on murdering the king. I cleared my throat and glanced to the left at a pair of males who were openly glaring at Toren.

Casting them a bored look, Toren leaned back in his high-backed chair. "Each piece can move like a rook from the chess you are used to playing. Your king's goal is to make it to one of his four castle spaces set into the corners."

The corner squares were marked with a dragon's head bordered in marks like castle crenellations.

"Is that your sigil?"

"It is. What would yours be if you chose one?"

I leaned my elbows on the table. "Hmm. I certainly never considered that."

"Maybe you should."

What exactly did he mean? I was no noblewoman and certainly nothing to the Fae. I frowned. But maybe he was simply having fun. It was a day of games after all.

"I'd choose a foot to represent my dancing and a ring of stars."

"Why stars?"

"Because they're beautiful. Not everything needs some serious reason."

Elbows on his chair's arms, he steepled his fingers and grinned. "Very true."

I took an unsteady breath. He had to stop looking at me like that. He had enough to worry about without flaunting his regard for a human in front of his court. Surely that wouldn't be everyone's favorite. But maybe they didn't look down on humans as the Seelie Fae did. Maja and Sofie treated me well. Of course, that might have been due to Toren's order to do so, but they seemed genuine. Flok hadn't liked me at the start. But I was beginning to think Flok was just a tiny bit of a grouch. And he was starting to not hate me too.

"Who goes first?"

"Attacking clans move first." He eased onto the edge of his chair and stared down at the board. "Let's see..."

With his thumb and middle finger, he lifted a knight and shifted him forward so that he was right up against one of my pieces. His talons were longer than the carved knights, but he didn't knock anything amiss. At this point, I shouldn't have been surprised at his grace in handling the small item, but it amazed me all the same. I'd probably knock the lot to the floor by catching my dress sleeve on the edge of the board.

"Can I jump your piece? I could trap you then and take you, yes?"

"No, sorry. You can't go over other pieces. It's not allowed."

"You're sure you didn't just make up that rule?"

"You'd never know."

"Unless I asked you straight out."

"If I deigned to answer." His eyebrow twitched.

"Fine. I'll beat you despite your convenient rules."

He snorted a laugh as a couple passed our table without bowing their heads or curtseying or anything.

"Aren't they supposed to show deference?"

"Not during the games. We are all meant to be equals during this casual part of the festival."

"Ah. Interesting." I moved a third knight across the board to surround one of his. "Captured," I said, lifting his little fellow up and setting him beside my arm.

"But perhaps that was a trap?"

Scowling, I studied the board. "You're bluffing."

"We aren't even betting. How can I be bluffing properly with no bets named?"

"Well, maybe we do need a bet."

"Oh, I like where this is going." He leaned forward and his silver eyes glittered.

For a second, I'd forgotten he was Fae. I laughed at myself. "Am I foolish to bargain with the King of the Unseelie?"

"It's no bargain. It's a bet. Completely different."

It was my turn to raise an eyebrow. "Right. Fine. If I win the majority of the next five games, you will sing a song for the whole room to hear."

His eyes went wide. "Of all the things..." Shaking his head, he chuckled. "And what do you wish for me to sing if the impossible happens and I lose to you?"

I rolled my eyes.

"You look like me dealing with him," a familiar voice said.

I glanced up to see Flok. He gave us a nod and continued on his way to join three females seated at the large table near the window. Toren left his chair and tended the fire with a golden poker. On his way back to his seat, he stepped beside me and spoke into my ear.

"Flok will watch my back. You can unclench your teeth. We are as safe as we can be for now."

I relaxed a fraction. I hadn't realized I was so tense, but he was right. Though most of my mind had been on Toren and our fun, a part of me had been coiled and ready to defend myself or Toren.

Toren resumed his position at the table and moved a piece, claiming one of my knights with a quick flick of his fingers. "What happens if I win the day, my lady dancer?"

"You tell me."

"I like your fire, human."

"And I like to win." I snagged another of his knights and added it to my growing collection.

He clapped his hands and laughed loudly as if he didn't have a care in the world.

"If I lose," I said quietly, "I have to teach Flok one of my dances."

Toren threw his head back and laughed again. "Now

I truly must seize every game and make it mine. He would be the absolute worst student a tutor could have."

I moved a piece, changed my mind, and slid the knight the opposite way. "Lots of eye rolling and snide remarks, I'm guessing."

"He can reduce a person to a sniffling pile of what-might-have-been with just words. I've seen it."

I glanced at Flok who met my gaze with a serious glint in his eye.

When I turned back around, Toren was watching a table of males and females two groups over from us. They were talking loudly about the border and some past battle.

I wondered what Toren had done when I was in my room earlier today. Had he met with his council? Had he spoken with his loyal folk here about what Hanina had done? He seemed so confident, but if he was having Flok watch his back, he wasn't completely sure of what came next in the real life game of ruling a kingdom.

Also, I had to appreciate the fact that I had just won and Toren was chuckling and setting up the board again. When I had played games with Gantu, who had been far older than me, he lost his mind when I won. He'd broken our Nine Men's Morris set. It was incredibly refreshing to play with a male whose ego wasn't so fragile as to crumble under the stress of losing to a female.

At the end of five games, I had won our little bet. Toren scooted away from the table, and with a wink to me, he spread his arms wide.

"The lady has won our bet. She is the master of Hnefatafl!" Placing a hand over his heart, he began to sing at the top of his lungs.

"A lady, she is in the wood,

No, a lady, she is on the wood."

Even I understood that one. Flok and a few others laughed and Sir Cat gave another yowl.

"Bring your cups,

Hail your kin,

All to bring life to the hall again..."

Toren's voice was deep and lilting and I wanted to listen to it for the rest of my life. Striding farther from our table, he glared over his audience, then lowered his chin and deepened the notes humming from his lips.

"The stars go dark, forest sinks into sea,

No sun rises in the misty sky;

Smoke joins the chaos,

Fire dances high and consumes.

Come to me. Rise for me. Be the flame in the night.

Fae fight Fae and spill blood on stones,

Kin bring no furs or mead.

The sacred land weeps and the Old Ones shriek,

All shudder and turn to ash."

Everyone had stopped breathing. The silence

pounded and buzzed in my ears. Chills ran rampant down my arms and suddenly Flok stood beside me. I hadn't seen him move. The courtiers stood and some murmured, sounding discontent.

"That is the voice of an Unseelie king," Flok whispered. "Do you feel that power as we do?"

"I most certainly do."

Flok nodded. "We stand for that second song. It is a war cry. A song calling all to arms. An ancient song that only a king may sing."

"Will it prove the truth to them?"

"No, but it does show he has power."

I bit my lip. "That's something."

"It is." Flok took my arm and led me to Toren as the nobles went back to their games and conversation.

With Sir Cat weaving himself through my legs, I laced my arm in Toren's.

"It's past time to take a break from these walls, Dancer. What do you say to a night out?"

Words tried to spill from my lips, but I held them back. None seemed good enough to praise his singing because that hadn't simply been the fulfillment of a bet and a fun bit of entertainment. That had been a sword drawn, a gauntlet thrown down, a fisted hand. Toren was more than ready for war if it came to it and I would stay by his side.

"Well?" he asked as we left the gaming hall and walked up a set of winding stairs.

"I wouldn't mind a break."

"We Unseelie can be a bit dramatic."

I barked a laugh that had little humor in it. "I wish that's all it was, but I'm no fool, Toren. I might not be an Unseelie Fae, but I know when a challenge has been issued."

He brushed a kiss over my temple and I felt a smile stretch his lips. "Do you wish I hadn't made such a spectacle?"

"Goddess, no. I loved every second of it."

"You really have been bored at that temple."

"You have no idea."

❦ 35 ❦

BRONWYN

I took Toren's arm, and we walked out of the inner bailey gates. He'd worn a heavy cloak and kept the hood raised. I assumed it was because he wanted to walk freely without letting everyone know who he was. My maids had set my fancier attire aside for the coming event and instead dressed me in a simple frock. They had added a half cloak that covered my head and came to my stomach, and thrust gloves onto my hands. They'd dusted me with a powdery glitter that they said would mask my human scent. No one would notice that I was human as long as I kept my face hidden and my gloves on. Thankfully, the evening was chilly so the extra coverage was pleasant.

The stars glittered overhead. Their emerald, diamond, and rose shine was breathtaking. The castle town spread out before us, and we strolled down a wide cobblestone road. A tavern spilled laughter, and the music of a strange-sounding fiddle and a horn.

"I'd bring you in there to introduce you to the hardanger violin and the bukkehorn, but we would create a rather big splash." Toren glanced backward at the guards that trailed us. They had kept to the shadows and weren't noticed in the flow of people, but in a tavern setting, they'd be recognized as guards for someone important.

"No, let's get to the market," I said. "You know that visiting a market has been a dream of mine for over four years. I want to touch everything and taste each stall's treats."

"We'll see. Some Unseelie foods might not suit a human. I noticed you didn't eat any of Flok's fire fish."

"It looks like it was still fresh enough to flop off the table."

Toren chuckled. "No, it was smoked, not raw."

"Smoked?"

"It's a way to cook the fish."

"I'll try it if we see it tonight."

I was headed to the night market with this amazing Fae king. I couldn't smile hard enough.

We turned a corner past a bubbling fountain and a group of Fae dancing around a male who played a lute. Small tables dotted the area, and elderly Fae sat tapping their feet. Or hooves. There were Fae in all sorts of shapes, colors, and sizes. All had pointed ears, but some also had black tails. Others boasted horns or dark purple skin. Most looked as Toren did, with varying shades of gray skin and pointed ears. Their smiles showed sharp fangs, and it seemed the custom to braid the hair away from the face.

My hands fell to my sides. So many colors. Such beauty. "It's a miracle."

Just as I'd seen in the portal at the temple, tiny lights sparkled over the maze of stalls like a second set of stars. One purple Fae sold azure cloaks and black bags that boasted embroidered and hand-tooled stars and trees. The stall across from him held an array of weaponry—swords, daggers, bows, arrows, and even small paring knives. A merchant with curly hair that didn't seem to want to stay in its braid offered small paintings. I picked one up from her table to examine it more closely.

The Fae growled, and I dropped the painting.

Toren touched my arm. His teeth gleamed white and his eyes shone quicksilver bright in the shadow of his hood. "In an Unseelie market, you ask to touch the items before buying. But still..." His words were laced with venom. Would he attack the merchant for being less than kind to me?

I had to fix this. Quickly. I looked at the angry merchant and worked up a smile. "I apologize. May I look at this painting?" I pointed to the one I'd let fall back to the table.

The merchant pushed her unruly hair away from her eyes and grinned. "As you wish."

I bowed my head in thanks and took up the painting.

"If you want, I can punish her for that behavior," Toren whispered.

"How was she to know I'm new in town? I'm covered from head to toe. She was only acting as any Unseelie would, right?" I set the painting back in place and gave the merchant a broad smile.

"I suppose. Protecting you makes me a shade wild."

Heat rose into my cheeks. I took his arm and smoothed my other hand over his shoulder, his muscles evident beneath the cloak's fine wool. "Calm down. I'm fine."

"I feel...possessive about you. Does that bother you? If it does, I will distance myself."

His protectiveness didn't bother me. In fact, his desire to shield me warmed my cheeks and sent a curling sensation of heat down my torso where it settled low in my belly.

"No, it doesn't bother me at all." I felt the same toward him. Though as a dragon shifter with four guards at his back, he needed little help in the area of protection.

The scent of cinnamon and something unusual hooked my nose and drew my attention to the next stall where rows of something bread-like steamed in the night air.

"Would you like one to try?"

"What are they?"

"Fyrstekake." He set a gladecoin much like ours but with a different pattern on the face—something leafy— into the wide-cheeked merchant's outstretched palm.

The merchant closed her gray fingers around the coin, then wrapped up a fyrstekake in a dark green leaf and handed it to Toren. Toren tore off a bite and set it against my lips.

"You'll have to lick my fingers to make certain you don't miss a crumb. Fyrstekake is divine."

My cheeks flushed again as I opened my lips and took his offering. The taste of almonds, sugar, and... I had tasted the other spice but I couldn't remember its name. "What is with the almond?"

"Cardamom," the merchant said, grinning as I chewed and moaned with delight.

We walked on, Toren feeding me bites as we went. I held his hand for the next nibble and licked his thumb and forefinger clean. A purring sound issued from the back of his throat, and the noise made my stomach tighten and my skin grow hot.

"I'll buy you a bushel of fyrstekake if you promise

continued attention from your lovely little tongue," he whispered.

I laughed quietly. "My tongue is the same as anyone else."

"Is it?"

He extended his tongue and I stopped, my jaw hanging. His tongue was forked.

"How did I not notice that earlier?"

Chuckling, he led me toward a stall that appeared to be a little bit on fire. "I'm not sure, but I'd be happy to further acquaint you with my tongue in the near future. You have only to command me, my perfect little dancer."

My heart fluttered. Feeling shy, I looked toward the flaming stall. Sparks flickered from the front poles holding up a tarp over the cart. "What is this about?"

"Firestars."

"Oh, all right." The sparks flying above were some sort of illusion—not actual firestars. But the items on the cart presumably were.

"These are just a bit different," Toren said. He asked the merchant if he could examine a black stick sitting under the tarp. The merchant nodded. "You light this end," Toren instructed, "and draw a rune onto it to time the explosion. You can also alter the color of the sparkling light with rune magic."

"I thought rune magic was rare?" I didn't want to

bring up my magic in front of the merchant just in case that led to Toren being exposed—surely gossip about me had spread through the Unseelie as quickly as a firestar would burn through a haystack.

Toren paid the merchant and slipped the firestar into his cloak pocket as we joined the flow of noisy folk headed down the road.

"Higher level rune magic is incredibly rare. Really only the Seelie's Druid can handle it properly. I've heard he has an apprentice too. The humans' Witch is capable in her own way. Rune dancers once wielded great runic power," he said, grinning at me from under his hood, "but no one has seen one in ages. But the runes used on these firestars is very low level magic. Any Unseelie can draw a low level rune and most see a result. It's nothing anyone could weaponize though unfortunately."

"Why is that a bad thing?"

"Because we could better defend ourselves from the monsters that roam our world."

"Oh, of course."

"Did you forget about the gargoyles so quickly? My, but you bore easily." He elbowed me.

I laughed and shook my head. "Well, it's not as if you used runes against the gargoyle. You used..." I leaned closer and lowered my voice. "You used your dragon form, and your warriors fired arrows."

"And if someone hadn't been distracted by an incredibly ill-visaged miniature lion, perhaps we would have seen runic fighting."

"You mean Sir Cat?"

"I'm never going to call him that."

I grinned, thinking back to what else he'd said. "Could I use my rune talent for fighting? Truly?"

"You used it on the Fae bear."

"But I only drove it away."

"Your hands dance as much as your feet. I would wager you could scribe runes on anything you choose and see most of them work quite nicely."

"I don't know any offensive runes," I said. "All of ours are inspirational."

"I wish you would have been taught. I'd love to have seen you set a particularly nasty one on that House Mother of yours."

I felt a wicked grin pull at my lips. "That would have made for a fine afternoon."

"Truly. Now, what would you like to taste next? Ah, never mind. I see exactly the thing."

He almost dragged me to a stall with a striped cloth hanging over the cart's table. The scent of fish punched at my nose, but all I could see were sheets of parchment.

"Merchant, may I look?" I asked.

The merchant waved which I guessed was a form of permission, so I lifted the parchment only to be greeted by a bunch of dried out fish.

"I suppose they're good for one's health?" I wrinkled my nose.

"They're called torrfisk. It's wonderfully crispy." He looked up at the merchant. "We will take a small bag."

After paying, we left with our bag of disgusting, crunchy fish snacks.

"I'm not eating that. I'm sorry."

"I swear they are actually very tasty. Salty and nice. Besides, you said you wanted to try everything. "

"Well, I'm human," I whispered. "And I can lie."

He guffawed at that and tucked the bag of torrfisk away. Thank the Goddess for small mercies.

Flok appeared in the crowd, smiled, and joined us. Toren offered Flok some of the fish even as he winked at me. Flok actually took a piece and chewed it happily as we wove through the crowd toward three long tables. Fae sat on low stools there, eating and drinking.

"So all of these people could use rune magic since they are Unseelie?" I kept my voice down so the music lilting over the crowd would cover my words.

"They are able, but most don't use it. It does take energy from the one doing the magic."

"I do sometimes feel fatigued after dancing. Not always though."

"We can take magical energy from the land here as Unseelie," Flok said. "By communing with the earth or a tree, we revive ourselves not only in the ways of magic but in the areas of general health. Many believe that is why we live such long lives."

"How long do Unseelie high Fae live?"

"Sometimes up to three hundred years," Toren said, his gaze snagging mine, a question in their depths.

He would go on after I died. It was a strange feeling knowing that. "I won't live that long here though. Do you think this world is bad for my health and longevity? Could I be shortening my life by living here?"

"I doubt it," Flok said as he watched two females dancing and laughing under the lights. "We have had humans here a few times in the past. The two that stayed clear of the monsters and made wise choices lived into their hundreds."

"Hundreds? I don't know any humans who have lived that long."

"Exactly," Toren said. "I think the Unseelie realm feeds everyone in one way or another."

"Maybe I can do more magic here. If it revives your power, perhaps it does so to mine as well."

"I hope so," Toren said. "But we won't know until we research your power further. You are a far different creature from anyone in this entire world. You are made for high magic, for ancient power. You," he said, reaching into the darkness of my hood and taking my chin between his thumb and forefinger, "are a goddess."

"No, I'm not. The Star Goddess battled evil and

subdued masses of monsters and healed the dying. She was a goddess."

"She had Fae blood too which made her live longer. She simply had more time to practice. You can bring wonders into your era if you choose to do so."

I swallowed, not knowing what to say.

Toren turned toward a horned Unseelie female with a tray of mugs. He gave her some coins, then took three mugs and handed them to Flok and me. The wind kicked up a little, and I had to hold on to my hood to keep it up.

"You know the scroll-keepers won't let her into the library," Flok said.

"They will if I demand it." Toren's hand slid into my hood, and he pushed a strand of hair behind my ear. I shivered at his touch.

Flok sipped from his mug. "The council runs the library though, don't they?"

Toren grunted and threw back his mug, finishing the drink in one go. "Let's get into some trouble. I tire of worrying about politics. It's too fine a night for such topics."

A grin spread Flok's lips wide. "What did you have in mind?"

Turning toward another set of tables tucked under a dark awning that stretched from a tavern's front windows, Toren chuckled. "I may have spoken too soon. Perhaps it is a perfect night to discuss the council."

I frowned, not understanding what he was getting at. Flok came close and discreetly pointed to a table of white-haired Fae males and females who wore tunics buttoned up to their chins and were scowling at those who danced and shouted around them.

"That's the council," Flok said. "Well, most of it. Seems Starssen and Hollan aren't in attendance."

I studied their pinched faces. "They don't seem to be enjoying themselves, do they? Do you have a solution to that problem, Toren?" I grinned.

"I might," he said, his tone jovial. "I spy their barrel of day beer."

A barrel sat beside the tavern's door and sure enough one of the council members rose and filled her cup from the wooden container.

"I might just have something to spice up their night," Toren said.

Flok finished his mug, set it on a passing server's tray, then rubbed his hands together. "Oh, do tell."

What kind of trouble was I about to be dragged into? I tried to worry about it, but honestly, I was far too excited. This was living, and I was more than happy to get tangled in all of Toren's wild plans.

36

BRONWYN

Toren's hand disappeared into the folds of his cloak and reappeared holding a copper flask. "Nightdregs." He wiggled the flask and liquid sloshed inside.

"What is it?" I asked as he led us in a circuitous route toward the back of the tavern.

"It's the most powerful drink one can find in the Realm of Night. Disgusting stuff, but if you take just one sip, well, let's just say you become the person you hide from everyone else," Flok said.

"Yes," Toren whispered as we edged our way along the back wall of the tavern. The barrel was just around the corner. "I realize you see this as childish, but I never promised to be wise."

I covered my mouth and choked back a laugh. "I never knew a king could act like this."

Flok leaned forward. "Younglings know how to have fun. In my opinion, everyone should be a little more childish."

"This is why we are friends. Or maybe because of that fancy bathtub you have," Toren said.

He slipped around the corner, but was back again in the blink of an eye. He pocketed the flask that no longer sloshed as he moved it. "Time to sit back and enjoy the show. Those uptight old codgers need loosening up. I'm doing them a favor really."

We slipped back to the area where we had been and took seats side by side at the end of the farthest table to watch the show.

While I loved being here and enjoyed the mischief because I'd never had a chance to be naughty on the farm at home or at the temple, my mind was on my magic and what Flok had said about the library.

"Why don't they want humans in the royal library?"

We bought another round of drinks from a merchant carrying a deep tray. This time the mugs were more like bowls and the drink tasted like berries and mint. It was wonderful.

Flok tapped a rhythm on his drinking bowl. "We don't want you humans finding out about our secrets."

"But the drumstones are sealed. No one else is coming through."

Toren eyed me over his bowl. "We did." He sipped and turned his attention to the council, all of which were lined up to refill their mugs. "Others will too."

"How can I prove I won't do anything against the Realm of Night if I find out any pertinent information?"

"You don't need to prove anything, my dancer. You are my guest, and they will permit it or die."

Smiling and looking into his drink, Flok shook his head. "You do not have the gift of subtlety, my friend."

Toren elbowed him in the stomach playfully. "Your teasing is going to ruin my alluringly dangerous reputation with the lady here."

It was interesting to see him joking around with Flok and letting his taunts go with a grin. I wished I had a friendship like they did. Loyal in every situation and fun-loving as they went through life.

"You're lucky," I said to them both.

"Why?" Flok wiped his mouth with the back of his hand. "Because I have to put up with this arrogant arsehead?"

Toren turned and raised an eyebrow at Flok. "Oh, I'm the arrogant one? If I remember correctly, you are the one who claimed to be the best lover in the history of the world at last year's Moonfest."

"I didn't claim. I stated the truth." He finished his drink, a smile tugging at the edge of his mouth.

"That goes against the account that the miller's daughter gave."

Flok's smile fell, and he slammed the mug down, his eyes wide. "The water was very cold in the river that night!"

Toren broke into guffaws and slapped the table. He wiped his eyes and grinned at me from under his hood. I couldn't help but laugh too. Flok muttered something about biology and nature, but a shout grabbed my attention before I could guess what he was saying.

Two of the council members were climbing onto their table.

"Oh, this is going to be good." Flok crossed his arms and leaned forward. His anger at Toren's poke had evidently fled quickly. "The female is Helga. She was a warrior in the wildlands for several years. The male is Arne. They both voted to reduce the amount of coin given to the borderland farmers after the last river flood."

"So I'm not to feel any shred of guilt at this... display?" I asked.

The council Fae were stomping their feet on the table, spilling their associates' drink, and singing a bawdy tavern song about a love triangle between a fox shifter, a landlord, and a troll.

The lyrics stunned me. "Would that work, anatomically speaking?"

Toren snorted a laugh and licked his lips. "I doubt it, but the song has me wondering too."

I couldn't tear my gaze from Toren's lips. What would they taste like right now? Sweet from the berries or fresh from the mint in the drink?

Flok put a fist to his mouth. "Don't look now, but they're calling a meeting."

I turned, feeling Toren watching me. I bit my lip, a fluttering rising in my stomach. "What are they saying? I can't hear over the two that are still singing."

Flok's eyes shone with tears of laughter. "They are admitting to every rule they've ever broken. Sten just said he believes himself to be the descendant of Njal the Giant."

"But he's not more than five feet tall. Short for an Unseelie male from what I've seen." I was chuckling again now too.

Toren huffed and rolled his eyes. "What a prick. He wants those northern lands so badly that he'd convinced himself his nanny's old stories are true and he has the old reigning blood of that area."

"Nanny told me!" the one named Sten called over the crowd. "She knew all. I tell you! I have the blood of the mighty giants! I will rule the north!"

Helga stopped singing and patted Sten on the head.

"Well, when you head up there to claim those lands, don't forget your stacked boots or they won't come close to believing you!" She cackled, and the crowd joined in.

Sten bent and shucked off his boot. He immediately stood a foot shorter, and I barked a laugh. He lobbed his stacked boot at Helga who ducked. The boot smacked the other singer, Arne, on the back of the head.

"Ow!" Arne swung around and punched Helga across the jaw.

She howled, then hauled back and threw a fist into Arne's stomach. He doubled over, then pitched to the left, falling onto Sten. They ended up in a pile on the ground, their fine council tunics flipped up over their heads and their small clothes showing beneath. The crowd clapped and cried with laughter. Then the bawdy song started up once more, and the rest of the council stood, linked arms, and began dancing terribly.

"This might be the best night I've had since I died," Toren said.

Flok nodded and stood. "If fate offers you this kind of gift when you face the end, you should try to die more often."

Rising with graceful, quick motions, Toren pretended to knee Flok between the legs. "Keep talking and I'll ruin your chance at fulfilling your Moonfest claim."

Toren offered me his arm, and I took it. We walked

along the night market's stalls, and Toren bought me a gold ring set with a large light blue stone. I worked it on over my gloves, careful to keep my humanness a secret.

"What type of stone is this?" I asked as we continued up a quieter side street. Somewhere a baby wailed, and the noise of the market faded behind us. Our shoes clicked on the cobblestones, and the too-bright light of a torch set near a home made me wince. I was glad I had Toren's arm because I couldn't see much at all.

"It's a memory stone."

"How does it work?"

"You press it to your temple and think on a moment from the past. If the rune is well-wrought, the memory should surface in your mind's eye."

"Whoa, I can't wait to try it." I'd want to see Beanie again with her warm smile and soft—but always excited —voice.

Flok stopped. "Someone is here."

Toren started to speak. He went silent and dropped to his knees with a groan.

"Flok?" He moved into the dark.

I held to Toren's arm. "Toren, what's wrong?" My heart flapped wildly inside the cage of my ribs.

Something hard slammed the back of my head, and the world disappeared.

❧ 37 ❧
TOREN

The view of the road, Flok, and Bronwyn blurred as Toren tried to speak. Bronwyn was trying to stand and she held a hand to the back of her head. His heart flipped over. Was she hurt? He would destroy these fools if she was hurt.

"Leave them alone," he tried to say, knowing the attackers were only truly after him. "Let them go. You have me."

Rough hands shoved him away from Bronwyn and Flok, and he fell backward. Pulling energy from the earth, Toren tried to clear his head and shift. Shouting rose from where Bronwyn and Flok were, but the sounds were disjointed, broken by the smack of fists and the grunt of taking strikes. The Unseelie earth's energy poured into him, up through his feet and torso and into his heart. He opened his eyes, and Hollan stood over him, knife in hand. The meaty-fisted fool's eyes were wide, and he looked from Toren to his associates. Toren leapt up and smashed a foot into Hollan's chest. He dropped back two steps.

Flok was finishing off a masked male at the turn in the road. Another male, closer, had grabbed Bronwyn by the hair. She stomped on his foot and tried to hit him between the legs.

Anger flowed through Toren like fire. "Release her or die."

He shifted into his dragon form, and the masked male let her go and ran off, the other two masked males joining him.

Bronwyn pointed behind Toren. "Watch out!"

Toren spun to see Hollan back on his feet and coming at him with a sword.

"Die, onde vardoger! I do this for our former king!"

Longing to burn him alive but knowing that the fool just believed he was doing right, Toren swept Hollan from his feet with the tip of a wing. The knight went flying over the cobblestones, his sword flung from his grip and spinning until it banged into a water barrel outside a home. Faces looked out from the house's window.

Toren shifted back into his high Fae form and

stalked over to Hollan. "Stop fighting me or I'll be forced to kill you. It's your choice."

"I'm dead anyway for striking the king. Unless you are not the king which I believe is the truth! Vardogers can lie!"

Toren kicked the water barrel and smashed it to pieces. He ripped the copper band from the barrel's remains. "Show me your hands."

Hollan did as ordered, his teeth bared and a vein throbbing in his forehead. Toren wrapped Hollan's wrists in the metal, bending it and twisting it so even this powerful Fae couldn't undo it without them noticing on their trip back to the keep. With Hollan restrained, Toren knelt and set a hand on the ground.

"Come, pixies, and do your king's bidding."

"This proves nothing. A vardoger has the powers of the one it mimics!"

"Shut it, Hollan."

Flok came up beside Toren and held out a strip of torn cloth. It was one of the runaway males' masks. "May I, my king?"

"Please do," Toren said.

Bronwyn had replaced her hood and stood watching as Flok gagged Hollan with the mask. Toren went back to his magic.

"Come, pixies, and watch over this foul Fae. Do not let him raise foot or claw to anyone on our journey."

He took a breath and stood. Holding out an arm, he studied Bronwyn's face in the shadow of her cloak's hood. "Are you all right?"

"Yes. Shaken, but yes. I hope I broke that arsehead's toe. I missed his more important parts unfortunately."

"I'm so glad you had the spine to fight back. If they had taken you..." His stomach turned, and he growled. "I don't know what I would have done."

"I do," Flok said. "You would've set the kingdom on fire trying to get her back."

Bronwyn glanced at him and gave him a sad smile. She looked ready to drop, probably from that adrenaline burst during the attack.

Pixies, their light blue and bright in the darkness, flitted overhead and dropped down to encircle Hollan.

"They're gorgeous," Bronwyn said, her eyes shimmering with wonder.

Toren raised his hood against the rising, chill breeze. "Let's hurry home and get this piece of shite to the dungeons."

Rain began to fall as they started back to the keep. The drops hit the cobblestones, and Toren couldn't help but imagine the worst—it could have been blood falling onto the street. Hollan and his cronies could have killed them all or injured them seriously. Bronwyn was human and incredibly susceptible to wounds. As they continued on, he silently chided himself for not paying better attention to her safety.

"Do you think anyone else will come after you?" Bronwyn asked as they walked the incline toward the gates. "Will those other three Fae try again?"

"Those Fae smelled of true fear. I don't think they'll be trouble again, and if they are, I'll be more prepared the next time they do something foolish. As for Hollan, he'll be safely locked up for the foreseeable future."

Flok glanced at Toren with knowing in his eyes. Both of them were very aware that more folk must be truly convinced that Toren wasn't the real king and was a spirit pretending to be him. Toren had to show them he was the true king somehow...

Even as he bid Flok and Bronwyn goodnight inside the keep, his mind continued kneading the problem. No solution illuminated itself to him, and he slept poorly, tossing and turning, nightmares of that Fae's hands on Bronwyn chasing him in the dark.

❦ 38 ❦

BRONWYN

The library stole my breath. The shelves were set into emerald stone walls, and they stretched from the thick carpets layered on the floor all the way to the skylights far, far above. With all the colors of the many, many books, it was as if the ancient giant Njal had placed tapestries here, and he was the only one large enough to truly take in the full beauty. The array of hues was nothing to my imaginings of what one could learn in this massive chamber. Through words and drawings, I could visit anywhere in the all the worlds here. Low couches made crescent shapes at each of the two hearths on either side of the room. Down the center, a row of scribes' desks and stools sat empty.

"It's the most amazing thing I've ever seen."

"I'd have thought watching the Unseelie King shift

into a dragon would win that coveted position in your heart, but alas." Toren was grinning when I turned to face him.

He wore a simple black shirt tucked into dark green trousers, and he'd tied back his black braids so that his sharp cheekbones and proud brow stood out. Blinking his silver eyes, he strolled to where I had wandered in my happy stupor.

"You'll be left alone here to research as you see fit."

"Can't you stay?"

"I would love to. I didn't want to intrude."

The Unseelie were so full of contradictions. Wild and dangerous but also full of calm intelligence, and with the long-seeing minds to create a place like this. It would take a lifetime to even begin to understand Toren and his people. I hoped to have that time.

"You're not intruding. I want help. Now, where do we start?"

The corner of his mouth lifted, showing just a quick flash of his fang. Then he was off, leading me around the library and grabbing various dusty tomes and scrolls wrapped in leather and bone cases. We set up at a low table near one of the fireplaces and sat side by side on a couch.

He spread a scroll out on the table and weighted the corners with silver animal heads that appeared to be designed for just this purpose. There was a dragon with horns just like Toren's, a raven, a wolf, and a stag.

"This scroll goes over the highest level runes that Unseelie have been known to use. It's incredibly rare for any of us to have the ability to work them these days. Long ago, it was the norm rather than the exception."

"Can you work any of these?"

The inscriptions were partially written in old Fae, a language I had only touched the surface of during my tutoring at the temple. Illustrations in faded ink showed the pieces of each magical symbol, and some had a visual representation of what the rune was meant to accomplish.

"I can. This, and this. But that's it. And I'm the most powerful Fae in any world."

"And you're so humble about it."

He winked and leaned over the scroll, studying the runes below the ones he could work. The two he'd pointed out showed illustrations of night creatures. The first rune had a bat and a host of insects advancing toward a half-drawn set of castle walls. Beside the second one, a tangle of thorns grew up and snared a Fae's slender ankle.

"So by your theory, I should be able to use this magic?"

Reaching for a book with a scarlet cover and worn gold lettering, he glanced at me. "This one talks about rune dancers. The others mention where most of them lived and how they died out, but this one has more information about the actual runic magic they wielded."

With careful hands, he flipped the tome open and chewed his lip as he sought a specific section. A smile tugged at my mouth. He glanced at me again.

"What?"

"You chew your lip when you are thinking."

His eyebrow twitched. "You find that entertaining?"

"I just like learning little things about you. Like how you are so careful when you hit Flok while you are joking."

"Well, he isn't as strong as I am. I don't want to hurt him."

"Also, you hate wearing shoes." I looked at his bare feet on the emerald and ruby colored rug.

He chuckled. "I do hate shoes. We Unseelie don't always wear them anyway."

"But many do."

"Yes. I like having direct contact with the earth as often as possible and going barefooted gives me that chance far more often."

"Of course."

He released the book, sat back against the couch, and crossed his arms. "What else have you noticed in your focused study of me?" His eyelids lowered a fraction and he tilted his head.

"That you have a dimple in your left cheek, and it shows up when you are quietly happy about something."

"What is quietly happy?"

"When something gives you a small joy. I don't know exactly how to explain it. You don't feel quietly pleased when someone saves your life or when a big dream you had comes true. It's when tiny details of life surprise you in a good way."

Leaning his elbows on his knees, he gazed at me with soft eyes. "Like when I noticed your joy at seeing this library?"

"Yes. I guess so." A bubbling feeling rose in my chest. I felt light enough to float to the skylights.

He reached up and ran his thumb over my cheek. "And the sensation I feel when I can just touch you here without worrying about those terrible runes." His fingers found my jaw, then he set his palm against the side of my neck.

I put my hand over his, enjoying the warmth of his skin and the gentle way he was handling me. A deep breath lifted his chest, and he came close, his gaze on my lips.

"But this." He pressed his lips to mine, and I shivered with pleasure. "This action is not a quietly happy sort of thing, is it? Because when I do this," he whispered, kissing me again, then nipping at my chin, "it leads to this."

He set his teeth on my throat and a wave of desire pulsed down my body. His hand slid over the neckline of my dress to my breast. His talon clipped at me, and I gasped. His silver eyes watched me closely. Fingers drifting easily over my skin, he drew a shudder of delight from me. My pulse beat between my thighs.

I took his other hand from my side and moved it onto my knee. With a wicked grin, he dragged his palm higher until his hand pressed against me firmly. I shifted my hips forward, and he began moving his fingers and hand slowly. Painfully slowly.

Snaking my hand into his tied-back braids, I leaned close to his ear. "Please, Toren. More."

"You see?" He increased the speed slightly. "I love the idea of quietly happy, but this is more of a loud happy, wouldn't you say?"

With a growl of frustration, I grabbed the shoulders of his shirt and attempted to drag him on top of me. The effort was laughable because he was enormous. His shirt ripped at one seam, and my hand slipped from the other. He had to catch me before I fell onto the books and scrolls.

A cough interrupted our laughter, and I bolted upright nearly knocking my head into Toren's nose. Only his Fae reflexes spared him that. My face felt as hot as summer midday, but I was having too much fun to be embarrassed.

A Fae male with wild, short hair and bushy eyebrows glared at us. "I was told the library was closed today."

Toren didn't look ruffled at all. He smiled. "It is. Get out."

The Fae hurriedly lifted a tiny circle of glass hanging on a chain, looked through the glass at Toren, then put a hand over his chest. "My king!" He fell into a low bow. "I didn't realize it was you. Please, forgive me, Your Majesty, and forgive me, lovely lady of the other realm."

"You're forgiven," Toren said. "Now, go."

The male hurried off, leaving us to our laughter.

"I'm pretty good at this seduction and love thing, aren't I?" I said, joking. Then I realized I'd said love. My face fell. Did it mean to him what it meant to me? I hadn't intended on saying that I loved him, but... Was I falling for him?

His lips stretched into a wide grin, then he studied my face for what felt like an entire day. What was he thinking?

"You are very good at being Bronwyn, and there is no other person in any realm with whom I'd rather be spending the day."

Yes. I was definitely falling for him. I had fallen. I was fully dropped into the beautiful danger that was King Toren of the Unseelie.

Feeling bashful, I faced the book he'd opened. "Before we ran off the road there," I said, throwing him a grin, "you were saying this book talks about rune dancers?"

"Yes." He scooted forward to the edge of the couch and flipped the page to a chapter titled *The Dancers of the Old Ways: Earth and Air Magic.* "'Rune dancers are capable of reaching the earth's power in ways others are blocked. They are open to the heart of the earth and its pulse and they can request various outcomes when in touch with that heart,'" Toren said, reading aloud.

"So that explains why my footsteps on the ground do things that yours don't."

He nodded and continued reading a little farther down the page. "'Dancers' hands tend to be capable of sensing the air's mood and can shift the way the future is blowing by shaping the ancient language of runes with their fingers and palms.'" Taking a breath, he moved back. "Want to try a new rune now?"

"I do. Which one?" I eyed the scroll. Toren moved the book so I could see the full set of writings.

"This is your magic. You tell me."

"All right." Every rune on the scroll was detailed with numerous lines, crosshatches, dots, and circles. "Do you have to draw the shapes on the ground when you use those two runes?" I pointed to the ones he had shown me earlier, the ones with the night creatures and the thorns.

"No, I simply press my palm into the earth. I think

it's because of my royal bloodline. Perhaps I have a different way of asking things of the earth."

"I guess so." My wandering finger stopped on a rune next to an illustration of sunbeams which appeared to... Well, I wasn't sure. "What do you think this does?"

"Ah, it shows the aura of the person on which you draw the rune."

"The aura that the Fae oak shows?"

"Yes, same thing. The light of a person's soul or essence. Depends on which philosopher you prefer."

"I'll try that. It says to draw the rune directly on the flesh. How does that affect the earth or air? Oh, maybe it's the up and down movement it details here. Am I reading that correctly? I'm supposed to draw this crescent shape, this set of five lines above me, and then echo the markings on my skin?"

"That's correct."

I lifted my dress so that my stockinged knee showed.

"I like how this is progressing thus far," he said, his voice a purr.

I smacked his chest with the back of my hand. "Quiet, you. This is serious work."

"Yes, my lady." He tickled the side of my leg, and I batted him away.

I rolled my stocking down so that I could touch bare skin.

"I like it very much." He eased back on the couch

and slung his arms over the back, his gaze half-lidded. "You have the king's approval."

"Be quiet, my lord king."

"As you command."

Following the scroll's instruction, I drew the rune above me and then on my knee. Warmth traveled from my fingertips up my arm. That same tingling sensation bloomed over the rune on my skin and flashed across my body. I gasped as an array of light poured from places where my fingers had drawn invisible shapes on my knee. The lightest pink, the darkest blue... The light flickered and settled into a pink glow through which gold threads shimmered.

I smacked Toren's shoulder. "It worked! It's the same as the Fae oak's leaves showed me when I found your terrifying mushroom!"

"Very good job, Dancer." He beamed at me and kissed my forehead. "You are probably the most powerful person in this realm. Remember us little folk when you're enjoying all your fabulous magic, all right?"

Laughing, I practically shoved my face into the book. "I'm going to memorize every one of these and try them all. Am I permitted to bring this back to my room?"

Toren rolled my stocking back into place. "Of course. Or I can arrange it that this becomes your bedroom."

"What?" I looked around at the sun, casting its

blessing over the multitude of books. "But there's no water closet. I always have to get up at night to..."

Toren barked a laugh. "My practical, ridiculously talented female. How I adore you." He swept me up into his arms and kissed me soundly.

Yes, I was in love. It was too fast. Utterly foolish. Completely true.

✻ 39 ✻
TOREN

oren paced his bedchamber, hands clasped behind his back. He was dressed for the ball, and Crommie said all had been set for the event in the great hall before Toren dismissed him for a night off. But the most important part of the evening— proving he wasn't an onde vardoger was as of yet unplanned.

A knock sounded, reminding him of the moment he'd had with Bronwyn in the library. Damn that librarian. He swung the door open.

"Finally," Toren said. "I thought perhaps you'd forgotten where my room was."

Flok entered, carrying two bottles of black wine— Toren's favorite beverage for such events. "I ran into Sir

Brighan. The old fellow is very worried about how the council will behave this evening."

"Screw the council. I just need the people, the court, to see me as I am. They can't do a thing if the people are behind me."

"Can't they?"

"Get that wine open, if you don't mind. I'm shaking with frustration. I needed a glass two hours ago."

Flok uncorked one bottle and set the other on the mantle above the snapping fire. He poured a glass for each of them. Toren took up his glass and drank down one healthy swallow. Black wine tasted like first love and made the whole world look rosy.

"I hope it improves your mood." Flok lifted his glass to Toren then sipped his wine loudly.

"You read my mind." He drank a little more, then started pacing again. "Do you have any ideas?"

"I do not."

"What did you come here for then?"

"To share in your misery as I always do, my king."

"You're a good friend." Toren clinked his glass against Flok's then finished his serving. He poured more into his own glass and then offered Flok more. He waved him off.

"I'm not going to dizzy myself up quite yet. Someone has to stay sober and keep the court from tossing you from the walls."

"I should have brought Harold here and spoken to him."

"That would have been a good idea."

Toren nodded, set down his glass on the table, then went to the door and flung it open. He grabbed the guard standing just outside. "Bring Harold here. Immediately. Don't stop for anyone."

The guard nodded and ran off as Toren went back inside and shut the door. He sat in the chair opposite the one in which Flok had made himself comfortable.

"I'll explain it all to Harold just so the lad knows what's afoot. I'll command him to remain in his rooms at double guard just in case things don't shift in my favor. I can offer the blood ritual? Would that display the validity of who I am?"

The ritual involved releasing a fair amount of blood into a bowl that had been crafted by the ancients. Supposedly, the bowl glowed a bright sapphire blue when the current ruler's blood touched the base of the container.

"Maybe. It wouldn't glow for a spirit's false blood even though the blood would look identical to yours to our Fae eyes. The magic would know. Sadly, I'm not sure anyone knows where it is."

Toren rubbed his chin, picked up his wine glass, then thought better of another drink and set it back on the table. He needed his wits tonight. "I've ruffled our librarian's feathers, and it's too bad because I bet he's the only one who might know where that old bowl is."

"True. I'm curious. What in the world could you have done to upset the librarian? He can barely see anything anyone does."

"I used his precious library for activities that had nothing to do with books or scrolls."

Flok chuckled. "It would be good for that dusty chamber to see some action."

Toren wanted to laugh and enjoy his friend's good humor, but the situation was dire and time was running out. If he couldn't stop this rumor, he would need to give up his throne and give it to Harold to ensure the peace of his people. And that would prove his enemies' story of the onde vardoger. They would find a way to have him killed.

When Harold arrived, he began speaking and wouldn't stop until Toren physically sat him down in the chair and sct his hands on the sides of the lad's face. He was flushed to a dark gray and trembling.

"I hate upsetting you like this, but you deserve to know what's happening in the kingdom that will someday be yours. I'm going to make this right," Toren said, interrupting Harold's spew of fears and worries. "I didn't intend to be caught up in the Seelie realm, and for that, I apologize for my recklessness."

Flok shook his head and offered his wine to Harold.

"You were caught up in the troll hunt, and no one can blame you for that. They had killed so many..."

Harold took a quick sip then returned the glass. His big eyes were just as they'd been when he was born to Toren's cousin, Rhina. *He'll grow into those eyes, right?* she'd said when she'd introduced Harold to Toren. She'd been joking and had kissed the babe all over his bald head. Harold had not grown into those eyes, and instead, he looked a bit bug-like. Seven hills of hell. This lad couldn't take the throne. He wasn't ready. Maybe Hanina hadn't been so mad taking control.

"King Toren," Harold stuttered. "I... I don't know what to do. Are you truly you?" He paled as if horrified by his own question.

Toren knelt in front of the lad. "I am Toren, your uncle. I promise you that. Remember the day we went hunting and saw the badger climbing Flok's garden fence?"

Harold let out a nervous laugh. "Yes."

"An onde vardoger wouldn't bother with such a memory."

Honestly, Toren only thought that was true; he didn't actually know if that's how it would go with a monstrous copy of himself. Toren didn't lie—he'd only stretched the truth. But Harold's chest moved in a deep breath and his color returned to normal so it was worth the slight deception.

"All right, Uncle," Harold said. "So tonight you will take care of General Hanina and the council? You'll make everything good again?"

"I will." Toren pulled the lad to standing and hugged him quickly. "Now, go back to your chamber with Flok and stay there tonight. The ball will most likely get a bit chaotic."

"As you order, my king." Harold gave him a smile as he left the room.

Flok was right behind him, rolling his eyes at the young Unseelie.

When Flok returned, he had a loaf of bread which he handed to Toren. Toren ate as Flok explained how he'd set a triple guard at Harold's doors to keep him safe.

Toren wiped crumbs from his mouth as he finished his portion of the loaf. Flok took one more bite of his half, then set the rest on the side table.

"Now, to the library. We have no time to waste." Toren led Flok through the keep and down to the library's sunken entrance.

INSIDE, THE LIBRARIAN WAS WORKING AT HIS DESK like there wasn't a ball about to begin.

"You don't even take a night off for the Star Festival?" Flok asked as they came up behind him.

The male jumped and hurried from his stool to bow. "How can I be of service?"

Toren's gaze went to the couch, but he forced himself to focus. "Do you know where we stored the blood ritual bowl?"

The librarian's brow furrowed, and he rubbed his hands together. Ink had stained the ends of his thumb and first fingers. "The ancient vessel of King Thorinian."

"Yes, that's the one."

The old Fae's gaze flicked to Toren's face, and his expression said he didn't care for Toren's lackadaisical approach to discussing relics. "I believe it is in the second vault. I can get it for you now, my king."

"Thank you. That would be perfect. Please deliver it to me in the great hall. I'll be the one on the throne."

Flok rolled his eyes and started for the door. Toren followed him and ran his hands through his unbraided hair.

"I don't think he," Flok said, jabbing a thumb over his shoulder, "knows where that bowl actually is."

Toren paused and turned back to look through the partially open library door. The librarian was tossing parchment from a drawer like he'd lost his mind.

"Damn it. You're right. I'm doomed."

Flok clapped a hand on his shoulder as they walked back toward his chamber. "If tonight is your last, make it a good one."

"You're a lot of help, friend. Such a support."

"You're so welcome."

Toren lobbed a fist into Flok's kidney. Maybe he could just say forget it all, shift into his dragon form, and force the court to obey and submit. He never wanted to rule with fear, but it might be the sole route to a solution.

"Get me back to that bottle of wine, Flok."

"At your service, my king."

And may the Old Ones have mercy on my soul.

❧ 40 ❦

BRONWYN

With Sir Cat wound into a ball of purring orange fur beside me, I spent all afternoon sprawled across my feather-stuffed duvet, studying the scarlet rune book. By sundown, Maja and Sofie were practically kicking me out of bed.

"Please let me toss that cat out. It is past time to prepare for the Star Festival ball." Maja's white eyebrows drew tightly together as she began her lecture. "This event opens the festival and is very important to our people."

"Sir Cat stays, but yes, I'm ready to dress." I let them pull me into the bathing chamber with their clawed hands. I wasn't afraid of the Unseelie at this point, but I wasn't about to test an angry one if I didn't have to.

Sofie yanked my hair free then while Maja undid the laces on the back of my dress.

"There will be bonfires," Maja said, "deliciously naughty dancing, and many laughs and delights in the dark."

"That doesn't sound like any ball I've ever heard about."

Both females paused in their grooming attacks and eyed me.

I held out my hands. "But I'm glad! Human and Seelie balls sound so terribly dull."

They traded smiles and got back to work. Sofie tested the warm water they'd already brought in while I was reading, and Maja pulled my loosened dress over my head. As she folded the dress, I slipped out of my shift, then climbed into the tub. Maja used a sea sponge to scrub my arms while Sofie washed my hair with soap that smelled like honey and patchouli—the librarian at the temple had always preferred that scent of incense. Goddess, I was so relieved to be out of that place. What if someday I had to leave? What if...

Maja and Sofie halted their scrubbing.

"Is everything all right, my lady?" Maja asked.

I shook my myself. "Yes. I'm fine. I-I'm just so happy to be here, and I don't want to have to leave."

Sofie moved so she was looking me in the face. Her teal hair had fallen over one eye, and she pushed it behind her pointed ear. "If King Toren wills it, you will remain as long as you like. If he is truly the king."

Maja smacked Sofie's shoulder. "Hush!"

I closed my eyes as they started washing me again. "Thank you both for everything."

Once I had been scoured to within an inch of my life, the females gave me a choice between two fine dresses. One was black and appeared to be the type that fit close to the body. Embroidered stars danced down the center of the fabric, then spread like a carpet at the bottom hemline. The second dress was dark green, but when I lifted the fabric, the candlelight in the room split the emerald green into many shades—the red of a rose, the exact indigo of the floating Fae pastlights, the hue of the sky before dawn, the gray of the Fae mice who Toren had sent to me...

"It's the most beautiful dress in any world."

Maja and Sofie grinned and helped me into a shift and then pulled the dress over my head. They braided half of my hair into a crown-like shape and let the rest fall over my shoulders.

"But the Unseelie always wear theirs fully in braids." I didn't want to offend anyone or look out of place.

Maja placed a gentle hand on my arm. "You are human. You should be who you are here. A human who loves an Unseelie."

My cheeks heated, and I nodded. She was right. No

more being who others wanted me to be. I was myself—a rare rune dancer, a woman who adored this foreign world, and inside, a girl who only wanted to live her life in peace.

"Thank you. It's perfect."

Sofie set a mask on the top half of my face. In the mirror, I looked like a forest flower come to life. The dress shimmered in all of its lively shades. Silk petals in scarlet, rose, and gray covered the mask and extended beyond the edges at my temples. Maja set her fingertip in a pot of lip stain, then dotted the color onto my lips.

I stood and spun, wanting them to enjoy this with me. "I can't thank you enough."

They curtseyed, joy gleaming in their eyes.

"You will be the loveliest human at the ball!" Sofie said, raising her eyebrows.

I bent laughing at her cheeky joke, and then I was off, escorted by the guards Toren had set at my door.

TORCHES BLAZED ALONG THE STONE WALLS, AND bonfires licked the air of the great hall. Massive trees made of velvet and linen grew over the room. Leaves as big as beds sat low enough for the Fae to lie on which they did, oftentimes with a partner of their choice. Some laughed and told stories as I walked by, and others were busy with lips and hands. Tiny sapphire lights twinkled under the highest boughs of the fabric trees, and I couldn't for the life of me figure out how they'd managed that. Maybe rune magic.

At the end of the room, Toren sat on his throne flanked by post torches as tall as him. He had his hand on his chin, his elbow propped on the throne's arm.

I walked forward, and the crowd parted, their whispers rising like the wind of a coming storm around me. Toren's hand fell, then he stood slowly, his powerful body unfolding to full height. Silvery liquid eyes shone through a mask with horns that mimicked his own when in dragon form. His gray shirt—loose and showing a triangle of his sculpted chest—had beautiful silver-embroidered sleeves that caught the firelight. His black trousers fit tightly, embroidered silver thorns and dragon scales drawing the eye down the outer thigh. His boots were polished to a high shine. Boots, hmm. Unlike him.

I had to take a moment to admire him. He was just so devastatingly alluring.

At the base of the dais, I curtseyed, feeling heat in my cheeks.

He came down the steps and offered his arm. "You look like a dryad, like a forest spirit come to seduce me."

His gaze pressed against the neckline of my dress, then slid over me to my hips before sweeping up once more to study my mask and eyes. My heart thumped loudly in my ears and warmth curled down my body to gather low.

"And is my seduction working, King Toren?"

Setting his lips on my ear, he whispered, "If it worked any better, we would need to find a corner immediately."

He glanced over his shoulder at the second throne on the raised platform. It sat empty beside his.

"That one's yours," he said, jerking his chin in the direction of the additional throne.

Was he serious? Moths by the thousands fluttered in my stomach. "Are you sure I can sit there?" I didn't move. I felt every pair of eyes on me. "I don't want to cause a riot. The crowd seems...uneasy."

A grunting sort of sound issued from the back of his throat. "They are and so am I."

"I know."

"How? Is my uneasiness that obvious?" he asked, his gaze behind the mask genuine.

I pointed at his boots. "You're wearing shoes."

He snorted a laugh. "I'm kissing up to the council so I don't have to burn them all to a crisp."

"Here I thought this ball might be dull."

"You did?"

"That was a joke, love."

"Love?"

I felt my cheeks go red. "Yes. So did you figure out a way to prove to your court you are who you are?"

"Flok and I thought we had the problem solved, but alas, the blood ritual bowl has not been located."

"I'm not sure I want to know," I said. "Blood ritual?"

Waving a dismissive hand, he grinned at me but sadness pulled at his features. "It's not happening so don't worry about it."

"But you have no other solution?" What if they turned on him in full?

"Not yet. I'll think of something."

He pressed his lips to my wrist and a dark blur shot from the shadows and hurled Toren to the steps. His mask clattered to the floor. I stumbled back, my breath caught in my throat. Toren and his attacker rolled down to the floor, punching and grappling. A line of smeared blood showed on the last step.

It was General Hanina. I'd heard her described enough times, and she wasn't wearing a mask.

My heart was in my mouth. I ripped off my mask and lunged forward to grab the general's belt, but they turned again.

"Why is no one helping us?" I glanced at the crowd to see an unmasked Flok fighting to get to the front.

I looked back at Toren and his attacker. Blood poured down the side of Toren's face, and his mouth was slack as the general yanked them to a stop and held a blade to his throat. Toren's eyes were shut, and his color looked like a blend of snow and ash.

"Move and I end him now." Hanina's voice was quiet and calm, utterly serious. This wasn't a crazed person but someone who truly believed she was doing the right thing.

"You actually believe he is an onde vardoger," Flok said.

I hadn't realized he'd come up beside me. He held his hands out like Hanina was a horse that needed gentling.

Hanina's lip was bleeding. She spat on the ground. "He is."

My head spun, and I widened my stance to keep from tumbling. What could we do?

"He's not," I said. "I've been with him in the human world and almost every moment since we came back through the portal at the Star Goddess temple in Veilbury."

"A portal in Veilbury?" Hanina laughed cruelly. "That's a lie, human."

"It isn't. We uncovered it in the ruins beneath the temple where I lived. I am a temple dancer."

"She is more than that," Flok said. "Lady Bronwyn is a rune dancer."

Whispers erupted in the hall, and Flok glanced at me, his eyes wide with panic. His gaze said, *Do something*, but I didn't know what I could do. The general called for silence and was obeyed.

"I am sad to see King Toren's reign end in this way,"

Hanina said. "We never saw eye to eye, but I wouldn't wish an onde vardoger's curse on anyone. Who knows what other foul deeds this creature has done to our king's loved ones, to his subjects? Still, it is difficult to kill the beast."

Her words overflowed with genuine concern, and once again I was reminded that Unseelie, like humans, were incredibly complicated and layered. We all changed from moment to moment, drawn by the lines of fate and the whims of the Old Ones.

The general's elbow moved as she shifted the knife into position to kill Toren with one simple, deep cut at the side of his throat.

"Wait!" a familiar, deep voice shouted.

An arrow hit the general's shoulder, and she fell from Toren and dropped backward onto the floor. Her body shivered and blood oozed from her wound, blackening the white of the linen shirt under her leather vest. The arrow's fletching was the same as the Seelie's who had shot Toren.

Toren's knights drew their swords and pointed them at the shadow behind the throne, the direction from which the arrow had been shot.

My mouth fell open. Drefan, city guard and my childhood friend, walked out of the shadow behind the throne, another deadly arrow nocked in his bow.

"Your king is your king." Drefan addressed the

knights and the crowd. "There is no onde vardoger. I've been watching and came through the same portal myself. King Toren isn't the monster I thought he was. He is a good person, good enough even for the woman I have always loved." Drefan's gaze flicked to me and my chest ached at the loss and love in his eyes.

"Drefan." I'd said it all with just his name.

He wasn't here to ruin the heaven of this place, to force me to return, or to hurt the male my heart had chosen. He had stayed his hand. He'd been the one following us all this time, and he'd waited to watch if my decision to trust Toren was wise or not. He'd trusted my judgment enough to refrain from attacking Toren in the forest when he could have easily killed him.

"Thank you, Drefan." Tears burned my eyes.

Flok and I ran to Toren's side. He blinked, then gazed at me through half-opened eyelids. Flok put a hand behind his back, and I took his arm as we helped him sit up.

"Your head is bleeding. Perhaps you should remain on the ground," Flok said.

"I'm fine. Thank you, Captain Drefan." Toren didn't seem surprised at all to see him.

I looked from Drefan to Toren. "Did you know he was our stalker?"

"I did. I wanted him to witness how I treated you and to be assured I would care properly for the woman he loved." A wince came from Toren as he pushed himself to standing.

Drefan bowed deeply, his bow and another bloodiron arrow at his side.

Toren's knights pulled General Hanina to standing.

"See to her wound," Toren ordered his knights. "Fetch a Destroying Spirit mushroom, crush it, and feed it to her in whole. She will either make it or she won't, but I will give her the chance to live."

The knights hesitated, their glances peppering Toren's face, mine, and Drefan's. They remained unsure that Toren was not a foul copy of himself. They weren't going to let him keep his throne.

The council walked through a break in the crowd.

An idea slithered into my head.

I had studied the rune book Toren had given me. Perhaps there was something I could do here.

Help me, Star Goddess. If you are real, help me save this good king.

A rune shimmered in my mind. The rune for exposing truth or for uncovering mysteries. I didn't fully understand how it worked, but maybe...

Could I show Toren's truth somehow too?

I stepped forward and all gazes turned to me. "King Toren, allow me to draw the rune of Truth on you."

❧ 41 ❧
BRONWYN

"Are you sure this is safe?" Flok hissed. I knew him well enough now to realize he wasn't angry with me; he was worried about his best friend and this potentially explosive situation.

"They won't believe unless we show them," I said.

I glanced at Drefan who gave me an encouraging nod. He'd always believed in my power and been awed by it.

Toren cocked his head, not understanding what I was planning, but a smile kicked up one side of his mouth. Then his face cleared as he figured it out and mischief glinted in his eyes.

"Is this a rune we found during our lovely after-noon?" he asked.

"Yes. I'll need to draw it over your throat, heart, and solar plexus to expose the truth of your identity," I said.

"Sounds fun."

Facing the throne, Flok rolled his eyes. "Only you could turn the possible loss of your reign and your line's entire right to the throne into a pleasure show," he whispered.

Toren grinned wickedly and shrugged, moving to the top step and sitting on the bare stone. "Why not make everything in life as fun as possible? Council, in the name of my mother and father, I call on the favor of time."

I wasn't familiar with this custom, but the council members nodded as if they were well acquainted with it. No one moved to arrest or strike Toren. He removed his shirt, revealing the beautiful lines of his strong chest and well-honed stomach. His hip bones showed above his belt. Biting my lip, I walked up the dais steps and sat behind him on my knees so everyone could witness the rune's work.

If it worked.

"I would ask you to send up a prayer that this insane plan works, but I think you've used up all of the Old Ones' favor at this point," I said, rubbing my chilled hands.

Toren huffed a laugh and stretched out on his back before me like a feast. My body warmed pleasantly, and I truly hoped we had a future in which I could satisfy the hunger I had for him.

I shut my eyes against the beauty of him, the attention of the mistrustful crowd, and the questions I still had for Drefan. Bringing to my mind the shapes and lines of the complicated Truth rune, I set both hands on Toren's warm throat. A barely audible purr issued from him, and it buzzed under my fingertips. I swallowed. I swear I could taste the salt of his skin on my tongue. My body hummed with magic and want.

With the side of my hand, I drew an invisible arc from just below his sharp chin to the hollow above the collarbone. Humming a strange tune that entered my mind, I flipped that hand over and smoothed the back of my hand over the top half of the rune, then used my left hand to drag a wide line through the arc. Magic tugged at the place between my eyebrows and tingled in my palms as I kept on humming. The song seemed to soak into my arms and thread down into my hands. The tune turned my movements into dance—into emotion and desire portrayed in motion.

I opened my eyes and positioned my hands over Toren's heart. The proud muscles of his chest moved under my fingers as I worked the rune into his flesh again. Fatigue pulled at me slightly; it was like going to bed near dawn.

Taking a deep breath of the vetiver and leather scent

of him, I moved to his solar plexus, just below his rib cage. He pulled in a quick breath and made that purring sound once more. It was so quiet that I wasn't sure I'd heard it, but I glanced up at his face and his half-lidded eyes told me he wished my hands would continue their journey farther on.

Humming the tune my intuition brought forth, I shut my eyes and drew the rune one last time over the tight musculature of his abdomen. His skin was velvet and warm as a hearth's glow. I wanted to lean into him, to feel his body against mine. Magic shivered its way from my head into my hands, and Toren trembled once, a quick shake of his torso.

Looking at the runes, I waited to see if the magic would take and how exactly the truth of his identity would be exposed. He got to his feet and held a hand out to me. I stood beside him, praying this would work. The knights still had their swords drawn. This could all turn around on us if the runes didn't take.

Strangely, I had the urge to lead him to his throne. I tugged him that way and gestured to the high-backed chair carved with all the powerful symbols of the Unseelie.

He sat and gave me a mysterious grin as I took his black, gold, and silver crown from the nearby pillow stand and set it on his brow. He had to be nervous. Even the reckless, death-defying, dragon-shifter Unseelie King had to see that this was the only moment he had to win back his reign.

The council members stepped forward, and one of them opened their mouth to speak.

Shouts of "Intruder!" echoed from the great hall's entrance.

The double doors flew open, and I couldn't believe what I was seeing.

Painted by the bonfires' tumultuous light, Seelie King Lysanael Oakthorn and Seelie Queen Revna of Isernwyrd stood armed and accompanied by my nemesis.

House Mother locked me down with her steely gaze. "We come to claim what is ours."

I straightened my spine and glared back. "I am not yours."

❦ 42 ❧
BRONWYN

Hissing and growls issued from the crowd, and all the knights turned their blades to the Seelie who cracked the gathering in two with a unit of warriors. The Seelie warriors' large frames blocked my view of House Mother. Their bloodiron arrows were nocked and ready to fire.

Toren's gaze was lazy, and he leaned against the arm of his throne, casually taking my hand and stroking the back of my knuckles with his thumb. I shook, not just with fear but also with rage.

King Lysanael's crown was a near match to Toren's. Both were crafted of adamant. Though the Seelie king's was decorated with square-cut sapphires instead of gold and silver leaves. Queen Revna—a human with rare berserker blood—wore a cloak the color of ice reflecting a blue sky. Her crown was of solid gold, and it glimmered brightly in the firelight.

King Lysanael surveyed the crowd, then focused on Toren and me. Distaste narrowed his eyes, and his hand never left the hilt of his sheathed sword.

"This human is a subject of the kingdom of Saxonion," he said, "and we claim her in service of the treaty we have with that kingdom's queen."

"She is not a prisoner here." Toren kissed my hand. "Ask her."

King Lysanael's straight, silky hair caught the light. The ferocity in his expression and stance was such a contrast to his fine looks. "We can't trust her words," he said. "You have most likely set some magic on her."

Drefan bowed. "May I speak, King Toren?"

Toren nodded.

Drefan faced the king and queen of the Seelie realm. "I am Captain Drefan of the Veilbury City Guard. House Mother knows me well. I followed King Toren and Lady Bronwyn through the portal and watched their progress through this dangerous land. King Toren treated Bronwyn with respect and care, as did his friend, Flok, and his court."

Standing where Toren and Hanina had fought and where Drefan had shot the general, Queen Revna raised an eyebrow. "If everything is perfectly fine, why are you covered in blood?"

Toren waved a lazy hand toward his injured head and blood-slicked cheek, his signet ring catching the light. "There was a bit of drama here that is of no concern of yours."

"It does concern them," a council Fae said. "We believe him to be an onde vardoger. Lady Bronwyn," he said with a sneer that showed me exactly how the council felt about me, "set some runes on his body, but they didn't work to show us the truth of his identity."

King Lysanael drew his sword and marched forward, his knights fanning out and holding the Unseelie fighters at bay with nocked arrows of bloodiron. Frost shot through my veins.

I stepped between Toren and King Lysanael. Drefan and Flok joined me, their faces grave. The Seelie king stopped, his calculating gaze sliding over us.

"I give you," King Lysanael said, "to the count of three to move away from the onde vardoger. After that, your deaths will come swiftly, and I will not feel guilt for spilling your blood alongside the monster's."

House Mother's features twisted as she joined the Seelie king. She had deep scratches all around her hands, arms, and face, and I couldn't help but wonder if Toren's thorn magic was responsible for that.

"I demand the return of my acolyte in the name of the Star Goddess," House Mother said.

"Go," Toren whispered to Drefan, Flok, and me. "Don't die on my account. Go. I command it."

"Too bad," Flok whispered back. "You're stuck with us."

"I refuse to bend when it comes to justice," Drefan said.

I smiled. "I'm not about to give in. I've had a taste of freedom." Giving House Mother a cold stare, I stood my ground even though my knees shook. "I am in no way yours. I belong to no one, and I am now a subject of the Realm of Night."

Queen Revna walked forward and leaned toward her king. "The city guard has been runed to avoid all magical sway. Captain Drefan acts of his own accord."

King Lysanael pursed his lips but didn't sheathe his steel.

Another idea sparked inside my mind. I had rights here; Toren would back me up. "As a subject of the Realm of Night, I claim protection from my enemies."

The Unseelie knights glanced from me to Toren and to the council.

Queen Revna pushed through the Unseelie knights as if they were more likely to ask for her favor than threaten her with their swords. I wished for that kind of confidence. Someday, perhaps. I smiled at her, liking her for all the stories I'd heard about how she'd helped her people at Fjordbok. Beanie had told me all about Queen Revna. To me, she was a hero from a storybook.

"You really do love this king, hmm?" Queen Revna asked. "You believe him to be who he says he is?"

"Yes, and yes."

The queen glanced backward at her Fae husband.

King Lysanael was studying those of us on the dais. "He must be a good king if he has such friends as this, who would risk death for him."

"This is a sacrilege!" House Mother ran for me, and the knights stopped her, one with a hand to her arm and the other with a sword's edge. She halted abruptly, wheezing in shock and staring at the sword as if they wouldn't dare to kill her. "Sacred Sister Bronwyn must be returned to the temple!"

I left Toren and walked down one step. "You are at my mercy now, House Mother. And honestly, I'd like to see you beg forgiveness from me and swear you will leave your position at the temple."

She torqued her painted lips into a foul grimace. "I will do no such thing."

"Fine by me. Knights?"

The knight with the sword lifted his arm to deal the killing blow.

House Mother threw out her arms and bent slightly, crouching like a cornered animal. "Stop! No, I-I call on the protection of the Seelie king and queen!" Her gaze dashed from me to King Lysanael and Queen Revna.

Queen Revna crossed her arms. "I'm not sure your temple would miss you very much. Sounds like you created some problems. What do you think, brave captain?" She looked to Drefan who flushed, obviously shocked at being addressed.

Drefan cleared his throat. "House Mother should be required to work off the debt of her crimes as we do in Veilbury. Ten years of hard labor at the quarry should be sufficient, if that pleases you, Queen Revna, King Lysanael, King Toren, and Lady Bronwyn. I could pass it by the local magistrate."

Gratitude swelled inside me.

"I like it," Queen Revna said. "But Lady Bronwyn gets the final say or I end the evil thing now." Her tone brooked no argument.

I loved that she'd called House Mother *evil thing*. I was honored to have the queen's trust and the support of another woman.

"Thank you," I said, then I turned toward Toren.

"Do as you see fit, my lady." His low voice promised violence in my name. I knew that all I had to do was ask, and he would risk everything to fight for me or beside me.

I circled House Mother, recalling how she'd stolen power from Beanie and ruined the sanctity of the temple. This woman had beaten me for no good reason. She had mistreated the other acolytes and priestesses too. She had committed murder.

"You are the worst sort, you know." Rage tinged my words with fire. "Hiding behind a false holiness and committing evil against those you are meant to support and foster."

She gazed at the floor. "I only did what I thought was best in the name of the Star Goddess. Your mind has been twisted by the monstrous Unseelie."

A chorus of growls and hissing issued through the crowd. I guessed they were allowed to disrespect him, but humans and Seelie were not.

I glanced at Toren who watched House Mother like a cat eyes a bird. He was more than ready to pounce.

Taking her chin, I lifted her head so she had to look at me. "Beanie ran the temple in a way that honored the Star Goddess, who by the way, was an Unseelie queen."

Her eyes widened.

"Yes, I found the truth of it in not one but two mentions in the rune book from King Toren's library." The fact hadn't shocked me. Along with Toren's mention that many of our gods were simply Unseelie from the days of old, I guessed my heart knew somehow. Perhaps my magic had told my heart the truth long ago and I'd only just now accepted it.

Tension as taut as the Seelie knights' bowstrings

worsened with every moment that the runes on Toren didn't work and the standoff between the Seelie and Unseelie continued.

"You will do as Captain Drefan suggested as long as the magistrate agrees. If I hear that you have returned to the temple or communicated with those there in any way, I will come through that portal and find you." I glared into her face, showing her I meant exactly what I said. "I will seek you out at night when you are asleep and unaware. You will remain alive only at my mercy. Tell me you understand and address me properly."

Her jaw tensed. Her lips pulled back from her teeth, and the color on her lips smeared over the tip of my thumb. I didn't blink.

"Don't make me kill you," I said. "I don't care to have any more blood on my hands, but I will do it. We slay monsters daily here in the Realm of Night, and you will die easier than any of those."

She trembled, shut her eyes, and whispered, "Yes, Lady Bronwyn Greensmith."

I felt as though a heavy weight had been lifted from my chest. Could this be real? It felt like a dream, watching her cower beneath me. Releasing her and stepping back, I looked to Toren so he could show power.

"My lady has made her order," he said, standing and looking around the hall. "King Lysanael, Queen Revna, if you would please return this filth to the human kingdom." His gaze slashed across House Mother before returning to the Seelie rulers. "I appreciate your concern for Lady Bronwyn. If you like, you're welcome to stay, and we will feast to celebrate a new relationship between the Realm of Night and the Realm of Lights."

The council murmured and one male raised a hand. "We cannot allow this. Take this onde vardoger and shut him in the cells until we can discover the truth of how our true King Toren died."

I clutched my dress as my pulse hammered in my throat and temples. I couldn't lose him now, not when we were so close to the happy future I'd dreamed of these last weeks.

"Wait!" Flok stared at Toren. "The runes. I saw something."

"He is your friend," the council male said. "It is understandable you would see what you wish to see in this case."

But then I saw it too.

The runes flickered with a faint golden light.

Toren touched the rune over his heart, and suddenly, the magical symbols flared as bright as flame. A gasp went up from the crowd.

A female spirit appeared over Toren's head.

The spirit's shimmering jade hair rippled in an invisible wind, and her face shone like a star. Her eyes were silver like Toren's and ghostly Fae fangs showed in her open mouth. A dress with pinpoints of light fluttered around her form and a crown of stars glimmered across her brow.

Everyone froze. No one breathed. The silence was louder than any noise could possibly be.

It was the Star Goddess.

"Here stands the heir to the Unseelie throne," the spirit said, her voice echoing with power and making the hairs on the back of my neck stand. "With ancient blood in his veins and a dragon's heart, this male is your king and protector. He has found love with the last living rune dancer." Her shining face turned toward me and I shivered. "With that knowledge, he will reign in peace until his last day."

Face painted in silver and gold, Toren was looking up at her, the runes on his exposed throat shimmering brightly before pulsing in flashes down his torso to the other symbols again. His crown glittered with the spirit's light.

"Thank you for your blessing, Star Goddess, Great Ancestor, Old One."

The spirit almost smiled at him, and then she disappeared, leaving the hall in silence once more.

Toren faced the crowd, the council, the Seelie, and his knights.

Flok bowed, and those gathered followed his lead,

every head save King Lysanael and Queen Revna, bowing low.

"We have much to discuss, King Toren," King Lysanael said. He looked to his knights. "Stand down for the evening."

As he gave them orders, the crowd broke into excited conversation and the ball resumed its wild joy. I released a gust of breath and nearly fell over with relief. Music rose into the air, and soon servants were bringing in trays of roasted meat and glazed vegetables.

I joined Toren beside the throne and he took my arm.

"We did it," I whispered.

"You are hero here, my lady dancer." He kissed the inside of my wrist and I shivered, ready to have those lips on every inch of my body.

I kissed him, claiming the Unseelie King as my own in front of everyone.

Once I broke away from the kiss, Toren gave me a sly grin, then he shouted out, "Let the feasting begin!"

I had found my freedom and a great love too. I thought of fifteen-year-old me and imagined telling her the good news. *We are free now. Finally free of the temple, of the mistakes we made, of that lost and lonely life. Thank you for surviving and seeing us to this day.*

❦ 43 ❧

TOREN

Throughout the night, Lysanael and Revna made conversation over the dancing and drinking.

"I was taught," Lysanael began, "to believe the Unseelie high Fae were no less violent than Unseelie monsters such as gargoyles." The Seelie ruler held his goblet to his lips with his pale hand, but Toren could tell he wasn't actually drinking.

Toren took a breath to keep himself from losing his temper. "The monsters from here are animals. Bloodthirsty animals, but they are only following their nature to kill. High Unseelie Fae such as myself have minds just as you do and we can be evil or good depending on all the same sort of factors. Also, I did not poison your cup."

Lysanael dipped his head in some show of respect. "I was completely mistaken about the Unseelie. Though I know some to be evil, it seems not all are."

"Just like Seelie high Fae." An argument burned in Toren's throat, but Lysanael's face held truth and humility. Toren swallowed the fiery words he longed to speak.

"I apologize for my prejudice," Lysanael said.

The knots in Toren's chest loosened and he nodded, taking a sip of his wine.

Revna sniffed her goblet, then drank it down. Toren recalled hearing that she had been trained as an assassin before her ruling days. The queen wiped her mouth with the back of her hand.

"Why are you angry about us killing the Unseelie monsters if you do the same thing?" she asked him.

This new queen of the Seelie didn't miss much. "Because they are my creatures, under my rule," Toren answered. "It is my job and mine alone to decide when their existence is best undone. You could have corralled them or chased them off instead of killing them so quickly."

Lysanael raised an eyebrow. "They were attempting to murder our wedding guests."

Toren shrugged. "As I have said, they are animals just like your moss deer and your Fae bears."

Bronwyn joined them and her gaze went from the Seelie to Toren like she could sense the danger in the conversation. "Why do you believe the portal was covered up?"

A smile pulled at Toren's lips. Smart subject change.

"I'm not sure," he said. "Do you have any ideas?" He looked to Revna and Lysanael.

"Perhaps monsters were coming through as they do with the drumstones," Revna said.

Lysanael at last drank a sip of his wine. "I would bet my ancestors worked to hide knowledge of the portal. They were even more prejudiced than me. That brings me to a point I'd like to discuss. Did you know we are related?"

Toren did know. They went on to discuss Toren's father and the strange happenings that occurred before they were born.

Once the talking had run itself out and the Seelie and Revna had left for their world, Drefan hugged Bronwyn once tightly, then bid farewell. Toren wanted to rip his arms off for touching her, but of course, he didn't. And finally, the time had come to enjoy his dancer.

Toren spun Bronwyn around and around between the bonfires until they were both sweating and laughing. She took a sweet from one of the servants' trays and placed it between his lips. Toren chewed the sugared plum and licked the stickiness from her perfect fingers. A sultry look simmered in her eyes.

He dragged her to a dark corner on the far side of the hall and wrapped his arms low around her hips. She hummed with delight, sending desire shooting through him like a well-placed arrow. Her lips found the tip of his ear and she nibbled the point. Longing shivered down the length of him. He tried to breathe normally, but it was impossible. Digging his claws into her dress and her hips, he pulled her even closer. He kissed her soft lips and drew his tongue over hers as she shifted her body against his, rubbing herself over him.

"A moment, my perfect dancer."

He hated the confusion in her fire-lit eyes, but this was worth the pause. Withdrawing the ring he'd secretly procured from the night market, he prayed she would be as excited about this vow as him. Opening his palm, he looked up and felt more exposed than he had ever in his entire life.

"If you wear my blood ring," he said, "you and I will be mates for life."

Lips parting, she gasped quietly and took up the ring. She ran her slender fingertip over the runes set into the gold and silver. "What is a blood ring?"

He had to smile. She was always so curious. "It's an Unseelie tradition. The jeweler forms a ring with the male's blood mixed into the gold and silver. It symbolizes me giving you my life."

Tears glistened in her gorgeous doe eyes. "How did you get this ring so quickly?"

"When you're king, you get what you want when you want it." He winked and she grinned.

Her throat moved in a swallow as she studied his face. "You're certain you want this?" Her voice was hardly more than a whisper.

"Want you? Yes, my love. I am more than certain. It's all I want. Forever. You, me, and the wilds of our realm until our final days. From this day forward, command this monstrous king as you see fit, Darling Dancer."

She threw herself against him, her arms clutching his neck and her mouth attacking his. He dove into the kiss to show her he felt as strongly as she did.

As she pulled away, he slid the ring onto her finger. Satisfaction warmed his entire body.

"My mate," she said tentatively.

He nodded. "And you are mine."

She laughed, her eyes wrinkled with that innocent joy she had no matter what she went through. It was addictive, this happiness she carried with her.

"You are the only star in my sky. I love you with every breath, every step, and every day I greet."

He pressed his mouth to hers. She melted against him. Shuddering with pleasure, he bit her lip gently and gripped her hips. She pulled his head toward her collarbone, urging him to kiss her where her restrictive runes had once marred her skin. He flicked his tongue over the hollow in her throat then began lightly kissing his way down her chest.

Looking up at her gorgeous face, he whispered, "I'm going to teach you so much, my dancer. You just wait."

He felt her body tremble. "I will be the best student," she whispered into his ear. Her teeth found the tip of his pointed ear again, and she bit down until it was just slightly painful.

Swallowing, he restrained himself from tossing her to the floor and finishing this here and now. "You remembered the Unseelie way."

"I doubt you'd die if I bit your ear, but I'm learning."

He chuckled. Old Ones save him from this female. He adored her more with each passing moment.

"Shall we leave the festivities and find our mating bed?" he asked.

"I don't know what that entails in this realm, but I have some guesses and am quite finished with the party."

Grinning against her throat, he whispered, "Come with me, my lady. I will give you an early coronation gift."

"What?"

The crowd at the back of the hall parted for them, and he pushed open a small door to the side of the dais to escape the noise. Torches lit the private passageway to a door to which only he had the key.

"You will be crowned, if it pleases you, as soon as I can have a proper diadem created for you."

She smiled, her cheeks as pink as roses. "I think I'll enjoy that. But not as much as I'm going to enjoy tonight's gift."

He unlocked the back door to his bedchamber, kicked it open, and shut it again once they were inside. With the hearth fire throwing gold over his massive four poster bed, he tossed Bronwyn onto the numerous silken pillows. She laughed and held her foot out to him. He slipped her shoes off and massaged her heel and arch with his fist. Her head fell back.

"That feels amazing."

"The dancer must take special care of her feet." He moved to the other foot, spending time kneading each delicate toe.

Once she was relaxed, he climbed on top of her. Her chest rose and fell in quick breaths.

"We will take our time, yes?" he asked, not wanting to frighten her unless she wanted that. "At your word, I will stop, and we can simply sleep side by side."

"I won't be calling this off, my dark king. Now, show me the Unseelie way of mating."

He drew a claw across the neckline of her dress, then raked it downward. The fabric ripped from neck to waist, laying her beautiful body bare. She gasped.

"You are starlight made into flesh and I will happily lose myself in your glory."

She gave him a dangerous grin, then gripped his hair and yanked his head back to expose his throat. He let out a surprised growl. She was incredible. Pulling him to her, she bit down on his throat. With her free hand, she snaked her fingers down his torso and slipped them under his waistband. His skin pebbled under her touch. She held him tightly and he shuddered, trying not to lose control.

Her teeth released his throat. "I have read about this," she said quietly.

Her fingers moved one by one and pleasure sparked across his body.

Leaning on his elbow, he raised an eyebrow. "I had no idea the temple would include such material."

"I don't think anyone knew that particular scroll was present in the library."

He grinned and smoothed his palm over her navel and settled his hand over her lovely breast. Her swallow was just audible over the crackle of the fire. He moved his hand so it rested over her heart, and he set his claws into her flesh, not hard enough to break the skin but firmly so she would know the damage he could do but never would.

Her answer was in the shift of her hand cupping him low. He gasped and desire lashed wildly inside him. He knew her golden heart. For reasons he couldn't fathom, this beautiful soul loved him. Her eyes had shown that love time and time again tonight. He was safe with her, and she with him. They could play and challenge one another with no fear.

Pulling away from her, he set to yanking the dress and shift from her completely, leaving her only in stockings that were tied with ribbon at her delicious thighs. He tore the ribbons with his teeth and drew the silk down each leg slowly before dragging his mouth up her leg until he found her warmth and savored it. She gripped his hair in her hands and moaned as he flicked his tongue over her so, so slowly. He wanted nothing more than to serve her, to pleasure her until she was fully sated. His body grew demanding, and he asked her a question with his gaze.

"Yes," she whispered with a rasping voice. "Take me, King Toren."

❧ 44 ❧
BRONWYN

I gasped as Toren lifted me. He was on his knees, and with rough movements, he urged me to wrap my legs around his narrow waist. I liked that he knew I was strong and wasn't afraid to touch me. It was heaven to be drowned in sensation.

Toren's eyes were molten silver, and I couldn't catch my breath as my blood thrilled at his attention. He set his teeth against the bend between my neck and my shoulder and held fast. The prick of his two fangs was sharp and scintillating. He gripped my hip with one hand and tugged his trousers down. Standing on the bed, he shucked the trousers to the floor and pressed me against the tall headboard. With his teeth still at my throat, he drove forward, and I cried out as chills of pleasure cascaded through me.

"My perfect dancer," he murmured against my skin. His forked tongue flicked over my flesh, and he nipped my chin. "I adore you more every moment we are together."

My body hummed with want for this dragon king. I kissed him and dragged my hands through his tangled braids, loosening them until I could hold tightly again.

"My love, my dark king, my mate, you have given me a life I thought I'd only see in my imaginings."

He moved back, and I moaned against his shoulder. With one last kiss, he found my neck and shifted his hips. Thrusting forward again and again, he murmured my name over my skin.

"Bronwyn, my love. My love."

His pace increased, and the fury of pleasure inside me built to a peak. He paused, and I snarled and dug my nails into his shoulders. With a purr, he rolled his hips and the coiled tension in my core unwound in a wild spiral of the most amazing feeling. At the same moment, his body tightened, his muscles shaking under my grip and between my thighs. He growled and thrust hard. I was melting, dissolving, soaring.

Lowering me to the bed, he studied my face. My heart was still beating too quickly, so I tried to take a full breath. He moved his weight from me, leaned on an elbow, and kissed the tip of my nose.

"You are quite a monster," he said.

I laughed, my body feeling both light and heavy at the same time. "Takes one to know one."

I set a hand against his cheek, loving the feel of his skin and the glow of happiness in his eyes. He cradled me in his arms, and I knew we would have a full life here in the Realm of Night. A life bursting with joy and danger, adventure and discovery—a life I had always dreamed of.

❧ 45 ❧

EPILOGUE: A YEAR LATER

The day's court business was about to begin. Outside the closed doors of the throne room, our people waited to speak with Toren and me. But Toren's focus was not on our work.

I leaned over the arm of my throne and gave Toren a nice glare. "We will allow all of them to stay."

Toren was staring at the litter of bright orange kittens mewing under his throne. Sir Cat and his mate, Lady Stripe, meowed in unison.

Reaching down to pet Sir Cat, I marveled at the tiny bodies squirming beside his lady. "They're such proud parents. We will not be moving them until they are ready."

"Your wish is my command, Queen Bronwyn," Toren said, begrudgingly. He gave me a stern look and raised a black eyebrow. "But if the Night Realm rises against me again because I'm in league with a creature domesticated by humans, it's on you."

"How do you think Sir Cat found Lady Stripe?" I asked. There weren't any cats besides these two in the Unseelie world. At least, not that I'd seen.

"I think he knows of another portal somewhere or is somehow immune to King Lysanael's sealing of the drumstones."

"Really?"

Toren shrugged. "How else would they be here?"

"Perhaps they have a mysterious magic we aren't yet aware of," I said.

Toren stretched out an arm and stroked the under-side of my chin with a taloned fingertip. Pleasant shivers danced down my neck.

"What do you say to creating our own mewling offspring?" His voice was a purr.

My heart lifted and I grabbed his hand. He didn't know about my mystery yet. "You mean…"

"Yes, I'd love to make children with you." He kissed my knuckles.

My grin stretched my cheeks. "Well, now that you mention it, I have news…"

He was up and lifting me into a spin before I could say another word. His lips pressed against mine.

"You are with child?" His silver eyes sparkled like stars.

"I am."

Toren spun me again, laughing as the doors opened for today's audience.

"If you keep spinning me, you're going to be wearing my breakfast."

Laughing, he settled me onto my throne. His hands cupped my face. "I love you, my brave dancer. I love you with everything I am."

I kissed him, not caring a whit about those watching and simply savoring the feel of his presence enveloping me. This male was all mine and I was the luckiest woman in all the worlds. "And I love you, my Unseelie monster."

READERS,

Thank you so much for joining me on this adventure with Toren and Bronwyn! If you haven't read the other standalone in this world, The Fae King's Assassin, go check it out here. The Fae King's Assassin It's the story of how Fae King Lysanael and his Queen Revna met (and tried to annihilate one another haha).

If you'd like bonus materials such as an interview with Bronwyn and Toren as well as a library of free reads

from me, join my newsletter here https://www.alishak
lapheke.com/free-prequel-1

See you around!

Alisha

P.S. Stick around for a sample of The Fae King's Assassin!

REVNA

Assassinations and spying had never been my preferred missions. Fights with fists and teeth and steel were refreshingly honest when compared to plotting seduction or slipping herbs into drinks. Which was why

I was thankful that my current assignment had nothing to do with gold-hemmed dresses and everything to do with stalking an Unseelie gargoyle through the forest alongside my dragon familiar. I had lost the Unseelie in the heavy underbrush, but the snap of a twig behind me stilled my breath.

I spun and sliced my iron and adamant blade across the gargoyle's abdomen, loosing a stream of smoking black blood. The monster's ratty wings flared wide as he leaped from the brush, lashing a clawed paw at my head. I rolled under his arm, but the Unseelie still clipped my shoulder and I let out a hiss. Pain slithered over the injury. Springing up behind the gargoyle, I gritted my teeth and rammed my sword into its back. The monster fell to the blood-soaked ground.

Steely clouds billowed beside the autumn sun as I stepped over the dead Unseelie monster. Another day, another assignment. And while I might have preferred one mission over another, my master didn't care about my opinion. He owned me in every sense of the word, the curse rune on the back of my neck ensuring my obedience. With one ancient word, he could kill me even from afar. I wiped the gargoyle's stench from my blade and surveyed the skies, seeking a particular pair of dragon wings.

"Where are you, terrible beast?" My dragon, Arkyn, had grown impatient waiting for the gargoyle to show and had flown off to survey the area. Lucky for him, he'd missed the fight. "If you're lolling about in a field of blueberries, I'm going to roast you for my dinner."

Arkyn was a good companion, but he had one weakness. Food.

A shadow blocked the sun, then Arkyn was landing beside me, his color the same hue as the surrounding oak trunks, his eyes as bright as torches, and his wings buffeting me with wind. The dragon was roughly the size of three horses, and when he nudged my stomach, I widened my stance to keep from toppling backward. I rubbed the smooth scales of his head, my heart warming.

"You're lucky I'm still alive." Maneuvering my round shield onto my back, I found a patch of dark moss. I dragged my dirtied sword along the ground to clean it, then I tucked a leg into one of Arkyn's stirrups and hauled my tired arse onto the dragon's back. "No one else would sneak Cook's scraps to your nest. She values those scraps more than all the lives at Isernwyrd."

Arkyn sniffed as if he didn't agree that he had only me to find his favored meal. He spread his bat-like wings and ran over the rocky ground, and we took off. Leaves brushed my boots, and branches tried to snag my cloak as we drove up and away from the forest floor in uneven bursts of forward movement. Above the broken canopy of green, the coming storm blew a chilly wind across my face.

Below, a drumstone's deep blue surface flickered with emerald light and I turned my face toward home. Hopefully, that stone was finished causing trouble for a while. At least long enough for my nap and a meal. I didn't mind the drumstones and the way they spit out Unseelie monsters from hidden realms—killing off things like the gargoyle paid for my keep and gave me coin to save for my ultimate goal. But I needed a day off.

Arkyn flew over the toothlike walls of Isernwyrd. Black pennants snapped from the five towers, the color denoting the Hunters' collective grief over losing the crown princess. The shouts of my fellow Hunters rose as Arkyn landed in the courtyard. Ignoring the other Hunters' kind calls to Arkyn, I slid out of the saddle and ran both hands down the dragon's body, checking for wounds.

"So tell me, was it blueberries or a lady friend?" I made it to his snout and picked a dark blue bit from one of his viciously long canines. Holding it up for him to see, I raised an eyebrow. "Really? I mean, I had guessed... But you truly left me to die for a snack?"

He exhaled a heavy, damp breath into my face, blowing my brown braids back, then bumped me with his snout.

I flicked his nose gently. "You might not believe one

gargoyle could have taken me down, but you underestimate my need for a nap."

Wishing the other Hunters would leave us be, I glared at our audience.

"Ah, come off it, Revna." The newest of the Hunters, Cuthnor, a recruit with far more brawn than brains, stalked around Arkyn. His swagger and smirk said he didn't know the story of my dragon and the last arsehat who'd tried his patience. "Let someone else take this beast into the skies. Someone whose strength matches his."

I sighed. I wanted ale and to sit the hells down. "Fine. Let's get this over with." I motioned to Cuthnor. "Take me down and I'll ask Arkyn nicely if he'll take you on a mission. Which he won't."

Cuthnor snorted and tugged at his ragged beard. Inside and out, the man was as ugly as they came. He lunged at me, then went left, trying to take my back. I put out onc boot and tripped the fool. With a grace that showed why Master had recruited him this late in life, he caught himself. Normally, we started here as children. Easier to manipulate that way.

Cuthnor grabbed my hair and laughed as he attempted to wrap an arm around my exposed throat. I took hold of the fist tangled in my thick, messy braids, pressed it down onto my scalp to hold him there, and donkey-kicked the moron in the stones. He howled as everyone else guffawed.

"Want another one or are you finished?" I kept both my hands on his fist on the top of my head, not allowing him to use the hold to his advantage.

He let out a few garbled words and spat on the toe of my boot. Fire simmered in my blood.

"These are my favorite boots." I twisted, skipped closer a step, then slammed my heel onto his instep.

He roared and released me to the cackling of the other Hunters.

"It's not the dragon you need on your next job, Cuthnor," the gangly Tynin called out as I used a rag from my pouch to clean spittle from my finely stitched gray leather boots.

Cuthnor stood, still cupping his man bits. "Berserker bitch."

The slur had always pleased me because I took pride in my Berserker blood. I didn't know how many folk still possessed the battle rage magic of my people, but the gift had to be rare. *The king had seen to that,* I thought darkly.

"That's right," I said to Cuthnor. "Don't forget it."

Cuthnor stalked away toward the horse stables as the rest of the Hunters gave me space. I smoothed my hands down Arkyn's belly and unbuckled the saddle. Drawing it over him, I was careful not to clip his wing. Sure, he could handle the pain of a scratched wing, but those lovely appendages were sensitive. I handed the saddle off to a stable boy, then walked alongside Arkyn across the mud-slick cobblestones of the courtyard.

In the sanded square near the entrance to the mess hall, Raulian fought Vi bare-knuckled. Raulian's gaze flicked to me as we passed. Vi knocked him hard with a nice right cross.

"Better focus on the training, Raul." I snorted a laugh.

He came back at Vi with a series of expert strikes. Raulian wasn't the sharpest fellow, but he was a good person and the nearest thing to a friend aside from Arkyn.

Servants in crisp linen aprons and tunics carried baskets of dirtied laundry from the arched doorways of the barracks and into the servants' hall near the chandler's workshop. I'd always thought it ridiculous that Master insisted the servants remain so tidy when he didn't give a rat's foot about what we Hunters looked like.

A shudder rippled through my bones and I swallowed a familiar sour taste on the back of my tongue. Arkyn nudged my shoulder and his tongue darted out to touch my cheek.

"Stop, you little beastie. You know I hate that."

With the sleeve of my tunic, I wiped dragon drool

from my face. Though Arkyn's concern over my long-standing full-on fear of Master was sweet, I had no space for it in my life. Hunters had to be cold and show no trepidation—even in front of the man who beat us when we failed in a mission and who controlled the death curse runes inked at the back of our necks.

When we reached the corner of the lower kitchens building, Arkyn lifted his head and sniffed loudly right next to my ear. I shoved him away a step as the scent of freshly baked bread and venison stew filled my nose.

"Don't worry. I'll get you some later." Master would pay me well for killing that monster so quickly. I'd have enough to feed us both for at least two days.

Wide stone steps led up to the abandoned scriptorium, which was now Arkyn's nest. Master had ordered the entrance torn down and a new one crafted of roughly hewn wood, wide enough to permit Arkyn easily. Three slender windows let in some of the approaching storm's metallic breeze and a portion of the day's weak light. Fresh hay sat in a large circle in the back corner of the empty room, along with a trough I filled with water every day before sunrise. Beside that, a wide copper bowl showed the remnants of Arkyn's squirrel and crabapple breakfast, cores and small bones discarded neatly into two piles.

I grabbed the dish and dumped the contents into the rubbish bin that the servants would discard for me later.

They did it for free because Master ordered them to keep Arkyn's nest clean. Master didn't give food freely to people, but he did provide a portion for the only dragon Isernwyrd had housed as a Hunter's familiar in two centuries.

A knock sounded behind me and I turned toward the entrance to see Raulian.

"You look even paler than usual." The man was as fair as a summer's day. Though I hailed from Fjordbok, I wasn't as light-skinned as him.

Raulian pushed his curly white-blond hair away from his face and swallowed. "Master calls for you. The king is here and asking for you."

I dropped the copper dish and it clanged against the flagstone floor, making Arkyn draw back and hiss.

"What? Now?" I hadn't even washed the gargoyle muck off my hands.

"Immediately. Need me to get Arkyn some grub?"

I scratched the only soft spot on my dragon's body—a tiny square of hide behind his ears—then left him with a lazy fist-to-the-chest salute. Starting out of the room, I clapped Raulian on the shoulder.

"Yeah, that would be good. Thanks, Raul. But watch your fingers."

I grinned wickedly and Arkyn took his cue, bristling so that the spear-sharp spikes on his tail fanned out and upward.

"Good dragon," Raul murmured as I left them to it.

I enjoyed teasing Raul, but it was only a weak distraction from the buzzing in my head and the tingling of my fingers. Why was the king here and asking for me? I had never met our ruler. The king always gave his assignments to Master, who then passed them on to whichever Hunter fit the job best.

Hurrying across the courtyard, I eyed the cut on my arm. It wasn't deep, but I needed to clean it soon to avoid infection. Gargoyles were nasty beasts.

Two guards stopped me at the door to Master's chambers. One pointed to my forehead. "You've got Unseelie blood on your face."

"All the better to show him I've been hard at work." I gave the man a nod and he opened the door.

Standing in a pool of sunlight that was as gold as spilled dragon blood, Master spoke in quick whispers to the king. Road dust caked the hem of King Darrew's ruby-red cloak and made his salt-and-pepper hair look brown. He turned as I walked in, his eyes already studying every inch of me.

I didn't know which one I'd rather run through. Both, if my dreams ever came true. I laughed silently at myself and sank into a low bow, my fist against my shoulder in the Hunter fashion, waiting until they spoke to me.

"The dragon Huntress with Berserker blood." The

king's voice slid across the chamber's dark stone floor like a snake. His boots sounded his approach while the slap of Master's bare feet marked his movement. "Rise," King Darrew said.

I did so but kept my eyes cast downward. "As you order, my king."

Master poked my ribs with his walking stick. "Show him your ice eyes, Huntress Revna."

Standing perfectly still, I looked at the king, whose eyes flickered with interest. But what kind of interest? A man's lust? A rich man's desire for that which is rare? Or was he only here for a job and my pale blue eyes—the mark of Berserker blood—meant I could do what he needed done?

The king's gaze left my face and found Master's. "Will she do it?"

Master set a heavily ringed hand on his stomach and raised a thick eyebrow. "If you order it so."

"This job will require an especially strong focus to complete successfully and with grace."

"If she doesn't complete this mission, she dies." Master shrugged.

The king smiled and he crossed his arms. "I like the way you work, Master of the Hunters. It's simple. Clean."

"Effective," I said.

Both men's eyes momentarily widened, but respect

shone in the king's look. I guessed he would like a show of my bold nature. If he wanted a Berserker, he wanted the death of someone difficult to kill. And he'd come here in the flesh instead of sending a missive. Whatever this job was, it sure wouldn't be a walk down the flowered lane.

"I am your servant, my king." I bowed again. Groveling to these monsters was disgusting, but I had no desire for a beating before my nap and meal.

The tip of Master's stick found my chin and he lifted my head. "Shall I tell her, my king, or do you want to?"

King Darrew's smile turned my stomach. He met my gaze. "You, my rare Huntress, are to kill the King of the Fae."

My mouth fell open and cold swept through me like winter had fallen on Isernwyrd with that one sentence.

My life was over.

GET THE FAE KING'S ASSASSIN TODAY!

AFTERWORD

Hello! Can't get enough, huh? I like that about you.

So when I started writing this novel, I had to figure out what would inspire both settings—Bronwyn's temple and Toren's realm.

I binged The Makanai: Cooking for the Maiko House and decided to use pieces of geiko/geisha traditions to inspire the Star Goddess temple. Now, listen when I say that the terrible way that House Mother acts and the rituals and behavior is not the way things are at a geisha house. I simply saw things like the names on the boards, the tiny foods, and the dancing as a jumping off point for my own world. I have so much respect for other cultures and would never want to make anyone think I was representing them as a person outside their culture. It is only for very loose inspiration and for the good parts of that setting.

As for Toren's realm, I let my newsletter folks vote between several countries to inspire the Night Realm. They chose Norway and I couldn't be happier. Once again, the Unseelie world definitely isn't Norway and nor did I try to make it a copy. I simply was inspired by their food and a few behaviors—all good things.

By far, most of the elements of each setting and every bit of each character are from my own head. But I do think it's fun to share some inspiration.

I hope you enjoyed it!

ACKNOWLEDGMENTS

A thousand thank yous to my Uncommon Crew ARC team, my Dragon Diva betas, the amazing Tessonja Odette, the Shield Wall baddies, my fabulous Facebook group, Alisha's Dragon Den, my editor, Jen, Julia Dea for art, Melissa Wright for saving my arse last minute, Miblart and JV Arts for design work, to Soraya Corcoran for the map of the world, and to the wonderful writing community of the Midsouth SCBWI and our local Not A Real Retreat Retreat folks.

As always, thank you to my amazing family for the love, listening, and support. I could never do this without you.

ABOUT THE AUTHOR

USA Today bestselling author Alisha Klapheke wants to infuse readers' lives with unique magic and cozy fantasy romance. Her inspiration springs from an obsession with history, years of world travel, and the fantasy she grew up reading when she was supposed to be doing her math homework.

When she's not writing, Alisha teaches Muay Thai kickboxing, Brazilian Jiu Jitsu, and Krav Maga to kids, adults, and the occasional country music star at her school just south of Nashville. That may be why writing fight scenes is her favorite.

Printed in Great Britain
by Amazon

41631036R00209

Do No Evil (Large Print)

An Oxford Murder Mystery

Bridget Hart Book 3

M S Morris

CHAPTER 1

Her footsteps rang sharply against the flagstone floor of the antechapel. As Alexia Petrakis crossed the south transept she felt the chill that emanated from the old stone building, even though August had only just passed. The daughter of a Greek father and an Italian mother, Mediterranean blood ran hot in Alexia's veins, and she favoured sunny climates over the typical British fare of damp summers, drizzly autumns and cold, wet winters. The chapel air was cool and musty, and she pulled her cashmere cardigan tight across her chest and hugged her upper arms.

Pausing in the centre of the antechapel, she tilted her head up to gaze at the empty space above her. The belfry tower. Whatever Oxford might lack in decent weather, it more than made up for with its buildings. Towers, spires, battlements, domes, quadrangles, gargoyles. The architectural flights of fancy made the university an inspiring place to live and study. Walking around the city yesterday she'd noticed some new buildings that had appeared since her undergraduate days: the Mathematical Institute, the Blavatnik School of Government, the Jesus College development on Cornmarket. But here at Merton College, one of the university's oldest colleges, little, if anything, had changed in the twenty years since she'd matriculated, seventeen since she'd graduated. For a college that had stood for over seven hundred and fifty years, twenty years was merely the blink of an eye.

But for Alexia it had been a long time.

Armed with a degree in English Language and Literature (first class) from Oxford, she'd completed a postgraduate course in Journalism at Goldsmith's University in London, coming top of her class. She'd quickly got her foot on the first rung of the ladder as a reporter on The London Evening Standard. But she'd always aspired to loftier goals. By dint of long working hours and a tenacious grip on every story that came her way, she was soon freelancing for national papers, uncovering stories of corruption in the corporate world, miscarriages of justice in the legal profession, and scandals in political life. She quickly gained a reputation as a crusader, a defender of the truth, someone who would stand up for the public good. But now she had a story to tell that would rock the centuries-old foundations of the institution in which she was currently standing.

That was why she had taken the unusual step, for her, of seeking advice before she went ahead with publication. By nature she was impulsive

2

and even reckless, not given to self-doubt. But for once in her life, she was filled with uncertainty. Could she do it? And if so, why would she?

To assuage her own guilt, of course. To do now what she should have done so many years ago. And yet the repercussions would be like an earthquake for everyone involved, including herself.

It was at times like these that she mourned the loss of her own Catholic upbringing, and the comfort given by the rite of confession. Bless me, Father, for I have sinned. To be absolved by the priest and to leave the confessional free of the burden of sin was a luxury too good to be true.

She didn't believe it anymore.

Alexia knew that there was only one way to put right past wrongs and that was through action. And for a journalist, action meant exposing the truth for the world to see. The pen is mightier than the sword. But before she wielded her pen once more in the service of truth, she deemed it prudent to consult.

The college chaplain had agreed to meet her at half past three in the chapel. She had arrived early, still unsure what she was going to say to him. She needed more time to collect her thoughts and to work through her feelings.

She turned pensively into the quire and walked up to the altar alongside images of apostles and evangelists. The quire was the oldest part of the chapel, dating back seven centuries, and stood on the foundations of an even older church. Alexia was soothed by the deep sense of connection with the past. It helped to put her own problems in perspective. Autumnal light filtered through the stained glass of the huge Gothic window that filled the eastern wall. Muted in comparison to the elaborate gilt churches of her Greek and Italian heritage, the chapel was still breathtaking in its quiet beauty.

The door to the sacristy was closed, so she supposed that the chaplain hadn't yet arrived. She turned and headed back down the aisle towards the gleaming pipes of the Dobson organ which sat in silent contemplation. No doubt those pipes would be brought to thunderous life later in the day as part of the evening's celebrations.

As she browsed the plaques and statuary in the north transept of the antechapel, the door in the south transept opened and closed. She turned and saw a figure enter and advance towards her across the flagstone floor. Once again, the great chamber echoed with the sound of footsteps.

'It's been a long time,' she said to the new arrival, but her visitor did not speak in reply. Instead, strong hands gripped her shoulders and a cold wire looped about her neck.

Caught off guard by the swiftness of the attack, Alexia had no time to struggle before the wire was drawn tight and she was gasping for breath. She sank to her knees and her vision began to blur. Just before she finally blacked out, a familiar voice whispered in her ear.

'See no evil.'

CHAPTER 2

The wheels of the suitcase bounced wildly over the cobbles of Merton Street as Detective Inspector Bridget Hart hurried on her way. Having left her bright red Mini convertible parked at home in Wolvercote and caught the bus into central Oxford, she was now running late for registration to the college gaudy.

'A gaudy what?' her teenage daughter Chloe had asked when informed that Bridget would be spending Saturday night at her old Oxford college. 'Are you going to wear something outrageous?' Chloe's eyes glinted with good-natured mischief.

'Not gaudy as in showy or tasteless,' Bridget explained to her. 'It's a noun, from the Latin gaudere meaning to rejoice. It's a reunion dinner for everyone who joined the college twenty years ago.'

'You mean it's a piss-up for middle-aged people?'

'Language!'

In truth, Chloe wasn't far wrong. Formal dinners at Oxford colleges invariably involved copious amounts of wine followed by more drinking down the college bar. The evening would probably end up being gaudy in both senses of the word.

The wheels of the suitcase finally jammed to a halt in a gap between two particularly troublesome cobblestones, almost causing Bridget's arm to be yanked off. In frustration she picked the case up by the handle and lugged it the final twenty yards to the college gate. The case, though small, was surprisingly heavy. Rather like Bridget herself in fact, despite her desperate attempts to shed a few pounds in preparation for the dinner.

Unsure of what to wear for the occasion, she'd lost her nerve at the last minute and bundled in several extra outfits, which was one of the reasons she'd been late catching the bus. That and the fact that she'd spent the morning writing up a report for her ever-demanding boss, Chief Superintendent Alex Grayson.

But now she was taking the rest of the weekend off and Thames Valley Police would have to manage without her. Detective Sergeant Jake Derwent and Detective Constable Ffion Hughes were more than capable of dealing with anything that came in. As for Chloe, she was only too happy to spend the night in London with her dad, Ben, and his girlfriend Tamsin. Perhaps the youthful and gorgeous Tamsin would give Chloe some more of her "cool" fashion advice, something which Bridget was incapable of providing.

A feeling of irrational jealously always crept up on her whenever she thought of Chloe spending time with Ben and Tamsin. Although, wait, there was nothing irrational about it. Any reasonable middle-aged divorcee would feel exactly the same as she did about her ex-husband's latest girlfriend. Especially when her own daughter had taken so quickly to Bridget's newer and younger replacement.

Meanwhile, her own love life had barely got off the ground. Her sister Vanessa had recently introduced her to Jonathan Wright, the owner of a contemporary art gallery in Oxford, but her police work had repeatedly thrown up roadblocks in their budding relationship. They had at last managed to go out to dinner together on a proper date. But now any hopes of romance were on ice after a serious injury that had required Jonathan to have abdominal surgery at the Royal Brompton hospital in London, followed by time spent convalescing at home. Bridget felt terrible about the incident, which had been partly her fault. She'd offered to spend the weekend looking after him but he wouldn't hear of it. Instead, Jonathan had given her strict instructions to go to the gaudy and enjoy herself.

'Have some fun,' he'd told her. 'Just try not to discover any skeletons hiding in the closets.'

So here she was, back at Merton College where she had spent three years studying for her degree in History. It was twenty years since she'd first

8

joined the college and it was hard to believe so much time had passed. Her undergraduate years had been a blissful time, cruelly marred by the family tragedy that had occurred straight after her final examinations and which still cast a long shadow. Was that the reason she'd never been back, until now?

Stepping into the lodge she was instantly transported back to the first time she'd arrived for her interview as a naive seventeen-year-old. She remembered the eagerness of wanting to demonstrate her academic ability, and the feeling of being overawed by the centuries of learning and tradition that seeped out of the ancient stonework. The history tutor had run rings around her during the interview, but had nevertheless offered her a place. She'd discovered later from the second- and third-year students that the harder the interview, the more Dr Irene Thomas rated you. She didn't waste time challenging those she considered unlikely to make the grade. Was Dr Thomas still around? She would be well into her sixties by now, but some Oxford academics refused to give up. As long as they had their wits about them, they might carry on studying and teaching until they died. Bridget didn't think that Dr Thomas would allow a minor inconvenience such as old age to stop her from continuing her life's work.

'Can I help you?' The sound of the porter's voice brought her back to the present. 'Are you here for the gaudy?' The young man in a college-crested sweater was peering at her from behind the reception desk. She wondered what had happened to Stephenson, the head porter during her student days. One of the old guard, he'd addressed all the female undergraduates as 'Miss' and all the male undergraduates as 'Sir'. Retired long ago, no doubt.

Bridget wiped away the beads of sweat which had formed on her brow after struggling with her overstuffed suitcase. 'Yes, I'm here for the gaudy. Bridget Hart.'

She had been Bridget Croft in those days, of course, and almost completely inexperienced with the ways of men, after coming straight from an all-girls school. Part of her still yearned for those simpler times.

The porter ticked her off his list and handed her a large white envelope with her name and room number on it. 'All the information about the gaudy is in there. The first event will be tea with the warden.'

The warden of Merton College was the equivalent of the master of other colleges, or the dean in the case of Christ Church. The old warden that Bridget remembered had now retired and his position taken by Dr Brendan Harper, a much younger man who was something of a celebrity. Bridget was looking forward to meeting him.

'Your room is in the Grove Building. Do you know the way?'

She thanked the porter and assured him that

she remembered the college layout very well. Then, wheeling her suitcase once more, she stepped out of the lodge and into Front Quad.

Built in a mish-mash of architectural styles, the buildings that made up the main college quadrangle nevertheless achieved a sense of unity through their use of yellow Cotswold stone. Every wall, gable and archway gleamed golden in the September light, and the leaded windows sparkled wherever the sun caught them. To her right rose the Gothic east window of the college chapel, and ahead of her a flight of stone steps led up to the medieval dining hall where tonight's dinner would be served. To the left, a double archway led through to St Alban's Quad, and the rather gloomy arch of the Fitzjames Gateway marked the entrance to Fellows' Quad. Crenellations and chimneys peeked gleefully down at the architectural jumble from on high, and behind her towered the castle-like turret that adorned the gatehouse.

Other colleges might be bigger, or grander, or more famous, but Merton's more modest proportions and eclectic mix of styles had the power to move Bridget deeply. This was beautiful architecture on a human scale.

A narrow walkway past old stone walls brought her to the peculiarly named Mob Quad. If Bridget had to choose her favourite place in the whole of the city of Oxford, then this would be it. Tucked away out of sight of the tourists and shoppers that thronged the crowded streets,

Mob Quad's thirteenth- and fourteenth-century buildings enclosed a perfect square of bright green lawn.

The tranquillity of Oxford's oldest quadrangle caused her to slow her pace. What was the hurry? If she was here to enjoy herself then she would do so by taking the time to soak up the atmosphere. She took a deep breath and felt the tension in her shoulders ebbing away. On an impulse, she left her suitcase at the bottom of one of the staircases and climbed the stairs to the college library.

With the undergraduate term not yet started, the library appeared to be empty. Bridget wandered down the central aisle, pausing briefly to glance at the various alcoves – English, Modern Languages, Law, Classics, Mathematics, and History. They were arranged just as they had been in her day. The oak bookcases were crammed with so much learning, it was tempting to pick a title off the shelves at random and just start reading. She had so little time for books these days. Being a parent – and a single one at that – had taken that part of her life away from her. She felt a tinge of regret at what she had lost. But then she remembered what she had gained in its place – a daughter, Chloe. She wouldn't undo the choices she had made.

Paper rustled from the farthest alcove and she realised that she wasn't alone after all. Peering around the shelves she couldn't stop herself from exclaiming in pleasure.

Dr Irene Thomas was sitting at one of the tables, surrounded by piles of history books. An expert on the Elizabethan and Jacobean periods, she had made her name with a book on Sir Francis Walsingham, spymaster to Elizabeth I. She was busy writing in her notebook in a flowing cursive script. Bridget had guessed correctly that her old tutor would keep going until the day she died.

At Bridget's approach Dr Thomas took off her reading glasses and looked up, her face lighting up instantly in recognition. 'Well, goodness me. Bridget Croft. How are you, my dear?'

'Very well, thank you,' said Bridget. Her tutor's ability to remember faces and names had always been impressive, and clearly had not diminished with the passing of time. 'Although it's Bridget Hart now,' she added.

Quick as a flash, Dr Thomas's eyes darted to Bridget's ringless left hand and she knew that her former tutor would at once have deduced the facts of the case. Wasn't that what the study of history was all about? Looking at the available evidence and drawing conclusions. Rather like police work in fact.

Diplomatically, Dr Thomas made no mention of Bridget's marital status. 'I take it that you're here for the gaudy?'

'Yes, I thought I'd just pop into the library before going to my room. I wasn't expecting to find anyone here, but it's lovely to see you.'

'Sit down and tell me what you've done with your life.' Dr Thomas indicated the chair opposite. 'I do like to hear what my students get up to once they escape from this place into the real world.'

Bridget gladly sat down opposite. After rushing to get here, it was a pleasure to spend time with a woman for whom she had the greatest respect and admiration. It was hard to pin down her tutor's precise age. The last time Bridget had seen her, Dr Thomas's hair had been grey, and had now turned white, and her skin had taken on the powdery look of advanced age, but her eyes still sparkled with that fierce inquisitive intelligence that Bridget remembered so well from her weekly tutorials. In her heyday, Dr Thomas was known to be able to complete the Times crossword in under fifteen minutes. Bridget doubted that her ability would have faded.

'Well, I'm afraid that I didn't really make use of my History degree,' said Bridget. 'I joined the police. It seemed like the only thing to do after… after what happened to my younger sister, Abigail. Now I'm a detective inspector.'

'Of course,' said Dr Thomas. 'I remember that dreadful business. And the police never caught her killer?'

'No,' said Bridget. 'But at least I now have the opportunity to bring other criminals to justice.'

Dr Thomas nodded her head approvingly. 'I always knew you would do something

14

worthwhile with your life.'

'And you?' asked Bridget, wanting to change the subject. 'Are you still teaching and writing?'

Dr Thomas waved a hand over the piles of books and papers in front of her. 'We have so much to learn from the Elizabethans. It was a time when Britain had to establish its place in the world after the chaos caused by the break with Rome. There are so many parallels with the present day. And if we cannot learn from history, what hope is there for the future? I sometimes fear that what the Spanish Armada failed to achieve in destroying this nation, we will achieve ourselves.' She paused. 'You do of course remember the date of the Spanish invasion?'

'Er... um, yes, it was 1587. No, 1588.'

Dr Thomas held Bridget's gaze for several excruciating seconds before nodding. 'Yes, I see you haven't completely forgotten everything you learned here. Now don't allow a gloomy old woman to keep you from your revelry any longer. I expect that tea is already being served.'

Bridget looked at her watch. It was nearly four o'clock, the time scheduled for tea to start. She rose to her feet. 'It was lovely to see you again, Dr Thomas. Maybe we'll have a chance for a longer chat later on.'

'I do hope so.'

Bridget collected her suitcase from where she'd left it at the bottom of the staircase and made her way to the Grove Building, a nineteenth-century addition to the college that

15

resembled a baronial manor house with stone gables and leaded bay windows. She lugged her suitcase up the stairs and found her allocated room on the second floor. She'd had a room in this very building in her first year in college, but times had changed and this room now boasted an en-suite bathroom shoe-horned into one corner, a small fridge under the desk, and an internet connection. She dumped her suitcase on the bed and looked out of the window.

The south-facing room overlooked Dead Man's Walk, a sandy footpath that ran east-west between the old city wall and Merton Field. Once used as the route of medieval funeral processions from the old Jewish quarter to the Jewish cemetery outside the city walls, legend had it that the walk was haunted by the ghost of Francis Windebank, a colonel executed at that spot during the English Civil War in 1645. The ghost was supposedly visible only from the knees up, due to the change in ground level since the seventeenth century.

Bridget didn't believe in ghosts, at least not the chain-rattling sort that stalked castle ramparts demanding vengeance for past wrongs, or that turned up as unwelcome guests at the dinner table. But she was only too familiar with the power of memory and guilt to haunt the present. It was why she had ignored previous invitations to college gaudies. It was now twenty years since she'd matriculated at the university as a fresh-faced eighteen-year-old, and seventeen years

16

since she'd graduated with a two-one degree in History. She was divorced with a fifteen-year-old daughter, and her career as a detective inspector with Thames Valley Police was at last getting going. Things were even tentatively looking up on the romantic front. It was time to face the ghosts of her past and see if she couldn't put some of them to sleep.

She opened the envelope the porter had given her and pulled out a timetable of the day's events. Tea with the warden (informal) was now being served in the foyer of the TS Eliot Theatre. She was already late and needed to get changed out of her jeans and T-shirt. But what exactly was an informal dress code? Was informal the same as casual? She strongly suspected it was not. She had a sudden nightmarish flashback to a college dinner at which she had turned up in a short cocktail dress when all of the other women were wearing long gowns. God, she had always found social events to be sartorial minefields.

She opened her suitcase and started pulling out clothes. She'd brought three different dresses, any one of which might (or might not) be suitable for dinner later that evening. The dress code for dinner was specified in the programme as black tie. That was all very well for the men, for whom black tie meant a black dinner jacket, a white shirt and a black bow tie. But what did it mean for the women? She would tackle that decision later.

In addition to the three formal dresses, she had

packed several other outfits to give her options for the various other social events of the day. But options meant choices. Difficult choices. She checked her watch. Tea with the warden (informal) had started fifteen minutes ago. At this rate it would be over by the time she'd decided what to wear.

The dinner at seven would be preceded by a short service in the chapel, for which no particular dress code was specified. And after dinner the college bar would be open until midnight, by which time everyone, including her, would be too inebriated to care what they were wearing.

For now, a pair of black trousers and a stripy Breton top would have to do. By Bridget's standards they were smart, not informal, but it was safer to be over-dressed than risk looking like a slob.

She quickly ran a comb through her short, dark bob, applied a dash of nude lipstick and checked her appearance in the mirror. For better or worse, she was ready to face the world.

CHAPTER 3

Bridget hovered nervously at the edge of the large crowd, her tea cup and saucer in hand, a small Danish pastry balanced precariously on the saucer's edge. She scanned the theatre foyer for a familiar face but could see none.

Being only five foot two never helped in these situations. It was simply impossible for Bridget to see over other people's shoulders. But at least that allowed her to hide from view. She had never been good at large social gatherings. She took a bite out of her pastry to give her courage.

She hadn't kept in touch with any of her old college friends, and people had changed noticeably in two decades. She was struck by how old everyone looked. Well, they were all approaching forty. Middle-aged, according to Chloe. Many of the men were already going bald, and some of the women had obviously dyed their hair. Nearly all of them had fuller figures.

She knew that she had changed too. Grey strands had begun to appear in her own hair recently, and she had never managed to shake those extra pounds she'd acquired since having

Chloe. Not that she had expended a huge amount of effort trying. Her high-pressure job and her responsibilities as a single parent left little opportunity to exercise or to eat healthy, well-balanced meals. And it didn't help that she was uncommonly fond of pasta, sticky desserts and a glass or two of wine. She took another nibble of the Danish pastry. It really was delicious.

She inched her way sideways past a group of men now running to fat who were fondly reminiscing about their college rowing days. It seemed that getting up at five o'clock every morning in the middle of winter to run down to the boathouse for training had been the happiest time of their lives. If that was the case, she wondered why they didn't still do it.

She felt a tap on her shoulder and turned around.

'Bridget! I thought it was you.'

'Bella!' exclaimed Bridget, relieved that there was at least one person here that she recognised. Bella Williams had shared a house with her during her second year at college, together with four other girls. They had all been good friends once, but Bridget had seen none of her former housemates since graduating. Her sister's murder had wrenched her away from university just as she should have been celebrating, and she had simply lost touch.

Bridget kissed Bella on the cheek, then stepped back to take a proper look at her old friend. She was taken aback by what she saw, but did her best not to show it.

Bella had been very pretty once, but the years had not treated her kindly. Now her mouth was turned down in a permanent scowl and her skin showed signs of premature ageing. Her hair – like Bridget's – was turning grey, but unlike Bridget she had made no effort to restore it to its original colour.

Bridget couldn't help noticing that if her own attire might be described as informal, then Bella's outfit was definitely casual, even a tad scruffy. She was wearing a pair of faded denim jeans and a loose sweater with fraying cuffs. An old canvas bag was slung loosely over one shoulder. It hardly seemed like the right thing to wear to Tea with the warden. But then what did Bridget know about clothes? Her own life consisted of one wardrobe gaffe after another. Chloe was the one who dished out fashion advice in her house.

'How are you?' asked Bridget.

'Oh, you know.' Bella tucked her hands into her jeans pockets and gave a noncommittal shrug of the shoulders. 'So, so.'

Bridget had no idea what Bella meant by that. It wasn't exactly the sort of reply you were supposed to make when someone asked you how you were. Even Bridget knew that.

'But what about you?' asked Bella, obviously keen to turn the focus of the conversation onto Bridget. 'I haven't heard from you in years. What are you doing with yourself? Married? Kids?'

Bridget gave Bella a quick synopsis of her life – a brief marriage, resulting in one daughter, followed by a messy divorce, and a career now finally beginning to get going.

'Wow,' said Bella. 'So you joined the police? I would never have expected that.'

Bridget laughed. 'Me neither.' She took a sip of her tea. 'And what do you do these days?' Bella had studied Classics at university and Bridget wondered if she had pursued a career in academia.

'Me? Oh, I ended up going into teaching.'

'In a university?'

Bella gave a hollow laugh. 'In a school. It's not really what I'd hoped for.'

It certainly wasn't what Bella had hoped for. At university she had been a rising star, expected to get a First and to pursue a glittering academic career. Bridget had fully expected her to be a lecturer at Oxford or some other prestigious university now. But life had a way of throwing up surprises and diversions, as she well knew.

'I'm sure that teaching's hard work,' said Bridget. 'But very worthwhile.' With a teenager of her own, she had total respect for anyone prepared to spend their working day controlling a classroom of kids followed by an evening marking homework and producing lesson plans for the following day. Maybe that was why Bella was looking so downtrodden. 'And at least you get nice long summer holidays,' Bridget added brightly.

Bella smiled wanly and Bridget thought it best to change the subject. 'What about boyfriends or husbands?'

Bella shook her head. 'Nothing to report there either, I'm afraid. I guess I never found the right person.'

'Well, neither did I,' said Bridget. 'It just took me several years to find out how wrong he was.' She decided not to say anything about Jonathan. It felt like tempting fate, to talk about her new relationship which had only just got off to such a very faltering start. Instead she asked about the other housemates. 'Have you seen Meg, Tina or Alexia here?'

'I haven't seen Alexia. But Meg and Tina are over there.' Bella indicated the far corner of the room where two women – one blonde, one brunette – were standing with their backs to each other, each engaged in animated conversations with other people. Their poses suggested that they were very deliberately ignoring each other.

'Have they fallen out?' asked Bridget. Meg – Margaret Collins, to give her full name – and Tina Mackenzie had always been the best of friends during their university days.

Bella shrugged dismissively. 'Who knows with those two? You know what they're like – they're as stubborn and pig-headed as each other.'

Bridget was surprised to detect such an undisguised note of hostility in Bella's voice. The three women – Meg, Tina and Bella – had all been inseparable at one time. She wondered what had happened in the intervening years to drive a wedge between them.

As if sensing that they were being discussed, both Meg and Tina looked over to where Bridget and Bella were standing. Meg was the first to abandon the person she'd been talking to and stride across the room in her brightly coloured dress adorned with big, expensive-looking jewellery. Her long, golden hair bounced over her shoulders. A pair of over-sized sunglasses were perched on top of her head as if she had just flown in from somewhere exotic and was attending the gaudy as part of a world tour.

'Bridget!' she exclaimed in her louder-than-life voice. 'How wonderful to see you, darling.' In her six-inch red stilettos Meg towered over Bridget and Bella. Bridget, who had never got on with heels, wondered how she could possibly walk in them. Meg bent down ostentatiously to Bridget's level and planted two noisy air kisses, one on either side of Bridget's cheeks.

Meg had studied Biochemistry at Oxford, and had always talked of starting up her own company one day. Bridget was about to ask her what she had done since graduating, but she didn't get the chance. Clearly not wanting to be left out of the grand reunion, Tina appeared the next moment at Bridget's side.

Whereas Meg favoured bold colours – bright scarlet with clashing pink accessories – Tina was tastefully turned out in an exquisite figure-hugging black dress. Her slim youthful figure suggested to Bridget an unattainable degree of self-control, and her short, elegantly-cut hair and impeccable makeup completed the vision of perfection. If this was informal, Bridget couldn't imagine what Tina might choose to wear for dinner.

'Bridget, you haven't changed a bit,' said Tina, planting a kiss on Bridget's left cheek.

'I don't know about that,' said Bridget. 'But you don't look a day older.' Yet that wasn't strictly true. Although Tina was just as thin as she'd been at twenty, the jeans-wearing student that Bridget had known had been replaced by a mature and supremely confident woman she barely recognised. Tina had studied Law at university. Perhaps she was now a high-flying lawyer with a big London firm as she'd always hoped to be.

'Well, here we all are again,' said Meg, beaming at everyone, although her smile dimmed noticeably as it reached Tina. 'It's just like old times.'

'Except that Alexia's not here,' said Bridget, looking around the room. Alexia Petrakis was the fifth member of their circle. With her exotic background and striking good looks, Alexia had always been the most glamorous of the group. She had stood out among the other students with her glossy black hair falling in curls, her dark eyes and olive skin, and she had broken more than a few male hearts during her three years at Oxford.

Even as an undergraduate she had enjoyed a jet-setting lifestyle, travelling to her family homes in Greece and the Amalfi coast during the summer vacations. She had once invited Bridget to stay with her, but Bridget had been too timid to go. Now she wondered what on earth she had been so afraid of. 'Has anyone heard from Alexia? Where is she now? Is she coming today?'

'I'm sure she is,' said Bella.

'Knowing Alexia, she's probably in someone else's bed,' said Tina.

Meg's face turned to thunder. She glared angrily at Tina. In response, Tina shrugged and sipped her tea.

Bridget waited to see if anyone would explain this exchange of hostilities, but instead the two women turned their backs on each other once more, saying nothing.

Bella caught Bridget's eye as if to say, 'Honestly, those two.'

Bridget sipped her tea, feeling decidedly uncomfortable at the way the reunion was progressing. She had expected people to have changed, naturally, but hadn't counted on this open warfare between her old friends. As she pondered their behaviour, she was reminded of another reason for her growing feeling of disquiet. Whatever might be going on between Meg and Tina – and Bella, for that matter – there was an elephant in the room that no one had yet mentioned. The sixth member of their household, Lydia Khoury.

Lydia, of course, would not be returning to college today. Lydia would never be returning.

The awkward silence that had descended on the group was broken by the arrival of the warden and his wife who were circulating among the guests. Both Meg and Tina eagerly turned back as the couple approached.

The warden of Merton College, Dr Brendan Harper, had been the tutor in Archaeology and Anthropology when Bridget was a student. He had since gone on to achieve a degree of celebrity presenting documentaries on the National Geographic Channel, the History Channel, and more recently the BBC where he was credited with making old bones look sexy. A real-life Indiana Jones, he was the sort of man whose appeal to women seemed only to increase as he aged, particularly when he was striding around the desert in a pair of khaki shorts and sturdy walking boots, his lightly stubbled features leaning earnestly into the camera as he explained the significance of some rare and important artifact.

While Dr Harper was in his mid to late fifties, his wife, Yasmin, was much younger. Bridget guessed maybe mid-thirties. With her long neck, finely carved features and deep-set eyes, she made Bridget think of the famous bust of the Egyptian queen, Nefertiti.

Meg was the first of the group to step forward and shake the warden's hand, switching her beaming smile back on. 'Warden, I hear we should be wishing you luck with your quest to become vice-chancellor of the university.'

Dr Harper returned her exuberant welcome with a smile of false modesty. 'Thank you. It's all in the lap of the gods now. Or at least the governing body of the university, which as you know is the nearest we have to divinity, here in Oxford.' He paused while Meg laughed rather excessively at his quip. 'Congregation will make its decision in a week's time,' he concluded. 'Of course, I don't hold out too much hope for myself. The other candidates are such worthy luminaries.'

'But so are you, Warden,' gushed Meg sycophantically.

'You're very kind to say so,' said Dr Harper.

The news that the warden was being considered as vice-chancellor was news to Bridget. She knew that Dr Harper was a highly respected academic, as well as being a shameless media tart. But the position of vice-chancellor was the university's most senior executive position and the warden was relatively young for the task. She wondered how he would fit it in around his busy TV schedule.

'An intrepid adventurer is just what this university needs,' said Meg. 'Shake things up a bit. Dust off the cobwebs. You'd be perfect for the role.'

The look of admiration on his wife's face suggested that she thought so too.

★

It was a relief for Bridget to return to her room in the Grove Building for some peace and quiet before the evening got going. She kicked off her shoes, banished her many and varied outfits to the room's small wardrobe and flopped down on the bed. The narrow mattress had seen better days and she doubted it would give her a good night's sleep. She stared up at the ceiling and pondered what she'd witnessed during tea.

She had been looking forward to renewing old friendships, but the atmosphere between Meg and Tina had been visibly hostile, even toxic, and Bella had seemed rather downbeat, and not exactly charitable towards the other two. They seemed such a disparate bunch, it was hard to remember how they'd managed to get along so well as students.

She sat up and checked the seating plan for dinner. The hall comprised three long tables running lengthwise, with high table placed perpendicular at one end. Bridget's name appeared at the top of the central table, with Bella opposite. Meg was seated next to Bridget, and Tina was next to Bella. Alexia was placed next to Meg.

Bridget gave a sigh of relief. So Alexia would definitely be at dinner. Her exuberant friend had always livened up any social gathering and helped to put everyone in a good mood. And once the wine started flowing, any awkward social tensions should hopefully be eased.

It was just as well since, for the duration of the dinner at least, there would be no escaping the group of women with whom Bridget had shared a house in East Oxford during her second year as a student. The house, she recalled, had been typical student digs. They'd paid a small fortune for a property with a severe damp problem, mould on the bathroom walls and a roof that leaked when it rained. Ah yes, those were the days.

On impulse she dialled Jonathan's number. She still felt guilty about abandoning him for the weekend.

He picked up on the third ring. 'Bridget, how's it going?'

'Just great. Two of my friends have fallen out with each other, one appears depressed and the other hasn't shown up yet. Looks like it's going to be a fun evening. What are you up to?'

She imagined him lying on the couch at home, reading a book or watching television.

He hesitated just a moment before replying. 'Actually I've just popped into the gallery. I know that you told me not to, but we've got a new exhibition opening on Monday.'

'It wasn't me who forbade you from going into work,' said Bridget. 'It was the doctors. And with good reason.'

'Yes, well, Vicky has been running the shop all on her own while I've been off work. It wasn't fair to leave everything to her. Organising an exhibition is a big job.'

'That's what worries me,' said Bridget. 'Don't lift any heavy paintings. I don't want you to injure yourself again.'

Any romance in their embryonic relationship had so far been limited to gentle hugs and chaste kisses. It was hard to do more than that with Jonathan recovering from his injury, especially since they had only just begun to get to know each other properly. But the time she had spent visiting him in hospital had helped them to cement their friendship. Bridget hoped that once he was fit and well, they would be able to move their relationship forward to the next stage.

'I promise,' said Jonathan. 'Now you must do what you promised me. Go and enjoy yourself with your grumpy friends. And remember what I said – no finding skeletons in closets.'

'I'll do my best.' She ended the call, smiling to herself. Jonathan's easy-going nature always managed to make her feel better.

She flicked through the contacts list on her phone, her thumb hovering briefly over Chloe's name. Should she give her daughter a call? She was tempted to, but in the end she managed to resist. Chloe hated it when she thought her mother was checking up on her. The two of them had not always seen eye to eye recently, and it would do them both good to have a little space. Besides, Bridget was supposed to be enjoying herself at the gaudy. When was the last time she had taken a weekend off just for herself? Or even part of a weekend? She could barely remember.

It was time to make a decision about what to wear for dinner. She retrieved her three dresses from the wardrobe and laid them out on the bed, eyeing them nervously. Whichever one she chose, she could never hope to look as glamorous as Meg, or match Tina for refinement. When you were five foot two and carrying too much weight around your middle, you had to set realistic expectations. She knew that whatever she wore would be a disappointment, so she might as well not worry.

It was a choice between a black velvet dress with a neckline that showed off her décolletage to its best advantage, a red satin dress that made the most of her skin and hair colouring, and a pale blue dress in gauze and chiffon which, on reflection, she decided made her look like the mother of the bride. After trying each one in turn, she decided on the black velvet dress.

She touched up her make-up with a dab of foundation, a smidgen of mascara, and a smear of lip gloss. Then she squeezed her feet into a pair of heels that gave her a much-needed height boost. Walking would be tricky, but hopefully she'd be sitting down for most of the evening.

She checked her phone once more for any messages from Chloe, but as expected, there were none. Then, slightly unsteadily, she made her way down the stairs and over to the chapel for the pre-dinner service.

CHAPTER 4

The rich harmonies of the Dobson organ reverberated off the ancient walls of the antechapel and floated up into the belfry, filling the space with glorious sound.

Bridget picked up an order of service and proceeded into the main quire of the chapel, taking a seat in the back row of pews. It was common in Oxford college chapels for the pews to mirror each other across a central aisle, instead of facing forward towards the altar. All the better for quiet contemplation. She closed her eyes and let the music of the Bach fugue wash over her, soothing away the tensions of the day.

Organ music in an ecclesiastical setting always had the power to transport Bridget back to her own childhood. She'd enjoyed a traditional Church of England upbringing in the nearby town of Woodstock where her mother had arranged the weekly flowers and taught in the Sunday School. Bridget had sung in the choir, and the church had been central to her existence. Life didn't get much more middle England than that. On coming to university in Oxford, she'd found a natural home in the chapel choir, participating in the weekly ritual of evensong with its musical settings of the Magnificat and Nunc Dimittis.

But that safe and comfortable world had come crashing down when her younger sister had been abducted and brutally murdered. Abigail's death had shaken Bridget's foundations to the ground, and pushed her in a totally new direction. Regular church attendance had fallen by the wayside as her faith struggled unsuccessfully to survive the cataclysm. Forced to confront a much darker reality than the world in which she had grown up, Bridget had joined the police force, beginning as a uniformed constable, before applying to become a detective. It was her way of trying to put things right. Not that Abigail's death could ever be put right, even if her killer were caught and brought to justice, which he never had been.

The final chord of the organ music died away and Bridget opened her eyes. The chapel was half full – none of her former housemates had turned up, although the warden was seated in the opposite pew – and the chaplain had taken his place in front of the altar. He was young – much younger than her – and had probably still been at school while she was a student at the university. She wondered if the floor-length cassock he wore concealed a pair of trendy jeans beneath.

'Welcome to our Gaudy Service,' he intoned.

Bridget imagined Chloe sniggering at that.

Was the organist wearing rhinestones? Would a flashing neon cross descend from the rafters, with angels adorned in Gucci sunglasses? That would certainly liven things up.

'We will start by singing the hymn All People that on Earth do Dwell, which is printed on your orders of service.'

As the organist played over the melody at full volume, the congregation rose to its feet. Familiar with the four-square tune from her choral days, Bridget joined in heartily, even though those around her were mumbling the words. There was nothing like a good sing to lift the spirits – indeed the first verse exhorted them to Sing to the Lord with Cheerful Voice – but these days her musical endeavours mostly consisted of singing along to her collection of operatic CDs. Her daughter was always telling her to upload her CD library to her phone, but that was a technological challenge that Bridget was forever putting off.

After the hymn, the chaplain spoke amiably about how a gaudy was a chance to review old acquaintances and friendships, and how friendships formed during university could, if properly nurtured, last a lifetime, helping us through the trials and tribulations of life.

He was too young to have seen many trials and tribulations. Still, he made a good point. So why had Bridget allowed her friendships with her old housemates to lapse after leaving university? Was it simply Abigail's death that had made her cut off all previous ties and start afresh at police training college? Or was it what had happened to the sixth member of their little household? Lydia. The only member of the group who could not be expected to attend the gaudy. Because she was dead.

'We read in the gospel of John, chapter fifteen, verses 12-13' – the chaplain was getting into his stride now and his voice had risen in a fervour of evangelical zeal – '"This is my commandment, That ye love one another, as I have loved you. Greater love hath no man than this, that a man lay down his life for his friends."'

Or her friends, mused Bridget. Would she lay down her life for Bella, Meg, Tina or Alexia? Given that she hadn't seen any of them during the last seventeen years, it seemed a pretty tall order. Would they do the same for her? She very much doubted it. But for her sister Abigail, that was a different matter.

'But maintaining friendships takes work,' said the chaplain. 'None of us is perfect, and so when problems arise we must be prepared to forgive each other. As St Paul wrote in his letter to the Colossians, chapter three, verse thirteen, "Forbearing one another, and forgiving one another, if any man have a quarrel against any: even as Christ forgave you, so also do ye." Amen.'

'Amen,' mumbled the congregation.

It was the lesson that Bridget had grown up with – Forgive us our trespasses as we forgive those who trespass against us – but it was a bitter pill to swallow. How could she ever forgive the person who had taken Abigail away from her, and who had destroyed her perfect family, driving her parents to the brink of despair?

Maybe that was the real reason she didn't go to church anymore. She couldn't stand being constantly told to forgive.

The organist was already thundering through the rousing melody of the final hymn, Guide Me, O Thou Great Redeemer. Bridget rose to her feet and joined in, but was unable to find the same joy she'd experienced singing the first hymn, even though this was normally one of her favourites. All that talk about dying for one's friends, and of forgiving one's enemies had stirred up too many painful memories and dark thoughts. It was hardly a great start to what was supposed to be a joyous evening. Maybe things would start to look up after a glass or two of wine.

On her way out, she shook the chaplain's hand and thanked him for a lovely service. It was the expected thing to do, and she had no wish to be discourteous. Up close he looked even younger. A sprinkling of freckles covered his nose and cheeks. His eyes were blue beneath a shock of sandy coloured hair.

'How long have you been the chaplain here?' she enquired politely.

'Since last Trinity term.' He grinned. 'Still finding my feet.'

'You're doing fine.' She moved on so that

other people could have a chance to greet him.

Outside, the evening air was growing cooler. The university term wouldn't start until October, but Chloe had already been back at school for three weeks. As Bridget made her way slowly back to Front Quad – these heels were going to kill her – she reflected that maybe it was time to properly renew old acquaintances. She resolved to enjoy herself over dinner and start rebuilding bridges.

★

With its high vaulted ceiling, stained-glass windows, and long wooden tables set for a banquet, the thirteenth-century dining hall could not have looked more magnificent if Queen Elizabeth I herself had been the guest of honour. Small table lamps the length of the hall created a cosy atmosphere reminiscent of the days when candles had provided the only illumination. Each place was set with an elaborate arrangement of cutlery, three differently-sized wine glasses, and a linen napkin artfully folded into the shape of a bishop's mitre. Gilt-framed portraits of centuries-old scholars and clerics gazed down sternly from the walls, as if envious of the four-course feast that was promised.

Bridget walked the length of the hall to take her place at the top of the middle table. Meg arrived soon afterwards, sitting down next to her. Tina and Bella followed, taking their seats opposite.

Each setting was marked with a name card printed in fancy lettering.

The three women had all changed their clothes since Bridget had last seen them, undergoing a transformation from informal to black tie. Both Meg and Tina looked as if they'd spent the time between tea and dinner having a fashion makeover. Meg was wreathed in a concoction of purple silk and flowing organza. The elaborate dress, combined with her ample bosom, threatened to knock over one of the many wine glasses every time she leaned forward. Tina had slipped into an off-the-shoulder black dress that displayed to advantage her chiselled collar bone and toned upper arms. Bella had at least managed to change out of her jeans and jumper into a plain blue dress which she had teamed with a black jacket. For Bella's sake, Bridget was glad that she herself hadn't overdressed, not that she could have hoped to pull off either of the looks adopted by Meg or Tina.

'We'll have to behave ourselves, sitting so close to the warden,' joked Meg, glancing up at the nearby high table where places were reserved for the warden, his wife and other college dignitaries. 'Although since we're no longer students, we can't get sent down.' She grinned wickedly. 'So perhaps this is our chance to behave badly.'

'What are you planning on getting up to?' asked Bella.

'Me? Nothing,' said Meg, adopting a look of

wide-eyed innocence. 'But perhaps Tina is going to stab someone in the back with a knife.'

'That may be your style, Meg,' countered Tina archly. 'I always stab my enemies from the front.'

Bridget groaned inwardly. She'd hoped that the two women might have brought their hostilities to an end by now. She still had no idea what their problem was, and didn't think that asking them outright would help to calm the mood.

'Come on, girls,' she said jokingly. 'You'd better watch out. Remember that Bella's a teacher. I'm sure she knows how to deal with unruly children.'

'Please don't remind me about it,' said Bella gloomily, and the group fell into an uneasy silence.

The hall was rapidly filling up, but the place next to Meg remained empty. It looked as if Alexia might not make it after all, which was a shame. Bridget hoped that Meg and Tina were not going to snipe at each other across the salt and pepper grinders all evening.

'Bella tells me that you're a police inspector these days,' said Meg. 'Is that true or was she pulling my leg?'

'It's true,' said Bridget.

'So if you're a detective inspector that must mean you're a plain clothes officer?'

'Correct.'

'So you could be on duty right this minute and no one would know.'

Bridget laughed. 'I can assure you that I'm definitely not working this weekend. I'm here to enjoy myself. I wonder what they're serving,' she said brightly, picking up one of the college-crested menus that were placed at regular intervals along the tables. Immediately her mood improved. A watercress and cucumber soup with pea shoots and saffron oil served with Broglia Gavi 2016 was to be followed by a butternut squash, sage and Gorgonzola risotto. The main course was a three-bone rack of lamb with fondant potato, baby vegetables and shallot jus served with Château La Sergue 2005. Dessert would be praline chocolate croquant, raspberry compote and sweet Persian pistachios served with Dow's late bottled vintage, 2012. Tea, coffee and mints to follow. She'd have to spend the rest of the week on the cabbage soup diet, but it would be worth it.

'They do a very similar thing at The Ivy in London,' said Tina, glancing briefly at a second menu before passing it to Bella. She made it sound as if she was rather bored with fancy food.

'Is that where you hold your client meetings?' asked Meg. 'No wonder lawyers charge such a bloody fortune.'

Bridget, who had never dined at The Ivy, felt her mouth watering at the prospect of the food.

'You should count yourself lucky,' Bella told Tina, echoing Bridget's thoughts. 'I don't get to eat in posh restaurants on a teacher's salary.'

'Of course not,' said Meg warmly. 'And some

people take posh food too much for granted. I'd be more than happy with fish and chips served from a newspaper.' She glared at Tina. 'Quite frankly, The Ivy is not all it's cracked up to be.'

Tina looked ready to respond with a caustic remark of her own, but was interrupted by the arrival of the warden and his wife leading a procession of tutors and assorted college VIPs to their places on high table. Once the new guests were standing by their places, the warden rapped on the table with a wooden gavel. Everyone in the hall fell silent and then, en masse, rose to their feet. They had followed this arcane routine so many times as students, they didn't need to be told what to do. In a sonorous voice, the Classics tutor proclaimed the Latin grace that was printed on the back of the menu, with a helpful English translation for those who, like Bridget, were not fluent in the tongue of Virgil and Cicero.

'Oculi omnium in te respiciunt, Domine, tu das escam illis tempore opportuno...'

The eyes of all wait upon thee O Lord, and thou givest them their food in due season...

Hearing Latin spoken had been one of those things Bridget had become accustomed to as a student. As a member of the chapel choir, she had done plenty of singing in Latin and could still, if pushed, just about recite the Latin version of the Creed. The matriculation ceremony in the Sheldonian Theatre in which students were inducted into the university had been conducted entirely in Latin, as had the degree ceremony three years later. The university motto was in Latin – Dominus illuminatio mea – The Lord is my light. In fact, a formal qualification in Latin had once been a prerequisite for studying at the university, even if your chosen subject was Chemistry or Mathematics.

'...Per Jesum Christum Dominum nostrum. Amen.' Through Jesus Christ our Lord. Amen.

'Amen,' intoned the one hundred and fifty voices of the assembled guests. Or one hundred and forty-nine, thought Bridget, given Alexia's absence.

With the formalities of grace out of the way, the black-waistcoated dining staff who had been standing in the wings now sprang into action, serving warm bread rolls with butter – real butter, thought Bridget, who had spent years consuming tasteless low-fat spread with little benefit to show for it – and pouring the first wine of the evening in a carefully choreographed routine designed to be fast, efficient and almost invisible.

As if the setting wasn't theatrical enough, the first course dishes were delivered to the tables covered with silver domes which were removed with a flourish. In eager anticipation, Bridget unfolded her napkin and picked up her soup spoon. She intended to enjoy the food however sour the company may be.

An ear-splitting scream from high table caused her to drop her spoon before she could taste the soup.

In the silence that followed, all eyes in the hall turned to the cause of the disturbance. The warden's wife was on her feet, her hands to her face, her eyes staring in horror at something on the table before her.

The warden rose too and angrily threw his napkin down on the table. 'What is the meaning of this outrage?' he bellowed.

'Whatever it is, I'm not to blame,' whispered Meg to Bridget. But no one laughed.

The tutors and college staff on high table were getting to their feet and peering at the warden's bowl of soup.

'Goodness me!' exclaimed the Classics tutor in alarm. 'When I said the words Oculi omnium, I never thought...' His voice trailed away.

Bridget's mind was no longer on her soup. This might be her day off, but a police officer was never really off duty. It was her job to respond to people in distress. It wasn't just her job, though, it was part of her nature. She rose to her feet and rushed over to the high table where the warden and his wife had been seated.

She didn't know what she'd been expecting to see, but it certainly wasn't the sight that met her eyes.

Staring up at her from the warden's soup bowl were two very round and very real eyeballs.

'Is this supposed to be a prank of some kind?' demanded the warden. 'Who would think that putting sheep's eyeballs in my soup was funny?'

His wife had resumed her seat, and was

fanning herself with one of the menus. She looked almost as green as the soup.

The Biology tutor who had been sitting at the far end of the table came over to examine the floating orbs as if they were specimens in his lab. 'Warden, I can categorically state that these are not sheep's eyeballs, but human,' he announced, sounding intrigued by the discovery. 'If you look closely you can see how the shape of the iris –'

Whatever knowledge he had been intending to impart was curtailed by another wail from the warden's wife. The rest of the hall now erupted in a cacophony of shouts and exclamations. Almost everyone seemed to have an opinion on the matter. Quite a few people were knocking back their glasses of wine, but not many people were touching their soup.

Bridget was acutely aware of the need to restore some order and preserve what looked like potential evidence of a crime, although no actual crime had as yet been uncovered.

'Everyone remain seated,' she shouted in her most commanding voice. The hubbub that had exploded faded away. 'I am a detective inspector with Thames Valley Police and I am assuming charge of this situation.'

She turned to address the college butler, who had delivered the soup to high table and was standing nearby, a look of absolute horror on his face. 'Call the police and inform them that a crime has been committed. Ask them to send an investigating team to the college immediately.

You can give them my name. In the meantime, cover the soup with one of those silver domes. We need to preserve the evidence.'

'Evidence of what precisely?' asked the warden. 'Is this some sick joke?'

'I don't know yet,' said Bridget. 'But I intend to find out.'

The chatter in the hall had begun to grow in volume again, but was suddenly disrupted by a new and unexpected noise. The ringing of a bell.

'It's the bell in the chapel,' remarked the Classics tutor. 'Who can be ringing it at this time of day?'

The bell rang once, twice, three times. It paused briefly, then continued, clanging loudly and ever more wildly.

'Make sure that no one touches this,' Bridget instructed one of the serving staff, indicating the bowl of soup containing the eyes, which was now mercifully covered by a silver dome. She turned, passing Meg, Tina and Bella, who were regarding her with something approaching awe, and strode out of the hall.

Outside, the ringing of the bell was even louder and more frantic. She hurried as quickly as she could in her heels and dress to the chapel entrance. Pushing the heavy door open, she stepped inside the antechapel.

The young chaplain stood in the belfry, desperately tugging at the bell rope. As soon as he saw Bridget, he abandoned his task and ran to meet her. The shock on his face was plain to see.

'What is it?' asked Bridget. 'What's happened?'

'Over there,' said the chaplain, pointing towards a row of wooden cupboards at the end of the north transept. 'I was just about to put my vestments away after the service. She fell out when I opened the door.'

'Who fell out?' asked Bridget, struggling to keep up with him as he hurried away towards the place he had pointed to. Damn these shoes. She kicked them off and ran the rest of the way to catch up with him.

'There.' The chaplain pointed at the woman's body lying sprawled across the floor by the open door of the furthest cupboard.

'Don't go any closer,' warned Bridget. 'We have to preserve the crime scene.'

'I don't know who she is,' said the chaplain.

'I do.' Bridget gazed down sadly at the corpse. Even with the amount of blood covering the dead woman's face, she could see quite clearly that it was Alexia Petrakis. Her eye sockets were two bloody holes.

CHAPTER 5

'Six pints of Yorkshire Bitter please, mate, and a jumbo pack of bacon fries.'

Detective Sergeant Jake Derwent had to raise his voice to make himself heard over the noise in the pub in Leeds. It was Saturday night in the city centre and it looked as if half of West Yorkshire was out partying.

He'd driven up to his home town from Oxford on Friday night, arriving late after doing battle with the latest set of roadworks on the M1 motorway. His mum had fussed over him, reheating the shepherd's pie she'd saved and then cooking him a big breakfast fry-up in the morning, just the way he liked it.

Today he'd taken his parents to Harlow Carr Garden in Harrogate for his mum's birthday, doing his best to answer his dad's questions about crime in Oxford and fending off his mum's not-so-subtle enquiries into whether or not he'd found himself a nice girl yet, and why didn't he consider moving back up north, the price of houses being what they were in the south? There were some nice new developments in Leeds city centre, down by the river, just right for a young man like him. He should get in now before prices shot up.

He had to admit it was tempting. Oxford house prices were insane, and buying a place of his own was out of the question. Even renting was expensive, and all he could afford was a flat above a launderette on the Cowley Road, sandwiched between an Indian restaurant and a Chinese takeaway.

But for some reason he found himself resisting his mum's suggestions. He liked his flat in Oxford, despite it being a bit cramped. He liked the hustle and bustle of Cowley Road, even if it could be seedy and rough at times. But there was more keeping him in Oxford than just his flat. There was his pride. There was his job. And it was only when they'd stopped for tea and scones at Betty's Café and his mum said, 'It's not as if you have anyone special in Oxford,' that he almost blurted out, 'There's Ffion Hughes.'

But he held his tongue. Any mention of the sexy Welsh detective constable at Thames Valley Police would have opened up a whole new can of worms that he wasn't yet ready to deal with. His mum would pounce on any female name as a potential girlfriend, wife and future mother of his children, and would want to know everything about her. She'd been almost as upset as he had at the break-up of his long-term relationship with his previous girlfriend. Maybe even more so.

Right now, he and Ffion were getting along

just fine, both as work colleagues and, tentatively, as friends. She had definitely mellowed towards him in recent weeks, and especially after the most recent case. When he'd first got to know her she'd been as prickly as a Welsh porcupine. Did they have porcupines in Wales? They had plenty of sheep, but Ffion was certainly no lamb.

Anyway, she'd recently confided in him that she was bisexual, and he was still chewing over what to make of that. Could he ever be comfortable with a girlfriend who was attracted to other women? Ffion had told him she found women easier to get on with because men were so often insensitive. Jake understood that she was setting him a challenge, and wondered if he could be the sensitive guy that Ffion wanted him to be.

'Things are going very well for me in Oxford,' he found himself telling his mum and dad. 'Since my promotion I've worked on a couple of big cases.'

That was true enough. There had been the murder of the wealthy student at Christ Church, and then the strange case of the artist shot dead in cold blood on the High Street. Both murders had made the national news.

'And you say you've got a female boss?' his dad asked, spreading a generous portion of clotted cream onto his scone.

'Yeah, DI Bridget Hart. She's all right actually,' said Jake through a mouthful of buttery

50

scone.

'Is she married?' asked his mum. 'I don't suppose she has a family, doing a tough job like that.'

'She's divorced with a teenage daughter,' said Jake. 'And she does a good job. She's fair and she doesn't take any crap from anyone.'

He found himself wanting to defend his boss. It couldn't be easy for her, heading up murder enquiries and looking after her daughter at the same time. Especially not when her ex-husband was a senior detective in London. DCI Ben Hart had turned up unexpectedly in the middle of their last murder investigation, causing quite a discordant atmosphere in the incident room for a while.

'Shall we go and look around the Alpine House next?' he asked to change the subject.

They'd driven back to Leeds with a car boot packed full of potted plants and shrubs, and Jake had promised to give his parents a hand planting them in the morning before heading back to Oxford.

Now he was out in Leeds city centre catching up with his mates from school. They were doing the round of pubs and bars in Call Lane, Duncan Street and Lower Briggate. Next stop would be an Indian restaurant for some much-needed carbs to soak up the alcohol. It had been a while since Jake had been out on such a monster pub crawl, and he would welcome the break.

'That'll be £23.40 please,' said the barman in

a thick West Yorkshire accent.

Jake paid for the round with a grin. It wasn't just the house prices that were cheaper in Leeds – pints were cheaper here too. Buying a round in Oxford, he'd have been lucky to get any change out of thirty quid.

'Cheers, mate.' He picked up the tray of glasses and snacks and carried it over to the table where his friends were waiting for refills. The table was already overflowing with empty pint glasses. The lads quickly cleared a space for him.

'What took you so long?' asked Dan. 'Did the barman have trouble understanding your posh southern accent?'

'Six pints of your very finest ale, please, barman,' said Matt, mimicking a ridiculously upper-class voice.

'And make it snappy, you working class oaf,' added Scott.

A gale of drunken laughter greeted their mockery.

'I haven't got a southern accent,' said Jake crossly. Back in Oxford, the guys at Police HQ poked fun at him for his short Yorkshire vowels. He passed the beers around. 'Cheers.'

Dan was eyeing up a girl sitting at the bar, whose skirt was almost non-existent. 'What do you reckon?' he asked the lads.

'Not bad,' said Scott.

'Slapper,' said Kieran.

'Minger,' said Reece.

Jake took a quick gulp of his pint so he

wouldn't have to volunteer his opinion on the girl. He wondered what Ffion would think if she could see him now. His mates would confirm her very worst fears about coarse, insensitive males.

'So, mate,' asked Dan, dragging his attention away from the woman at the bar. 'How do you rate the girls in Oxford? Are all the rumours about posh girls true?'

'I don't know what you mean,' said Jake. 'Oxford's not full of posh girls.'

'Come on, I bet they're all stinking rich.'

Jake thought again of Ffion. He wondered how he could describe her to the lads, without them making fun. Ffion certainly wasn't the kind of horse-riding, jolly hockey-sticks girl they crudely imagined. She had gone to an ordinary school in a Welsh mining village. In many ways she was more working class than his mates, and yet she had studied at Oxford University and was one of the smartest people he had ever met. There was no way he could begin to explain her to the lads. He wasn't even sure how he would describe her to himself. Ffion was different to any girl he'd ever known.

He sipped his beer thoughtfully while Dan began telling the others a dirty joke he'd heard at work. It had felt good to meet up with his old friends again, but now he felt as distant from them as if they were a hundred miles away. They had been wrong about him losing his northern accent, and yet it was true that a gulf had opened up between them. He'd felt the same when he'd first moved to Oxford – all those medieval quadrangles and dusty libraries and students on bicycles everywhere – but he'd never expected to feel that way in the city where he'd grown up. Was he, in fact, becoming a "soft southerner" like the lads joked, or was he now stuck in some no-man's land, no longer fitting in to either of the cities he called home?

His phone buzzed in his pocket and he pulled it out to see who was calling. Ffion! His heart began to race and he felt the tips of his ears growing hot – a sure sign that they were flushing pink. He hoped his mates wouldn't notice. What could Ffion possibly be phoning him about on a Saturday night? It was almost as if she'd sensed his discomfort and had called to rescue him.

It was too loud in the pub to talk on the phone, and he had no desire for his mates to listen in, so he got up and headed outside to shouts of, 'What's her name, then? Is it Lucinda? Or Camilla? Perhaps Lady Henrietta?'

'Hi,' he said to Ffion, leaving the din of the pub behind him. 'What's up?'

Ffion wasn't one for wasting time on small talk. 'There's been a murder at a gaudy in Merton College,' she said in her Welsh accent. 'You need to get yourself back down here right now.'

'Christ,' said Jake. 'I'm at the pub.'

'So I can hear. The thing is, the boss was one of the guests, so Baxter's been put in charge of the case.'

'Baxter?' Jake had encountered Detective Inspector Greg Baxter in the office a few times, but hadn't worked with him before. The DI was older and more experienced than Bridget, and gave the impression of being gruff and humourless.

Jake suddenly felt stone-cold sober. Hearing Ffion's voice over the phone had answered one question for him – Oxford was definitely his home now, not Leeds. The second question still hanging over him – could he be the right man for Ffion? – was one that she would have to answer for herself. It was up to him to prove to her that the answer was yes.

'I'll head off first thing in the morning,' he promised. 'I'd leave right now, but I'm over the limit.'

'Okay,' said Ffion. 'I'll see you tomorrow.'

It was only afterwards that he realised he had forgotten to ask the obvious question, 'What the hell's a gaudy?'

CHAPTER 6

Uniformed police from the local St Aldate's station had secured the college chapel, and scene-of-crime officers in their white suits were now crawling all over the place, rigging up arrays of bright lighting, dusting for prints, taking photographs and carrying out fingertip searches of the chapel and antechapel.

Vikram "Vik" Vijayaraghavan, the head of SOCO, was in charge of the operation as usual. 'You look as if you had other plans for this evening,' he said, indicating Bridget's dress and heels with a grin. 'Or maybe CID are just better turned out these days?'

'Ha, ha!' It wasn't the first time Bridget had attended a crime scene in wholly unsuitable clothes. In fact she was beginning to make a habit of it. This time, she wasn't even going to attempt to pull one of the white protective suits over her dress, so she was keeping her distance. A ribbon of crime scene tape was strung across the antechapel from the organ to the quire entrance, dividing the north and south transepts. All the main action was taking place in the north transept where the body had been found.

Vik's face grew serious. 'Sorry, it must have been a terrible shock for you.'

'Yes,' Bridget acknowledged. 'I knew the victim well from my student days. We were good friends, although I hadn't seen her in a long time. I was looking forward to catching up with her this weekend.'

That would never happen now, of course. Those lost years would remain forever lost, and she would never have the chance to catch up with her old friend.

'Perhaps you should go and sit down. Let others do the work this time.'

'No,' said Bridget adamantly. 'I want to help.' The reunion that she had looked forward to so much was no longer possible, but she was determined to find out who had committed this terrible crime. It was the least she could do for Alexia.

She had quizzed the chaplain immediately after discovering the mutilated body, but he had been too distraught to tell her much. According to him, he'd been tidying up after the service and had been about to put his vestments away. On opening the wooden cupboard in the north transept where the robes were kept, the woman's body had fallen out on top of him. In terrified panic he had rung the bell to summon assistance.

No one else was being allowed inside the chapel, and Bridget wondered what the other guests were doing now. The dinner itself had been brought to an untimely close, first by the discovery of the eyes in the warden's soup, and then by the ringing of the bell, and she imagined that the guests had probably made their way to the college bar. Maybe the horror of Alexia's murder would enable Meg and Tina to get over their differences. Then again, maybe not.

'What can you tell me about the murder?' she asked Vik.

'From the marks on her neck, it looks like she was garrotted. We found a piece of wire in the cupboard, which was most likely the murder weapon. We also found a small sharp knife, the sort you'd use for paring vegetables. You can guess what that was used for.'

Bridget shuddered as she remembered the sightless sockets in Alexia's bloody face.

They were joined at the tape by Dr Sarah Walker, the medical examiner who Bridget had worked with on several murder investigations. She had clearly just finished her examination of the body, and Bridget was hoping she would be able to provide some more detailed information.

Dr Walker was never the chattiest of Bridget's colleagues. Now she regarded her with a look of professional aloofness. 'I understand that the murder victim was known to you.'

'Yes,' said Bridget. 'She was an old university friend. What can you tell me about how she died?'

'Are you sure you want to know?' There was an element of warning in Dr Walker's voice.

'Yes.' Whatever had happened to Alexia, it was vital for Bridget to find out as much detail as she could.

'I'm afraid that it was a particularly gruesome murder. Death by garrotting is always unpleasant. It's been used as an execution method since Roman times, and also as a means of torture. There are many variations, but in this case a length of wire was used. Simple but effective. The wire was looped around the victim's neck and then pulled tight, resulting in death by asphyxiation. The victim would have been completely unable to cry out, and any attempt to free herself would simply have drawn the wire tighter.' Dr Walker pulled off her latex gloves with a snap. 'The enucleation was carried out using a kitchen knife.'

'Sorry?' said Bridget. 'The what?'

'Enucleation. The removal of the eyes, leaving the eyelids, eye muscles and other structures intact. In this case the eyeballs were gouged out with a knife and hacked from the optic nerve. Quite messy.'

Bridget swallowed hard, struggling to maintain her poise. She was used to attending post-mortems, but had always found them the most difficult part of her job. Now she was dealing with a friend, it was hard to keep her emotions under control. 'Were they –'

'I think that the eyes were almost certainly removed after death,' said Dr Walker. 'You'll be wanting to know the time of death, no doubt.'

Bridget nodded. 'Yes, if you can give me an estimate.'

'It's hard to say precisely,' said Dr Walker, hedging her bets as Bridget had known she would. 'But I would say she's been dead for at least three or four hours.'

Bridget felt her blood run cold at the news. If Alexia had been dead for three hours, it was almost certain that her body had been concealed in its hiding place before the chapel service had begun. All the time that Bridget had been sitting listening to the chaplain's words and reflecting on her own dead sister, her friend's corpse had been slumped in the cupboard just yards away from her.

She remembered Jonathan telling her not to go looking for any skeletons in cupboards. If only he knew.

'Look sharp,' said Vik. From where he was standing he had a clear view of the main chapel door in the south transept. 'The cavalry's arrived. I'd best go and see how my guys are getting on.'

Sarah Walker also made her farewells and left, leaving Bridget standing on her own by the crime scene tape as DI Greg Baxter and DC Ffion Hughes entered the antechapel and strode towards her.

The detective inspector and the young detective constable made an incongruous pair – Baxter in his mid-fifties, grey, balding, round-shouldered and overweight, dressed in a badly fitting suit and a pair of slip-on shoes; Ffion in her mid-twenties, tall, slim, with a pixie haircut, dressed in tight-fitting black jeans, green emerald leather jacket and a matching pair of snakeskin ankle boots with two-inch heels. Bridget couldn't help smiling to herself. The first time she'd encountered Ffion she'd been leaning against Bridget's desk clad in green motorcycle leathers, texting at breakneck speed on her mobile phone. The young constable didn't excel at interpersonal skills, but Bridget had come to value her technical ability, encyclopaedic knowledge and near-photographic memory, even if Ffion's sharp tongue could make her colleagues flinch at times.

Bridget had worked with Baxter in her days as a detective sergeant, but since being promoted to DI earlier in the year, their paths had not crossed, except in department meetings. Bridget had been glad of that. Although she and the older DI were now the same rank, he still seemed to think he was her superior, either because of age or gender, or both.

Besides, they had very different styles of working. Baxter was a competent detective, but something of a stick-in-the-mud when it came to procedures. He got the job done, but wasn't known for his flashes of inspiration. He was an old-school detective, the sort who enjoyed a pint down the pub at lunchtime. In the old days of policing, liquid lunches had been the norm, and Baxter didn't change his habits in a hurry.

Right now he wore a frown on his face. 'Only on-duty police officers and members of the SOCO team should be in the chapel,' he told Bridget.

'I am a police officer,' she said, standing as tall as she could. 'And I can be on duty whenever I'm needed.' For the first time that evening she was glad of the extra couple of inches afforded her by her uncomfortable shoes.

'Well you're not needed now, thank you,' said Baxter, 'In the context of this investigation you're a private individual attending a college gaudy and therefore I have to ask you to leave the crime scene. You'll be questioned in due course along with everyone else.'

'Come on, Greg. Are you saying I'm a suspect?'

Baxter chose his words with care. 'I'm not making accusations. It's far too early in the investigation for that. But from what I understand, you knew the murder victim personally and were the second person on the scene. Besides, everyone is a suspect until proved otherwise.'

'Oh, come on!' She knew he liked to do things by the book, but this was ridiculous. 'I can help you out here if you'll let me.'

'I'm sure you can, but it's a question of following procedures,' said Baxter. 'Don't make me tell you a second time to leave this to those assigned to the case.'

'All right then,' said Bridget. 'have it your own

way. But I want to be kept fully informed. Alexia was a good friend of mine.'

'That,' said Baxter, 'is precisely the problem. Now, if you'll allow me to get on with my job, I have a murder enquiry to run. DC Hughes, come with me.' He marched off towards the body.

Ffion turned to follow him. As she went, she gave Bridget a wink, and Bridget knew that she had at least one ally in the detective team.

★

Despite having been dismissed from the chapel, Bridget was in no mood to join her friends down the bar just yet. Gossip and rumours about what had happened would no doubt be rife, and Bridget might learn something of value there later, but for now she wanted facts and evidence, not wild speculation. She made her way back to the dining hall where the waiting staff were clearing the tables. Not surprisingly under the circumstances the meal had been abandoned. Bridget didn't think she could eat anything just now, and certainly not soup.

The butler was busy clearing the crockery and cutlery from high table. 'How can I help you?' he asked as she approached. He was a tall man with a commanding presence who very much looked the part in his black waistcoat and bow tie. Bridget could imagine him leading a team of staff in an old country house with footmen and scullery maids and a cook presiding over the kitchen.

She showed him her warrant card, which she always carried with her, whatever the occasion.

The butler put down the dishes he was holding. 'I've already been interviewed at some length by one of your colleagues,' he said defensively, not sounding as if he relished being grilled for a second time.

Bridget gave him a reassuring smile. 'I'm sure you won't mind answering just a few more questions.'

'Well, I suppose not.'

'Let's start with a bit of background, Mr...'

'Kernahan. Nick Kernahan. What is it you'd like to know?'

'How long have you been doing this job, Mr Kernahan?' The butler was clearly too young to have been around when Bridget was a student here.

'Ten years now. I came here after a short stint at Wadham College.'

'And what exactly is your role in an event like this?' She indicated the dining hall and the places still laid out for dinner.

'Well, the menu for a formal dinner is decided in a meeting between myself, the chef and the bursar. The bursar controls the budget. As you'd expect, the chef is in charge of the menus and all the food preparation. I'm responsible for the service.'

'What about staff? How many work for the chef and how many work for you?'

'The chef has a team of six who prepare food and do all the cooking. I have eight staff serving the food, that's two per table. Plus another four serving the wine.'

Bridget did a quick calculation in her head. Including the butler and the chef, that made a total of twenty people involved in the preparation, cooking and serving of the food and wine. It made Downton Abbey look rather low-key.

'And are these all regular staff?'

'Not really. A lot of them are temps. They tend to work for short periods then leave. We use an agency to supply them. Only the chef and I have permanent positions with the college.'

'Tell me, who would have had access to the bowl of soup that was served to the warden?'

'I've already explained this to your colleague,' said the butler with some obvious irritation. 'Anyone could have had access to it. Any of the kitchen or waiting staff, and anyone else too, for that matter.'

'What do you mean, anyone else?'

'The watercress and cucumber soup was a cold dish, a gazpacho. It was prepared well in advance and placed on a table at the back of the hall. If you're trying to find out who might have had an opportunity to put the… eyeballs… in it, then the answer is everyone who was attending the dinner this evening.'

Bridget recalled seeing the food on the table when she had entered the hall, each bowl covered by its own individual silver dome.

'I see,' she said. She tried another angle. 'A knife was discovered in the same location as the body. It looked like the kind of implement that might be used for preparing vegetables.'

'Yes, I've been shown it,' said the butler. 'It's one of ours. The college's I mean. But don't start getting the idea that one of the kitchen or serving staff must have taken it. I explained this to your colleague. The kitchen isn't kept locked. That knife could have been removed at any time. Again, anyone could have done it.'

The butler's answers weren't exactly helping to narrow things down, but something else occurred to Bridget then. 'One more question. Could the bowl of soup containing the eyes have been delivered to anyone? I mean, all the dishes looked exactly the same to me. If someone intended the warden to receive the eyeballs, how would they have known which was his dish?'

'The warden has a gluten allergy. His food is always labelled.'

'Interesting.' As Bridget considered this fact she heard a commotion at the entrance to the dining hall. DI Baxter had left the chapel and was striding down the length of the hall, a look of fury on his face.

'DI Hart,' he bellowed. 'Did I not make myself clear in the chapel?'

The butler, discreet to a fault, resumed clearing the table as if nothing was amiss.

'You asked me to leave the chapel,' said

66

Bridget, 'which I did.'

'I asked you to back off and leave me to run my investigation.'

'I'm not getting in your way.'

Baxter ground his teeth together. 'You have no authority on this case, and it is not your job to be questioning members of staff or any other witnesses.'

Bridget wondered if she should tell Baxter what the butler had said about the warden's gluten allergy, but decided that he wasn't in the mood to listen to her. He could ask his own questions and find out the answers for himself.

'Fine,' she said. 'I'll leave you to do it your way. But what is going to happen now to all the guests?'

'No one leaves the college until I say so. Including you. Is that clear? We'll be interviewing everyone. Now, if you don't mind, I've work to be getting on with.' He folded his arms and waited for her to leave the hall.

Bridget decided it was time for a drink. As she left the hall and crossed the quadrangle on her way to the college bar, she noticed uniformed officers guarding the stone gatehouse. The college had become a prison.

CHAPTER 7

Merton College bar was just as barely furnished and seedy-looking as it had been in Bridget's student days. There were no bar stools or chairs, just long wooden benches and functional tables positioned along each wall. In Bridget's time, the college rugby players had enjoyed sliding their pint glasses up and down those long tables on a Friday night. An oar was fixed to each of the low ceiling beams, and the walls were covered with photographs of sports teams from days gone by. Unsurprisingly, Bridget's face didn't appear in any of the photos. She'd never been any good at sport, being too short for netball, and too lazy for hockey.

It seemed like every single dinner guest had relocated to the bar, and the room was completely packed. Bridget pushed her way through the crowd to the bar itself. 'A large glass of Pinot Noir and a packet of pistachios, please,' she shouted over the noise. Having interviewed the butler, she decided that she was hungry after all. She handed over a five-pound note and was delighted to receive a few coins in change. Even at these sorts of events, the college still charged student prices.

Meg, Tina and Bella were seated at the very end of one of the tables. Judging from the number of glasses and bottles covering the surface of the table, they'd downed a fair few drinks already. Meg and Tina had always been formidable drinkers.

Bella made room for Bridget to sit at the end of the bench.

'I see that not much has changed here,' said Bridget. 'I don't think they've even updated the prices.'

'Nor the décor,' said Tina. 'It looks no better than when we were first here, and that was twenty years ago.'

Bridget nodded. The bar might not look much different, but her three friends had altered in many obvious ways. Not only were they older, they had clearly moved on with their lives, in directions Bridget couldn't guess. She wished now that she'd made an effort to keep in touch with her old friends. She didn't even know where they lived or what jobs they did, except that Bella was a teacher.

At university, Bella had studied Classics and had hoped to pursue a career in academia. Tina had studied Law and had been determined to become a lawyer. Meg had been a Biochemist. She'd wanted to become an entrepreneur and start up her own biomedical company. Bridget wondered whether she had achieved her ambition. With her designer dress and expensive handbag, she certainly gave the impression of affluence and success. Tina too.

But before she could ask them what they'd been doing with their lives, Meg had an urgent question for her. 'What's happening in the chapel? No one's told us anything, but there are plenty of rumours circulating. You're a police detective now. You must know what's going on.'

'That's right,' said Bridget. 'But I can't tell you much about the murder enquiry. I won't be allowed to get involved with the investigation.'

Well, at least not officially, she thought.

'So it's true then?' said Tina. 'It was murder?'

'Yes.'

'And the victim was Alexia?'

'I'm afraid so.'

'God, that's awful.'

Tina and Meg exchanged glances, their earlier quarrelling brought to a halt, at least temporarily, by shared grief.

'I can't believe she's dead,' said Bella. 'Alexia was always so full of life.'

It was true. Of all the friends, Alexia had been the most vivacious, and the life of any party. Like Meg, she was an extrovert, always dressing in bright colours, seeking out excitement and adventure. But she'd had a serious side too – campaigning for worthy causes and going on marches for or against various issues. As Bella said, it was almost impossible to process the fact that she was dead.

'And then there were four,' declared Meg, looking ominously around the group.

'Honestly, Meg,' said Tina. 'Don't be so melodramatic. Try to show some respect for once.'

In response, Meg raised her glass solemnly. 'To Alexia. To Lydia. Let's drink to the dead.'

It was the first time that Lydia's name had been mentioned, and Bridget felt a kind of relief that the sixth member of the group had been acknowledged at last. Unlike the others, who had left Oxford behind them and moved on with their lives, Lydia Khoury had not been able to grow and change. She had taken her own life shortly after Finals, at the end of that last fateful summer term, and had never even graduated from the university.

For Bridget, that period of her life had dealt her a double tragedy. First her own sister, Abigail, had been murdered, and then Lydia had committed suicide, all within the space of two weeks. The shock had been too much for her to handle, and it was perhaps no wonder that she had cut herself off from the four surviving members of the group. But she had never stopped thinking about them all, especially poor Lydia. Her friend might be gone, but had never been forgotten. And now Alexia was gone too.

Bridget lifted her glass to Meg's. 'To the dead.'

Tina and Bella joined in too, raising their glasses and clinking them together across the table. 'To the dead.'

'And to the living,' added Meg before downing her wine in one.

Bridget took a careful sip of her own drink. She was as fond of a glass or two of wine as anyone, but she had no intention of trying to match Meg's alcohol consumption.

Meg wiped a trickle of wine from her chin with the back of her hand. 'God, I need another bottle. Anyone else?'

'Gin and tonic, please,' said Bella.

'You can get me another bottle of Cabernet Sauvignon, if you like,' said Tina, emptying the last of her wine into her glass.

'Nothing for me,' said Bridget.

Meg disappeared into the crowd, using her formidable bulk to muscle her way through the heaving mass of bodies that crammed the small space.

'So how exactly was Alexia killed?' asked Bella, once Meg had gone.

Bridget hesitated. There was a definite air of morbid curiosity underpinning Bella's question. No doubt everyone had already guessed that it was Alexia's eyeballs that had been so horribly gouged from their sockets and placed in the warden's soup. She saw no need to share any further gruesome details about the murder with them. They would find out for themselves in due course.

'I don't think I should say anything more for the moment,' she told them. 'I shouldn't really be talking to you about the investigation at all.'

'Well, what else do you think we want to talk about?' asked Bella. 'Look around you. Alexia's murder is the only topic of conversation in this entire bar.'

That was probably true, but Bridget had annoyed Baxter enough for one day, and didn't want to run into any more trouble with him. If he found out that she'd been releasing privileged information to potential witnesses, he would be incandescent, and rightly so.

'What I'd really like to find out,' said Bridget, helping herself to a handful of nuts, 'is what each of you has been doing since we last saw each other.' She hoped her attempt to change the subject wasn't too obvious. 'Tina, you're looking really well.'

Tina did, in fact, look amazing. In her student days, she had always dressed casually, and had rarely worn makeup, but now she looked immaculate with her strapless dress and polished, beauty-salon styling.

'And you, too, Bella,' Bridget added politely, even though Bella looked not much better now than she had done earlier in the day.

Tina seemed happy for the conversation to switch away from Alexia's murder. 'Yes,' she said. 'There's a lot to catch up with. Shall I begin? Or do you want to, Bella?'

'I'll go first,' said Bella. 'My story won't take long.'

'You said that you're a teacher now,' prompted Bridget.

Bella took a half-hearted sip of her drink before responding. 'Yes, well, it wasn't my first choice of career. As you know, I always wanted to stay on at Oxford and become a lecturer. But the academic world is fiercely competitive, and who you know is just as important as what you know. I didn't know the right people.' Bella made little effort to hide the resentment she obviously felt at the perceived injustice. 'So now I teach. There isn't a big demand for Latin teachers these days, but I managed to find a position in a small girls' school close to Peterborough. Everyone tells me it's a noble occupation.' She tried to inject a note of brightness into her final sentence, but looked utterly disheartened.

Bridget felt embarrassed and sorry for her friend. 'I'm sure that teaching can be very rewarding. But hard work, and challenging too. A bit like being a police officer, perhaps.'

'Maybe. So why did you choose to join the police force?'

Bridget knew that her usual defensive reply of, 'What else could I have done with a degree in History?' would be too flippant for the circumstances, so she opted for the truth instead. 'I wanted to try and put the world right, after Abigail's murder. And after Lydia's death too, I suppose. There was too much evil in the world. I needed to try and redress the balance.'

'And have you succeeded?'

It was a good question. Bridget had been promoted to detective inspector a few months ago, so she was obviously doing something right. And she had certainly made a difference, bringing criminals to justice, and finding answers for victims' families. But how could you truly measure success if your goal was to save the world? 'Well, I suppose I've done some good,' she concluded.

'That's all any of us can hope for, isn't it?' said Tina earnestly. 'To do more good than evil.'

Meg returned from the bar then, clutching fresh bottles of Chardonnay and Cabernet Sauvignon and a gin and tonic for Bella. She sank heavily onto the bench and sloshed more wine into her glass, spilling some over the edge. 'Wow, you lot look bloody miserable. What have you been talking about?'

'Bella was just telling me about her job as a teacher,' said Bridget.

Meg gulped down a large mouthful of her wine. 'I see. So we're filling in the gaps, are we? Summarising our lives in nice neat biographies and leaving out all the messy parts that we don't want people to know about. Apart from Bella, of course, who's desperate to tell everyone how her life went so badly wrong.'

'Stop being such a bitch, Meg,' said Tina.

'Sorry, can't help it,' said Meg. 'Well, I'll happily go next. As you know, I never need an excuse to talk about myself. I might even tell you some of the messy parts too.'

She manoeuvred her large bottom into a more comfortable position on the bench in readiness to tell Bridget her story.

'So, where were we last time we met? We'd just finished Finals when your sister was murdered and you had to run off back home. That really put a dampener on the end of term celebrations, I can tell you.'

'Oh, Meg,' interrupted Tina again. 'How can you be so insensitive?'

'Very easily. It's a knack I have. So, after Bridget left and Lydia topped herself, I decided I couldn't stand any more of this God-awful place. I moved to Cambridge and continued with postgraduate research in biochemistry. My doctorate was in gene therapy cures for congenital and hereditary blindness.'

Bridget decided to ignore Meg's tasteless references to Abigail's murder and Lydia's suicide. She knew that Meg meant no real harm. Gallows humour was just her way of dealing with topics that were too difficult to discuss. 'What's gene therapy?' she queried.

'It's a technique for repairing genetic mutations in patients. We extract a sample of the patient's chromosome, replace the defective gene with a corrected version and then inject it back into the patient. It's a life-changing treatment. We can literally make the blind see. Anyway, after I finished my doctorate, I started my own biomedical company. I didn't just want to do research, I wanted to deliver real results to patients. And so GenMeg Therapeutics was born. I had to name the company after myself, of course.'

'Of course,' said Tina. 'With an ego as big as yours, what choice did you have?'

'Exactly.' Meg took another gulp of her Chardonnay. 'So, now the clinical trials of the company's first treatment are almost complete, and we should be able to bring it to market as soon as we get regulatory approval.'

'That sounds wonderful,' said Bridget. 'Curing blindness.'

'Yes, I think so, but not everyone seems to agree.' Meg slid a sidelong stare at Tina, who turned away.

'What about your personal life?' asked Bridget. 'Where do you live now?'

'I have a house in Cambridge and an apartment in London. Half my time I'm a scientist, the other half I'm a CEO.'

'It sounds like you have a busy schedule. Are you married?'

'I was,' said Meg acidly. 'But sadly not anymore. What about you? Are you married?'

'Divorced with a teenage daughter.'

'And is there anyone special in your life right now?'

Bridget debated whether or not to tell them about Jonathan. As wonderful as Jonathan was, her relationship with him was at such an early and tentative stage, she didn't want to say too much. 'There might be. I'm not entirely sure yet.'

'In other words, you've met some amazing hot

guy, but you haven't shagged him yet,' said Meg. 'What?' she demanded, when Tina gave her a sharp look. 'I only said aloud what everyone was thinking.'

Tina sipped her glass of wine. 'My turn, then. It won't surprise you to learn that I became a lawyer. I work for one of the big London law firms, specialising in corporate liability.'

'A parasite, in other words,' sneered Meg.

Tina continued as if Meg hadn't spoken. 'My clients are victims of corporate greed and arrogance.'

'You mean they're pawns that you can use to bring massive lawsuits against hard-working honest businesses,' said Meg.

'I see myself as a champion for those who suffer abuse by large corporations that believe themselves to be unaccountable.'

Meg clapped her hands together sarcastically. 'The woman's a saint. Someone should give her a medal.'

Tina turned a fiery gaze on Meg. 'I don't need a medal. Seeing my clients receive their rightful compensation is reward enough.'

Bridget decided it was time to intervene before the two women came to blows. It was apparent that the pair had some ongoing personal quarrel, presumably related to Tina's work. Was it possible that her firm was bringing a lawsuit against Meg's company?

Bridget did her best to change the subject. 'So tell me, what was Alexia doing?'

'Alexia became a journalist, like she'd always wanted to,' said Bella. 'She obviously had all the right connections.'

At university, Alexia had written articles for student newspapers. Her ambition had been to work for one of the big national newspapers as a campaigning and investigative journalist. Bridget seemed to recall reading one of her articles in a magazine.

'She was bloody good at her job, too,' said Meg. 'She started out working for The London Evening Standard, then went solo as an investigative journalist, uncovering big stories and selling them to whichever newspaper was brave enough to publish them. Remember that politician a few months ago who was caught accepting bribes from big business? It was Alexia who broke that story.'

'Right,' said Bridget. 'What about her personal life?'

The three other women exchanged glances.

'You know Alexia,' said Tina. 'Her life was a whirlwind of romances and affairs. Every time I saw her she had a new boyfriend. It was impossible to keep up with her.'

Meg's face darkened. 'She certainly never missed an opportunity in that department.'

'Come on, Meg,' said Tina, 'don't speak ill of the dead.'

'Speaking's nothing to be ashamed of, in my world,' said Meg fiercely. 'Sleeping with your friend's husband is, however.'

Bridget stared at Meg in astonishment. Was she really saying that Alexia had slept with her husband? The hurt expression on her face left little room for doubt. 'Oh, Meg, I'm so sorry.'

'It was probably my own fault,' said Meg gloomily. 'We all knew what Alexia was like. She would pounce on anything wearing trousers. I should never have let her get near to Michael.'

'She was the worst kind of sexual predator,' said Bella. 'But what she did to you was shocking, even by Alexia's standards.'

'You really can't blame yourself for what Alexia did,' said Tina. 'Seducing Michael was an unforgiveable thing for her to do.'

For the first time that day, it seemed that the three women were finally in agreement with each other.

'You're right,' said Meg. 'I don't blame myself. I blame my ex-husband. And I blame Alexia too. I'm not saying she deserved to die, but the truth is that she was a selfish bitch.'

'Exactly,' said Tina. 'She had no sense of loyalty. She may have been a good journalist, but she was a lousy friend.'

'Treacherous,' agreed Bella. 'Let's not pretend we're going to miss her that much.'

Bridget was shocked at what she was hearing. Alexia may have had a string of boyfriends and a complicated love life during her student days but Bridget had assumed she would settle down eventually. It was distressing to hear that her old friend had seduced Meg's husband, and to hear the raw anger in Meg's voice. The cold venom in Bella and Tina's final remarks was perhaps even worse.

'Well,' said Meg bitterly, 'now you know the truth. I hate Tina. Alexia and I hated each other. And Bella hates all of us, including herself.' She sloshed more wine into her glass. 'So let's get drunk.'

'I'll drink to that,' said Tina. She downed the rest of her glass and poured another.

Bridget didn't think she could stand a second more of this. She'd been so looking forward to catching up with her friends, but now she wished she'd never come. She rose to her feet.

'It's been a long evening,' she said. 'I'm turning in for the night.'

★

Bridget made her way out of the noisy, crowded bar and into the cool night air. The sky was clear, and an almost-full moon watched silently over the college, lending a cold lustre to its yellow stonework. The sinister effect only added to her sense of unease.

Bridget's conversation with Meg, Tina and Bella had left her deeply unsettled. So many sorrows and grievances had come to light that her mind was reeling. Poor Bella seemed quite despondent with her life. Meg and Tina's feud had driven a wedge between them, perhaps an irreparable one. And this business of Alexia and

81

Meg's husband was perhaps the most disturbing revelation of all.

Bridget walked through the tiny stone enclosure of Patey's Quad next to the hall, and continued into Mob Quad. As she passed the chapel, a small group of figures emerged from the darkened archway that led from the south transept, rolling a gurney across the bumpy flagstones. Bridget knew without looking that Alexia's corpse lay on the trolley. She stood to one side to let the mortuary workers and uniformed officers pass. Thankfully, the body was sealed within a bag, so she was spared another view of Alexia's sightless eyes.

When they had gone, she hurried on beneath the arch and onto the path that led to the Grove Building. She would be glad to get back to her room for the night.

A lone figure sat on a bench to one side of the path, its face in darkness, shaded from the bright moonlight by a tree.

'Bridget? Is that you?' Bridget recognised the voice of her history tutor, Dr Irene Thomas. 'Will you join me?'

Bridget left the path and crossed the well-trimmed Chapel Lawn to join Dr Thomas on the bench. Up close, the old woman's features were clear, her eyes shining bright in the night. 'I often come here to think,' said Dr Thomas. 'Especially at night. It's so peaceful.'

'It is,' agreed Bridget, taking a seat on the bench.

'I am so very sorry for your loss,' said Dr Thomas. 'I know that you and Miss Petrakis were good friends – in your university days, at least.'

'Thank you,' said Bridget. 'We were. But I have to admit, with some regret, that I had allowed our friendship to lapse. In fact, I hadn't seen Alexia in seventeen years, not since leaving university.'

'It's quite understandable,' said Dr Thomas, 'considering your personal circumstances at the time.'

Bridget nodded. Her old tutor's mind was so sharp, there was never a need to explain anything to her. Unless she demanded an explanation, of course. But that was another matter.

'What are your thoughts on tonight's events?' enquired Dr Thomas. 'As a police detective, I mean.'

Bridget tried to choose her words with care. Dr Thomas was far too intelligent to be fobbed off with platitudes along the lines of, It's too early to say.

'I'm not allowed to be part of the investigating team, because the victim was known to me.'

'Of course.'

'So I'm not privy to all the details.'

'Naturally,' said Dr Thomas. 'Just as in historical research, one never has access to all the source material one would like.'

'No,' agreed Bridget.

'Nevertheless, one must form an opinion based

on the evidence available.'

'It's certainly an unusual case,' admitted Bridget. 'Quite unlike anything I've ever encountered in the past.'

'Are you referring to the murder method itself – garrotting, I understand – or the removal of parts of the body?'

'I see that you're as well informed as usual.'

'I have my sources within the college.'

'I'm sure you do. Well, since you ask, I've never encountered either the method of the murder, nor the mutilation of the body after death.'

'No. What do you think they imply?'

Bridget fell silent. She had resisted thinking too deeply about the way Alexia had been killed. She didn't want to imagine how she must have felt as the wire pulled taut around her throat and she struggled ineffectually to throw off her attacker. She tried to suppress her emotional reaction and to think clearly and logically, as Dr Thomas had always implored her to do in their weekly tutorials. 'Death by strangulation isn't particularly uncommon,' she said. 'Although the use of a wire suggests a degree of premeditation.'

'Indeed. Go on.'

'The eyeballs are the most disturbing aspect. Removal of body parts is an act most commonly associated with sexual crimes. It's sometimes used as a kind of signature by serial killers. And yet...'

'Carry on.'

'In that case, the killer usually retains the body parts as trophies. I've never heard of a murderer placing them where they will be found.'

'No. Does it remind you of anything?'

Bridget had the sense she was being tested. Even in the darkness beneath the tree, Dr Thomas's eyes seemed to sparkle with curiosity. 'No, I can't say it does. Sorry.'

The history tutor sighed with disappointment. 'Body parts served at a feast is a common trope in revenge tragedy of the Elizabethan and Jacobean eras.'

'It is?'

'Really, Bridget, think of Shakespeare's Titus Andronicus.'

'Right,' said Bridget, who wasn't as familiar with Shakespeare's bloodiest play as she felt she ought to be. She much preferred the playwright's lighter works such as A Midsummer Night's Dream and The Tempest. 'Remind me what happens in that?'

'A great deal, but the most relevant part is where Titus slays his enemies and bakes their heads to serve to his guests at a feast.'

'Now I remember why Titus Andronicus isn't my favourite play.'

'And yet, just like a good historian, a police detective must not be afraid to face the facts,' remarked Dr Thomas.

As always, the tutor was right. 'You're suggesting that this was a revenge killing, then?'

'It's not for me to say,' said Dr Thomas.

'That's for the police to determine. I'm merely pointing out the similarities.'

'I won't be determining anything,' said Bridget glumly. 'The detective in charge has warned me to stay well clear of the investigation.'

'Hmm,' said Dr Thomas. 'Both you and I know that isn't going to happen.' She rose to her feet. 'Goodnight, my dear. It's past my bedtime, and at my advanced age I find that late nights sap my energy terribly.'

Bridget watched her tutor walk away. There was no indication that Dr Thomas's energy had been the least bit sapped. The old woman was as sharp as she had ever been, and in her youth her intellect had been as sharp as a knife. Bridget suspected that the history tutor had been sitting on the bench solely with the intention of catching Bridget as she returned to her college room. And although she had asked Bridget several questions, it was clear that she had already known all of the answers. Her purpose had been simply to plant the idea of a revenge killing in Bridget's mind.

Bridget sat on the bench for a while longer. The Elizabethan and Jacobean periods had been violent, bloody times, and the revenge tragedy had been a popular form of entertainment in those days. The playwrights of the time had not felt any need to hold back in their crowd-pleasing productions, packed full of sex, violence and dismembered body parts.

Bridget found her thoughts returning

unbidden to Meg and her ex-husband. Adultery was as good a motive as any for revenge, and if Meg had indeed murdered Alexia, she would not be the first jealous wife to exact vengeance in a bloody and violent manner.

But Meg was perhaps not the only person who held a grudge against Alexia. As a journalist exposing corruption and abuse of power by people in high places, no doubt Alexia had made a number of enemies over the years. It was certainly an interesting idea to explore.

The air was growing chilly, and Bridget returned to the Grove Building deep in thought. Back in her room, she went to the windows to draw the curtains. The moonlight cast an eerie glow across Dead Man's Walk and the playing fields beyond. If any ghosts haunted the footpath, they would surely be walking it tonight. But there were no ghosts outside, only the ones in Bridget's head. She drew the curtains tight and got herself ready for bed.

Before turning out the light, her thoughts turned to Chloe and Jonathan, and to her older sister, Vanessa. She prayed that they were safe and sound.

CHAPTER 8

DC Ffion Hughes poured boiling water onto her pomegranate and raspberry tea in the staff kitchen, then took her mug decorated with a Welsh dragon through to the incident room where DI Baxter had called an early morning meeting to review yesterday's murder at Merton College.

It was clearly too early on a Sunday morning for some people. DS Ryan Hooper looked as if he'd spent last night getting hammered. He rubbed his bloodshot eyes and sipped a cup of strong black coffee. DS Andy Cartwright also looked like he'd have preferred a few more hours in bed. Only DC Harry Johns looked bright and ready for action. Ffion knew that the young detective constable was into healthy living and liked to go for a run on a Sunday morning. Ffion herself went running most days. She had missed her morning run today in order to come into work, but would hopefully manage to find time this evening instead.

She thought of Jake, and wondered if he'd managed to get away early as he'd promised. If the roads were clear it would take him about three hours to drive from Leeds to Thames Valley Police HQ in Kidlington. Sunday morning was a good time to do the journey. She pictured him bombing down the motorway in his tastelessly-painted orange Subaru, his dreadful music blasting from the souped-up speaker system, and smiled to herself. What on earth did she see in the guy?

'All right, everyone, let's get started.' DI Baxter stood in front of the noticeboard in a light grey suit that looked like it had seen better days. A bit like DI Baxter himself, in fact. Baxter's hair matched the colour of his suit, and the man's beer belly threatened to burst his jacket wide open. The brown shoes on his feet did nothing to improve the overall effect. Ffion was reminded of a particularly uninspiring maths teacher she'd had at school, who would have killed the subject for her if she hadn't taken the text book home and taught herself.

Ryan stretched and yawned without bothering to cover his mouth. Andy put down his mug of builder's tea and took out his notebook and pencil, waiting to see what Baxter would say. Ffion also picked up her notebook. She knew that doing so made a good impression, but in truth she could remember everything without ever needing to write it down.

'So, the dead woman,' said Baxter, 'is Alexia Petrakis, a journalist. Thirty-eight years old. Former student of Merton College. Lived in

London and did freelance work for a number of national newspapers, investigating miscarriages of justice, that sort of thing.'

Andy was jotting down every word Baxter spoke. Ffion doodled a mandala as a way of focusing her attention.

'The victim was murdered in the chapel of Merton College, where she was attending a college dinner to be held later that evening. She was strangled to death with a length of wire that was discarded at the scene. Then her eyeballs were cut out.' Baxter delivered this shocking fact in the same monotone he'd used from the start.

Ffion glanced across the room at Harry. His face had turned white at this latest piece of information and he looked as if he might be sick any minute. She would offer him a ginger tea if he was still feeling queasy after the briefing.

'During the dinner, a pair of eyeballs were found in the warden's soup,' continued Baxter, indifferent to Harry's discomfort. 'DNA tests will confirm whether or not the eyeballs that were found did indeed belong to the murder victim.'

Ryan raised a hand. 'Sir, do you think that the eyeballs may have belonged to someone else?' His tone was as deadpan as Baxter's despite the obvious insolence of his question.

Baxter responded with exaggerated patience. 'That is what the DNA tests will confirm, Sergeant. Until then we should not make any assumptions one way or the other.'

'Very good, sir. We'll keep our minds open. And our eyes too.'

Baxter frowned but said nothing to that. Instead he consulted his notes. 'We interviewed all the kitchen staff last night, including the chef and the butler. The chef and his team spent most of the day preparing the food. There were to be four courses in total, although of course the dinner was abandoned during the starter. This was a cold soup, which was prepared during the afternoon.'

'A gazpacho,' said Ffion.

Baxter studied her, perhaps wondering if she was poking fun at him. 'A gazpacho, that is correct, Constable. It was dished up and the bowls were covered and left on one side ready to be carried to the tables. The staff who served the soup swear blind there was nothing amiss.'

Baxter hesitated, perhaps wondering if he had selected the right word. He swept his gaze around the room, looking for anyone who might find his choice of vocabulary amusing, but everyone held their faces straight. He resumed his lecture. 'No one can explain how the eyeballs came to be in the bowl of soup. However, we have established that the warden's soup was labelled and kept separate from the others due to his gluten allergy.'

'Croutons,' commented Ryan. 'The warden can't eat croutons.'

'Croutons, indeed,' said Baxter. 'Thank you, Sergeant.'

'I'm guessing he isn't too fond of eyeballs, either, sir.'

Harry lurched unsteadily to his feet. 'Excuse me, sir,' he said, then rushed from the room with his hand covering his mouth.

Ffion sighed. It looked as if not even ginger tea would help Harry now. She took advantage of the interruption to raise her hand.

'Yes, what is it now?' growled Baxter.

'I was just wondering, sir, if the eyes were intended to convey a special message. I mean, why eyes? Wouldn't it have been easier for the killer to cut off a finger instead?'

'An eye for an eye,' quipped Ryan.

Baxter glowered at both Ffion and Ryan as if they were a couple of unruly schoolchildren. 'DC Hughes, we cannot possibly know the mind of the murderer, and we're not here to speculate or come up with fanciful notions. We gather evidence and interview witnesses, and we solve this case by good old-fashioned police work. I don't want anyone running away with ideas of their own. Got that?'

'Got it, sir,' said Ffion.

DI Bridget Hart would have welcomed suggestions at this stage. She always encouraged her team to think creatively and to use their initiative. In fact she'd probably have had a few ideas of her own by now.

'We need to start filling in the blanks,' said Baxter. He turned to Andy, who had already filled a whole page of his notebook. 'DS

92

Cartwright, I'd like you to find out the victim's movements from the time she arrived in Oxford to the time she was last seen alive.'

'Yes, sir,' said Andy, writing it down.

Baxter pointed to Ryan and Ffion. 'DS Hooper, DC Hughes, since you two have so much to say, you can go to the college and start interviewing the guests. There were one hundred and thirty former students at the dinner last night, plus twenty tutors and other senior college members on high table. What time did they arrive at college? Where were they during the course of the afternoon and evening? What connections did they have to the dead woman? Get all the facts.'

Ffion grimaced at the prospect of carrying out interviews all day long with Ryan and his smart-arsed comments for company.

Ryan, on the other hand, seemed happy enough with his allotted task. 'Aye, aye, sir,' he said, giving Ffion a wink.

Baxter rounded on him. 'Sergeant, if I hear one more joke like that from you, I'll have you conducting a fingertip search of the entire college.'

'Yes, sir. Sorry, sir.'

'So watch out,' Baxter added. 'I've got my eye on you.'

Ryan struggled to keep his face straight. Wisely, he said nothing in reply.

Ffion sighed. Working with Baxter was going to be a trial, but teaming up with Ryan threatened to be even more of an ordeal. She wished that Jake was back already.

'Where is DS Derwent?' asked Baxter, seeming suddenly to notice Jake's absence.

'In Leeds,' said Ffion. 'Visiting his mum. He should be back by lunchtime.'

Baxter grunted. 'Good. We need as many people on this investigation as possible.'

'What about DI Hart, sir?' suggested Ffion hopefully. 'Could she join the team?'

Baxter fixed her with a look like thunder. 'May I remind you that Detective Inspector Hart is a witness in this investigation, and is to be treated as such. I will be interviewing her myself as soon as I arrive in college, and I don't want anyone speaking to her without my permission. Is that understood?'

'Yes, sir, very clearly.'

Harry returned to the room just as everyone was getting ready to leave. He looked a more normal colour now. There were damp patches on his collar where he'd splashed his face with water.

'DC Johns,' barked Baxter, 'you can come with me. I've already interviewed the kitchen staff, but I want you to take full written statements from each of them. That will be twenty statements in total, and I want them all entered into the system by the end of today. Detailed paperwork – that's how we're going to crack this case.'

'Yes, sir.'

'Given that the kitchen staff prepared the soup, and that a knife from the kitchen was used to remove the dead woman's eyes' – Harry flinched, but Baxter seemed not to notice or care – 'the kitchen staff have got to be our most obvious suspects at this point in time. Talk to them individually and try to nail down their movements throughout the day.'

'Yes, sir. Right, sir.'

'And no one leaves the college until we're done,' bellowed Baxter.

Ryan joined Ffion as she made her way out of the incident room. 'All right, Fi? Want a lift in my car?'

'No need,' she said. 'I'd rather take my bike.'

She went into the bathroom to change into her green motorcycle leathers, then headed out to the car park, where her neon green Kawasaki Ninja awaited her.

CHAPTER 9

After a disturbed night of sleep in which the ghost of Alexia Petrakis had invaded her dreams, chasing her sightlessly down Dead Man's Walk, Bridget rose, showered quickly in the tiny en-suite bathroom and got dressed.

It was still early on a Sunday morning but Bridget knew that her sister, Vanessa, who had two young children – eight-year-old Florence and six-year-old Toby – would be up and about. She had probably already baked a cake by now and peeled all the potatoes ready for roasting later. Vanessa worked miracles in her kitchen, and never left the smallest detail to chance. She would be desperately disappointed to hear that Bridget couldn't make it for Sunday lunch.

She called Vanessa's mobile in case she was out walking Rufus, the family's Golden Labrador.

As soon as Vanessa answered, Bridget could tell from the barking in the background that she was indeed out walking the dog. 'Be quiet, Rufus!' said Vanessa. 'Hi, Bridget. This is early for you. How was the gaudy?'

Bridget thought it better not to answer the question directly. 'Vanessa, I'm sorry to bother you, but I've got a favour to ask.'

'Oh?' Sounding suspicious.

'Something happened at the gaudy last night. Something… unfortunate. Now I'm stuck here in college and can't leave. Chloe will be travelling back from London this morning and I won't be able to pick her up from the train station. Could you collect her please and take her to your place until I can get away?'

'Oh, don't say that you won't be able to make it to lunch,' said Vanessa irritably. 'You're always cancelling at the last minute. What could be so important that you can't leave the college?'

Bridget debated whether or not to reveal what had happened. Her sister always worried about Bridget's job, and would be dismayed to hear about a murder. But it would be better for her to find out from Bridget directly than to hear about it on the news.

'There was a murder here last night,' said Bridget, dropping her voice. 'We have to stay here until we've been interviewed by the police.'

'Oh, Bridget!'

'So that's why I need you to look after Chloe for me.'

'Yes, of course,' said Vanessa, sounding flustered. 'I see that. I'll get James to meet her at the station in the Range Rover.' James was Vanessa's husband and was quite used to being bossed about by his wife. 'I'm going to be far too busy in the kitchen. You know how it is.'

Bridget didn't know. Her own version of Sunday lunch was a shop-bought pizza or the microwaved leftovers from the previous night's takeaway, but she knew how seriously Vanessa took her domestic affairs. 'Yes, of course. Thank you very much.'

'By the way,' said Vanessa. 'Who was murdered? Was it anyone you knew?' Now she sounded as if she wanted all the juicy gossip.

'It was, actually. It was one of my old housemates from my student days.'

'One of your housemates?' Vanessa sounded appalled.

'Yes. Her name was Alexia Petrakis.'

'The journalist?'

Bridget was surprised that Vanessa knew Alexia's name. 'That's right. Did you know her?'

'I didn't know her. I just read her articles. She wrote for The Sunday Times and The Telegraph. The Guardian too, I believe. She was something of a campaigner. You know – social justice, that kind of thing.'

'Right.' To Bridget's shame, it seemed that Vanessa knew more about Alexia than she did herself, at least in terms of her work as a journalist.

'Well, I'm very sorry to hear about it. How absolutely ghastly. That must have rather spoilt your evening.'

Bridget supposed that was her sister's way of offering her condolences. Vanessa had never been good when it came to expressing her feelings.

'You could say that,' said Bridget. She wasn't going to tell Vanessa the precise way in which the dinner had been spoilt. Eyeballs in the soup would be too much for her to handle this early in the morning. 'So, you'll make sure that Chloe's all right?'

'Of course I will.' Vanessa liked nothing better than to organise other people and sort out their problems. Now that she had got over the shock of Bridget's news she was probably secretly pleased that she'd be able to mother Chloe for the day. 'I'll make sure she's properly fed and looked after until you can collect her.'

'Thanks.' Bridget wasn't sure if that was an implied criticism of Bridget's own ability to feed and look after her daughter. If it was, it was probably justified. Juggling a full-time career with being a single mother was a skill Bridget hadn't yet mastered and probably never would. 'Take care,' she said before she hung up.

Next she sent Chloe a quick message to say that something had come up at work and that Uncle James would be meeting her at the station. She didn't think that Chloe would mind in the least. Lunch at Vanessa's would be far better than anything Bridget might rustle up. And Chloe always had a nice time with Florence, Toby and Rufus at Vanessa and James's huge detached house in leafy North Oxford.

All this talk of lunch suddenly made her realise

how hungry she was. She'd missed out on the four-course dinner last night, and the bag of pistachio nuts she'd eaten in the bar had only gone so far in filling the void. She slung her bag over her shoulder and headed down to the dining hall, hoping that normal service would have resumed and that breakfast would soon be served.

★

Bridget was in luck. As she walked up the steps to the dining hall the smell of grilled bacon and toast wafted into the quadrangle. Breakfast was a much less formal affair than dinner, and Bridget queued with her tray at the hot counter. The college had always put on a good breakfast, and she happily filled her plate with bacon, scrambled eggs, beans and toast. She grabbed herself a cup of piping hot coffee and looked for a place to sit.

The long tables of the dining hall were beginning to fill with small groups of guests. The atmosphere in the hall was subdued, but she overheard murmurings of "murder" and "scandal". Bridget kept her head down and found a space by herself at the end of one of the tables. Her appetite had returned with a vengeance and she tucked into the hot food.

'Mind if I join you?'

She looked up to see Meg carrying a tray piled high with food. Meg didn't wait for an answer, but sat down on the bench opposite and began unloading the various plates and dishes from her tray. This morning she was dressed casually, but still managed to exude a sense of glamour in a bright pink shirt and a pair of designer-label jeans. Her eyes were red, however, and her coffee was black. 'Too much to drink,' she explained to Bridget. 'The story of my life.' The after-effects of the alcohol didn't seem to have dented her appetite, however, and she began to devour the various food items with gusto.

'How are you feeling?' asked Bridget.

'If you mean my hangover,' said Meg in between mouthfuls of sausage and beans, 'it's nothing that a couple of aspirin and half a dozen cups of coffee won't fix. But if you mean how I feel about Alexia's murder, I'm still coming to terms with it.' She set down her knife and fork. 'Look, Bridget, about last night. I just want to apologise for any bad behaviour on my part. I'd had a terrible shock. Well, we all had, obviously.'

'Of course. Forget it.'

'And I was half drunk too, although that's no excuse. I said some cruel things that I wish I hadn't.'

Bridget took Meg's hand in sympathy. 'I was so sorry to hear about what happened between Alexia and your husband.'

Meg snorted. 'Ex-husband, and good riddance. Let's not talk about him. He's gone. And so, now, is Alexia. Let's talk about something else. Did you say you had an ex-husband too?'

'Ben, yes. He lives in London now. My daughter, Chloe, stayed with him last night.'

'And how old is she?'

'Fifteen.'

'A teenager. Unlucky you. At least I have no children of my own. That's one blessing. I've never been able to stand kids. You know I have no patience for that kind of thing.'

Meg had never been a patient person. She'd always been restless and driven. Perhaps that's what it took to start up your own pharmaceutical company. Bridget had always been restless too, yet she couldn't imagine herself running a business. Perhaps other qualities were needed too.

Meg continued to cram food into her mouth as if she hadn't eaten in days. 'When do you think we'll be able to leave this place?'

'I think you'll be allowed to go as soon as the police have interviewed you.'

'Well, let's hope that doesn't take too long. I have a meeting in Cambridge after lunch. I wish I'd never come to this gaudy now.'

There was a question Bridget needed to ask Meg before Tina or Bella turned up. She glanced up and down the hall, then lowered her voice. 'Meg, tell me what's going on between you and Tina. You used to be such good friends.'

An irate look passed quickly across Meg's face. 'Oh, that. Tina's suing me. Can you believe it? What a bitch.'

'I guessed it was something like that. Can you tell me what she's suing you for?'

'I don't suppose it will do any harm to tell you.' Meg finished her food and let her cutlery clatter onto her plate. 'I explained to you that my company is developing a gene therapy treatment.'

'A cure for blindness, yes.'

'Well, bringing a new treatment to market is a long and complex business. That's why new drugs are often so expensive. We have to run various trials, and there are a lot of regulatory hurdles to overcome. We've just successfully completed our phase III clinical trials, which means that hopefully we'll be able to start rolling out the treatment next year. But ten years ago, when we were first testing the treatment, we had a problem during our phase I trial.'

'What kind of problem? What's a phase I trial?'

Meg slurped noisily at her coffee. 'A phase I trial is the first time that a new treatment is tested on humans. Its purpose is to find out if there are any dangers or serious side effects. The testing is carried out on a small number of volunteers before getting the green light to proceed with larger-scale phase II trials.'

'Okay.'

'Tina's firm is representing one of the volunteers who took part in the original trial. He developed a problem very soon after receiving the treatment. It started out as an allergic reaction, then quickly developed into multiple organ failure. He was given emergency treatment, but ended up with a serious brain injury. He never recovered.'

'Oh, Meg.'

'These kinds of adverse effects are rare, but they do sometimes happen. That's the whole point of the phase I trial – to find out if the treatment is safe. Anyway, it turned out that the reason for the adverse reaction was that the volunteer had a serious pre-existing medical condition that he failed to disclose to us. If we'd known, we would never have accepted him onto the study.'

'It sounds like you have a strong defence, then.'

'Our lawyers think so, yes. But Tina is arguing that because our recruitment process offered a financial incentive to volunteers, the patient, who was experiencing financial difficulties, was motivated to sign up for the trial without taking the time to understand the risks. Or perhaps the financial incentive encouraged him to conceal his pre-existing medical condition from us.'

'I see,' said Bridget.

'But the technique we've developed could give thousands of people the gift of sight,' said Meg, her voice rising as she became more passionate. 'What Tina's doing could destroy not only my company but the possibility of a cure. She could ruin everything I've spent my entire career working for. So you can see why we're not seeing eye to eye at the moment.' She gave a weak smile. 'Sorry, no pun intended.'

Eye to eye. Bridget's thoughts went back to Alexia's empty eye sockets, and the eyeballs in the warden's soup. A cure for blindness. A woman with her eyes removed. Could it be more than a coincidence?

An official-sounding voice at the entrance to the dining hall alerted her to the arrival of Detective Inspector Baxter and his team.

'Is that the police?' asked Meg. 'Can you ask them to interview me first, so that I can get away?'

'It doesn't work like that,' Bridget told her. 'Inspector Baxter has his own way of doing things. You might be waiting a while.'

'God, what a bore,' said Meg. 'I'll have to work on my laptop.'

Heavy footsteps approached the table. 'DI Hart,' said Baxter without any greeting or preamble. 'I'll see you first.'

CHAPTER 10

Bridget accompanied Baxter to a room in the Fellows' Quadrangle that he had commandeered as a temporary office. From the books on the shelves she surmised it was normally an English tutor's room. The room had an excellent view over the Fellows' Garden to the east. The garden, which occupied the area of land between the houses of Merton Street and Dead Man's Walk, had once filled the entire south-eastern corner of the original medieval walled city of Oxford. It was a beautiful, private space, famous for its ancient mulberry tree. Bridget had often enjoyed walking and sitting in quiet contemplation there when she had lived in college.

She sat down on a faded sofa where hundreds of students had no doubt sat before her, and waited while Baxter took a seat opposite and arranged his notes on a low table. It was just like being back in a tutorial, except that tutorials with Dr Irene Thomas had been stimulating affairs, whereas she suspected an interview conducted by Baxter would be relentlessly dull and tedious.

'My team will be interviewing all the guests who were present at the gaudy,' he explained to her. 'No doubt we'll be here all day. But, as the second person at the crime scene and an acquaintance of the deceased, your input at this early stage in the investigation could be valuable. Therefore I would be grateful if you could answer some questions before I conduct any other interviews.'

She wanted to smile at his formal way of talking but suppressed the urge. Baxter was only doing his job. She supposed she should be flattered that he'd come to her first and hadn't expected her to wait her turn with the other guests. 'Of course,' she said. 'Happy to help.'

When he'd finished shuffling and rearranging his papers to his satisfaction, he cleared his throat and looked up again. 'I'd like to start with an apology for last night. If I came across as a little short with you, then that was not my intention.'

'Thank you,' said Bridget, surprised at the apology, but pleased to receive it. 'Apology accepted.'

'However,' and now Baxter's voice lost its conciliatory tone, 'I must make it perfectly clear to you that I am the investigating officer here and you must allow me and my team to do our job without interference.'

Well, that put her in her place. The apology had just been an excuse for him to reassert his authority over her.

'Understood,' she said coolly. If that was how

he wanted to play it, she would be professional too.

'Good. Now that we understand each other, let's get down to business. First, I'd like you to tell me how you knew Alexia Petrakis.'

'Okay,' said Bridget. 'We were both students here at the college twenty years ago. I studied History, and Alexia was studying English, but at Oxford it's common for students studying different subjects to socialise together in their college.'

'I understand the Oxford college system perfectly well,' said Baxter. No doubt he was reminding her of his many years of experience as a detective working in the city. 'You say that you studied History?'

'That's right.'

'Hmm,' was his only reaction to that.

'So,' continued Bridget, 'in our second year, a group of six of us shared a house together in East Oxford.'

'Six of you?' Baxter's pen was poised over his notebook.

'Yes. Alexia Petrakis, Tina Mackenzie, Meg Collins, Bella Williams, Lydia Khoury and me.'

Baxter wrote down the names, then picked up a copy of the guest list for the gaudy and ran his thick finger down it. 'I see five of those names here, but no one called Lydia Khoury.'

'No,' said Bridget. 'Lydia's dead.'

'When and how did she die?'

Bridget cringed at the abruptness of the

question. She had prepared herself to talk about the circumstances of Lydia's death, but it was still painful to be questioned about her old friend by someone as insensitive as Baxter. 'Immediately after Finals in our third year. She committed suicide.'

Baxter was scribbling furiously in his notebook. 'Why did she do that?'

'I don't really know all the details,' said Bridget. 'I... had my own troubles to deal with at that time. I had already left Oxford when Lydia took her life.'

'Oh?'

'My sister Abigail was murdered during that final term.'

At that, Bridget thought she detected a slight softening in Baxter's demeanour. 'I'm sorry to hear that.'

'That's why I didn't keep in touch with any of my friends from university. In fact I hadn't seen any of them for seventeen years. Not until yesterday.'

Baxter wrote it down. 'Tell me what you know about Alexia Petrakis.'

Bridget pondered where to begin. It was the kind of question she had been taught to ask during her training at police college. An open question, designed to elicit the most information, not to limit the response. But faced with it herself, she hardly knew how to frame her answer. How could you reduce a person's entire life down to a few sentences, especially when they had lived their life as fully as Alexia Petrakis?

She did her best to convey the essential facts in a form that Baxter would understand. 'Alexia was the only daughter of a Greek father and an Italian mother. Her family was very wealthy, and Alexia travelled a lot. Her parents owned homes in both Greece and Italy, but they sent her to a boarding school in England because they believed that was the best possible education for her.'

Baxter was scribbling down every word.

'Alexia was a stereotypical Mediterranean type. She was warm, open, passionate and always spoke her mind. She was very idealistic too, and believed that she should use her privileged upbringing to fight to make the world a better place.'

'Fight?'

'Not literally. Alexia's weapons were words. She studied English Language and Literature and was determined to become a journalist. She believed that by revealing truths she could expose corruption and abuses of power around the world.'

'Was she politically active?'

'She didn't follow party politics, but she would often get involved in causes that caught her attention.'

'What were the negative aspects of her character?'

Bridget paused. She felt like she was being asked to betray her old friend, but Baxter was right to ask the question. Character flaws exposed weaknesses that could get people into trouble, or lead them to take questionable actions. It was only right that he had a fully rounded picture of the murder victim.

'Although Alexia could be warm-hearted and generous, she could also be cruel and cold-blooded. I saw the way that she would dump boyfriends without a second thought for their feelings. And when she became passionately interested in some cause or other, she would pursue it relentlessly. She was like a bulldozer. I wouldn't have wanted to stand in her way.'

'Can you think of any specific reason why someone would want to murder Miss Petrakis?'

Bridget thought carefully. She wondered if she ought to tell Baxter about Dr Irene Thomas's idea of a revenge killing. But she doubted he would be impressed by a possible connection between the gruesome events at the dinner and revenge tragedy of the Elizabethan and Jacobean eras. That would be far too fanciful for a straight thinker like him. Besides, she had no concrete evidence to back up any theory. Baxter was looking for means, motives and opportunities. She considered telling him how Alexia had seduced Meg's husband, but she had no desire to provide Baxter with a reason to harass Meg. 'I wondered if...'

'What?'

'Just that since Alexia was a journalist and wrote articles exposing powerful people, perhaps she would have made some enemies.'

'It's possible. Do you have anything more definite? Names, for example?'

'No, sorry.'

Baxter nodded. 'Tell me about the warden.'

'The warden?' Bridget was surprised by Baxter's sudden change of direction. She guessed that he was simply reeling off a list of prepared questions. 'Dr Brendan Harper. He's a leading expert in archaeology. You've probably seen him on TV?'

'No.'

'Well, he presents documentaries, mainly from countries in the Middle East and around the Mediterranean Sea. He talks about the Ancient Egyptians, the Romans, the Phoenicians... that sort of thing. He's very popular.'

Baxter stared at her blankly. 'Never heard of him.'

'His wife, Yasmin, is very glamorous too. She's Egyptian-born and quite a bit younger than him. She's a great beauty.'

'I haven't had the pleasure of meeting her yet.'

'When I was a student,' said Bridget, 'Dr Harper was the senior tutor here. In fact, he was also Lydia's tutor. Now he's running for vice-chancellor of the university.'

Baxter looked more interested by this nugget of information. 'Aha! A man with a reputation to protect.'

'I suppose so,' said Bridget.

'So why were the eyeballs presented to him?'

asked Baxter. 'And why eyeballs?'

'I don't know the answer to either question,' said Bridget. 'At the moment, your guess is as good as mine.'

Baxter held her gaze for several seconds before responding. 'DI Hart, I would like you to know that I never make guesses.'

CHAPTER 11

It was the equivalent of a door-to-door enquiry, except that in a door-to-door you at least got to stretch your legs and move around. Ffion preferred to be out and about, or doing tasks that utilised her technical skills. But here they were just sitting at high table asking the same repetitive questions over and over again.

DC Harry Johns was busy doing the same thing in the kitchen, interviewing the kitchen and serving staff. From what Ffion had observed, half of them seemed to be from overseas and spoke very little English.

A uniformed constable had been given the task of rounding up the guests for interview, and two other detectives were conducting interviews at the other end of high table. The questions they were asking were the same as Ffion and Ryan.

What time did you arrive at college yesterday?

Where were you between the hours of three and seven o'clock?

Did you see Alexia Petrakis yesterday afternoon?

How well did you know the deceased?

Ryan was doing most of the talking and had assigned Ffion the job of taking notes. But he wasn't as good at putting people at their ease as Jake. Ffion hadn't previously appreciated Jake's gift for connecting to people and getting them to open up. To her surprise, she found that she was missing him.

'Did you see anyone tampering with the bowls of soup prior to the meal?' Ryan asked the latest witness, a bored-looking woman. He seemed so eager to hurry through the many questions that each one sounded as if it were being fired from a machine gun.

The witness shook her head.

It seemed that no one had seen anything interesting. Most people knew who Alexia was but hadn't kept in touch with her. A few claimed never to have spoken a word to her in their three years as a student. Those who'd studied English recalled her as particularly ambitious, not a character trait that seemed to have endeared her to any of them. And so far, everyone they'd spoken to had been at the tea between four and five thirty and then getting changed for dinner at seven. A few had gone to the service in the chapel at six thirty.

There was a huge gap in the afternoon when almost everyone had been getting dressed for dinner and no one had seen anyone else. That was the window of opportunity when the murderer had most likely carried out their work.

Ryan dismissed the current witness with a plea

for her to tell them if she later remembered anything that might be significant. The uniformed constable scurried off to fetch the next witness.

'God, this is dull,' said Ryan. He studied his list. 'And we've hardly started. There's another sixty-three more people for us to interview.'

'We'd better get on with it, then,' said Ffion caustically. 'At least we don't have the job of interviewing Bridget.'

'Right,' agreed Ryan. 'Interviewing the boss. That would be awkward.'

The next witness took a seat opposite them. To Ffion the woman looked like something of an old maid, if such things still existed. There was a dowdiness to her, and even though she must be the same age as DI Hart – around thirty-eight – she had the look of a much older woman. The grey hair, the stoop to her shoulders, and the general air of neglect all spoke of someone who had largely given up on life.

'Name?' asked Ryan.

'Bella Williams,' said the woman, tucking a limp strand of hair behind her ear.

'What time did you arrive at college yesterday?'

'Just after three o'clock.'

'Where were you between the hours of three and seven o'clock?'

'I took my bag up to my room, then went to tea. After that I went back to my room to get ready for dinner.'

'You spent the whole one and a half hours

getting ready?' queried Ryan.

'No. I was reading a new translation of Hesiod's Theogony.'

Ryan hesitated, as if about to ask what that was, before thinking better of it. 'Can anyone vouch for your movements during that time?'

'Only while I was at tea, and then again during dinner.'

'Did you see Alexia Petrakis yesterday afternoon?'

'No.'

'How well did you know the deceased?'

'We shared a house together in our second year.'

Ffion put down her pen and looked up. At last. Someone who might be able to tell them something useful.

'So would you say that you and Alexia were good friends?' she asked, ignoring Ryan who was frowning at this deviation from the prepared script.

'No,' said Bella. 'I mean, real friends would send each other Christmas cards and maybe visit each other from time to time. Alexia and I were never like that.'

'Why was that?'

Bella shrugged. 'Alexia Petrakis wasn't the kind of person who valued friendships. She was only interested in people who could be useful to her.'

'And you couldn't? Be useful to her, I mean. What is it that you do for a living?'

'I teach Latin in a girls' school in Peterborough,' said Bella defensively.

'And Alexia Petrakis was a beautiful, glamorous woman with a successful career in journalism. She travelled all over the world and met famous people. You're right. How could someone who's just a teacher at a little-known girls' school possibly be of interest to her?'

Bella glared back indignantly. 'You know nothing about me.'

'Only what you just told me yourself,' said Ffion. 'So, did you feel that she'd abandoned you after university?'

'Perhaps. Yes.'

'You didn't like her,' said Ffion bluntly.

'Not very much.'

'Did you want to kill her?'

At that, Bella looked amused. 'If I did, I would hardly tell you.'

'Can you think of a reason why anyone would have wanted to kill her?'

'No.'

'What about in her career as a journalist? Had she made enemies?'

'I'm sure she made a lot of enemies. Her articles were all basically hatchet jobs. She liked to find people's faults and tell all the world about them. In Ancient Greek, Alexis means defender or protector. I think that's how she saw herself. She imagined she was a kind of guardian of the truth. It's a shame the world didn't know the truth about her.'

'And what truth is that?'

'Like I already told you. She was a selfish person who cared little for others.'

After she'd gone, Ryan leaned back in his chair and stretched out his arms. 'Blimey, you know you're in Oxford when someone helpfully translates some Ancient Greek for you.' He shot Ffion a quizzical look. 'She's a bit of a psycho, actually. You reckon she did it?'

'You know Baxter hates speculation. But I think he probably ought to speak to her himself.'

'Yeah, right.'

'There were a couple of things she said that were very interesting,' said Ffion.

'What? The Ancient Greek?'

'No. The fact that she'd obviously read all of Alexia's articles, even though she claimed to dislike her so much. Also, what she said about Alexia having made lots of enemies.'

'Some people make enemies easily,' said Ryan. 'But most of them don't end up dead with their eyeballs in the soup.'

'True.'

'And speaking of soup, I'm starving.'

'You're always starving.'

'I'm a man with a healthy appetite,' said Ryan. 'When's lunch?'

'Later. Look out, here comes Baxter.'

The detective inspector had appeared at the entrance to the hall, wearing his usual grouchy expression. He began to stride past the dining tables towards them.

'Just when I thought the day couldn't get any worse,' grumbled Ryan.

But Ffion's day was suddenly looking up. A tall ginger-haired figure appeared at the far end of the hall in Baxter's wake. Jake. He followed in the older man's footsteps, quickly catching up with his long gait.

'Right,' said Baxter brusquely when he arrived at high table. 'Detective Sergeant Derwent has joined us at last, so I'm rearranging the teams.' He turned to Ryan. 'I want you to pair up with Derwent here' – he indicated Jake – 'and bring him up to speed on everything that's been going on. Who you've spoken to so far, etc.' He turned to Ffion. 'DC Hughes, I'd like you to join me in interviewing the former housemates of the deceased. DI Hart has already provided me with a list of their names.'

Ffion groaned inwardly. She'd hoped that she might be paired up with Jake, but instead it seemed that she had simply swapped Ryan for Baxter. 'DS Hooper and I have just interviewed one of them, sir,' she said.

'You have?' said Baxter. 'Well, good. That will make our job quicker. All right, everyone know what they're supposed to be doing?'

'Yes, sir,' they all chimed in unison.

'Right, let's get to work.' He headed for the exit.

Ffion lingered behind for a moment. 'You got here quickly,' she whispered to Jake. 'I hope you stuck to the speed limit.'

'I made an early start.' Jake grinned. 'Not much traffic around at seven o'clock on a Sunday morning.'

'I believe you,' said Ffion. 'But thousands wouldn't.'

She hurried to catch up with Baxter.

★

After her talk with Baxter, Bridget strolled through the college wondering how she was going to fill her time if she wasn't allowed to go home until all the interviews had been completed.

Police officers were bustling around the college and she nodded to those she knew. It was frustrating to be so closely immersed in a murder investigation but not to be allowed to take part in it. She wandered aimlessly through Mob Quad and into Front Quad before an idea occurred to her.

At the gatehouse the porter was sitting in his lodge reading the sports section of The Sunday Times. He put it aside as soon as he saw Bridget. 'Morning. How can I help you?'

'I was just wondering if you still have the guest list for yesterday showing what time everyone signed in?'

'Certainly,' said the porter. 'I have it right here.' He reached into a tray on the counter and pulled out a sheet of paper. 'I had to give the police a copy, but this is the original.'

She considered telling him that she was police too, but stopped herself. As Baxter had made abundantly clear to her, she had no authority in this investigation, but was just another civilian attending the gaudy.

'Do you mind if I take a quick look?' she asked.

'I don't see why not.' He slid the sheet across to her and went back to perusing the newspaper.

Bridget worked her way through the guest list, noting what time everyone had signed in. She wasn't surprised to see that she had been one of the last to arrive at the college. No matter how careful her plans, she always seemed to arrive everywhere at the last minute.

Alexia had been one of the very first to arrive, signing in at just before three o'clock. Bridget wondered why had she got here so early. Alexia had never been one for arriving early to any social event. She had normally taken great care to be fashionably late.

Bridget made a mental note of the arrival times of everyone else she knew. Meg, Bella and Tina had all signed in between three and three thirty. After Alexia, in other words, but well before Bridget. But then, so had almost everyone else attending the gaudy. She thanked the porter and handed the sheet back.

There was one name that wasn't on the list, however.

'Were you on duty all day yesterday?' she asked him.

He seemed surprised by the question, but

happy to answer it. 'Yes, I was working from nine in the morning right through to seven in the evening.'

'Can you tell me what time the warden arrived in college?'

'The warden? Dr Harper never passed through the gate yesterday. Not while I was on duty.'

'But how is that possible?' asked Bridget. 'He was here for afternoon tea and then again for dinner.' And, she recalled, he had changed out of his lounge suit into black tie at some time between those two events.

The porter grinned at her. 'Dr Harper has no need to enter or leave college through the gatehouse. His lodgings on Merton Street have a back entrance that leads directly into the Fellows' Gardens.'

'I see,' said Bridget. 'So he can enter and leave freely without anyone seeing him.'

The porter glared at her. 'Why would that be of any importance?'

Bridget gave him a parting smile. 'No reason. Thanks for your help.'

★

Ffion caught up with Baxter just as he was disappearing through the archway leading into the Fellows' Quad. The quadrangle was of a classic Oxford design, with a pristine square of lawn in the centre mowed to within an inch of its life in uniform stripes. The three-storey stone buildings that encompassed it were topped off with square battlements. At a guess Ffion would have said the architecture was early seventeenth century.

Baxter walked through one of the doorways and climbed the stairs. 'One of the English tutors is away on sabbatical,' he remarked. 'The warden's given us permission to use her room.'

Ffion couldn't complain about her working environment. The well-proportioned suite of rooms was much nicer than the incident room at the police station in Kidlington. It would have been an idyllic place to work, had it not been for the presence of Baxter himself.

'I want to make it clear from the outset that I will be leading these interviews,' he told her. 'There's no need for you to ask any questions. In fact, I'd rather you didn't.'

'I see, sir. Then, what exactly would you like me to do?'

'Just... try to put the witnesses at their ease. You know... woman to woman, so they talk more openly.' He peered down at his notes, avoiding her gaze.

'I'll do my best, sir,' she said stiffly.

She wondered if she should point out the blatantly sexist nature of his request. She could tell him that he'd misjudged her, and that just because she was a woman it didn't mean she was good at empathy. If he'd wanted an empathetic side-kick he'd have been better off asking Jake. But she held her opinions to herself. Helping to interview the women who had counted the murder victim as a friend was bound to be a lot more interesting than sitting in the hall taking notes for Ryan.

There was a knock at the door, and a uniformed PC popped her head round. 'I've got a Ms Collins here for you, sir.'

'Show her in,' said Baxter.

Ffion recognised Meg Collins immediately. Meg had been interviewed earlier by the other detectives and, with her loud voice and brightly-coloured clothes, tended to attract attention.

'Are you the detective in charge of this investigation?' she demanded as soon as she entered the room.

'I am,' said Baxter. 'Detective Inspector Baxter.'

Meg stood in front of the doorway with her hands on her hips. 'Why am I here? I've already spoken to your sergeant this morning. I was led to believe that I'd be allowed to leave after that, not kept back for further questioning.'

'As a person of interest to the enquiry,' said Baxter, 'we just need to ask you a few more questions.'

A look of indignation flooded Meg's face. 'What do you mean, a person of interest? I think I should call my lawyer.' She whipped her phone out of her handbag.

Versace, Ffion noted.

'That really won't be necessary,' said Baxter hurriedly. 'You are not being interviewed under caution. Please, take a seat.' He indicated a sofa in front of the fireplace.

Reluctantly, Meg replaced her phone in her bag and took a seat on the sofa.

Baxter settled himself into a wingback chair opposite, crossing one leg over the other.

Ffion pulled up the wooden chair from the desk. She opened her notebook and studied Meg carefully. The woman had clearly decided to focus her attention on Baxter since he represented the seat of power in this meeting, and Ffion was happy with that arrangement. It gave her the opportunity to scrutinise the witness without being noticed. From the top of her coiffured hair to the tips of her stiletto shoes – Louboutin, if Ffion wasn't mistaken – everything about Meg Collins screamed "successful businesswoman". And she wanted you to know it.

'We'll start at the beginning,' said Baxter, turning to the first page in his notes. 'You studied here at the same time as the deceased.'

'We all did,' snapped Meg. 'Last night was a reunion for everyone who started here twenty years ago, so if that's your criterion then everyone's a suspect.'

'And moreover,' continued Baxter, 'you shared a house with the victim during your second year.'

'As did four other girls.' Meg paused. 'Although, as I expect you've already heard about Lydia, you'll know that there are only five

126

of us now. Well, four,' she corrected herself.

'Tell me about Lydia Khoury.'

'Lydia? What would you like to know about her?'

'Anything that you think may be relevant.'

'I'm not sure that Lydia is relevant to your enquiry at all,' said Meg. 'She's been dead for seventeen years.' When Baxter said nothing, she sighed and continued. 'Lydia was in the same year as the rest of us. She was an immigrant, the daughter of Lebanese parents. She moved to this country as a child.'

'Her family came from the Middle East. Was she a Muslim?'

'No, Christian. Almost half of all Lebanese are Christian. She was a devout Catholic, in fact. She was very interested in her cultural background and always wanted to return to Lebanon. At university she studied Archaeology and Anthropology and was able to travel to Lebanon in her final year on a research trip.'

'I understand that the warden, Dr Brendan Harper, was her college tutor?'

'Yes, that's right.'

'What do you think of him?'

'I think he's done an excellent job as warden of the college and would make a fine vice-chancellor. The university needs people like him, keen to engage with the public.'

'Is he universally popular?'

'I don't know. I suppose that some people might think he's too populist in his approach.

They'd prefer archaeologists to stay in dusty libraries or go on digs instead of explaining and showcasing their work to a larger audience.'

'You mean television?'

'Yes, he's a bit of a TV star. Some people are envious of that kind of success.'

'Are some people envious of your success?'

'Yes,' said Meg, her eyes narrowing. 'I'm sure they are.'

'Why did Lydia Khoury take her own life?'

Meg seemed taken aback by the suddenness of the question. Ffion had to give Baxter some credit for his interview technique. His direct style was very different to Bridget's but just as effective. It was rather like Ffion's own style, in fact.

'Why does anyone do such a terrible thing?' said Meg, recovering her composure. 'She was obviously deeply unhappy. Final exams at Oxford can be extremely stressful.'

'Was Lydia under any particular kind of stress?'

'Not that I'm aware of. But she was an extremely private person. I doubt that she would have shared her concerns, even with her close friends.'

'Don't Catholics consider suicide to be a mortal sin?'

'Yes, I believe they do.'

'So Lydia must have been in extreme emotional turmoil to have even considered taking such a course of action.'

'I'm sure that's true of anyone who chooses to end their own life, Inspector,' said Meg drily.

Baxter paged through his notes. 'Did your friendship with Alexia Petrakis continue after you'd both left university?'

Meg seemed relieved to move on to a new topic. 'Yes, it did, for a time.'

'For a time?'

'After graduating, I spent three years in Cambridge completing my post-graduate degree. I didn't see much of Alexia during that period. But then I moved to London and we started to see a lot more of each other again. We went to the same parties, had the same friends, that sort of thing. We moved in similar social circles for a few years.'

'What sort of social circles?'

'Young, ambitious professionals starting out in their careers. The parties were networking opportunities as much as anything else. If you want to get on in life it's a question of who you know.'

Ffion detected a hint of scorn in Meg's voice, as if she pitied Baxter for not having been allowed to enter into the right "social circles". Baxter appeared not to notice the slight, or if he did, not to care.

'When and why did you and the victim cease to move in the same circles?' he asked.

Meg stretched out the fingers of one hand as if examining her manicured nails for flaws. 'It was shortly after I got married.'

Was that a hint of colour rising in Meg's cheeks? Ffion watched her closely, observing her body language, which seemed suddenly to have become a lot more defensive.

Baxter was also watching her closely, but said nothing.

'If you must know,' said Meg, 'Alexia and I stopped being friends after she had an affair with my husband.'

'When was this affair?' asked Baxter, a note of interest creeping into his voice.

Meg waved a hand in front of her face, dismissing his question. 'More than ten years ago now. Ancient history. I got a divorce and moved on with my life. I've built a successful company all on my own.'

Hell hath no ambition like a woman scorned, thought Ffion. She wondered how much of Meg's business success was down to the need to achieve more than her ex-husband and her former friend.

'Would you say that you harboured a grudge towards Miss Petrakis?'

'A grudge? No. I'm not a petty-minded person.'

'Forgive and forget, eh?' suggested Baxter.

Meg leaned towards him, placing her elbows on her knees. 'Inspector Baxter, I can assure you that I never forget anything, nor forgive anyone. But if you're not-so-subtly suggesting that I murdered Alexia Petrakis, I can assure you that I didn't. Her affair with my husband took place many years ago, and as I've explained to you already, I have far more important matters to occupy my attention than a desire for revenge.'

'Where were you yesterday afternoon between the hours of three and seven?' asked Baxter.

Meg leaned back in the sofa. 'My train arrived from London at two forty-five and I took a taxi here from the station. You can check with the porter but I think I signed in just after three. I collected the keys to my room in Front Quad and made a call to the office. Then I went for tea in the TS Eliot Theatre. After that I returned to my room, made some more phone calls, and got myself ready for dinner.'

'What time did you leave your room again?'

'About five minutes before dinner.'

'You didn't attend the service in the chapel?'

'God, no. I'm a scientist, not a believer in myths and fairy tales.'

'Did you visit the chapel at any time during the day?'

'No.'

'What is it that your company does exactly?'

'GenMeg Therapeutics is a bio-medical company developing gene therapy treatments for common causes of congenital and hereditary blindness.'

The statement sounded to Ffion like an elevator pitch that had been delivered hundreds of times before.

'Blindness?' Baxter's interest had clearly been piqued again. 'Bit of a coincidence, wouldn't you

131

say, that the victim had her eyeballs removed?'

'Hardly, unless it was intended as some kind of sick joke.'

'I expect that a bio-medical expert would know how to carry out such an operation?'

Meg looked disgusted at the insinuation. 'My company specialises in advanced therapeutic treatments, not butchery.'

'Tell me, why would someone have wanted to kill Alexia Petrakis?'

'Besides the fact that she was a self-centred, selfish bitch?' Meg shrugged. 'Lots of people probably wanted to kill her. In her personal life she treated the people she knew as disposable commodities. She wrecked marriages, Inspector. She used and then discarded men as if they were toys. In her professional life, she was an investigative journalist who made a living from digging up dirt on other people. I imagine she'd made quite a lot of enemies along the way.'

'Do you know what she was working on when she died?'

'I've absolutely no idea,' said Meg. 'Is that everything?' She pushed back her sleeve to reveal an expensive smartwatch. 'As I've already told you, I have a pressing engagement in Cambridge to attend this afternoon.'

'I've got a question,' said Ffion. 'Why do you think the victim's eyes were presented to the warden?'

'Were they intended for him?' asked Meg. 'I assumed that was just chance. Surely the soup bowls were identical. Any one of us might have made the grisly discovery.'

'Apparently not,' said Ffion, ignoring the scowl that had appeared on Baxter's face. 'The warden's bowl was labelled, due to a food allergy.'

'Well, I honestly don't know,' said Meg. 'Are we done here? I really need to get away.'

'We're done for now,' said Baxter. 'But don't leave the college. We might need to speak to you again.'

Meg glared at him, then slung her bag over her shoulder. She rose onto her towering heels and strode towards the door.

CHAPTER 12

Forbidden from poking her nose into the investigation, and keen to avoid running into Baxter, Bridget was at a loss about how to spend the rest of the morning. She didn't fancy returning to her room to sit twiddling her thumbs, so after leaving the gatehouse she headed over to the Junior Common Room. Some of the guests were sitting there reading newspapers and magazines, but no one that Bridget knew well enough to talk to. Instead, she tried to immerse herself in the Sunday papers, a large pile of which had been delivered to the college that morning.

The JCR hadn't changed much since Bridget's day, except that it now boasted a huge flat-screen TV on one wall instead of the 'box' that had sat in the corner. The room still had the same saggy sofas and dark brown carpet designed not to show spillages, and that air of a place where students could hang out and relax. At the far end of the room, a couple of people were killing time with a game of table tennis.

She forced herself to plough through the main

news sections of The Sunday Times, diligently keeping herself informed about the world's big stories, although she would much rather have moved straight on to the arts and culture sections inside. A new production of The Magic Flute had just opened at the Royal Opera House in London, and she wondered if she might persuade Jonathan to go and see it with her.

She was skimming through the news review section when she suddenly caught her breath. A double-page article, complete with photographs, was entitled Miscarriage of Justice, Again! But it was the byline that really grabbed her attention. Alexia Petrakis. This must be Alexia's last published piece of work. The newspaper could have been rolling off the printing press even as the journalist drew her last breath.

Bridget started to devour the words on the page. She no longer heard the tap of the table-tennis ball or the exasperated sighs of the less-than-competent players every time one of them missed. Could this article be the reason Alexia had been killed?

She only looked up when she became aware of a large figure looming over her. Baxter. And from the look on his face, he wasn't in the best of moods. Not that he ever was. Ffion stood behind him, looking as if she'd rather be somewhere else.

Baxter dragged a chair over to face Bridget and sat down heavily, leaning forwards so he could talk to her without anyone else hearing.

'Why didn't you tell me when I interviewed you this morning that Alexia Petrakis had an affair with the husband of Meg Collins?'

'I didn't think it was relevant,' said Bridget. 'It happened such a long time ago.'

'You didn't think it was relevant,' repeated Baxter. 'I would say it's highly relevant. We're looking for someone who held a grudge against the victim. Marital infidelity leads to the biggest grudges of all in my experience.'

Bridget had to concede that he had a point. She didn't harbour many warm feelings towards her own ex-husband, Ben, who had slept with several women during their relatively short marriage. But she hadn't turned into a killer because of how she felt, and she couldn't believe Meg would either. 'Have you seen the newspapers this morning?' she asked.

'I haven't had time to read the papers,' growled Baxter. 'I'm trying to solve a murder enquiry, in case you hadn't noticed.'

'I think you should take a look at this.' She folded back the pages of the article she had been reading and held it out for him to see.

'What is it?' asked Baxter impatiently.

'It's an investigative piece written by Alexia Petrakis. She claims to have uncovered a miscarriage of justice that occurred some years ago.'

'A miscarriage of justice?' Baxter took the newspaper from her and glared at it as if he found it a personal affront. 'Just tell me what it says, will you?'

'What it says is that five years ago the lawyer Tina Mackenzie deliberately fabricated evidence in a high-profile lawsuit against a paediatric cancer specialist. The doctor in question was accused of professional misconduct and struck off as a result of the lawsuit. In this article, Alexia claims to have gathered witness statements that contradict the false evidence used by Tina in the original case. As a result, the doctor now hopes to be vindicated and allowed to practise medicine again.'

Baxter was still staring at the newspaper. 'Tina Mackenzie was one of the women who shared a house with you and Alexia Petrakis. What precisely is she supposed to have done?'

'According to the article, she drummed up fraudulent claims from people who stood to benefit financially from a successful lawsuit.'

A cold shiver ran down Bridget's spine. Could Tina really have been involved in such a gross miscarriage of justice? Getting a children's cancer specialist struck off, just so that she could win a lawsuit? It was horrible to think that she could be so ruthless. And even worse, could she have killed Alexia in order to secure her silence?

Baxter was oblivious to Bridget's distress. 'I was planning to interview Tina Mackenzie next, but the constable I sent to look for her hasn't been able to find her.' He waved Ffion over. 'DC Hughes, do you recall seeing Tina Mackenzie any time this morning?'

'No, sir.'

Now Bridget thought about it, she hadn't seen Tina this morning either.

Suddenly Baxter was on his mobile phone, shouting to whoever was unlucky enough to be on the other end. 'Her name's Tina Mackenzie... Yes... I want her found straight away... Bring her to my room for questioning.'

The table tennis game ceased and the players turned to stare at the commotion.

'If you know where she is,' Baxter said to Bridget, 'find her and bring her to me.' He stomped out of the common room, taking the newspaper with him. Ffion gave Bridget a quick nod before following her boss.

'I thought you didn't want me working on the case,' Bridget muttered to herself. But still, she needed to find Tina. Where could she have gone?

She remembered that Tina had liked taking long solitary walks along the river. She said it helped her to think. Right now, no one was allowed to leave the college, so if Tina wanted to find quiet and solitude there was only one place she could have gone. The Fellows' Garden.

★

Bridget slipped out of the common room, ignoring the questioning looks of the table tennis players, and walked quickly over to the entrance to the Fellows' Garden, passing the wrought iron Water Gate that led down to the river via

Deadman's Walk. With its extensive informal lawns, mature specimen trees and abundant herbaceous borders, the garden at Merton was the perfect spot for a private moment of tranquil contemplation. It didn't take Bridget long to spot a solitary figure in black standing before an exuberant display of pink chrysanthemums.

'Tina?'

The figure turned and Bridget could see that she had been crying.

'I thought I might find you here.'

'Where else?' said Tina sadly. 'You know me too well.' She knelt down next to the flowers and inhaled deeply. 'These are beautiful, don't you think? The world of nature is so simple compared to our murky world.'

'I've just read the article in The Sunday Times,' said Bridget gently. 'Do you want to talk to me about it?'

Tina glanced up. 'In your role as a police officer?'

'I'm not working on this case,' said Bridget. 'I'm here as your friend.'

Tina seemed to accept this. 'All right. Let's find a place to sit.'

They crossed the lawn to the foot of a flight of stone steps that led up to a gravel walkway. From the top it was possible to see the entire garden spread out around them. The sun was shining brightly in the blue September sky and just for a moment Bridget could remember how they had been as fresh-faced teenagers, full of hopes and dreams, their lives as yet unwritten. Now the choices they had made had caught up with them, shaping them in ways they could never have imagined in their youth.

'I still can't really believe that you joined the police force,' said Tina.

'What did you think I would do?'

'I don't know. I couldn't really imagine what you might end up doing.'

'My ideal job would somehow have combined history with opera and visiting sun-drenched Italian piazzas.'

'I don't think that job exists, Bridget.'

'No. So I had no choice, really. Becoming a police officer was the next best thing.'

The path led them along a raised terrace, bounded on the south side by the parapet of the old city wall. After a short distance they reached a semi-circular bastion set within the wall with broad views over Merton Field and Christ Church Meadow. Wooden benches were set against the curved boundary wall around a hexagonal stone table.

According to college legend, the author JRR Tolkien had sat at this table to write Lord of the Rings. It was fun to imagine him sitting right here, crafting his epic tale of good versus evil. The writer had been Oxford's Merton Professor of English Language and Literature, and had clearly drawn inspiration for his books from the city's medieval architecture. Bridget sat next to Tina on one of the benches and waited patiently for her to speak.

'A colleague phoned me early this morning to tell me that the article had been published,' said Tina. 'I came to the garden to get away from everything and to think things through. I wasn't trying to run away, if that's what you were thinking.'

'Is there any truth in the article?'

'Unfortunately, yes,' sighed Tina. 'I was led astray by people who saw the court case as a quick way to make a lot of money. If I'm honest, I was naive and over-ambitious. For me, it wasn't really about the money. Mostly I just wanted to make a name for myself, and this was a golden opportunity. I'm not sure that I even lied as such, just massaged the truth a little. Every lawyer does that to some extent.' She looked Bridget straight in the eye. 'As a detective you probably believe that your job is about discovering the truth.'

Bridget nodded. 'That's generally what we try to do.'

'Well the law's not like that. People think the law is about right and wrong, but it isn't. It's about winning and losing. And I've always hated losing.'

Bridget digested this for a moment. She could see how the battles that were fought in court between defence and prosecution lawyers could easily turn into win-or-lose situations where something as fragile as the actual truth could fall victim to one side's ego or greater powers of persuasion. Tina had been right to say that it was a murky world.

And yet blaming her own actions on the system or on her colleagues didn't feel like a very satisfactory answer. Tina was a highly intelligent woman. She must have known exactly what she was doing, and what the consequences would be for the doctor accused of malpractice. But she had done it anyway. Everyone made mistakes, but this one wasn't so easy to excuse.

'Did you know that Alexia was writing this article?' asked Bridget.

'No. I had absolutely no idea. The first I heard about it was this morning.'

Bridget nodded. At least that was something. If Tina had known about the article in advance, it would have given her a very clear motive for wanting to see Alexia dead. And yet... 'What exactly did you mean last night in the bar when you said that Alexia was a good journalist, but a lousy friend?'

'Well, she was a lousy friend, wasn't she? Look what she did to Meg. How could she have seduced her best friend's husband? She was shameless.'

Bridget resisted the temptation to comment on Tina's own disloyalty in pursuing a lawsuit against Meg. Instead she asked, 'Tina, did you see Alexia yesterday?'

'No. I saw her name on the register when I signed in, so I knew that she was already in college, but I didn't see her.'

'Okay. And just one last question, because the

police are going to ask you this, can you account for your movements between the hours of three and seven yesterday, and can anyone provide you with an alibi?'

'I made a few work-related calls from my room and then I went down to tea. Well, you saw me there yourself. Loads of people did.'

'Yes, said Bridget. 'That was between four and five thirty.'

'After tea I went back to my room, caught up on my messages and emails, and got ready for dinner.'

'That still leaves over two hours of time when you were on your own.'

Tina stared at her. 'Surely you can't think that I had anything to do with Alexia's murder?'

Bridget evaded the question. 'I'm just telling you what the police will want to know. You need to have your answer ready.'

'I understand,' said Tina.

'Now, will you come with me and tell DI Baxter everything you've told me?'

Tina nodded. 'Lead the way.'

CHAPTER 13

After delivering Tina into Ffion's capable hands, Bridget decided to get a spot of lunch in the dining hall. The serving staff were clearly working under a lot of stress due to the continued police presence in the hall. Through the open doorway leading to the kitchen, Bridget spotted DC Harry Johns attempting to speak to one of the kitchen assistants, who was wielding a lethal-looking meat knife. After watching for a second she decided that the situation was not life threatening, and turned instead to examine what food was on offer. With all the disruption in the kitchen, only cold sandwiches were available.

Bridget selected a wholewheat baguette filled with tuna and sweetcorn mayonnaise and gave herself a mental pat on the back. Having missed an entire four-course meal last night, the weekend was turning into a much lower calorie affair than she'd anticipated. She could almost feel her waistline shrinking by the hour. Chocolate muffins and portions of cream-covered cheesecake were also on display, but she hurried past them with iron resolution, selecting a low-fat yoghurt instead.

She thought she might take her lunch outside to eat in the gardens, but a voice called out to her.

'Bridget, come and join me.' It was Bella, sitting at a table nearby with a sandwich before her.

Bridget sat down opposite and unwrapped her baguette from its plastic covering. 'Hi, Bella. How are you?' It was the first time for Bridget to see her since the previous night in the bar.

'I'm all right,' said Bella, 'under the circumstances. Do you know what's happening? When are we going to be allowed to go home? No one seems to know anything.'

'I haven't heard,' said Bridget. 'I'm not officially on the case.'

'I was interviewed this morning,' said Bella, 'by two of your colleagues.'

'DI Baxter?' enquired Bridget, taking a bite out of her bread. 'He's the senior investigating officer.'

'No. A young sergeant and a Welsh constable.'

DS Ryan Hooper and DC Ffion Hughes, Bridget deduced. She tried to imagine the two of them working successfully together as a team and couldn't quite picture it. 'What did you think of them?'

Bella pulled a face. 'The sergeant was all right, I suppose, although a bit blokeish. That Welsh woman was positively rude, though.'

Bridget suppressed a smile. Ffion could be

rather abrasive and direct at times. Bridget would have to send her on a suitable training course to try to remedy that. 'In what way?'

'After I said that I knew Alexia, she asked me if I was jealous of her success as a journalist when I was "just" a teacher at a little-known girls' school.'

'That was rather insensitive,' admitted Bridget. 'But Ffion was just doing her job. She was probably trying to establish whether you had a motive for killing Alexia.'

'Huh. That doesn't sound much of a motive to me. Like I don't have enough problems to worry about, what with marking schoolwork and keeping up with changes to the exam syllabus. Being insanely jealous of my friends isn't something I have a lot of time for.'

'Right, yeah,' said Bridget. 'I think that other people may have had stronger motives.'

'You mean Meg,' said Bella. 'I know she's still angry about the affair between her husband and Alexia, but do you really think she's capable of murder?'

'No, not really,' said Bridget. Although one thing she had learned during her time as a detective was that everyone was capable of extraordinary acts under extreme circumstances. 'I was actually thinking about Tina.'

Bella seemed surprised. 'Tina? What about her?'

'You haven't heard, then. An article written by Alexia appeared in one of today's newspapers, naming Tina in a miscarriage of justice.'

Bella covered her mouth with her hand. 'Today? Written by Alexia? Oh my God. That's too weird.'

'Yeah, I know. Talk about reaching out from beyond the grave. The article accuses Tina of lying in a legal case some years back.'

'Well, I wouldn't put it past her,' said Bella. 'Tina has always been ruthlessly ambitious. When it comes to her career, she never lets anything stand in her way.'

Bridget chewed thoughtfully at her tuna sandwich. It did seem that her friends were unusually ambitious. Meg, Tina and Alexia had all excelled in their respective careers. Bella, too, had been an ambitious academic high-flyer who everyone had expected to stay on at Oxford and become a Classics tutor one day. But she had fallen by the wayside and settled for a different kind of job, teaching Latin to schoolgirls, not undergraduates. Bridget wondered if Ffion was right about Bella harbouring resentment of her old friend. But that really didn't seem to be a strong enough motive to have committed murder.

'You don't really think that Tina murdered Alexia to prevent the article being published, do you?' Bridget asked Bella.

'Well, if someone was going to do something that threatened to destroy everything I'd worked for, I'd probably feel like killing them. But there's a world of difference between feeling and doing.'

'Of course.' Bridget returned again to the thoughts she'd had about Ben, in the dark days after she discovered he was cheating on her. Violent and grisly murder had certainly featured prominently among her thoughts. But she had never considered acting on those impulses.

'Do you remember how close we all were when we shared that house in our second year?' asked Bella. 'It was such a dump, but it brought us together in adversity.'

'I remember how the roof leaked when it rained and we had to put a bucket on the landing to collect the drops.'

'Yes. And how in the middle of winter we would wake up to frost on the inside of the windows.'

'The best times were when we cooked huge pots of pasta and opened bottles of wine and talked late into the night.'

'We were going to change the world, weren't we?'

Bridget was almost feeling nostalgic for the old days. 'When you live with someone as closely as that, you think you know them. But now I'm not so sure I really did. Or is it just that we've all changed so much in the last seventeen years? I'm sure I have.'

'You haven't really changed,' said Bella. 'You're still the same old Bridget.'

'Am I?' Bridget wasn't so sure. Seventeen years ago she hadn't been a mother. She hadn't even met her future ex-husband. Her sister, Abigail had still been very much alive. Bridget suspected that these days she was an almost entirely different person. As for Alexia, Meg and Tina, they were certainly not as innocent as when she'd first met them. And what about Bella? How had she felt when her grand dreams of academic success were brought low? She seemed to have picked herself up and carried on, but she was no longer the happy, confident woman she had once been.

Around her, Bridget could hear people muttering about being kept in the college and how they should be allowed to go home. She couldn't disagree with them, although she understood Baxter's wish to keep everyone around until he had completed his interviews. It was strange being on the other side of the fence for once, observing a police investigation from the witnesses' point of view.

Although she was not really an outsider. Despite being forbidden from getting involved, she couldn't stop herself from thinking and behaving like a police detective. Spotting Ryan and Jake in the lunch queue, she excused herself from Bella and went over to say hello.

'Morning, ma'am,' said Jake.

'You can call me Ms Hart today. I'm off duty.'

Jake grinned. 'Yes, ma'am. If you say so.'

'I thought you were taking the weekend off to go up to Leeds?'

'I was, but I was called back to help out with the case.'

'Then maybe you could help me out.' She looked around to make sure that Baxter wasn't anywhere in the vicinity then turned to Ryan. 'Both of you.'

'Sure,' said Ryan. 'What do you want us to do?'

★

Bridget left the hall and made her way back towards her room in the Grove Building. It was high time that she made contact with Chloe to make sure she'd returned from London safely and had been picked up by James. She checked her phone to see if Chloe had sent her a message, but of course there was nothing. Expecting your teenager daughter to be helpful and informative was a certain road to disappointment.

At least she felt confident that Jake and Ryan would keep her informed of any news. They had both cheerfully agreed to update her on any significant developments in the investigation, despite explicit instructions from Baxter not to do so. She had obviously succeeded in building a loyal team. Of course she couldn't say she was exactly happy with the way things were going, not with one of her friends having been horrifically killed, and another being questioned on suspicion of the murder. But at least she would find out as soon as anything new happened.

She was approaching the entrance to the

chapel when the chaplain emerged. He wasn't wearing his cassock this time, and she was delighted to see that he really was wearing a pair of jeans, along with a black casual shirt and clerical collar.

He stopped to greet her, brushing his long sandy hair from his eyes. 'Ah, um, Bridget – do you mind if I call you that?'

'Not at all.' Although she had only met the young chaplain the previous afternoon, she already felt that she knew him quite well. Being the first two people at the scene of a grisly murder was enough to establish a lasting bond.

'How are you bearing up?' he asked, an expression of concern on his face. The look came naturally to him, as if he'd always been destined to be someone that those in need could turn to in a crisis.

'I'm all right,' Bridget told him. 'This isn't the first time I've had to face a tragic death. It tends to come with the job.'

'Ah, yes, of course. Police officers and the clergy – we have a lot in common. You might say that death is our business.'

'I suppose so. I'd never thought about it that way.'

He smiled weakly. 'Although in the church we cover births and marriages too.'

'Yes,' said Bridget. 'And we do robberies and assaults. On balance, I think you have a better deal.'

'Um, yes. I suppose so.' The chaplain seemed

distracted.

'Was there something you wanted to talk to me about?' Bridget asked.

'Well, yes, there was, actually. I'd like to ask your advice. It's quite a sensitive matter, in fact.'

'It's usually the other way around,' remarked Bridget. 'People normally go to a chaplain to ask for advice, not to give it.'

'Oh, yes, I suppose you're right.' He looked around. Several people were meandering through the quadrangle, and others were sitting on a bench enjoying the sun. 'Maybe we could go somewhere more private?'

'Of course.'

She followed him back inside the chapel to a door to the right of the altar.

'We shouldn't be disturbed inside the sacristy,' he said, opening the door and stepping aside for her to enter. 'Please, after you.'

She descended a couple of steps into a square, wood-panelled room that looked like a storeroom for ecclesiastical accessories. A silver chalice stood on a table, surrounded by a pile of hymn books. Various items of clothing were scattered about.

'Sorry about the mess,' said the chaplain, removing a heap of white surplices from the back of a wooden chair. 'I ought to keep it tidier, but no one else comes in here normally. Do have a seat.'

'So what's the problem?' asked Bridget, sitting down on the wooden chair.

'Well,' said the chaplain, pulling up another chair and sitting down opposite her. 'It's rather awkward.'

'Yes, I already had that impression,' said Bridget. 'But it's always better to talk.'

'Yes, yes, that's exactly what I tell people.'

Bridget waited patiently for him to begin.

'On the day that Alexia Petrakis died – yesterday that is – I was due to meet her. Here, in the chapel.'

Bridget struggled to keep the surprise from her voice. 'You were meeting Alexia? I wasn't aware that you two knew each other.' She stopped, puzzled. 'When you discovered her body you told me you had no idea who she was. You said you'd never seen her before.'

'I hadn't,' he said hurriedly. 'We had never met. But she emailed me on Friday and requested a meeting in my capacity as college chaplain. Obviously, I agreed to see her.'

'Did she say what she wanted to talk to you about?'

'No. Well, not precisely. She didn't want to put any details in an email. She was going to tell me more in person. We arranged to meet in the chapel on Saturday afternoon.'

'At what time?'

'She told me she'd be in college for the gaudy, and would be arriving at about three o'clock. I said I'd meet her here at three thirty. Only the thing is, I was delayed in a meeting at Brasenose College, and by the time I reached the chapel there was no sign of her. I assumed she'd decided to call the meeting off or she'd just got bored waiting for me. I sent her an email to apologise, but of course I didn't get a response. She must already have been dead.'

A cold feeling gripped Bridget as she was reminded again that Alexia's body had probably been shut into the cupboard throughout the chapel service on Saturday afternoon. Bridget had been singing her heart out, completely oblivious to the fact that her dead friend was just a short distance away from her.

'What time did you arrive at Merton chapel yesterday afternoon?' she asked. 'Please try to remember exactly.'

'It must have been around four o'clock.'

'And what exactly did Alexia tell you about what she wanted to discuss?'

'Well, that's the crux of the matter. She explained that she was an investigative journalist and she was sitting on a story – a huge story, in her words – but she wasn't sure if it ought to be published. She was conflicted about whether to proceed.'

'And this story was about Tina Mackenzie?'

'No,' said the chaplain in surprise. 'Alexia's story was about the warden.'

'The warden?' Bridget's mind was doing somersaults. 'You must be mistaken. Alexia published a big story in today's newspaper revealing that her friend, Tina Mackenzie, was guilty of perpetrating a miscarriage of justice.'

154

'I'm sorry, but I don't know anything about that,' said the chaplain. 'This was definitely about the warden of Merton College, Dr Brendan Harper. That's why Alexia wanted to talk to me. She thought that publication of the story would quite possibly destroy Dr Harper's career, not to mention bringing an end to his hopes for the vice-chancellorship.' He brushed the hair from his eyes. 'That's the reason I didn't mention anything about this to the police. I was worried about getting the warden into trouble.'

Alexia had certainly been busy digging up dirt on people. Bridget wondered what kind of article could be so damaging that it might be career-ending for the warden.

'What did she tell you about the substance of the story?' she asked the chaplain.

'Nothing. Perhaps she would have told me more if we had met. All I know for sure is that she was undecided about whether or not to go ahead and submit the story for publication. She rather hinted that the warden had used his contacts in the media to help her get her first job. I think she may have been torn between loyalty to him and a desire to tell the truth.'

'I see.' No one had helped Bridget get a start in the police force, but she wasn't so naive as to think that these things didn't happen. If the warden had used his influence to kickstart Alexia's career in journalism, it certainly helped to explain her meteoric rise. 'And do I take it that you haven't mentioned this meeting to the police?'

'No. That's why I wanted to ask your advice first. You see, I would hate to get Dr Harper into any kind of trouble. I mean, with the new vice-chancellor due to be appointed very soon, any suggestion that he'd behaved badly in the past could be disastrous for him. And since I have no information about what he is supposed to have done wrong...'

'It's not your job to decide,' said Bridget. 'Your duty is simply to tell the police everything you know and let them determine whether it's relevant to the investigation. Remember that a woman has been brutally murdered.'

'Yes.' The chaplain nodded gratefully. 'When you put it like that it suddenly seems very simple. These things usually are, I find. Sometimes people come to me with problems that seem insurmountable to them, and yet, when they tell me what's on their mind, the answer is very often quite clear. More often than not, they already knew what they needed to do, they just wanted someone to tell them to do it.'

'I think that's the case here,' said Bridget. She could understand why the chaplain had chosen to come to her though, rather than Baxter. DI Baxter might not want her involved in the case, but she could hardly be blamed if witnesses found her a more approachable figure than him.

The chaplain was nodding his head vigorously. 'Yes, absolutely. Thank you so much for listening to me. I'll go and tell the police everything I've told you.'

CHAPTER 14

DS Jake Derwent had been away from Oxford for little more than twenty-four hours, and in that time a lot had happened. Over a hurried lunch, Ryan Hooper had briefed him on the juiciest aspects – woman strangled, eyes gouged out, eyeballs found floating in a bowl of soup, that's about it, mate – and he was now mostly up to speed with events at Merton College.

Thanks to Ffion, he'd also discovered that gaudy was a Latin word for a reunion of former students – or alumni, as Ffion insisted on calling them – the highlight of which was a slap-up meal in the medieval dining hall. If there was one thing Jake could rely on in Oxford, it was that the people here never called a spade a spade. He wondered what the Latin word for spade was. He would have to ask Ffion. She always seemed to know everything.

It was good to see Ffion again, even though he hadn't really had a chance to speak to her alone so far. Her slim, elfin features were as usual completely unperturbed by the presence of dismembered body parts and the other gruesome aspects of the murder. Her emerald eyes regarded him calmly from across the dining table as she explained some of the more obscure background details of the case to him and Ryan.

'Merton College has a valid claim to be Oxford's oldest college,' she informed them over lunch. 'It was founded by Walter de Merton in 1264. University College was founded fifteen years earlier by William of Durham in 1249, but didn't have a written constitution until some years after Merton was established.'

'Really?' Ryan was diligently working his way through his second chocolate muffin. 'And how do these fascinating facts help us to solve the case?'

Ffion turned her piercing green eyes on him. 'Solving a murder is all about uncovering the events of the past.'

'Yeah, maybe. But I don't reckon we're going to be arresting this Walter de Merton or William of Durham for the murder of Alexia Petrakis.'

'You never know how far back you need to go,' said Ffion, as if that proved everything.

After lunch the three of them trooped across to the temporary incident room in Fellow's Quad, where they'd been summoned by Baxter. Jake sat down on a sofa, squashed between Ryan and Harry, struggling to find room for his long legs, while Ffion took a chair opposite, crossing one leg neatly over the other. The other detectives working on the case squashed themselves onto a second sofa, while Baxter took up a stance in front of the fireplace, top button undone, tie askew, watching over them like a bird of prey.

'Right,' he said, when they were all in position, 'let's get started. And I don't want any interruptions from anyone while I'm speaking.' He directed a hard stare at Ryan before proceeding to pace the rug in front of the fireplace like a caged animal as he conducted the team meeting. Or, more accurately, delivered a monologue.

'Right,' he said again, 'So far we have two likely suspects who are both looking as guilty as each other.' He held up one stubby finger. 'First off, Meg Collins, former friend of Miss Petrakis, and founder of a bio-medical company based in Cambridge. Ms Collins had a clear motive for wanting Miss Petrakis dead, on account of her having an affair with her ex-husband. Wives who've been cheated on are always near the top of my list. There's also a possible link with the eyeballs placed in the soup, since Ms Collins's company is working on a cure for blindness, although quite how that fits with removal of the victim's eyes isn't clear. Second' – he raised a second digit – 'Tina Mackenzie, a partner in a London law firm. She also knew the victim, and in fact is now facing the threat of professional death as a result of Miss Petrakis's article which appeared in this morning's Sunday Times. Miss Mackenzie claims she didn't know that the article was in the pipeline, but we only have her word for that. If she did know about the article, but not when it was due to be published, then she had a clear motive to murder Miss Petrakis before the article could appear.' He paused and stuck out a third finger. 'Another possibility is that these two women were in it together. They're both former housemates of the victim. They could have cooked up the plot between them.'

He ceased his pacing and scowled angrily at everyone in the room, as if one of them had interrupted his flow.

'But all this is pure speculation. And I'm sure you're aware of what I think about speculation. I'm not interested in finding possible motives for the perpetrator. Let's leave that for the lawyers to argue about in court. I'm looking for means and opportunity.'

He held up one finger again and resumed his pacing. 'The means here is clear enough. A short length of wire was used to strangle the victim, and a knife taken from the college kitchen was used to remove the eyeballs.' A second finger shot up. 'Opportunity. From what we know so far, damn well every single person in the college had an opportunity to commit the murder. We have established that the murder took place between three and five o'clock, and the college chaplain claims that he was in the chapel from around four o'clock preparing for the service that began at six thirty. That indicates that the murder – and the removal of the victim's eyes – took place sometime between three and four o'clock. Hardly a single person appears to have a convincing alibi for that time, not even Inspector bloody Bridget Hart, who, incidentally knew every single person of interest in the case and was even in the chapel service, probably just a matter of hours after the murder took place.'

He paused for breath, then launched back into his summary, which seemed to Jake more like an extended rant. 'Also, the placing of the eyeballs in the soup. Again, anyone might have been able to carry this out, since the soup bowls were left unattended for most of the afternoon. However, the kitchen and serving staff seem to have had the greatest window of opportunity here.'

Ffion raised a hand to say something, but Baxter waved her down in annoyance before continuing. 'Those are the facts. What we're missing so far is any real evidence that links those facts to a possible suspect. Fingerprints, DNA samples, footprints, clothing fibres, strands of hair, phone records.' Baxter reeled them off on his fingers like a litany. 'We don't have a single bloody one of them.'

Ffion raised her hand again.

'Not now,' growled Baxter through gritted teeth.

He swept his dark gaze around the room as if holding his team responsible for the absence of physical evidence. He lifted a pile of papers from the desk and held it up for all to see. 'Most of you have spent the last five hours interviewing the guests and the various college staff. I've interviewed several key witnesses myself, including both Meg Collins and Tina Mackenzie. And this is the result. Ink and paper. Questions and answers. Good, solid police work. What does it prove? Nothing. Not a God-damn thing.'

Jake wondered if Baxter was going to allow anyone else to contribute to this so-called team meeting, or if they were just supposed to sit there like idiots. Maybe he just wanted an audience for his soliloquy. It was a very different approach to DI Hart who always welcomed and encouraged suggestions from her team and was willing to listen to fresh ideas. Jake turned to Ryan, who shrugged. On his other side, Harry just looked bewildered.

Ffion raised her hand for a third time.

'What?' demanded Baxter. 'What is it?'

'It's just that, I wonder if we should re-interview Bella Williams?'

'What for?'

'Well, it's just that she's one of the group of people who shared a house with Alexia Petrakis during her second year. She's obviously a person of interest.'

Baxter consulted his notes. 'According to this, DC Hughes, you interviewed her yourself this morning, together with DS Hooper.'

'That's correct, sir,' said Ffion. 'But I wondered if you ought to speak to her again yourself, given your greater experience at conducting interviews.'

'Don't try to flatter me, Constable. I promise you, I'm immune to all kinds of flattery.'

'I wasn't, sir. I was just trying to be helpful.'

Baxter seemed to be thinking her suggestion through. 'You do have a point. Maybe I'll –'

A knock on the door brought him to a juddering halt mid-sentence.

'What now?' bellowed Baxter. 'Who is it?'

The door opened and Bridget walked into the room. It seemed to Jake that she took in the scene at a glance – the various detectives perched on the sofas and chairs, and DI Baxter holding forth like a Shakespearean actor – and understood immediately what was going on.

Baxter looked livid at her sudden intrusion. 'DI Hart, I told you –'

'I'm sorry to disturb you,' said Bridget, not sounding particularly sorry to Jake's ears. 'But I've just had a very interesting conversation with the college chaplain.' She motioned for the chaplain to follow her into the room. 'I think you should hear what he has to say, and then go and speak to the warden, Dr Harper.'

★

Bridget couldn't help smiling to herself as she made her way back to her room. The look on Baxter's face when she'd ushered the chaplain into the room to tell his story had been priceless. Baxter had made it clear that he was leading the investigation and would not tolerate any interference from her – had, in fact ordered her to keep out of the case – but she'd just supplied him with a valuable new lead that he was duty-bound to follow up. In fact, she was a little surprised to discover that he hadn't spoken to the warden already. After all, the eyeballs had been found in his soup. That had to be significant.

She pulled the desk chair over to the window of her room and watched the tourists strolling along Dead Man's Walk as she called Chloe on her phone. It was strange to think that those people were free to come and go as they pleased, whereas she and the other guests at the gaudy were trapped inside, like animals in a zoo.

'Hi, Mum. All right?'

'I'm fine. I was calling to find out how you were. Is everything okay? Did you get back from London all right? Did Uncle James pick you up from the train station?'

'No,' said Chloe. 'I was abducted by men in black balaclavas who took me to a secret underground lair and held me hostage.' She paused. 'Just kidding. Of course I'm all right. To answer your questions, I'm good, yes and yes. Stop panicking. It's all cool.'

Bridget felt a weight of anxiety lift from her shoulders. As long as she knew Chloe was safe, everything else was bearable.

'Did you have a nice time in London?' Bridget braced herself for the worst. She was torn between a desire to know that everything had gone well, and fear of hearing that her ex-husband and his new girlfriend were the coolest people ever.

'It was so amazing. We went to the Sky Garden restaurant and, ohmygod, you could see for miles right across London in all directions, and we had cocktails before dinner in the bar that's more like a nightclub.'

'Cocktails?'

'Don't panic, Mum, strictly non-alcoholic. For me, anyway. Then for dinner I had roast quail followed by cod with mussels and then black fig and orange Bakewell tart. It was delicious! But Aunt Vanessa says there's been a murder at Merton College. You're not in any danger are you?'

Bridget marvelled at the ability of the young to switch effortlessly from one subject to another without pausing for breath.

'I'm fine,' she told her daughter. 'And, no, I'm not in any danger.'

'So when are you coming home? I'm not going to have to stay with Aunt Vanessa overnight, am I?'

'I'm not entirely sure,' admitted Bridget, secretly pleased to hear that Chloe would rather be at home with her than spend another night away. 'But I'm sure I'll be allowed to leave this evening once the police have finished interviewing everyone.'

'Who was it who was killed?' asked Chloe. 'Was it someone you knew?' There was a ghoulish interest in her voice which Bridget didn't like.

'Yes, it was actually. It was an old friend of mine. Someone I used to share a house with.'

'Oh, God, I'm really sorry.' Chloe sounded quite upset. 'That must be horrible for you.'

'It was a bit of a shock,' said Bridget. 'But I hadn't kept in touch with her. I don't suppose we were really friends anymore.'

'Still…'

'Anyway,' said Bridget, changing the subject, 'stay with Aunt Vanessa for now and I'll pick you up later this evening. I'll let you know if there's a change of plan.'

'Okay.' Chloe was back to her usual cheerful self. 'I think we're going to take the dog for a walk now.'

'All right. Take care. Speak to you soon.' Bridget ended the call and put her phone back in her bag. She longed now to just go home and see her daughter again. With any luck, Baxter would have his initial enquiries wrapped up very soon.

CHAPTER 15

A gravel path led from the Fellows' Gardens to the rear entrance of Dr Brendan Harper's lodgings, the complimentary residence that came with the job of warden. Baxter had asked Ffion once again to join him for the interview, and since there was no need for any "woman-to-woman" assistance this time, she speculated that Baxter might have begun to appreciate her abilities as a detective. Or maybe he was such a dinosaur that he thought only a woman would be capable of taking notes during an interview. Either way, she was pleased to have been asked.

She'd noticed the look of relief on Jake and Ryan's faces that they didn't have to sit in with DI Baxter. It was no fun working alongside someone who didn't appreciate other people's input. Ffion wasn't unduly concerned though. She was glad of an opportunity to observe the warden at close quarters. It had been obvious to her from the very start that the warden was somehow involved in the mystery, otherwise why had the eyeballs turned up in his soup?

The warden's wife was pruning rose bushes in

their private garden behind the lodgings, ruthlessly cutting back the thorny stems to just a foot above ground level in preparation for winter. At the crunch of their feet on the gravel, she stood up and turned to face them, secateurs in hand.

It was the first time for Ffion to see her. Throughout the investigation, both the warden and his wife had been noticeably conspicuous by their absence. Now, close up, Ffion was struck by Mrs Harper's exquisite beauty and elegance. She knew from her background reading that Dr Harper had first met the woman who would become his wife during an archaeological dig near Cairo. Yasmin Harper came from a wealthy Egyptian family, and was the daughter of a government minister. Quite how the couple had become acquainted, Ffion didn't know, but they had apparently fallen in love at first sight, got married six months later and had returned to live in England. At least, that was what Yasmin Harper had told the writer of a celebrity gossip magazine, when recently interviewed.

'Inspector Baxter, how may I help you?' Mrs Harper appeared very relaxed and at ease in her Oxford environment, yet Ffion sensed that she did not welcome this intrusion into her personal realm. She took up position on the path before them like a guardian.

'Is your husband in?' asked Baxter gruffly. 'I'd like a word with him.'

Yasmin Harper raised one perfectly-pencilled

eyebrow at the inspector's poor manners. 'You'd like to speak to Brendan?' She glanced from Baxter to Ffion and back to Baxter again. 'Is there some kind of problem? Perhaps it's a matter I can help you with?'

Ffion could sense Baxter's impatience coming off him in waves. 'No, Mrs Harper, there's no problem. But I'd appreciate it if we could speak to your husband straight away please.'

'Well, yes, of course.' She pulled off a pair of leather gardening gloves. 'Come on inside. I'll see if I can find him for you.'

She led them through a spacious kitchen – Ffion noticed the old-fashioned Aga that was pumping out a gentle but persistent heat, surely not an environmentally-friendly way to cook in this day and age – into the hallway and then through into a comfortably furnished lounge. 'If you don't mind waiting here a moment, I'll go and find Brendan.'

Despite Yasmin Harper's surface ease and charm, Ffion detected an undercurrent of anxiety at this unannounced arrival of the detectives in her house. Perhaps that was understandable – nobody welcomed a surprise visit by the police – but perhaps it betrayed a deeper-rooted concern. Ffion wondered if she should mention it to Baxter, but on reflection decided that it didn't seem solid enough for him to take seriously.

Baxter paced the room, picking up and scowling at photographs of Brendan Harper on archaeological digs, looking suntanned and rugged. Ffion spotted the couple's wedding photograph in a silver frame on a side table. They'd married in the college chapel by the looks of it, him looking handsome in black tails, her in a shimmering silk gown with an Egyptian tiara on her head that made her look like Cleopatra. Her bridal bouquet contained an exotic collection of lilies and orchids.

The door opened and the photogenic couple appeared in person. 'Inspector,' said Dr Harper, striding across the room, his hand outstretched, a smile fixed to his face. He was even better looking in the flesh than in his TV appearances. He was a good two inches taller than Baxter, and in much better shape, despite being of a similar age, and his energetic physicality seemed to fill the room. Here was the leader of the pack, staking his claim to his territory.

Baxter too, was ready for combat. In the presence of the renowned archaeologist and college warden, he immediately pulled himself straighter, squaring his round shoulders and thrusting his chest forwards. The two men shook hands, engaging – in Ffion's opinion – in a quite excessive amount of eye contact.

Honestly, she thought, it was like watching two alpha males readying for a fight. Why couldn't they just discuss the matter without this needless posturing? Unless, of course, the warden had something to hide and was trying to cow his opponent into submission before he had the chance to deliver a fatal blow – or question.

Yasmin Harper hovered on the edge of the room, trying, but not quite succeeding, to appear relaxed and unconcerned by the display of macho behaviour.

'So, what can I do for you?' asked the warden, jumping in and taking charge of the conversation.

Baxter looked around the room. 'Do you mind if we take a seat?'

'Of course not. Where are my manners? Can I offer you a tea or a coffee? Perhaps a glass of water?'

'No, no,' said Baxter dismissively. 'I just want to talk.' He located a deep armchair and flopped down into it, pulling out his notebook as Ffion had seen him do at the beginning of every interview. She took a seat on a nearby sofa and readied her own notebook and pen.

The Harpers sat down opposite, Dr Harper making a show of casually crossing his legs and leaning back with his arms outstretched, his wife perching next to him, her eyes not leaving Baxter for one second.

'How is your investigation proceeding, Inspector?' asked Harper.

'As expected.' Baxter continued to page through his extensive notes. Eventually he looked up. 'Dr Harper, I understand that you are a world expert in ancient cultures and civilizations. Is that correct?'

Harper seemed pleasantly bemused by the

question. 'That's very kind of you to say so, Inspector. That is my area of expertise, yes.'

'Such as?'

'I beg your pardon?'

'Can you give me some examples of the kind of civilizations you study?'

'Ah, I see. Well, the field of ancient history covers the entire timeline from the very beginning of recorded history up to the beginning of the medieval period, but my particular interest is in the pre-Christian Near East and Mediterranean. The Romans, the Greeks, the Egyptians of course' – he smiled at his wife – 'the Persians, the Phoenicians…'

'The Phoenicians?' enquired Baxter. 'I don't know anything about them.'

'Ah, yes. Not many people do. What have the Phoenicians ever done for us, eh?' joked the warden.

Baxter regarded him without any apparent amusement.

The warden's jovial manner faltered, but he ploughed on gamely. 'Their civilization was based in the coastal cities of modern-day Lebanon, but they were great sailors, spreading their culture all around the Mediterranean coast. Their greatest legacy was the Phoenician alphabet, which formed the basis of the Roman alphabet, and therefore our own modern system of writing.'

'Very good,' said Baxter. 'Now can you explain to me why someone would want to send you a gift of two eyeballs?'

The warden's relaxed manner flickered for only a heartbeat. 'As I told you on Saturday evening, I haven't the faintest idea why anyone would do such a thing.'

Yasmin Harper wrapped her arms around her willowy frame. 'It was quite clearly the deranged act of a madman. I find it extraordinary that you haven't yet identified the person responsible, Inspector.'

Baxter seemed irritated by the interruption. His gaze flicked to her for a moment before returning to Brendan Harper. 'Dr Harper, are you aware that the deceased was planning to write an article about you for the newspapers?'

'No, I wasn't aware of that. I have no idea what such an article might be about, but from the sort of articles she normally wrote, I suppose it's reasonable to assume it was unlikely to be a flattering piece about my contribution to the world of archaeology?'

'I never make assumptions,' said Baxter. 'However, in this case even Miss Petrakis appears to have had some qualms about the piece she intended to write. In fact she was of the opinion that publication of her article might wreck your chances of becoming vice chancellor, if not your entire academic career.'

The warden batted away the suggestion with a faint smile. 'Inspector, I find that a fanciful notion. My past is an open book. There is nothing I have done that might cause me any concern, and certainly nothing that could potentially damage my career in the way you describe.'

Ffion turned to study the warden's wife who returned her stare with an inscrutable look. The two women locked gazes for several seconds before Baxter began to speak again.

'It would seem that Miss Petrakis felt a strong sense of loyalty towards you. She was conflicted over whether or not to publish this damaging article –'

'Allegedly damaging,' interjected the warden softly.

'– and felt the need to take guidance before proceeding. Why did she feel such a strong sense of obligation, do you think?'

'I really have no idea. Perhaps because she knew there was no truth in this story?'

'Might it be,' continued Baxter, 'that she felt indebted to you because you helped her out in some significant way at the beginning of her journalistic career?'

'Well, it's true that I did put in a good word for her when she was first applying for a job in journalism. I have contacts in the media via my television work. You know how it is.'

The expression on Baxter's face suggested that he had no idea how the world of media operated. 'So you introduced her to influential people. That's just the sort of break that can make the difference between a career rocketing off the starting block and plodding along at a mundane pace. I wonder what made you so generous with your help?'

'Are you suggesting some kind of impropriety, Inspector? I can assure you that every tutor does their best to help their students when they transition from academia to the world of work.'

Baxter's face took on the look of a hound that had scented blood. 'But Alexia Petrakis never was your student, was she, Dr Harper? She was a student of English Language and Literature. Nothing to do with you, whatsoever. So I'm interested to know whether she had some kind of hold over you. Did she?'

The warden smiled politely. 'Certainly not. At the time Alexia completed her degree, I was senior tutor at the college. My duty was for the welfare of all students, not just those in my own subject.' He looked ostentatiously at his watch – a gold Cartier, Ffion noted. 'Do you have many more questions, Inspector? I don't wish to be rude, but I have a busy evening ahead.'

'A few more,' said Baxter, his feathers unruffled. He turned another page of his notes. 'You hosted tea yesterday afternoon in the TS Eliot Theatre between four o'clock and five thirty. And you were present at the chapel service from six thirty to just before seven, and then at dinner in hall from seven o'clock. Can you give me an account of your movements during the rest of the afternoon?'

'Yes, let me see,' said the warden. 'I ate lunch in college at around one o'clock with several members of the college's governing body. Afterwards I returned here to write my speech for the evening. A speech that – regretfully – I didn't have the opportunity to give.'

'Perhaps you can use it for another occasion, sir,' said Baxter in a tone that suggested he didn't care one jot that the warden had wasted his time speechwriting.

'Yes, perhaps. Then, as you say, I hosted tea until five thirty.'

'Brendan sees it as an important part of his duty to host these kinds of events,' said Mrs Harper. 'Maintaining good relations with our alumni is one of the college's main methods of fundraising.' She trailed off under Baxter's glare, as if aware that she was providing extraneous information.

'That still leaves one hour before you attended the service in chapel,' prompted Baxter.

'Well,' said Mrs Harper, 'you were here with me all that time, darling. Weren't you?'

The warden looked grateful for his wife's prompt. 'Yes, absolutely. We were here, together.'

'Alone?' said Baxter.

'Together,' repeated the warden crossly.

'So in other words, for a whole two hour period before tea and another hour afterwards, you were alone or with only your wife as company?'

'I suppose, so, yes. Is there anything else you need to ask me, Inspector?'

'Just one more thing. Are you aware of anyone

who may have wished to harm Alexia Petrakis?'

'Kill her you mean? No, certainly not.'

Baxter stood up. 'Thank you for your time.'

The warden rose too. 'Actually, I have a question for you.'

'Yes?'

'When is everyone going to be allowed to go home? Many people have already had to make alterations to their travel plans. Some of our guests have travelled a long way to be here, you know. Some have even flown in from overseas. They have flights to catch.'

'I'm afraid that can't be helped, said Baxter unapologetically. 'But I expect to conclude my initial round of interviews by this evening.'

The warden grunted something that sounded like acceptance, if not actual approval.

'We'll see ourselves out,' said Baxter, heading towards the door and gesturing for Ffion to follow him. 'In the meantime, don't go anywhere. I might want to speak to you again.'

Ffion rose quickly. As she was leaving, she sneaked a final glance at the warden's wife. Yasmin Harper's features were worried and drawn, and there was a noticeable tremor in her elegant fingers. Ffion followed Baxter out through the back door.

★

It was a minute or so before Yasmin Harper crossed the room to where her husband stood with one hand leaning against the mantelpiece. Despite telling the inspector that he had work to be getting on with, Brendan hadn't moved since DI Baxter and his colleague had left. He was staring at an old photograph of himself, working on a dig, out in the hot sun. In the photograph he was smiling and relaxed, holding up a small statuette for the camera and obviously delighted with his find. How triumphant and fearless his young face looked.

Yasmin reached out to her husband, running her hand down the length of his spine. The tension in his muscles made her feel as if she was caressing rock, as smooth and unyielding as the stones he had once unearthed in the desert of her homeland. She leaned her head close to his left ear.

'Do you think he knows?'

Brendan turned towards her, his face grave. Perhaps for the first time she noticed how lined his forehead had become in the years since they had first met. Although he was more than a decade her senior, she had never before thought of him as old. He had seemed as unchanging and eternal to her as the desert itself. He cupped her cheek in his hand. 'What can he possibly know? He was bluffing, trying to trick me into letting something slip.'

'We can't afford even the tiniest error now, darling. We've worked so hard, for such a long time. This is the most critical moment.'

Brendan's hand moved back to his side. 'Do

you think I don't know that?'

'Of course not.' She could hear him breathing heavily, as if he had just returned from one of his tennis matches, not been sitting on a sofa, engaged in mere conversation.

'What about the journalist and her article?' she asked.

'She can't write it now, can she?'

Yasmin had nothing to say to that. Her husband had never once lied to her... but that didn't mean she knew everything about him. And he didn't know everything about her, either. Some questions were best left unasked.

As for the police, Brendan was probably right. The inspector was fishing for information, nothing more.

Then she remembered the look on the face of the young constable who had accompanied the inspector. DC Ffion Hughes had said nothing the whole time she was here. Yet her almond-shaped green eyes hadn't missed a single thing.

CHAPTER 16

'So, how are you getting on with Baxter?' asked Jake, when he next bumped into Ffion. He couldn't say that he envied her, accompanying the DI to interview the warden. Jake didn't generally get on well with authority figures, and Baxter plus the college warden were the two people in college he'd least like to spend time with. Ffion, on the other hand, was the person he'd most hoped to see. To say that he'd bumped into her wasn't strictly accurate. He'd been loitering in the dining hall for some time, keeping a look out for her. He hoped she didn't know that.

'Baxter's not as bad as his bark,' she said. 'And he's not as stupid as he first seems. In fact, I'm quite getting to like him.'

'Really?'

'Yeah, he's okay in a rude, sexist, obnoxious kind of way.'

'Uh, right.' Jake wondered what was going on there. Ffion had set him a challenge of showing he could be a sensitive guy who didn't conform to traditional male stereotypes. But was she secretly attracted to the worst kind of macho behaviour? The idea that she might find Baxter remotely appealing was pretty gross.

'It's Ryan who's been the worst,' continued Ffion.

Now that news was more to Jake's liking. Although Ffion had blown Ryan off when he'd asked her out one time, Jake couldn't quite dismiss the idea of Ryan as a potential rival. Even though the guy was obviously a dick.

'Yeah, he basically treats me as if I'm his secretary, getting me to take notes. I've had enough of his sarky wisecracks too.'

'I admired the way you spoke up to Baxter at the briefing,' said Jake. 'No one else dared say a word.'

'No. They didn't, did they? So how was your weekend in Leeds? Did you have a good time?'

Jake wondered if this was some kind of test. He was still a little embarrassed about his mates' behaviour in the pub, and regretted the fact that Ffion had phoned him when he was obviously out getting hammered in town. He tried a diversionary tactic. 'I took my parents out to the local gardens for Mum's birthday. I bought them tea and scones for a treat.'

That seemed to amuse Ffion. 'Well, how thoughtful. Was that your mum I could hear in the pub when I called you?'

'Uh, no. Listen,' he said hastily, 'I've been doing a lot of thinking.'

'Oh yes?' Her expression suggested she found

that hard to believe.

'Yeah, you know. About what you told me.'

'About me being bisexual?'

'Yeah. I just wanted to say that I'm cool with that.'

'Cool. And you're not just saying that because you think it might be an opportunity to try out something kinky?'

'No!' Why did Ffion always have to bring him down this way? Every time he tried to say something serious to her, she seemed to go out of her way to humiliate him. Maybe it was some kind of self-defence mechanism. 'I'm saying it because it's true.'

'Well, good. I'm glad. Then that's half our problem solved.'

'Is it? Good.' He wondered what exactly their problem was, and which half of it was still to be solved.

Ffion was happy to spell it out for him. 'The question still to be answered,' she said, 'is whether I'm cool with you being cool.' She gave him a mischievous wink. 'I'll keep you posted on that.'

★

There was a palpable sense of discontent amongst the guests as they gathered for dinner in the hall that evening. Like holidaymakers at an airport whose flight had been delayed beyond all bounds of reasonableness, they were starting to demand when they might be permitted to leave. Even the news of Tina's public humiliation had now been dissected and discussed to the point of boredom, and no longer provided a diversion from the growing sense of frustration.

Word had got round that Bridget worked for the police, and people seemed to expect her to know what was going on.

'I'm sorry,' she said on more than one occasion, 'but I know about as much as you do. However, I'm sure it won't be much longer now.' Although knowing DI Baxter, who was to say?

She was just as eager as anyone else to get away. She still had to collect Chloe from Vanessa's.

She joined Meg and Bella at the far end of one of the long tables. A handful of tutors, including Dr Irene Thomas, had gathered on high table, but there was no Latin grace this time. This wasn't a proper formal hall, given the circumstances. The butler was busily ordering his staff to serve plates of what looked suspiciously like yesterday's dinner menu hastily reconstituted into something indefinable. It certainly wouldn't win any Michelin stars. Bridget was reminded of the "bubble and squeak" her mother used to serve whenever she had leftover potatoes and cabbage.

'At least they've given us some wine with the meal,' said Meg, pouring herself a generous glass of white. 'Anyone else?' Both Bridget and Bella shook their heads. 'Please yourself,' said Meg. 'I honestly couldn't get through this hell without it.'

'Isn't Tina joining us?' asked Bridget. After the chat they'd had together in the garden that morning, Tina had seemed resigned to facing up to the consequences of her actions. She'd agreed to speak to DI Baxter, and obviously Baxter hadn't decided to arrest her, otherwise they'd have all been allowed to go home by now.

'I expect she's too ashamed to show her face after what appeared in this morning's papers,' said Meg.

'I bet she is,' said Bella, regarding the unidentifiable concoction on her fork with suspicion. 'I mean, lying to get a doctor struck off for malpractice is a pretty disgusting thing to do. Especially one working in paediatric cancer care.'

'That's lawyers for you,' said Meg bitterly. 'They're a ruthless bunch. Never mind the good that some of us are trying to do in the world.'

Bridget looked towards the door where a few latecomers were still arriving. Tina wasn't among them.

'Do you think she might have murdered Alexia?' asked Bella.

'Who knows?' said Meg. There was an unpleasant gloating in the way she asked the question, as if she hoped it were true. 'Whatever happens, I doubt her career will survive this news. She might even go to prison.' She leaned confidentially across the table and lowered her voice. 'I can tell you one thing. When I arrived in college yesterday afternoon, I saw Tina and Alexia arguing with each other in Front Quad. When they saw me, they both tried to pretend that nothing was the matter, but I'd heard enough to get the gist of the argument.'

'What?' said Bridget, her fork halfway to her mouth, astounded that this nugget of information had only just come to light. Tina had said nothing to her about an argument with Alexia yesterday afternoon. In fact, she'd categorically denied seeing Alexia at all.

'What were they arguing about?' asked Bella.

'Tina was accusing Alexia of betrayal. At the time, I had no idea what she meant, but with hindsight it seems obvious. They must have been discussing Alexia's newspaper article. Either Tina already knew about it, or Alexia was telling her. You know how Alexia loved to gloat. And an hour or so later she was dead. If that doesn't make Tina the prime suspect, I don't know what does.'

'Why didn't you mention this before?' asked Bridget. 'Did you tell DI Baxter about what you heard?'

'He didn't ask.'

'Well, you need to tell him. Urgently. This is hugely important information.'

Suddenly Bridget wasn't hungry anymore. When she had spoken to Tina in the Fellows' Garden, Tina had claimed not to have known anything about the planned article. But Meg's revelation shed a whole new light on the situation. If Tina had known all along that Alexia was working on an article about her, she had a very strong and obvious motive to have killed her. It would also explain why she had chosen to come to the gaudy despite her ongoing dispute with Meg. It also explained why she had made such barbed comments about Alexia in the bar on Saturday night.

Bridget needed to find Tina before she did anything stupid. She stood up from the table. 'I'm going to look for Tina. I'm worried about her.'

'You don't think she's done a runner, do you?' asked Bella.

'And left the college?' asked Meg, frowning. 'There are uniformed police guarding the gatehouse, but I suppose there are back ways out if you're desperate to escape.'

'The police don't actually have the power to force us to stay here against our will, do they?' asked Bella.

'No,' said Bridget. 'Not unless they decide to arrest everyone.' Knowing Baxter, that wasn't completely beyond the bounds of possibility. 'But they can be quite persuasive.'

'If I'd known that we were free to go,' said Meg, 'I might have left myself.'

'Do you want us to come with you?' asked Bella.

'No, it's all right. You stay here. I'll go and look for her. She's probably just moping in her room.'

★

Bridget hurried away before Meg or Bella could insist on joining her. Despite reassuring them that there was probably nothing wrong, she hadn't convinced herself of that. Tina had deliberately lied to her, and probably lied to Baxter too. And now she had vanished for a second time. Bridget had to find her, and quickly.

It was only when she left the dining hall that she realised she didn't know which room Tina was staying in.

Fortunately the porter appeared not to have heard of data protection and privacy rules. Or if he had, he'd decided they didn't apply to him. 'Tina Mackenzie? She's in Mob Quad,' he told Bridget cheerfully, giving her the staircase and room number.

'Thanks,' said Bridget.

She turned around to find Jake standing behind her. 'Evening, ma'am.'

'Hello, Jake. Have you got some news for me?' She set off across the quadrangle, talking as she walked.

'Not as such,' he said, falling into step beside her. With his long gait, he matched her pace with ease. 'But I thought you'd like to know that we've just about wrapped up here, and I think DI Baxter intends to release everyone in the next half hour or so.'

'Well, they'll be glad to hear that.' She continued to walk briskly across the quad, passing the entrance to the dining hall and continuing on to Patey's Quad.

'Going somewhere, ma'am?' inquired Jake.

'I am, actually. Perhaps you should come with me.'

'Ma'am?'

'It's probably nothing,' she said as they turned right into Mob Quad, 'but I'm a bit worried about a friend of mine. Tina Mackenzie.'

'The disgraced lawyer?'

'Yes,' said Bridget. She supposed that was how Tina would be thought of from now on. The rising star who had fallen from the heights and crashed to the ground in a heap of shame. 'She didn't show up at dinner, and I want to check that she's all right.'

'You think something might have happened to her?'

Bridget wondered what to tell her sergeant. She was only following a hunch, but Jake was a man with good down-to-earth common sense. She decided to tell him everything. 'I'm worried she might have tried to make a getaway. I just discovered that she knew in advance that Alexia was writing the newspaper article about her. In fact, the two of them were seen arguing about it just after they arrived in college yesterday.'

'You think she might be the murderer?' said Jake, picking up on her meaning.

'Let's just say that I want to reassure myself that she's in her room.'

'Of course,' said Jake. 'We should definitely look in on her.'

Another thought occurred to Bridget as they walked. Had the removal of Alexia's eyes been a message that her career built on exposing hidden secrets was now at an end?

With most of the guests at dinner, Mob Quad was quiet. A light shone out of the upstairs library window and Bridget wondered if Dr Thomas was up there, surrounded by her beloved books. Perhaps Bridget would drop in on her later, once she'd confirmed that Tina hadn't done anything stupid. If anyone could bring meaning and context to the ghastly events of the past twenty-four hours, then it was Dr Thomas with her honed analytical skills and her historian's perspective of mankind's tendency for self-destruction.

'This is the staircase,' said Bridget, stopping before one of the arched doorways. A light was showing through some closed curtains from an upstairs window. It looked as if Tina was most likely in her room after all.

Bridget led the way up the stairs and Jake followed. She paused outside Tina's room, listening. Like a lot of older college rooms, its doorway was fitted with two doors. The sturdy outer oak door stood open, pushed back against the wall, but the inner door was closed. All was quiet from within. Bridget tapped on the door.

There was no response. She knocked louder.

'Tina? Are you in there? It's me, Bridget.'

Silence.

Bridget's skin started to prickle. She tried the handle, but the door was locked. She hammered on the door. 'Tina, please open up. We need to talk.'

There was no response.

'I don't like this,' she said to Jake.

She had come here worried that Tina might try to run off, but now a worse fear gripped her. Might Tina have harmed herself in some way, or even tried to take her own life? Regardless of whether she had murdered Alexia, the shame of her professional downfall might have proved to be unbearable. Now that the thought had occurred to her, Bridget could have kicked herself for her own stupidity. Someone should have stayed with Tina at all times. Bridget herself should have stayed with her.

Jake was studying her intently. 'You really believe she might be the murderer?'

'Yes,' admitted Bridget, although it pained her to say so. 'And I fear for her safety.'

'In that case, please stand back, ma'am.'

She stepped aside and watched as Jake turned sideways and spun his right leg out, kicking at the door with the heel of his black boot. The wood splintered apart with a crack, and he reached through the gap to open the door from the inside, turning the key in the lock.

'Is that what they teach at police training

college these days?' asked Bridget.

'Ffion's shown me a few moves,' he said. 'Taekwondo.'

He pushed open the door and Bridget stepped through, Jake following close behind.

She braced herself to find Tina's body hanging from the ceiling, or lying in a pool of blood with her wrists cut. But nothing could have prepared her for the sight that actually met her eyes.

'Shit,' said Jake behind her. 'What the hell is this?'

'I've no idea,' said Bridget. She swayed on her feet and Jake steadied her shoulder with a firm hand.

'I need to call this in,' said Jake, taking his phone out of his pocket.

While Jake called Baxter to report what they'd found, Bridget tried to digest the scene in front of her. Tina was dead, all right. But she had certainly not taken her own life. Her body lay on the bed, neatly arranged with her arms folded across her chest. But there was nothing serene about the way she had been laid to rest. Where her ears should have been, two gaping holes stared back, dripping red blood onto the white linen sheets.

On the bedside locker was a plate of biscuits, an open bottle of Madeira wine and two glasses, one full, the other nearly empty. But that was not all. The killer had cut off Tina's ears and laid them neatly in the middle of the plate of biscuits. Propped up beside the wine bottle was a card on which had been printed the words, 'Hear no evil.'

CHAPTER 17

DI Baxter plodded up the staircase, breathless with effort and rage, clutching the wooden banister with his huge ham fist. 'DI Hart!' he bellowed when he reached the top. 'What are you doing here? I told you to keep away!'

Bridget regarded him with irritation. 'I was the one who discovered the body, together with Sergeant Derwent here.'

Jake stood beside her on the landing outside Tina's room. After finding the body and quickly checking to make sure that Tina was indeed dead, they had withdrawn from the room, leaving it untouched ready for the SOCO team to come and begin their careful examination. Bridget had been very grateful for Jake's solid presence while she waited for Baxter to arrive. The shock of discovering another of her old friends murdered was threatening to engulf her.

'You discovered the body?' Baxter looked like he was about to explode. His face had turned as dark as thunder and his eyebrows were bunched together in the middle of his brow. He jabbed a thick finger in Bridget's direction. 'Everywhere I go, you get there first. You were the first person on the scene at the first murder too.'

'Second,' corrected Bridget. 'It was the chaplain who found the body.'

'You were there when the eyeballs were discovered in the soup,' continued Baxter. 'You were friends with the first murder victim. You interviewed the butler immediately after I warned you off the investigation. You were the one who found the newspaper article, and the one who located Tina Mackenzie when no one else knew where she'd disappeared to.' He paused to take a few deep breaths. 'You were the one who the chaplain made his confession to, and now you've discovered a second murder victim, who, coincidentally was also a friend of yours.'

He stopped, red-faced, seeming to have run out of accusations to throw at her. Behind him on the staircase, Ffion and Ryan appeared, looking on in surprise.

Bridget matched Baxter's spluttering anger with a calm dignity. 'I think that maybe some sympathy is in order, and a "thank you" too. If it wasn't for me, you'd still be completely oblivious to the fact that a second murder has been committed.'

'I'm seriously considering having you arrested.'

'Don't be ridiculous,' snapped Bridget.

Jake stepped forward to defuse the tension. 'Sir, would you like to view the crime scene?'

Treating Bridget to one final glare, Baxter pushed past her to peer into the room beyond. 'Christ almighty. What the bloody hell happened here?'

Thirty seconds later he was back out on the landing, breathing heavily. 'Did you move anything?'

'No, sir,' said Jake.

'Nobody else has been in?'

'No.'

'Right then. SOCO have been informed of the situation and should be here any minute. Apart from them, no one goes in that room without my express permission, is that understood? DS Derwent, you stay here and guard that room. Don't move until I tell you. DS Hooper, DC Hughes, go and find Meg Collins and take her in for questioning at Kidlington. If she refuses to cooperate, arrest her on suspicion of murder. Do it now.'

'Yes, sir,' said Ryan, disappearing back down the stairs with Ffion.

'Why are you taking Meg in?' asked Bridget.

'Why? Because she had a clear motive for both murders.'

'What?'

'Do I need to spell it out? Alexia Petrakis slept with her husband, and Tina Mackenzie was engaged in a damaging lawsuit against her company!' He shook his head. 'Why am I even justifying myself to you? How many times have I told you, you're not involved in this investigation. Now get out of my sight before I lose my temper!'

'I think you lost your temper some while back,' said Bridget. 'And I hope that once you've calmed down you'll realise that you owe me an apology.'

'Apology?' Baxter's face was almost purple.

'In the meantime, what should I tell the other guests?'

'Tell them?'

'They were hoping that they'd be free to leave the college anytime now.'

'Don't you tell them anything,' said Baxter. 'I'll tell them myself.'

'Tell them what?'

'That my officers will be re-interviewing every single one of them. Someone must know something. I want to know where they were, what they were doing and what they were thinking. No one goes anywhere until they've accounted for every minute of today.'

'You intend to hold them here for a second night?'

'I'll hold them for as long as it bloody well takes.'

CHAPTER 18

It didn't take a huge amount of police effort to track down Meg Collins. When Ffion and Ryan arrived in the dining hall, she was chatting to other guests, and steadily working her way through a bottle of white wine. A Chablis Grand Cru, Ffion noted in passing. The college was obviously going the extra mile to keep the frustrated guests comfortable. Meg appeared relaxed and happy and certainly didn't give the impression of a woman who had just carried out a vicious and violent murder.

Or did she? Ffion had encountered some cold-blooded killers in her time with the police, and had read plenty more about serial killers in her own background reading. Taking the life of another human being wasn't as easy as most people imagined. But taking a second was a whole lot easier. Some things got simpler with practice.

'Meg Collins, would you please come with us?' said Ryan.

Meg's eyes narrowed suspiciously. 'What for?'

'We'd like you to answer some questions, if

you don't mind.'

'I've already been interviewed by DI Baxter at some length. I've told him everything I know.'

'He'd like to talk to you again. At Kidlington this time.'

'Where?'

'The police station.'

'You're arresting me?'

'I hope that won't be necessary,' said Ryan. 'I'm sure you'd much rather cooperate fully with the investigation.'

Meg downed the rest of her wine and fixed him with an angry glare. 'Don't be so sure of anything, young man.'

Ffion wondered if she was going to try and make a run for it. If she did, she wouldn't get far. Ffion was a keen runner, not to mention being a black belt in Taekwondo. She didn't get to use her skills very often in her job, but she was always looking for an opportunity.

But before Meg had a chance to do anything, a voice boomed out across the dining hall. Baxter had appeared. 'Ladies and gentlemen, I have an announcement to make. Unfortunately there has been a further development in the case. Consequently it will be necessary for everyone to be re-interviewed.'

A chorus of indignation and fury greeted this news. Baxter waited until the protests died down before speaking again. 'I cannot say with any certainty at this time how long you will be required to stay in the college, but I anticipate that it will be until tomorrow lunchtime at the earliest. I'm sure that the college will have no problem providing you with a second night's accommodation. If you have any questions, I suggest you direct them to the college authorities.'

The howls of protest began again as soon as he had finished speaking, but at that moment the warden appeared at the entrance to the hall. 'Inspector, may I please have a word with you?'

The two men disappeared briefly into the kitchen for a hurried conversation, before emerging a minute later. The warden's face looked pale. 'As the Inspector has said, the college will be happy to provide everyone with continued accommodation for as long as necessary. I hope that everyone here will recognise the seriousness of this matter and cooperate fully with the police enquiry. Please see me or one of the other members of staff if you have any specific requests or require assistance with travel arrangements. In the meantime the college will do everything it can to make you comfortable.'

The hall echoed with frustrated moans.

'And one last thing,' said the warden. 'The Inspector has assured me that in the interests of everyone's safety, uniformed police will be stationed throughout the college and will be on patrol during the night. I would advise you all to return to your rooms and to be careful who you admit. Thank you for your understanding.'

The complaints were immediately replaced by the feverish buzz of speculation.

'What's happened?' asked Meg, turning back to the two detectives.

'Another murder,' said Ffion in a low voice.

Meg was speechless for a moment. Then she whispered, 'Tina?'

Ffion nodded.

Meg sat in silence, recovering her composure. Then she rose to her feet, gathering her handbag. 'Well, it looks like I don't have much choice in the matter. Let's go to Kidlington, then. At least it will make a change from this place.'

★

The kitchen at Thames Valley Police headquarters in Kidlington was no match for the dining hall at Merton. There was certainly no butler to bring Ffion a cup of tea. Instead she made herself a mug of matcha green tea, suspending the pyramid-shaped teabag by its piece of string and swirling it around the boiling water. The finely ground powder of tea leaves was specially farmed and processed to maximise production of theanine and caffeine. Ffion had read that it was used by Japanese Zen monks to stimulate wakefulness, and controlled experiments had proven its ability to reduce stress and enhance cognitive function. It had been a long day and it was going to be a long evening.

It was a good job she didn't have anyone special in her life right now. In fact there hadn't been anyone special for some time. People assumed that it was easy to find a partner when you were bisexual. There was double the choice, right? But in fact she'd found the opposite was true.

Online dating was just about impossible for a bisexual woman. Ticking the box that indicated she was interested in relationships with either men or women simply led to an avalanche of attention from trolls. She had lost count of the number of men who'd messaged her on dating apps, asking if she was up for a threesome. Jerks.

It was far safer to try to get to know someone in the real world before considering the possibility of a more intimate relationship. But her job as a police detective often led to overtime and anti-social hours. It was difficult enough for her to maintain her exercise regime, let alone the degree of commitment required to support a serious romantic entanglement. Her ideal partner would be someone who understood that, and who perhaps even shared a similar hectic lifestyle. Another police officer, even. Jake Derwent, for instance.

She hadn't considered Jake as a prospective boyfriend when she'd first met him. He was good-looking, although not perhaps in an obvious way. He was a little too tall for comfort, and his long arms and legs reminded her of a gangling teenager. His ginger hair and thick beard wouldn't be to every woman's taste either. And then there was that ridiculous car he drove – a bright orange Subaru that clashed so badly with his hair and beard. But Ffion was attracted to off-beat, distinctive looks. She cultivated an unconventional appearance herself.

All the same, his initial behaviour had made her think that he was the usual stereotypical blokeish male she'd encountered so many times before. Beer, football and sex were all most men thought about, and Jake certainly spent a lot of time thinking about those three topics. But she'd known him a few months now, and he was growing on her. He wasn't as coarse as she'd first imagined, certainly not when compared to guys like Ryan.

Had she been unfair towards him? Had she actually been prejudiced? The thought made her feel rather uncomfortable.

He'd obviously been thinking about her too. A lot. What had he told her? That he was cool with her being bisexual. Well, that put him ahead of a lot of guys, who found it either kinky or intimidating to meet a woman who didn't think that a man was necessarily her only romantic option, or even her best one. He was trying hard to please her, and she had to admit that was a nice feeling. She could grow to like it.

But Jake was back at Merton, guarding the scene of the second murder. She shouldn't have allowed her thoughts to drift to him. Right now, she needed to stay focussed on the job in hand

and the interview with Meg Collins. This was her second chance to undertake the woman-to-woman role that Baxter had assigned to her. Perhaps she would even be able to rise to the challenge and deliver the one insightful question that would reveal whether Meg really had killed off two of her former friends. She hoped the matcha tea would work its magic soon and bring her back up to peak performance.

She carried her mug through to the near-deserted office and booted up her computer. There was something she wanted to look up before the interview started. There ought to be time enough. Meg's lawyer had only just arrived and was currently in interview room two talking to her client.

Through the glass walls of Chief Superintendent Grayson's office she could see Baxter updating the Chief Super on the latest gruesome turn of events. Grayson was seated behind his desk, a look of revulsion fixed to his normally stony face. Baxter, with his back to her, was on his feet. From his hand gestures she guessed he was explaining about Tina Mackenzie's ears.

As soon as her computer sprang to life, she switched her attention to the screen, quickly searching for the information she sought. It took a bit of digging online before she found what she'd been looking for. It was just as she'd expected. She printed it off with a sense of satisfaction, just as Grayson's glass door swung open.

Baxter marched out, looking grim. Ffion wasn't too surprised at that. Two gruesome murders in two days and not much to show in the way of evidence, apart from a pair of eyeballs and now a pair of ears. It was tempting to speculate what might be next. A nose?

No doubt the Chief Super had given Baxter a hard grilling and would be demanding results quickly.

'Is that lawyer here yet?' asked Baxter irritably, pushing his jacket sleeve up his wrist to look at his watch.

'She arrived ten minutes ago, sir,' said Ffion. 'She's with her client now.'

'She?' The look on the DI's face told her clearly what he was thinking. Not another bloody woman. But even he had the sense not to express his thoughts out loud.

'Should we leave them a little while longer, sir?'

'No.' Baxter treated her to a scowl. 'They've had ten minutes. That's more than enough. Let's get this show on the road.' He grabbed his papers from his desk and headed towards the door. Ffion picked up her tea and notebook and followed him to the interview room.

CHAPTER 19

Meg's lawyer was a diminutive Indian woman who Ffion had not met before. She introduced herself as Ms Gupta.

Ms Gupta was scrupulously attired in a striped business suit, and was so short that her elbows barely reached the level of the table. Her sharp bird-like eyes studied Baxter and Ffion in minutest detail as they took their places across the table. Next to her sat Meg Collins: large, flamboyantly dressed, and brooding like a gorilla preparing for a brawl. The contrast between the two women could not have been more striking.

'I have some questions for you, Inspector,' said Ms Gupta before Baxter had even had a chance to open his file and start proceedings. She had a very precise way of speaking, enunciating every word crisply and cleanly.

Baxter clearly didn't enjoy having the initiative taken away from him. 'Yes?'

'Is my client under arrest?'

'No. Ms Collins is not currently under arrest. However –'

'So she is here voluntarily and is free to leave

at any time,' interrupted Ms Gupta.

'Yes. I was about to explain that. However –'

'Do you intend, therefore, to interview her under caution?'

'If you will allow me to speak,' said Baxter through gritted teeth, 'I will tell you.'

Ms Gupta nodded as if she had expected nothing less. But she'd got her firing shot in first and shown that she was not to be messed with. Ffion liked her already.

Baxter shuffled his papers on the desk in front of him, marshalling his thoughts after the rude interruption. 'I will interview Ms Collins under caution and I strongly recommend that she chooses to cooperate and help us fully with our enquiries.'

'She is already fully cooperating,' pointed out Ms Gupta.

'Yes,' said Baxter, who clearly didn't think the same of the feisty solicitor.

'In this case,' declared Ms Gupta, 'you have reason to suspect her of committing a crime, but you lack sufficient evidence to charge her.'

'That's correct,' agreed Baxter. 'Is it all right if I say something now?'

'Please do,' said Ms Gupta.

Baxter started the recorder, named all those present, and read Meg her rights, asking her if she understood them.

'Of course.'

'Yesterday afternoon, Miss Alexia Petrakis was found strangled to death in the chapel of Merton

College. Today, Miss Tina Mackenzie was found murdered in her room.'

'Was Miss Mackenzie also strangled?' enquired Ms Gupta.

Baxter glared at her. 'I will disclose any relevant information at a time of my own choosing.'

When arresting Meg, Ffion hadn't mentioned the manner of the second murder, and Meg hadn't asked, a fact that struck Ffion as odd.

She also hadn't revealed that the victim's ears had been removed. That particular detail was troubling Ffion greatly. First eyes, now ears. The obvious symbolism of the body parts suggested that the murderer was sending a definite message, even if Ffion couldn't yet work out what it meant. Hear no evil. What was it that Tina Mackenzie had heard? What had Alexia Petrakis seen?

Baxter had obviously decided to go straight for the jugular. 'Both women were well known to you, Ms Collins. You were at university with them and shared a house together during your second year. Both victims had wronged you. Alexia Petrakis conducted an affair with your husband and broke up your marriage. Tina Mackenzie was pursuing a lawsuit against your company, seeking several million pounds of damages on behalf of a client. The college gaudy gave you the perfect opportunity to kill both of your enemies. Having returned to their former college for the weekend intending to enjoy themselves they would have let their guard down. You took advantage of that to attack them both in the most brutal manner possible.' He jabbed his ball-point pen in her direction. 'Means, motive and opportunity. You had all three.'

'That's ridiculous,' protested Meg. 'I did nothing of the sort.'

'Your story is pure conjecture,' said Ms Gupta.

Baxter consulted his notes. 'In the interview this morning you told me that your train arrived at Oxford station at two forty-five on Saturday afternoon. You then took a taxi from the station to the college and signed in just after three.'

'That's correct.'

'You then claim that you made a call to your office before attending tea in the TS Eliot Theatre at four o'clock.'

'Yes, I did.'

'After tea you returned to your room, made some more phone calls and got ready for dinner at seven.'

'Yes, that's exactly what I did,' said Meg.

'Where is this going?' asked Ms Gupta.

'I'm coming to that,' said Baxter. 'We have spoken to colleagues at your office in Cambridge. They have no recollection of you phoning them yesterday afternoon.'

'That's because I phoned my London office.'

Baxter turned a page in his notebook. 'We have established that you did speak to a colleague in London at around three fifteen. However, that conversation lasted no more than ten minutes. That leaves at least thirty minutes unaccounted for.'

'You think I just popped out to strangle Alexia and cut out her eyes before casually calling in for tea with the warden? That's absurd.'

'The window of opportunity exists,' declared Baxter. 'You do not deny it. And where were you this afternoon between lunch and dinner?'

'I was in my room, catching up on work.'

'Alone?'

'Of course I was alone.'

'Did you make any phone calls?'

'No. I was reading emails and working on a document.'

'How convenient. So again you have no alibi for the time of the second murder.'

'Lack of an alibi is not a valid reason to accuse my client of murder,' interjected Ms Gupta. 'The majority of guests at the college dinner probably also lack credible alibis. Unless you have some actual evidence, then I must insist that you bring this interview to a close.'

Baxter ignored her. 'Ms Collins, let's go through everything from the beginning, shall we? Tell me how Alexia Petrakis first met your husband.'

'Ex-husband.'

'Mr Michael John Kennedy. An investment analyst, currently working for Citibank in New York. A graduate of Magdalen College, Oxford, he previously worked at the London office of the investment bank Goldman Sachs.'

'You seem to know all about him already.'

'Only the bare facts. I'd like to hear your side of the story.'

Meg gave a resigned sigh. 'All right. I first met Michael when I moved to London after studying for my postgraduate degree in Cambridge. We had a lot in common. We were both Oxford graduates, we were the same age, we were ambitious people pursuing demanding careers. We just seemed to hit it off together.'

'How did you meet?'

'At a party. I went there with Alexia. Michael was a friend of hers. We got talking. Things happened quite quickly. We were married within a year.'

'At what age?'

'Twenty-six. Too young, really. People said it wouldn't last.'

'And how long did it last?'

Meg laughed bitterly. 'The honeymoon period lasted until about three months after our actual honeymoon. That's when I found out that Michael wasn't simply a friend of Alexia's. He'd been sleeping with her the whole time we'd been engaged. Getting married hadn't put an end to the affair either. By all accounts, Alexia had simply found Michael even more attractive after he became my husband.'

'I see. What happened then?'

'Michael told me that the affair wasn't serious. He and Alexia were just having a little fun on the side. He told me he was willing to give her up if that's what I wanted.'

'How did you respond to that?'

'I kicked him out and I never spoke to him again. He transferred to New York soon after our divorce came through. I haven't seen him since.'

'What about Alexia?'

'What about her?'

'Did you see her again?'

'No. She was the very last person I ever wanted to see.'

'And yet you must have known that you were likely to run into her if you came to the gaudy this weekend.'

'Really, Inspector, I split up with Michael more than ten years ago. I don't allow old arguments to ruin my life.'

Baxter consulted his notebook. 'That isn't what your ex-husband tells us. We spoke to him on the phone in New York. In his words, "Meg Collins is a vindictive bitch who never misses an opportunity for revenge".'

'Well, Michael always was a bit of a bastard. You shouldn't believe anything he says.'

'You said something very similar to me when I interviewed you this morning.' Baxter thumbed through his notes. 'Yes, here it is. You told me, "I can assure you that I never forget anything, nor forgive anyone".'

Meg shrugged.

'Did you see Alexia Petrakis on the day of her murder?'

'No,' said Meg, but Ffion thought she detected a slight hesitation before her reply.

Baxter must have noticed it too. 'Are you quite sure about that? Remember that your answers are being recorded and may be used as evidence against you in court.'

'I didn't see her to talk to,' said Meg. 'But I saw her with Tina. They were arguing.'

'What about?'

'I didn't hang around to listen. But I assume they were discussing Alexia's newspaper article.'

'Why do you assume that?'

'I heard Tina say something about treachery.'

'What precisely did she say?'

'I didn't hear her clearly.'

'I see. Did anyone else overhear this argument?'

'Not as far as I know. I didn't notice anyone else in the vicinity.'

'And did you see Alexia at any other time?'

'No.'

'Very well. Let's move on. I'd like to hear about the lawsuit that Tina Mackenzie was pursuing against your company. Your company has developed a cure for blindness, yes?'

'For certain types of hereditary blindness.'

'Does it work?'

Ffion smiled to herself. She was still not sure whether Baxter's habit of asking stupid questions might be a cleverly-cultivated interview technique, or if he was as brainless as everyone thought.

Meg stared at him in annoyance. 'Of course it works,' she snapped.

'Then why was your company being sued for damages?'

She gave an exasperated sigh. 'Because of a single unfortunate incident that occurred during our Phase I trial. I don't know how much you know about the regulatory process that governs pharmaceutical companies, Inspector' – her tone suggested that she didn't hold out much hope that he knew anything at all – 'but obtaining clinical approval for a new drug or treatment is a very time-consuming process. Phase I trials are designed to demonstrate the basic safety of the treatment. We tested the treatment on a small number of volunteers to see if there were any problems.'

'And were there?'

'One of the volunteers suffered a serious adverse effect. Tina's law firm was representing him. She was suing us for negligence. The case has been hanging over us for almost ten years now. It's like something out of a Dickens novel. Honestly, the legal system operates even more slowly than the biomedical regulatory authorities.' Meg glanced sideways at Ms Gupta. 'No offence intended.'

'No offence taken,' said Ms Gupta. She looked meaningfully at her watch. 'The way this interview is dragging on, I am inclined to agree with you.'

Baxter took no notice of their asides. 'And

214

what exactly is at stake in this lawsuit?'

'Everything,' conceded Meg. 'It isn't just the money. If we lose this case, not only will it cost GenMeg Therapeutics millions of pounds in damages, it will frighten off potential investors too. It might sink the company completely. If that happens, our cure will never become available.'

'I see.' Baxter spread out his fingers on the desk. 'So in both murders you had a very strong and obvious motive. In the first case for personal revenge. In the second, to protect everything you've worked for. The stakes could not have been higher.'

He directed his next remark at Ms Gupta. 'I hope it's now clear to you why Ms Collins is being interviewed here tonight, and not any of the other guests.'

Baxter turned yet another page in his notebook. 'We've talked about opportunity. We've talked about motive. Now let's discuss means. What do you think the circumstances of the second murder tell us, Ms Collins?'

Meg looked blank. 'I don't know anything about how Tina was killed.'

Ha, thought Ffion. Baxter had done his best to catch Meg out by springing the question on her unawares. But either she truly was ignorant of how Tina had died, or else she was an accomplished actor.

Baxter seemed unruffled by her response. 'Then let me enlighten you. Tina Mackenzie

215

appears to have been poisoned. We'll be running more tests, but the initial indications are that some form of cyanide was added to a glass of Madeira wine that the victim consumed. What does that tell you?'

'That Tina would never turn down the offer of a free drink?'

'I see no reason for flippancy,' said Baxter. 'What it tells me is that the person who gave her that drink had access to a deadly chemical. A biochemist such as yourself, for instance.'

'Cyanide isn't particularly difficult to get hold of,' said Meg. 'A school chemistry lab would have everything you needed to manufacture it.'

'If you knew how.'

'Have you ever heard of the internet, Inspector?'

Ffion could see that Baxter's relentless accusations were getting nowhere. Meg had a response for every line of attack. Ms Gupta looked as if she was about to raise an objection too. While Baxter flipped through his notes looking for another angle, Ffion decided to try a different tack. Baxter could berate her afterwards if he liked, but she didn't think he'd raise an objection in front of the suspect.

'You've worked hard to build a successful company,' she said.

Meg turned to her, perhaps surprised to hear the constable speak for the first time. 'Yes, I have. Bloody hard.' Her voice betrayed the ruthless determination that had enabled her to achieve her goals. Ruthlessness that might also have made her into a cold-blooded killer.

'It can't have been easy for you,' said Ffion, deliberately playing up her Welsh accent. She knew its musical quality had a calming effect on people, like a soothing lullaby. Like hypnosis. 'Persuading investors to back the project, obtaining the necessary capital, pushing through all the regulatory hurdles. I expect you encountered prejudice being a woman too.'

Meg nodded in agreement and the muscles in her face began to relax. 'It takes balls for a woman to set up a successful company in any field, let alone in the pharmaceutical industry. It's a testosterone-fuelled environment dominated by giant corporations and billion-dollar deals.'

Baxter shifted in his seat, showing obvious impatience at the way Ffion had taken over proceedings. Ms Gupta's face had assumed a hawk-like expression as if searching for a trap. But Ffion had Meg's full attention and she wasn't about to let it go.

'But you were fortunate, weren't you?' she said, pulling from her file the sheet of paper she'd printed earlier. 'You received a small but significant amount of seed capital at a crucial time in the company's history.'

Meg frowned, now on guard. 'What do you mean?'

Ffion turned the sheet of paper around so that Meg could read it. 'Merton College made an investment in your company during its very first year.'

'How is this relevant?' demanded Ms Gupta, staring crossly at the sheet of paper. 'What do my client's investors have to do with any of this?'

Baxter raised his eyebrows, obviously wanting to know the same thing.

'It's just that I find it surprising the college would take a financial stake in such a high-risk project,' said Ffion.

'You may find it surprising,' said Meg, 'but that's what happened.'

'Was it good luck?'

'I don't believe in luck.'

'Then why did the college invest money in your company?'

'Why? For the same reason that the college invests in many other businesses and commercial enterprises – in anticipation of making a return on their investment. As I'm sure you're aware, Constable, the college manages assets worth many millions of pounds.' Meg had adopted a didactic tone of voice now, as if explaining the matter to a child.

'I meant, why specifically in this company?' said Ffion impatiently. 'Putting seed capital into a start-up biotech company seems like a very odd choice for a risk-averse institution like an Oxford college.'

'There's nothing odd about it. Biotechnology is a strategic area of interest for Oxford. The university aims to support entrepreneurs who use science to do good for the world. If the CEO happens to be a college alumna, then all the better. In any case, the risk isn't perhaps as great as you might think. The sum invested was modest. The college routinely takes small stakes in relatively high-risk companies that offer the potential for substantial long-term growth. A proportion of these will fail, naturally, but some will grow into multi-million or even multi-billion-pound enterprises in the decades to come.'

'And what was the role of the college warden in taking the decision to make this particular investment?'

'Dr Harper? I believe he may have referred the matter to the college's investment committee for consideration. But he holds no special power. The committee's decision to invest was unanimous.'

'Is there a purpose behind this line of questioning?' asked Ms Gupta.

Reluctantly, Ffion shook her head. Meg was hiding something, she was sure of it. But no amount of questioning was going to persuade her to reveal anything more.

'In that case,' said Ms Gupta, gathering her briefing notes together, 'I think it's high time this interview was brought to a close.'

Baxter looked thoughtful. 'All right,' he said to Meg at last. 'You can go. But we'll be taking you back to the college for the night. Nobody leaves until I say they can.'

CHAPTER 20

With Baxter safely out of the way in Kidlington, Bridget saw no reason to confine herself to her room as he had suggested. Especially not when there was information to be gleaned from talking to the professionals.

Under Vik's supervision, the SOCO team had been crawling over Tina's room for nearly three hours now, and Dr Sarah Walker had arrived some while ago to examine the body. She was still inside the room.

Bridget loitered on the landing outside, waiting to catch them when they left. She was determined not to miss any opportunity to ask questions. Jake was still standing guard at the entrance to the room and she was glad of someone to talk to after the shock of finding Tina's body.

'This must be hard for you, ma'am,' he said, 'you being friends with both victims.'

'Yes, it is. But they were old friends. It's been seventeen years since I last saw them. People change.'

'Yes, they do, don't they?'

Jake seemed to be thinking about something else, perhaps reflecting on how his own friends had changed, following his short return visit to Leeds. But he was still a young man. How much could his friends have changed in six months?

'Even so,' he said. 'You still knew them. It can't be easy for you.'

She gave him a weak smile. It was good to have someone who seemed to understand some of the complicated emotions she was feeling. Loss. Sadness. Confusion. The weekend wasn't turning out remotely as she had anticipated. Not only had two of her friends been murdered, but she was having to come to terms with the fact that even if they had still been alive, she would no longer have had much in common with them. In reality she had lost Tina and Alexia many years ago.

She thought of Meg and Bella. They too had changed out of recognition from the young carefree women she had once known, and she found it hard to imagine wanting to keep in touch with them in the future. This weekend ought to have brought them back together, but instead it had driven them even further apart. It was not just the dead she was mourning, but the living too.

'Everyone changes,' she told Jake. 'It's what life's all about.'

Sarah Walker emerged onto the landing. 'Ah, Bridget. You're still here, are you?' The medical examiner's tone suggested she had been hoping to avoid this conversation. It was becoming apparent that Sarah wasn't very adept at handling emotional situations. In fact, Bridget was beginning to get the impression that she found it easier to deal with the dead than the living. Perhaps that was why Sarah was still single at the age of nearly forty.

'What can you tell me?' asked Bridget.

'You knew this latest victim too, didn't you?'

'Yes.'

Sarah dropped her gaze to the floor. 'Well, there are no signs of strangulation this time, or any other kinds of external marks on the body. Instead the cause of death would appear to be cardiac arrest brought on by cyanide poisoning. That's my best guess at this stage, anyway. The pathologist will have to measure blood concentrations of cyanide during the post-mortem examination to be certain.'

'Cyanide? Was it from the wine?'

'That's the most obvious source. Cyanide is a deadly poison. A dose as small as two hundred milligrams is enough to cause fatality within a few minutes of ingestion. In a glass of wine, it would be impossible to taste.'

Tina had certainly been a very enthusiastic wine drinker. How ironic that it had ultimately killed her.

'What about time of death?'

'Some time in the past three to four hours, I would say.'

That didn't help to pin things down very

much. It meant that Tina had been killed by her mysterious visitor some while after Baxter had interviewed her, and before dinner – a fact that was already obvious. Bridget had been in her room for most of that time, apart from her chance encounter with the college chaplain just after lunch.

Sarah made her way to leave, but Bridget stopped her. 'What about the ears?'

'They were removed after death with a sharp knife. That's really all I can say for now. I'm sorry.' She pushed her way past Bridget before she could be asked any more questions. Bridget watched her go.

'First eyes, now ears,' said Jake. 'I think the killer's trying to tell us something.'

'Us, or someone else,' said Bridget. 'But what exactly?'

Vik, the SOCO head, emerged from the room next. Fortunately he seemed much more willing to talk than Sarah had been. 'Bridget, have you been waiting all this time? You'll be wanting an update, no doubt.'

'You read my mind, Vik.'

'We've bagged up all the evidence and sent it off to forensics for analysis. Now we're going over the walls, furniture and other surfaces. There are prints everywhere, probably from every student who's lived there in the past hundred years.'

'Anything significant yet?'

'You already know about the wine, I take it?'

'Only that Sarah thought Tina had most likely been poisoned.'

'With cyanide, yes. Just like she thought. The toxicology tests from the lab have already confirmed it was in the wine.'

'That was quick work, especially for a weekend.'

Vik grimaced. 'The boys and girls at forensics weren't very happy to be dragged into work on a Sunday evening, but Baxter put a rocket up their arse.'

Bridget could imagine it. DI Baxter might not be the most pleasant person to work with, but he certainly made things move.

'Was the cyanide added to the bottle?' she asked Vik.

'No, it appears not to have been in the bottle itself, but one of the wine glasses was laced with potassium cyanide. It's a colourless compound that's highly soluble in water. It gives off a smell of almonds and has a slightly bitter taste, but mixed in with a strongly-flavoured wine like the Madeira, it would be difficult to taste.'

Bridget remembered that there had been two wine glasses on the bedside locker; one empty, one full. 'Presumably that was the empty glass?'

'That's right.'

'Do you think it will be possible to extract a DNA sample from the second glass?'

'I don't think so. The second glass doesn't appear to have been touched. Whoever did this must have known that we'd be able to extract

DNA from any saliva left in the glass. They took care not to leave any traces behind.'

'What about the knife that was used to cut off the ears?'

'Another knife stolen from the kitchen. Oh – and one more thing you might be interested in. The bottle of wine was taken from the cellar. It was stamped with the college crest.'

★

There was nothing more that Bridget could do in Mob Quad. Tina's body had been bagged and was on its way to the morgue at the John Radcliffe, ready for the post-mortem which Dr Roy Andrews would carry out in the morning. SOCO were clearing up, having finished scouring the room for fibres, strands of hair, fingerprints and anything else that might help the police to identify the killer. Now only the crime scene tape across the doorway remained. Jake had been given permission by Baxter to go home, and had been replaced by a uniformed constable who had the unenviable job of guarding the staircase overnight.

As Bridget descended the stairs she realised that Vanessa would still be waiting for her to return and collect Chloe. She quickly dialled her sister's number.

'Bridget? What's going on? I thought you'd be back hours ago.'

'I'm sorry. Something's come up.'

'What?'

'A second murder.'

'Oh my God. Who was it this time?'

'I can't really tell you any details right now.' Bridget pressed on before Vanessa could ask any more questions. 'Unfortunately the police are keeping us here for a second night. Would you mind looking after Chloe tonight and taking her to school tomorrow?'

To Bridget's relief, Vanessa didn't sound like she minded in the least. Her sister liked nothing better than providing hospitality for guests, and her house was plenty large enough to accommodate visitors with ease. 'No, of course I don't mind. I'll make up a bed for her in the spare room. I can drop her off when I take Florence and Toby to school.'

'Thanks, Vanessa. You're a star.'

'I know that already,' said Vanessa. 'Now you just take care of yourself. Stay safe. Lock your door and don't let anyone in.'

'Don't worry,' Bridget told her before hanging up. 'The police think they've already caught the culprit.'

When Baxter had taken Meg in for questioning, he had certainly seemed convinced that she had killed both Alexia and Tina, and Bridget had to agree that the evidence was compelling. Meg had clearly hated Alexia for sleeping with her husband, and Tina had made herself into Meg's enemy by pursuing the lawsuit against her company. It would be perfectly understandable for Meg to want both women dead.

Bridget recalled what Meg had told her at dinner – that she had seen Tina arguing with Alexia on Saturday afternoon. At the time, the information had seemed to implicate Tina as the murderer, but now Bridget wondered if Meg had been lying about seeing them arguing together in order to throw suspicion onto Tina.

Tina had categorically denied seeing Alexia on Saturday afternoon. Perhaps she had been telling the truth after all.

Either way, Bridget could do nothing about it now. With both Alexia and Tina dead, it would probably be impossible ever to know for certain.

Baxter had taken Meg to Kidlington, and would no doubt be doing his best to extract a confession from her, or at least to obtain some incriminating evidence. She wondered how that would work out. Baxter could be a bit of a bully, but Meg was as tough as nails. It was anyone's guess who would come out on top.

★

It was nearly eleven o'clock by now, and Mob Quad was clothed in darkness. The moon had not yet risen. A pair of uniformed police officers stood guard at each archway leading from the quad, and Bridget nodded politely to the two who were positioned at the western end. She was about to return to her room for the night and lock the door as Vanessa had instructed when she noticed that a light was still shining from the library window. There could surely only be one person up there at this time of night.

On impulse she turned and entered the darkened archway leading up the stairs. She climbed the wooden staircase, then made her way softly along the worn carpet that stretched between alcoves filled with dusty books. Just as she'd expected, Dr Irene Thomas was in her usual spot in the last alcove. A single desk light illuminated her books and papers.

'Hello, Dr Thomas. You're working late.'

The old tutor peered up at her, removing her reading glasses in order to see Bridget better. 'I work late every night. Work is what keeps me going these days. Where would I be without it?' She smiled. 'And please, call me Irene. There's no need to be so formal, otherwise I shall feel compelled to start asking you questions about the English Reformation or the Elizabethan Religious Settlement.'

'Please don't do that,' said Bridget. 'You'd be dismayed if you discovered how much I've forgotten of what you taught me. All those long hours of study, all for nothing.'

'Nonsense,' said Dr Thomas. 'No time spent studying is ever wasted. I'm sure it's all up there still.' She tapped the side of her forehead with one index finger. 'The subconscious mind is remarkably good at dredging up information from the murky depths when we need it.' She looked thoughtfully at Bridget. 'I understand there's been a second murder.'

'Yes. Another old friend of mine, in fact. Tina Mackenzie.'

'The lawyer.'

'Yes.' Bridget was relieved that Irene hadn't described Tina as the disgraced lawyer.

'You look like you could do with a drink. I was just about to finish here, anyway. Care to join me?'

'That would be lovely,' said Bridget. 'Let me help you with those books.' She scooped up a pile of dense tomes on Elizabethan politics and followed Dr Thomas to her suite of rooms in Fellows' Quadrangle.

To Bridget's knowledge, Dr Thomas had never been married, and had always lived in college. Her modest suite consisted of a living room which she used as a study, and a small bedroom leading off it. Bridget had attended her weekly tutorials in this study all those years ago, and the room looked almost the same as she recalled.

The shelves groaned under an even greater weight of books, but the same reproduction of a Canaletto hung above the fireplace. A View of the Grand Canal. Bridget remembered sitting on the sofa each week looking up at that picture of Venetian gondolas, and reading her essay aloud, waiting for Dr Thomas to mercilessly dissect the myriad discrepancies and weaknesses in her argument. The memory was enough to send a shiver down her spine. Each weekly tutorial had left her feeling like an abject failure.

She wasn't a nervous student anymore, and Dr Thomas had just invited her to use her first name. Yet she still felt a trepidation returning to this room. She would never be able to think of her former tutor as an equal.

Bridget sat down in her accustomed place on the ancient sofa while Dr Thomas – Irene – poured two generous measures of sherry. She handed one glass to Bridget. 'I understand that the latest victim was poisoned. With a glass of college Madeira wine.'

'I wonder how you could possibly know that?' asked Bridget.

'I have my ways and means.'

Bridget had no idea how Dr Thomas could have gained access to this kind of information. To her knowledge, no details of the murder had been officially released by the police. But it was possible that the college warden had been informed, and he had divulged the facts to the college's oldest tutor.

Dr Thomas sat down in her usual chair by the fireplace and took a long sip of her sherry, studying Bridget closely. 'They say that poison is a woman's weapon, don't they?'

'Do they?' Bridget regarded the glass of sherry in her hand, beginning to feel slightly uneasy. She had watched Irene pour the sherry from the bottle and drink a mouthful herself. But Vik had told her that the cyanide that had been used to poison Tina was not in the drink itself but had been added to the glass.

Irene saw her hesitation. 'Don't be afraid, my dear. It's a very fine vintage. From the college cellar, in fact. Drink up!'

It suddenly occurred to Bridget that she was being tested by the devious old tutor. Irene had deliberately raised the matter of poisoned college wine to see how much Bridget trusted her. In that case there was only one way to respond. She raised her glass and took a deep drink of the sweet, fortified wine. 'Cheers!'

Dr Thomas broke out in a broad grin. 'And cheers to you, Bridget. I must say, it's a nice change to have some company on these dark autumnal evenings. Especially when death stalks the college like an uninvited guest.'

'That's a rather melodramatic turn of phrase, Irene.'

'Ah yes, I seem to be getting somewhat histrionic in my old age. And yet I hear that the murderer also has a finely-tuned sense of the theatrical. First eyeballs, now ears.'

Again Bridget marvelled at how well informed Dr Thomas was about the latest crime. But it would be no use probing to find out how she had obtained her knowledge. She was obviously unwilling to divulge her sources.

'Yes,' Bridget confirmed. 'Poor Tina had both her ears cut off.'

'That doesn't surprise me in the least.'

'Really?' said Bridget. 'I can't say that I was

expecting anything like that to happen.'

Dr Thomas regarded her like an undergraduate who had failed to perceive an entirely obvious fact. 'As I said to you last night, the removal of body parts is one of the key tropes of revenge tragedy. I think you must now seriously consider the hypothesis that the murderer is familiar with these tropes and is acting out their own revenge drama.'

Bridget had to admit that she was intrigued by Irene's theory. 'What are the other tropes of the genre?' she asked.

It was obviously the right question to ask. Dr Thomas settled back in her chair in readiness to begin a lesson, and Bridget prepared herself to be educated. She had never left a tutorial with Dr Thomas without being considerably better informed than she had been beforehand.

'Some of the earliest examples of revenge tragedies can be found in the works of Seneca in the first century, who of course based many of his plays on earlier Greek tragedies. Plays like Phaedra, Oedipus and Thyestes all deal with the subject of revenge. In fact it seems to have been quite a hobbyhorse of both the Romans and the Greeks. Thyestes is an interesting example. In that play, Atreus takes revenge on his brother Thyestes after Thyestes has an affair with Atreus's wife.'

It was hard for Bridget not to make the connection to Alexia's affair with Meg's husband. 'A timeless theme,' she mused aloud.

She could certainly relate to vengeful feelings where marital infidelity was concerned.

'Indeed,' said Dr Thomas. 'There's nothing new under the sun. In this case the revenge takes a particularly gruesome turn when Atreus tricks Thyestes into eating his own children.'

'They certainly knew how to please an audience in those days.'

'Oh, yes,' said Dr Thomas, gleefully nodding her head. Bridget could tell she was getting into her stride. 'Dismembered body parts and cannibalistic feasts are ideas that Shakespeare uses centuries later in Titus Andronicus when various characters lose their tongue, their hands and even their heads. Chiron and Demetrius, who represent Rape and Murder in the play, have their blood drained, their bones ground to powder, their heads baked and served up in a pie. More sherry?'

'Just a little, please.' Bridget had been so engrossed by Dr Thomas's lecture that she'd finished her drink without even noticing. Dr Thomas had also emptied her glass. She refilled both glasses, then settled back into her chair.

'So you see, dismemberment is one of the key elements of the revenge tragedy. Tell me, if you would, where the latest victim's ears were discovered?'

Bridget knew she shouldn't really divulge any information about the murder to Dr Thomas, but as she already seemed to know everything else, she didn't think it would do any harm.

'Absurd as it sounds, they were placed in the middle of a plate of biscuits.'

Dr Thomas nodded vigorously. 'Yes, that proves my point. The killer is clearly adhering to the trope of serving body parts at a feast.'

'I suppose so,' said Bridget. She wondered if her old tutor really was onto something. First eyes, now ears. First soup, now biscuits.

'Now if this were a work of fiction, we would expect a ghost to make an appearance,' said Dr Thomas.

'A ghost?'

'Yes. Either real or imagined. Think of the ghost of Hamlet's father, who explains to Hamlet how he was murdered, and asks him to avenge his death. Or Banquo's ghost in Macbeth, who incidentally can only be seen by Macbeth himself. And there would also have to be a character who expressed the prevailing moral view of vengeance versus forgiveness.'

Bridget's mind darted immediately to the chaplain's sermon, in which he had quoted from St Paul's letter to the Colossians. Even as Christ forgave you, so also do ye.

'We'd also expect to see an authority figure presiding over the domain in which the drama was set. In this current case, that role is presumably being fulfilled by Dr Brendan Harper as the college warden. And also a mix of servants – let's say a butler, a chef and a college porter, for instance.' Dr Thomas smiled. 'But of course this is not a drama, but a real-life enactment of a series of brutal killings.'

'Yes,' said Bridget. She realised that at some point during this chat she had moved from polite scepticism to a gradual and growing acceptance of her tutor's ideas. Could she really have found herself in the middle of a revenge tragedy being acted out just like a play on the stage? The notion seemed too crazy to contemplate, and yet...

'So if what you say is true, which one of these characters should we expect to be the actual revenger?'

Dr Thomas shook her head. 'Ah, Bridget, you didn't expect me to solve the case for you, did you? It might be any one of them. But listen, there's more to understand about the genre. Another important element is that the act of revenge must invariably be in excess of the original crime. It's a little like modern-day road rage, where a relatively minor incident or accidental infringement can cause the injured party to retaliate disproportionately, inflicting massive harm on the other driver.'

'Yes, I see,' said Bridget. 'But these murders appear to be premeditated, whereas in road rage incidents, people are acting emotionally on the spur of the moment. Afterwards they often say they don't know what made them do it. It's as if they were taken over by a kind of madness.'

'Well, madness certainly plays a role in revenge,' said Dr Thomas. 'Look at Hamlet for example, where both Hamlet and Ophelia display clear symptoms of madness, although whether their madness is real or feigned is a matter of debate.'

'But if the revenge is planned in advance, what causes someone to go to such extreme lengths? Is madness the only explanation for their behaviour?'

'No, it's actually quite rational and easy to understand. The person seeking revenge acts in the way they do because they are unable to obtain justice through the normal means, for example when state-controlled forms of justice such as the police and the courts have let them down. They reach a point where taking revenge personally seems to be their only option. They are desperate and have nothing to lose.'

It was an argument that touched on Bridget's own personal feelings. After her sister had been murdered, she had initially placed her faith in the police, but the murder investigation at the time had led nowhere. With no help from the authorities, Bridget had felt helpless and frustrated. In her case, she had redirected her anger in a positive direction, joining the police force herself. But she could see that it could just as easily turn someone into a vigilante, taking the law into their own hands. As a serving police officer, she had witnessed countless occasions when justice failed or seemed inadequate to the wrong done. And what then? Revenge appeared to offer a type of retribution. It might be bloodthirsty and disproportionate to the original crime, but it answered a deep-seated, animal instinct that maybe wasn't so far beneath the surface in any of us. It was a sobering thought.

'The avenger takes a huge personal risk, though, don't they?' she said. 'They will lose their freedom if caught. In fact, in the Roman or Elizabethan age, they would probably have been sentenced to death.'

'Certainly,' said Dr Thomas. 'But that is of very little concern to them. You see, Bridget, in this type of drama, the revenger always ends up dead.'

★

It was dark at the top of the staircase, and John Bradley, chef of Merton College waited patiently in the shadows. Down below, he could hear noises as someone crept around the college wine cellars. A case of bottles clinked, and then he heard a grunt and the heavy tread of feet coming up the stairs.

The butler, Nick Kernahan, appeared from the cellars with a case of wine tucked under his arm. He shut and carefully locked the cellar door behind him, using one of the keys from the extensive collection that hung from his belt.

John Bradley stepped out of his hiding place.

'Bloody hell!' The butler jumped visibly when he saw him. 'What are you doing skulking about at night? I damn well nearly dropped these bottles!'

The chef smiled. He'd caught his quarry off-guard, just as he'd been hoping to. He said nothing, just looked the butler up and down, knowing that silence was the best way to unnerve the man.

The butler clutched the case of wine close to his chest. 'Bloody fool, get out of my way! As if I don't have enough problems to deal with at the moment.' He pushed past, setting off down the corridor at a brisk pace.

'Running away are you?' the chef called after him. 'It won't do you any good. I know your secrets.'

The butler stopped and slowly turned around. He cast a measuring eye over the chef, then took a step closer. 'You're a liar! You haven't worked here long enough to know anything about anyone.'

'Maybe not, but I keep my wits about me. And I hear rumours.'

'What kind of rumours?'

'You know what kind.'

The butler gazed at him malevolently. 'Maybe you have heard something about my past, but so what? The warden knows the truth already. You can't tell him anything new.' He turned to leave.

'He doesn't know everything. I've been watching you. I know what you did.'

Nick Kernahan spun back to face him. This time the butler's eyes held the unmistakable sign of fear. 'You're bluffing. You don't know a thing.'

'Are you sure about that? Do you want to take

the risk?'

The butler walked right up to him, the heavy case of wine still in his arms. Up close, he was a good two inches taller than the chef, and a heavily-built man too, with powerful arms and broad shoulders. 'If you really do know everything you claim you do, then you'll know what happened to the chef who was here before you.'

John Bradley faced him, only slightly intimidated by the butler's veiled threat. 'You don't scare me. If I were you, I'd be the one running scared, what with the police crawling all over the college. How long do you think it will take before they find out everything?'

The butler stood still for a second, thinking it over. 'What is it you want?'

These were the words John Bradley had been hoping to hear. He smiled inwardly but kept the expression on his face unchanged. 'To buy my silence? I'm not a greedy man. Two grand will keep your secrets safe with me.'

CHAPTER 21

Bridget's excessive alcohol consumption of the previous night was now taking its own revenge. Her head throbbed as she rose from her hard, narrow bed. Her tongue felt like sandpaper. She had stayed up late into the night, debating ideas of justice and vengeance with Dr Irene Thomas, and consuming way too many glasses of the college's finest Amontillado in the process. Drunk on sherry. Who in the world did that, apart from elderly great-aunts on Christmas Day?

Still, it had not been time wasted. If nothing else, she had received an intensive grounding in Classical, Elizabethan and Jacobean revenge tragedies. An evening with Dr Thomas was worth a whole course of study. By the end of the night, Bridget had been entirely convinced that she was living in a real-life enactment of a bloody Jacobean play, complete with ghosts, college servants, and gruesome feasts. Now in the cold light of the morning, such ideas seemed somewhat fanciful. This was no colourful drama, but the work of a vicious and possibly deranged killer, who had taken the life of two of her friends.

On the face of it, Meg did look like the most plausible suspect, but Bridget couldn't really bring herself to believe that anyone she knew could have carried out such horrible murders, let alone have butchered the victims after their death. She wondered whether Baxter's interview with Meg had revealed any new information. If so, her spies in the detective team would hopefully keep her informed.

As she showered herself back into the world of the living she wondered how Chloe was getting on at Vanessa's house. No doubt her sister would be fussing over Chloe like a mother hen, feeding her a spectacular breakfast (organic cereal with maple-syrup pancakes and freshly-squeezed orange juice, just like in a five-star hotel), and prompting her to get ready for school. She wasn't sure whether Chloe would be loving the attention, or desperate to get back home to a bowl of Corn Flakes and Bridget's benign neglect. She resisted the temptation to phone for an update and instead decided to concentrate on her own wellbeing for the day ahead. Looking at her red puffy eyes in the bathroom mirror she concluded that a light breakfast with plenty of strong coffee would be the best tactic to get started.

On her way to the dining hall she encountered Ryan sauntering across the Front Quad with his hands in his pockets. He grinned at her and came over for a chat. 'Morning, ma'am, I must say you're looking very well today. Your weekend off must have done you the world of good.'

'Thank you, Sergeant,' she said, perfectly aware of just how bad she looked, and ignoring his friendly brand of sarcasm. 'Can you fill me in on the latest?'

Since Baxter was nowhere to be seen for the moment, she was willing to endure any number of comments about her appearance if he could tell her something useful about the investigation.

'Not much to report, really, ma'am. We had to let Meg Collins go. She's still Baxter's number-one suspect, but there isn't enough evidence to charge her. She was brought back to college last night.'

'I see. So she didn't admit to anything?'

'No. Did you expect her to?'

'Not really.' Bridget had never known Meg concede that she was wrong about anything, and she would surely never admit to something incriminating during a police interview. 'Meg's going to be a tough nut to crack. Any news from forensics?'

'Well, it was definitely potassium cyanide in the wine, or rather in one of the glasses. But they can't say where it came from. Potassium cyanide is illegal to buy without a licence, but it can be obtained through illegal channels, and you can even manufacture it if you know how. But SOCO also recovered loads of fingerprints, hairs, fibres and other kinds of physical evidence, so we're hoping the perpetrator's left something useful behind this time.'

'Good. Is Baxter still planning to keep us here until he's re-interviewed everyone?'

'I think so, ma'am. That's what we've been told. In fact, that must be him now.'

The unmistakable sound of the detective inspector's raised voice could be heard from the porter's lodge.

'I'd better look busy,' said Ryan. He scurried away across the quad, eager to put as much distance between himself and Bridget as possible before his boss appeared.

Bridget too was keen to keep out of DI Baxter's path. With no progress after interviewing Meg, she guessed his mood this morning would be just as black as it had been last night.

She headed into the hall, where the smell of fried eggs and bacon threatened to turn her stomach upside down. Keeping well away from the hot food counter, she helped herself instead to a slice of wholegrain toast and a cup of black coffee, and went to join Bella, who was sitting alone at the far end of the middle table, in the seat she had occupied for the gaudy dinner itself.

'Hi, Bella.' Bridget took a seat opposite.

Bella also looked like she'd slept terribly. Her face was pale and drawn. She was wearing the same clothes that Bridget had seen her in when they'd first met on Saturday afternoon. No doubt all the guests would be struggling to find a fresh change of clothing, having been kept in the college for a night longer than they'd anticipated. Bridget was probably the only one who had come with three times as many outfits as she actually needed.

'Is it true?' asked Bella miserably. 'About Tina?'

No official announcement had yet been made about the second murder, but it was inevitable that news would have spread around the college.

'Yes, I'm afraid it is. I was there when her body was discovered yesterday evening.'

'My God. First Alexia, now Tina. And I heard they've taken Meg in for questioning.'

'Yes, but she's been released without charge.'

'Well, that's something, I suppose. I know that Meg and Tina were at each other's throats all weekend, but I can't believe that Meg could really have murdered Tina. And Alexia too. It's just too awful.'

'Yes,' said Bridget. 'I'm sure Meg's innocent.' She couldn't ignore facts, however. Baxter had arrested Meg with good reason. She would probably have done the same if she'd been in his position.

Still, Bridget's reassurance seemed to ease Bella's mind a little. 'So what will happen now?' she asked. 'How long do they plan to keep us here?'

'I don't know. Probably until lunchtime at least.' It would take at least the whole morning to interview everyone a second time, and Baxter would be keen to find out as much as possible from every person. In such a crowded community, surely someone must have seen something that would help to pin down the murderer's movements.

Bridget spread some marmalade on her toast and took a tentative nibble. Sugar and carbs were usually a good antidote to a late night. In fact, they were Bridget's standard solution to any kind of problem. She sipped some of the dark coffee and began to feel a little better.

Bella looked up and down the table, then leaned forward, dropping her voice lower. 'The thing is, Bridget, I wish I could leave right away. I just don't feel safe here anymore. After what's happened to Alexia and Tina, I can't help thinking that someone is targeting us.'

'Us?'

'You know who I mean.'

'Do I?'

'Of course you do. I'm talking about Alexia, Tina, Meg, you and me. Don't tell me the same idea hasn't occurred to you. And if I'm right, that means that you, Meg and I might be in danger too.'

'I hardly see why. There are many reasons why Alexia and Tina might have been murdered. What reason would someone have for wanting to kill you or me? Or Meg for that matter?'

'I don't know. But don't you see the pattern? What if whoever is doing this hasn't finished yet?'

Bridget chewed thoughtfully on her toast as she pondered Bella's words. She couldn't think of any reason why someone might be targeting the group of friends. Bella's theory didn't have any evidence to support it. The newspaper article that Alexia had written about Tina had established a clear link between the two women, and much as Bridget hated to admit it, the police investigation had identified a suspect with an obvious reason to want both Tina and Alexia dead – Meg Collins. But even if Meg turned out not to be the killer, both Alexia and Tina had pushed themselves into the public spotlight and had no doubt made a lot of enemies during their careers. There was no reason to suspect that anyone would want to kill Bella, or Bridget for that matter.

'But why, Bella? Why would anyone want to kill a group of people just because we were friends almost two decades ago?'

'I don't know. But it scares me.'

Bella leaned back as other people brought their food to sit nearby. She was clearly very nervous, perhaps even neurotic. Bridget knew that irrational fears were sometimes associated with depression, and Bella certainly showed symptoms of being clinically depressed.

But perhaps she shouldn't be too quick to dismiss Bella's theory. If it were correct, then there was still a risk that the murderer might not have finished their grisly business. The spectre of revenge that Dr Irene Thomas had conjured came again to mind. The act of revenge is invariably in excess of the original crime, the tutor had said. But what crime? Hear no evil, the message next to Tina's severed ears had proclaimed, but what could that possibly mean? What evil?

'And where is Meg, anyway?' asked Bella. 'Did the police let her go?'

'They released her from custody after interviewing her and brought her back to college.'

'Then where is she?' persisted Bella. 'Have you seen her this morning?'

'No. But to be honest, it's still very early for Meg to be up, especially if the police kept her at the station for a long time last night.'

'I suppose so,' said Bella. 'Even so, don't you think we ought to check that she's safe?'

Bridget didn't imagine that Meg would show her any thanks for dragging her out of bed this early. But Bella was insistent.

Bridget sighed. 'Okay.' She shovelled down the last of her toast, and swallowed a large gulp of coffee. She stood up. 'I'll go to her room now and make sure she's all right.'

'Wait,' said Bella. 'Don't leave me here on my own.'

Bridget sat back down. 'Bella, now you're being ridiculous. Nobody can possibly harm you here in the dining hall. There are dozens of people all around.'

But Bella didn't look the least bit reassured. 'Bridget, any one of these people might be the murderer. What happens when I go back to my room after breakfast? Tina must have thought she was safe in her room, but she wasn't. She was in terrible danger.'

'Well I can't stay here with you and go to check on Meg.' Bridget looked around the hall and saw Ryan helping himself to a large cooked breakfast. 'I've got an idea,' she told Bella. 'I'll ask Sergeant Ryan Hooper to keep an eye on you. Will that help?'

'That would be wonderful,' said Bella, her face flushing with relief. 'Thanks, Bridget.'

Bridget had a quick word with Ryan, who was perfectly happy to act as bodyguard to Bella, just so long as he was allowed to eat his breakfast without interruption. She left the two of them in the hall and headed off to check on Meg.

★

Bridget walked briskly across Front Quad to the staircase that led up to Meg's room. As she climbed the steep wooden stairs, she braced herself for a storm of abuse. Meg had never been a morning person and had always resented being disturbed before nine o'clock, even if she'd slept late for a lecture. Bridget checked her watch. It was still only eight.

Meg's bad temper was one of her least endearing features, and Bridget could only guess how aggravated she might be feeling after a gruelling late-night interview in the care of DI Baxter. Perhaps she would lash out at Bridget, as a representative of the forces of law and order.

It seemed strange for Bridget to think of herself in that way, viewed through the lens of her old friendships. After spending the weekend back in college with Meg, Bella (and Tina too, before her horrible death), the young, carefree women she remembered so vividly from two decades ago seemed almost within touching distance. It was difficult to accept that they were all now approaching forty and had moved on with their lives, taking on adult roles and responsibilities. Meg now ran a multi-million-pound organisation, with the fate of sufferers of congenital blindness in her hands. Tina, before her untimely death, had helped victims of corporate negligence (real or alleged) seek redress. Even Bella, despite her obvious discontentment with the way her life had worked out, was entrusted with the education of hundreds of children. What could be more important than that? And Bridget herself had a daughter to care for, and the duties that went with being a senior police detective.

The staircase that led up to the top floor seemed to have absorbed the dust of centuries. The stairs creaked loudly as Bridget climbed them. Perhaps it was the old musty smell of the staircase that had wiped away the years and made her remember the days when the college had been her home. Climbing it was like travelling back into the past.

She was caught suddenly in the grip of self-doubt, as if she and the others were really only pretending to be adults, and were simply dressing up and taking on parts. She felt an irrational fear of being called out as an imposter. Once again she was struck by the thought that they were characters in a play, and that this was mere fiction.

But two of her friends lay cold and dead in the morgue. Whatever was happening, it was deadly real.

Perhaps it was the presence of DI Baxter looming over the investigation that had sown the seeds of uncertainty in her mind. What she craved most was the freedom to take control of the investigation herself. But Chief Superintendent Grayson would never permit that. Not when the two murder victims and the prime suspect were all known to her.

However, she knew that whatever authority Baxter might believe himself to hold, she could count on the loyalty of Jake, Ffion and Ryan to keep her informed and allow her to remain close to the investigation even though she had no official involvement. Sarah Walker and Vik from SOCO would also hold nothing back from her. Besides, she held an advantage that Baxter would never have – an insider's view of the case and intimate knowledge of the people involved.

The top-floor landing led to a row of cramped attic rooms whose windows looked out across the quad. Bridget walked along the landing until she reached the door to Meg's room. The college had allocated Meg the same room that she'd occupied during her final year as an undergraduate. How many times had Bridget climbed these same stairs and knocked on this very door to meet Meg before going to formal hall, or for an evening out in the college bar, or to go punting on the river? Too many to remember.

Bridget tapped lightly on the door but there was no response. She waited a moment before knocking more loudly. There was still no sound from within.

'Meg?'

The silence stretched out.

A sudden feeling of disquiet gripped her and she was reminded of knocking on Tina's door in Mob Quad barely twelve hours earlier. A repetition of that horrible discovery was unthinkable, and yet she realised with a growing dread that this was precisely what Bella had feared. Why hadn't she listened to Bella from the beginning? And why hadn't Baxter thought to station a constable outside Meg's door?

She banged on the door much louder this time and called out at the top of her voice. 'Meg! It's me, Bridget! Are you in there? Open up!'

She grabbed at the door handle and to her surprise it turned. She pushed the door open tentatively. The room beyond was dark. 'Meg? Are you there?'

Nothing.

Steeling herself, Bridget stepped into the

room. Her eyes took a moment to adjust to the gloom. The curtains were drawn tightly closed, casting the room in dull sepia tones. A sickly, slightly cloying scent filled the air. As Bridget approached the bed she put a hand to her mouth to stop herself from crying out loud.

Meg was lying in her bed just as Tina had been. But whereas Tina had looked as if she were merely asleep, there was nothing restful about Meg's appearance. A weapon like a small pickaxe was embedded in her chest, and her eyes were wide and staring. The blade of the axe had been driven deep into her flesh, tearing her open like a slab of meat on a butcher's block. Blood had spread out across the bedclothes like a red carpet.

But Bridget's attention was drawn to an even worse horror. She inched closer to the body and saw that Meg's jaw hung loose, as if it had been wrenched open with a tool of some kind. Her neck and upper body were stained dark red, and where her tongue should have been, only a deep empty cavity remained. The tongue lay on her chest next to the pickaxe.

Bridget gasped, then finally lifted her gaze to the wall above the headboard. There, scrawled in blood, were the words, 'Speak no evil.'

She turned from the scene in shock and hurried away to the safety of the doorway, shutting her eyes and leaning against the doorframe for support. Her chest rose and fell, wracked by breathless sobs. It was at least a minute before she could compose herself enough to raise the alarm.

CHAPTER 22

Jake finished the last of his breakfast hurriedly and made his way out of the dining hall towards the temporary incident room that Baxter had set up in the Fellows' Quadrangle. Ffion had scolded him more than once about eating a cooked breakfast, saying he should switch to a healthier option. Apparently she kicked off each morning with a pink grapefruit and a bowl of porridge made with soya milk and a handful of chia seeds, whatever they were. But the full English breakfast on offer at the college was just too tempting. He resolved to try out her suggestion as soon as he'd finished this current assignment. Although… soya milk? Really? And what the hell were chia seeds anyway?

When he entered the incident room, he realised that he was the last to arrive, apart from Ryan who was nowhere to be seen, and that Baxter had already begun his daily lecture. He wished now that he'd curtailed his breakfast and perhaps not gone back for that second helping of bacon and egg. There was a sense of urgency in the room and Jake wondered what he'd missed.

Something important, obviously. He felt the tips of his ears begin to glow.

Baxter glared at him as he shuffled into the back of the room, but didn't pause in his delivery. 'So now both of our key suspects have been murdered,' he declared angrily.

Jake wondered if he'd heard right. *Both* suspects murdered?

'Meg Collins is dead,' Ffion whispered to him from the seat in front.

'Meg? Dead? Shit!' As far as Jake knew, their prime suspect had been alive and well not so many hours ago, in the hands of DI Baxter himself at Kidlington. How had it happened?

'Killed with a pickaxe,' whispered Ffion.

'A what?' Jake wondered if there was something wrong with his hearing this morning. Nothing anyone told him was making sense.

'DS Derwent,' warned Baxter sternly. 'I don't want to have to repeat anything because you're not paying attention.'

'No, sir. I am paying attention.'

Baxter looked terrible this morning, his hair sticking up at odd angles, his tie askew, and the scowl that often flitted across his face now permanently fixed there like a mask. It was hardly surprising, if this was now a triple murder enquiry.

The Chief Super would be spitting teeth. And mostly in the detective inspector's direction.

Baxter pointed testily at the photographs of the three victims pinned to his noticeboard. 'First victim. Alexia Petrakis. Strangled. Eyes gouged out. Second victim. Tina Mackenzie. Poisoned. Ears cut off. Third victim. Meg Collins. Killed with some kind of axe. Tongue cut out.'

Jake gaped at Meg's photo incredulously. Tongue cut out? He was seriously regretting his bacon and sausage breakfast, and would be sure to try out this porridge idea tomorrow morning. In fact, the idea of becoming a vegan seemed suddenly to be increasing its appeal.

Beside him, DC Harry Johns looked like he was about to throw up. The poor lad really needed to toughen up if he was going to last in a murder team.

'What I want to know,' growled Baxter, 'is what the bloody hell's going on?'

Ffion raised her hand. 'Sir, the messages.'

Baxter nodded. For once, he seemed grateful for Ffion's contribution. 'Thank you, DC Hughes.' He pointed to two more photographs. 'First, a printed card placed next to Tina Mackenzie's ears. *Hear no evil*. The card is of the type used by the college as name cards for dinner guests. It appears to have been taken from the college office, or perhaps from the dining hall where the butler kept his own supply of stationery. Second, a message written in blood on the wall above Meg Collins' s bed. *Speak no evil*. What the hell do they mean?'

Jake stared at the second photograph. The words had been written in what looked like red paint. In several places the blood had left trails where it had run down the wall. It looked like some kind of paintbrush had been used to daub the message on the wallpaper.

Ffion raised her hand a second time. 'Sir, the phrases come from the Japanese proverb, "See no evil, hear no evil, speak no evil." Traditionally the words are spoken by three wise monkeys, the first with his hands covering his eyes, the second covering his ears, and the third with both hands placed over his mouth.'

'Monkeys?' Baxter gave the distinct impression he suspected Ffion was winding him up.

'Yes, sir. The phrases obviously tie in with the body parts that were removed from the victims. There are two conflicting interpretations of the monkeys' words. The first is that they are commandments, instructing the wise to turn away from all kinds of evil behaviour. The second interpretation is that the words are intended as a rebuke of the morally weak person who fails to speak out when they witness evil in the world.'

Baxter grunted. 'Thank you for enlightening us, DC Hughes, although I fail to see exactly how that moves us forward.' He ran a hand through his already-dishevelled hair. 'Let's consider the facts. Alexia Petrakis was an investigative journalist. Her article exposing Tina Mackenzie as a liar was published in a national newspaper the morning following her death. Tina Mackenzie was obviously our prime suspect initially, but if she didn't murder Miss

Petrakis, why would anyone else want to? Tina Mackenzie was a lawyer bringing a lawsuit against GenMeg Therapeutics, the company owned by Meg Collins, making Ms Collins an obvious suspect in her murder. But since Ms Collins is now dead, who else had anything to gain from Tina Mackenzie's death? Thirdly, Alexia Petrakis once had an affair with the husband of Meg Collins. But with both women now dead, and the ex-husband half a globe away in New York, that also now seems to be irrelevant. What do we have left?'

Baxter didn't wait for anyone to answer his questions. 'Let's look instead at the physical evidence available. We now have a positive ID on the wire that was used to strangle Miss Petrakis. It seems that it was a length cut from wire used for electrical work in the college and was stolen from a college storeroom. The theft was reported by a workman when he turned up to work this morning. The knife used to remove the first victim's eyes was also college property, taken from the kitchen. In the case of the second murder, Miss Mackenzie was poisoned with Madeira wine from the college wine cellars and stamped with the college crest. Again, the knife used to cut off her ears was taken from the kitchen, perhaps at the same time as the theft of the first knife. Yet another college knife was used to cut out Miss Collins's tongue.'

Photos of the butchered body parts were pinned to the noticeboard, along with the various weapons and tools.

'In every case, college property was used both as the murder weapon and to remove body parts from the victim. Why? Was it simply a matter of convenience, or was the killer sending us, or someone else, a message of some kind?'

'Could it be an attempt to drag the college's good name through the mud?' suggested Jake.

'Or, if it was someone working in the college,' suggested Andy Cartwright, 'they would easily have had access to all the items. Perhaps they just used what was most easily available.'

'I like that theory,' said Baxter. 'It's obvious. It's practical. In that case, let's focus our attention on the kitchen and serving staff. That's where we should have been looking all along.'

'But what about the messages?' asked Jake. 'See no evil, hear no evil, speak no evil. What evil do the messages refer to? Did the victims commit some evil act, or did they fail to speak out about some evil?'

'Or were they being warned by someone not to speak up?' suggested Ffion.

Baxter shook his head. 'These melodramatic touches may be nothing more than a distraction, perhaps even a deliberate piece of misdirection by the perpetrator. No, we've already had enough distractions. From now on I want hard facts. No more speculation.'

'What about the axe used to kill Meg Collins?' asked Andy. 'Did that come from the college, and if so where?'

'Good question. SOCO have bagged it up and sent it off to forensics for analysis. They're working at the murder scene right now. The perpetrator must have left some kind of trace after such a brutal killing. The lab also has all the physical evidence that was recovered from the scene of the second murder. Hopefully we'll be able to get a fingerprint or a DNA sample, or at least some kind of clothing fibre that will pin down our killer. No one can carry out three murders and not leave something. Forensics are also trying to identify the type of axe used, and also a brush that was found at the scene. The indications are that it was used to paint the message on the wall.'

'The pickaxe looks like it might be an ice axe,' said Ffion. 'The kind used by mountaineers.'

'Maybe,' said Baxter. 'But remember what I said about speculation. Let's wait for forensics to come up with a firm ID.'

Andy cleared his throat and raised a hand.

'What is it, Cartwright?' demanded Baxter.

'You asked me to look into Alexia Petrakis's movements before she was killed on Saturday.'

'And?'

'She arrived in Oxford the day before the gaudy, on Friday. She travelled here from London by train, arriving at twelve noon. She checked into the Randolph Hotel where she'd previously booked a room for the night. Then on Friday afternoon she went to the Ashmolean Museum, which is just opposite the Randolph, where she had arranged to meet with somebody called Dr Philippa Atkins.'

'A visit to the museum? What in God's name has that got to do with anything?'

'It's what you asked me to find out, sir.'

'Well, yes, all right then. Good work.'

Ffion raised a hand. 'Sir, I have another idea.'

'What?'

'Last night, as you know, I discovered that the college made a small but very significant investment in GenMeg Therapeutics.'

'Yes,' said Baxter. 'If you recall, I told you after the interview that I thought it was irrelevant.'

'Yes, sir, you did, but I've been thinking. The investment was extremely helpful in enabling Meg Collins to get her company started. Alexia Petrakis also received a boost to her career when the warden introduced her to his media contacts. We don't know if Tina Mackenzie received any kind of assistance, but just suppose that she did.'

'What of it?'

'All three women are now dead. One of the other members of the same group of friends – Bella Williams – received no help at all, and her career failed to take off. What if Bella became resentful of the others' success and decided to get her own back on them at the twenty-year reunion? It would explain why they've all been murdered this weekend.'

Baxter made no attempt to conceal his anger at the suggestion. 'DC Hughes, I have already made it very clear what I think of wild theories and pointless speculation. And this is one of the least plausible theories I've heard so far. If envy was a motive for murder, half the world would be lying dead with a knife sticking in them. And the other half would be in prison.'

But Ffion was persistent as usual. 'Don't you think we should at least interview her, sir? Bella Williams, I mean.'

Baxter gave the matter reluctant consideration. 'All right. I haven't spoken to her myself yet. I'll have a quick word with her now. Meanwhile, I want the rest of you back in the kitchen interviewing the staff. Find out everything you can. Let's get to the bottom of this, and let's not waste any more time.'

The meeting ended in a flurry of activity, with a sudden scraping of chairs and a mad scrambling of feet. Everyone was eager to show willing and get some results. Jake was one of the first out of the door, anxious to make up for being the last one in, and just as keen to keep well away from Baxter.

CHAPTER 23

Ffion was surprised when Baxter called her back at the end of the briefing. 'I thought you wanted everyone to go and interview the kitchen staff, sir.'

'You can come with me instead, DC Hughes.'

'To interview Bella Williams?' Ffion was under the impression that after her unsolicited questions during the interview with Meg Collins, Baxter never wanted her in an interview with him again.

'I need someone,' said Baxter grudgingly. 'Everyone else is busy.'

'Very good, sir.' Ffion decided to take that as an endorsement. Maybe Baxter did secretly appreciate her suggestions after all.

'We're just going to talk to her, mind you. Nothing confrontational. She's not a suspect. But you're right that she was close to all three victims. She may know something useful. And let's find out if there really is anything fishy about the way that two of the murdered women received help from the college.'

Ffion was delighted that Baxter was taking her

idea seriously at last. 'Yes, sir. Absolutely.'

'Let's go to her room.'

When they reached the staircase in St Alban's Quad where Bella was staying, they found DS Ryan Hooper standing guard outside.

'What the bloody hell do you think you're doing here?' bellowed Baxter. 'I said I wanted everyone in the kitchen.' His face turned dark as he stared at Ryan. 'Were you present at my briefing just now, Sergeant?'

'Sorry, sir. No, sir. DI Hart asked me to keep an eye on Miss Williams. She's worried that she may be in danger.'

Baxter nearly exploded at the news. 'DI Hart? If you mean Ms Bridget Hart, I would remind you that she has absolutely no authority in this investigation and that I have given her explicit instructions to stop poking her bloody nose in. You take your orders from me, Sergeant, not her. And if anyone's in danger, it's you. Danger of being suspended for gross misconduct. Now go and help out in the kitchen.'

'Yes, sir. Right away, sir.' Ryan scurried off across the quad. Even Ffion felt sorry for the guy. But not too much.

Baxter took a deep breath, strode inside the building, and banged loudly on the door to Bella's ground-floor room.

The door was opened by Bella herself. She regarded Ffion and Baxter warily. 'Hello? Has anything happened?'

'We'd just like to ask you a few questions, if

that's all right with you,' said Baxter.

'Of course,' said Bella. She opened the door wider to allow them inside, before taking a seat by the window. A book was open on the window sill next to her chair. Hesiod's Theogony, Ffion noted. The book that Bella had mentioned when she'd been interviewed on Sunday.

'I hope you don't mind standing,' said Bella. 'This room doesn't have anywhere else to sit.'

'That won't be a problem,' said Baxter, who looked like he had far too much nervous energy to confine himself to a chair. 'We won't take up much of your time. No doubt you'll be aware that Meg Collins has also been murdered?'

Bella nodded glumly. 'Yes, your sergeant told me.'

Baxter offered no condolences on the loss of Bella's one-time friend. 'You once shared a house with all three murder victims?'

'Yes, along with two other friends.'

'DI Bridget Hart and Miss Lydia Khoury.'

'That's right.'

'Had you kept in close touch with the others since your time in college?'

'Not really. I bumped into them once or twice over the years, but I can't say that we remained friends.'

'Was there any particular reason for that?'

Bella shook her head. 'It's almost twenty years since we shared the house. That's half a lifetime. After Oxford, we all went off into completely different walks of life. I moved to Peterborough and rarely visited London, which was where most of the others lived. There was no reason for us to stay in touch.'

Baxter seemed satisfied by the explanation. 'It has come to our attention that two of the murdered women – Meg Collins and Alexia Petrakis – received help from the college at the beginning of their careers. Do you know anything about that?'

'No,' said Bella. 'What kind of help?'

'The college warden put Miss Petrakis in touch with his media contacts, helping her to get her first job in journalism. The college made a key investment in Ms Collins's company.'

'It doesn't surprise me,' said Bella. 'Alexia's career got started very quickly. And Meg was fortunate to obtain funding for a concept that was little more than a university research project at the time.'

'Might Miss Mackenzie also have received some kind of assistance from her former college?'

'I really have no idea,' said Bella. 'But she certainly became a partner in her law firm at an early age. Someone might have pulled some strings for her. Is it important?'

'Probably not,' said Baxter. 'Thank you for your time, Miss Williams. We'll leave you in peace to read your book now.'

'Just one more thing,' said Ffion. Baxter shot her a warning look, but she ignored it. 'You studied Classics at university, is that right?'

'Yes,' said Bella. She indicated the book she

was reading.

'The study of the literature, history and philosophy of the ancient Greeks and Romans. You were a scholar, weren't you?'

'Yes, I was.'

'And in fact you graduated with first class honours and strong hopes of embarking on an academic career.'

'Yes,' said Bella. 'But you'll know that my hopes came to nothing and I ended up as a teacher. "Just" a teacher, in your own words.' She made no attempt to conceal the resentment in her voice.

'So what went wrong?'

Bella shrugged. 'Nothing went wrong. Oxford is full of bright, young things. Ability isn't enough to succeed in the academic world. You also need luck, or at least the endorsement of someone with influence.'

'And you didn't have that?'

'No.'

Baxter's glower had become a scowl, but Ffion pressed on. 'But your three friends did receive the right kind of help, didn't they? You were forced to watch from the sidelines as their careers took off. It must have made you very jealous. You compared your own life to theirs and didn't like what you saw.'

'DC Hughes, I'm warning you,' said Baxter.

'Although you claimed that you didn't keep in touch with your old friends,' continued Ffion, 'you told me yourself that you'd read all of

Alexia's newspaper articles. And you just admitted that you knew all about Meg's company, and Tina's career as a lawyer. I think that you secretly watched them, keeping a tally of their various achievements. And then one day, nearly twenty years later, you finally found a way to level the playing field.'

Bella laughed, then gave Ffion a pitying look. 'All right, I admit that I watched them. There was plenty to enjoy, with all their petty rivalries and disputes. But if you think I murdered Alexia, Tina and Meg because I was jealous, I can assure you that I had nothing to be jealous of. Do you think that success made any of them happy? It didn't. Alexia wrote her nasty articles attacking all kinds of people, but it only brought her enemies. In the end, even her closest friends hated her. Tina was no better, living for years with the guilt of how she had lied and cheated her way to success. She was so consumed by ambition that she relentlessly pursued a legal case against her best friend, not caring what damage it did. Meg herself was tormented by both Tina and Alexia's selfish and thoughtless actions.'

Bella brandished the book she'd been reading. 'Hesiod relates the story of three women; vengeful and jealous sisters who were known as the Erinyes, or Furies. They dwelt in hell and had snakes for hair, the heads of dogs, the wings of bats, and bloodshot eyes. Not only did they wreak anguish on mortals who had transgressed the will of the gods, they tormented each other too. Meet Alexia, Tina and Meg.'

A silence fell across the room once Bella had concluded her emotional outburst.

'I think we're done here, Constable,' said Baxter to Ffion, as Bella began to weep quietly. 'I'm sorry to have disturbed you, Miss Williams.'

Outside, Baxter turned the full force of his fury on Ffion. 'DC Hughes, when I warn a junior officer to desist in a line of questioning, I expect to be obeyed. I do not expect them to continue as if I had said nothing. I certainly do not expect them to treat a witness as if they are guilty when there is no actual proof of any sort that they have committed a crime. And I have made it abundantly clear to you that I detest wild speculation of the kind that you just indulged in. Am I in any way unclear?'

'No, sir,' said Ffion. 'Sorry, sir.'

A figure was running towards them across the quad. DS Andy Cartwright.

Baxter turned irritably to confront him. 'What is it now?'

'Sorry to interrupt, sir,' said Andy breathlessly, 'but you asked me to tell you as soon as there was any news.'

'Well? What news?'

'I've just had a call from forensics,' said Andy excitedly. 'They've finished analysing all the fingerprints that were found in Tina Mackenzie's room. The only prints on the empty glass of wine were from Miss Mackenzie herself. The second glass was wiped clean, but they've managed to lift a print from the bottle.'

'And?'

'It's the butler's, sir. Nick Kernahan.'

Baxter glowered at him. 'That's not particularly surprising, is it, Sergeant? The butler is the only member of staff with access to the college cellars. Presumably every bottle has his prints on them.'

'Yes sir, but what is surprising is how the team knew that the print was his. Nick Kernahan's fingerprints were in the police database because he has a criminal conviction.'

Baxter's features sharpened into a predatory look. 'Conviction for what?'

'Assault, occasioning actual bodily harm. Apparently he attacked the previous college chef and broke both of his arms. He would have gone to prison, but the college warden put in a good word on his behalf and he was given a suspended sentence.'

'I never liked the look of that butler,' said Baxter. 'Come on. Let's get him.'

★

When DI Baxter stormed into the dining hall, Jake was engaged in a heated debate with the college butler. Nick Kernahan was a tall imposing man, dressed in a black waistcoat and bow tie. He had been busy supervising the clearing away of the breakfast things when the team of detectives arrived in the hall, intent on interviewing his staff and finding out their every movement during the past forty-eight hours. He reacted with undisguised hostility to the intrusion. 'You've already interviewed all the kitchen and serving staff at great length,' he told Jake. 'I've been interviewed myself at least twice. How am I supposed to do my job when you clowns keep swooping in and disrupting everything?'

For a butler, Jake found the man's behaviour to be somewhat aggressive. If he ever found himself in need of a butler himself – a situation that seemed extraordinarily unlikely – he would never choose one who displayed so much unbridled belligerence. 'Calm down, mate,' he told him. 'There's no need to get shirty.'

'I can get a lot shirtier than this. And don't you "mate" me. I'm no friend of yours.'

Jake wondered how to handle the situation for the best. He could sympathise to some extent with the way the man's job was being hampered by all the disruption. It was a difficult situation all round. But the guy had to understand that three people had been murdered. There was no place for such hostility.

He was relieved when Baxter swept into the hall like a miniature thunder cloud and slapped a meaty hand on the butler's shoulder. The man whirled in surprise, his face as dark as Baxter's own.

'Nick Kernahan, I am arresting you on

suspicion of the murders of Alexia Petrakis, Tina Mackenzie and Meg Collins. You do not have to say anything –'

'What? Get off me!' cried the butler in outrage. He tried to shake himself free, but Baxter rammed him roughly up against the wood-panelled wall and snapped a set of handcuffs over his wrists.

'– but it may harm your defence if you do not mention when questioned something you later rely on in court.'

'I didn't murder anyone!' shouted Nick Kernahan. 'I didn't even know those women!'

'Take him to Kidlington,' muttered Baxter. 'Andy, do it now.'

Jake watched in bemusement as Andy and two constables dragged the butler from the dining hall. That was certainly one way of dealing with the situation. But why on earth had Baxter decided to arrest him for murder?

Baxter offered no clue to his reasons. Instead, he swept his gaze around the dining hall, ignoring the startled stares of college staff, police detectives and guests, and looking happier than Jake had seen him all weekend. 'Now we're getting somewhere,' he declared.

'Very good, sir,' said Jake. 'What should we do now?'

'I'll be heading back to Kidlington to interview him,' said Baxter. 'In the meantime, I want this place turned upside down. Check every knife, fork and spoon. Question all the kitchen and serving staff again. Find out everything about them. By the time you're finished, I want to know the entire life story of every single person who works in this place. No more mistakes.'

Jake began to organise the junior detectives and other officers to carry out the orders. He was about to help too when the college warden appeared in the doorway. 'What on earth is happening now?' he demanded.

Baxter turned to confront him, drawing himself to his full height and puffing out his chest like a soldier readying for battle. 'I have arrested the college butler, Nick Kernahan, on suspicion of the murders of Alexia Petrakis, Tina Mackenzie and Meg Collins. Now my officers are conducting a search of the premises.'

The warden looked appalled. 'Meg Collins? Nobody informed me there had been another murder.'

'The third body was discovered just over an hour ago.'

'Good God. And you think that Mr Kernahan is responsible?'

Baxter glared at the warden. 'Does that surprise you? I understand that you were aware he has a criminal conviction for assault?'

Jake gaped at the news in amazement. A butler with a conviction for assault? Even with his limited experience of life, he guessed that wasn't common in the world of butlers. But after experiencing the man's aggressive behaviour for himself, he couldn't say he was totally surprised.

'Yes. But –'

'And yet you failed to mention this fact to either myself or any of my officers?'

'I was never questioned about the butler,' protested Dr Harper. 'I didn't see that it was relevant information.'

'Didn't you? And is it normal college policy to offer employment to convicted criminals? Violent criminals? What about your duty of care to your students?'

'The college believes in allowing people a second chance, Inspector. Nick Kernahan was given a suspended sentence on condition that the college continued to employ him. And apart from a single unfortunate incident that took place several years ago, his behaviour has been exemplary.'

'Until now.'

'Do you have anything to link him directly to the murders?' asked the warden.

Baxter looked pleased to have been asked. He began to reel off a list, using his fingers to count. 'College property used as murder weapons; college knives from the kitchen used to remove body parts; college wine – which, incidentally, only the butler had access to – used to poison one of the victims; the placing of eyeballs in the bowl of soup. Not to mention incriminating fingerprints. I expect that further evidence will be obtained once our forensic team has finished examining the material taken from the most recent crime scenes.'

The warden looked stricken. 'If I had any suspicions about Nick, I wouldn't have hesitated to mention them to you.'

'If you had done that, sir, then maybe two of your guests would still be alive,' retorted Baxter.

Dr Harper curled his lip but said nothing more. The two men glared at each other for a moment before Baxter left, followed shortly after by the warden.

After they'd gone, the hall was filled with silence. Ryan came over to Jake and whispered in his ear. 'I don't know why we didn't arrest the butler right at the start.'

'Really? How come?'

Ryan broke into a broad grin. 'It's always the butler, isn't it? Haven't you read any Agatha Christie, mate?'

CHAPTER 24

'I can't believe this has happened,' said Ffion to Jake after Baxter had returned to Kidlington to begin interviewing Nick Kernahan.

Jake wondered what she was talking about – the arrest of the butler, or the fact that Baxter hadn't asked her to accompany him for this latest interview. Whatever it was, she looked thoroughly miserable and dejected. He had to suppress an urge to put a consoling arm around her.

'I really thought she'd done it,' she said.

'Who?' he asked, blankly.

'Bella Williams.'

'Bella?' Jake's brain was struggling to keep up. 'You thought Bella was the murderer? But why would she have wanted to kill her own friends?'

'Jealousy.'

'You think so?' he said sceptically. 'I actually thought this was all about revenge.'

'What makes you say that?'

'Well, Tina hated Alexia for writing that newspaper article about her. Meg hated Tina for taking her company to court. Meg hated Alexia for sleeping with her husband.'

'But Meg and Tina are both dead now. And anyway, who hated Meg?'

'I don't know.'

'No,' said Ffion. 'There's something else going on.'

'Well, yeah,' said Jake. 'The butler.'

Ffion shook her head dismissively. 'Why would the butler have done it?'

'I don't know,' he admitted. 'But all the evidence points towards him.'

'Huh,' said Ffion.

Jake waited, but she seemed in no hurry to elaborate. 'Well,' he said, 'Baxter's convinced the butler did it.'

'You know what Baxter's like when he gets hold of an idea.'

'Like a bulldog.'

'Exactly.'

Still, Jake had to admit that the evidence was compelling. The fact that Nick Kernahan had been the one who served the soup containing Alexia's eyeballs to Dr Harper suggested some kind of personal grudge against the college warden. Maybe his three victims had been chosen simply at random, as part of an elaborate scheme to discredit the warden and stop him becoming the university's vice-chancellor. But that sounded far-fetched, even to Jake's ears. 'I don't think Baxter's too bothered about why anything happens,' he said. 'He's only interested in who, when and where.'

'Here's the question we should be asking,' said Ffion. 'What was the nature of the article that Alexia Petrakis was writing about the warden, and why did she spend the day before the gaudy visiting the Ashmolean Museum?'

'That's two questions,' grumbled Jake, 'and I don't really see why either of them matters.'

'Well, we won't know until we've answered them. And that's what you and I are going to do right now.'

'It is?'

'Yeah. Is your car outside?'

'Yes.'

'Come on, then,' she said grabbing his arm. 'Let's take a visit to the Ashmolean.'

★

Bridget watched from the far corner of Front Quad as first Baxter, then Dr Harper strode angrily out of the dining hall, heading off in opposite directions – Baxter stomping towards the gatehouse, the warden marching briskly in the direction of the Fellows' Garden, presumably returning to his lodgings. She had already seen the butler being led away in handcuffs by Andy. A major development had obviously occurred, and thanks to a rapid text message exchange with Ffion, Bridget was already fully up to speed on this latest twist in the investigation.

'Do you mind if I join you?' she asked, as the warden approached the archway where she was standing. She stuck out a hand. 'I'm DI Bridget Hart.'

Dr Harper's eyes flashed angrily at her for a brief moment before he collected himself together and replaced the look of annoyance with a polite smile. He took her hand, looking puzzled. 'I thought you were one of our alumni guests. Inspector Baxter didn't mention that you were involved in the investigation.'

'I'm not officially,' said Bridget. 'I'm here as a guest for the gaudy, but I'm also a detective inspector with Thames Valley Police.'

'I see. So how may I help you? I can give you a few minutes of my time, but then I really must get back to my lodgings. The police investigation is playing havoc with my schedule and the college's various activities. We've already had to cancel a conference that was supposed to be taking place here this week. Although,' he added quickly, 'I understand perfectly well the need for us to cooperate fully with the police.'

'Of course,' said Bridget. 'Perhaps I could walk back through the gardens with you, then we can talk as we go?'

'That seems like an excellent idea.'

They left the noise and bustle of Front Quad behind them and set off through the quieter surroundings of St Alban's Quadrangle. Bridget struggled somewhat to keep pace with the long-legged Dr Harper. It was easy to picture him striding around the rugged hills of Iraq or Jordan, a battered fedora perched jauntily on his head of fine silver hair.

'So, what is it you'd like to know?'

'It's rather a personal matter, really.'

'Oh?' Dr Harper slowed his pace.

'You may not remember this, but I was a good friend of Alexia, Tina and Meg when we were at college together.'

'I'm very sorry for your loss. How terrible for you, all three murder victims being friends of yours.'

'Thank you.'

'Yes,' said the warden, heading out into the green open space of the Fellows' Garden. I do seem to remember you now. You studied History under Dr Irene Thomas, is that right?'

'Yes,' said Bridget, relieved to discover that she had made some kind of lasting impression on the warden during her three years as an undergraduate.

'I was senior tutor at that time,' said Dr Harper. 'Although I'm sure you remember that. Dr Thomas stood against me for election to the post of warden soon after. But, as history records, the college's governing body chose me for the position instead. I don't think she's ever quite forgiven me.'

'Is that so?' Bridget wondered how best to broach the question she was hoping to ask. She had been tipped-off by Ffion that the warden had helped Alexia to get her career started in journalism, and that he'd probably also been responsible for persuading the college authorities to invest in Meg's fledgling company. She didn't think he would be willing to divulge the reason why he'd been so helpful, but she hoped to trick him into revealing whether he had done something similar for Tina.

'I know that you were a great help to them,' she ventured. 'To Alexia, Tina and Meg, that is.'

Brendan Harper swung his blue-eyed gaze on her. 'A help? What do you mean?'

'The way you got Alexia started in journalism. Meg too, with her company. They always said how much they appreciated your kindness.'

The warden seemed happy to hear it. 'Did they? Good. I'm very glad I was able to help them. I always do what I can to assist former students of the college.'

Bridget didn't recall that the warden had offered any assistance to her. It was obvious that he barely knew who she was. Bella, too, would no doubt have been very grateful if he'd given her some help getting her career established.

'Tina appreciated your help too, of course,' she said.

'Ah, yes. Well, it was really Brian Mellor, the professor of jurisprudence, who put in a good word for Tina. Brian's retired now, you know.'

'Yes,' said Bridget. 'Although Tina knew that you'd asked him to do it.'

'Well,' said the warden modestly, 'I do have some influence in the college.'

They had arrived now at the rear of the warden's lodgings in the Fellows' Garden. Mrs

Harper was sitting in a chair next to a beautifully-trimmed yellow rose bush, reading a book. She glanced up as they approached.

'So, what was it you wanted to ask me about?' asked the warden.

'It doesn't matter now,' said Bridget. 'I can see you're very busy. Perhaps we'll talk again another time.'

★

The roughly cobbled road of Merton Street was no place to drive his beloved Subaru, but Jake didn't have any choice in the matter. Parking on the streets of central Oxford was close to impossible, even with the police permit that allowed him to park on double yellow lines. He had been obliged to leave his car just outside the college gatehouse.

With Ffion in the passenger seat, he set off slowly, bumping and bouncing his way along the ancient road surface, doing his best not to scrape the car's custom body kit on the lumps of stone that stuck up through the mortar like dinosaur teeth. Why any city council would insist on maintaining a road like this when horse-drawn carriages had been phased out a century ago was beyond his understanding.

'Come on, get a move on,' said Ffion impatiently. 'If you drive like this all the way, it'll be quicker to walk.'

'I'm not going to scratch my bodywork just for

282

the sake of a hunch. Anyway, we shouldn't be doing this at all. Baxter wants us in the college. How are we going to explain a detour to the Ashmolean Museum? He'll do his nut if he finds out.'

'Baxter should be back in Kidlington by now. If we're quick he won't even know we're gone.'

Jake hoped she was right about that. He certainly didn't fancy facing DI Baxter's wrath. 'Remind me again what we're hoping to find?'

Ffion shrugged. 'I don't know exactly. But someone needs to follow up on what Andy found out. Alexia Petrakis travelled to Oxford a day early and made an appointment to meet one of the museum curators. She wasn't just going there as a casual visitor. She was doing research.'

'But research for what? I thought Alexia Petrakis pursued stories about miscarriages of justice and abuses of power. Why would she be interested in a museum?'

'That's what we're going to find out. Since Baxter doesn't have the imagination to think outside the box, we'll have to do it for him.'

'Fair point.' Jake was prepared to take Ffion's word for it. Especially if it meant an opportunity to spend some time in her company. It was certainly more appealing than hanging around the college, interviewing a load of kitchen staff. 'So, this Ashmolean, what kind of museum is it exactly?'

Ffion looked at him as if he had the brains of a donkey. 'You're kidding me?'

'No. I've heard of it, obviously –'

'Obviously,' she retorted, 'since it's Oxford's most famous museum.'

'– and I've been meaning to go and visit it. I just haven't got round to it yet.'

Ffion snorted as if she found the idea of Jake visiting any kind of museum hard to credit. She wasn't wrong. Jake had always hated being dragged around museums as a child. He had visions of row upon row of glass cases stuffed with broken fragments of pottery, ancient cooking utensils, and misshapen lumps of rock.

'The Ashmolean Museum is the university's museum of art and archaeology,' lectured Ffion. 'It was founded in 1683 and originally housed the collection of curiosities donated to the university by Elias Ashmole.'

'Elias Ashmole, that's right,' said Jake. Who? he thought. He probably hadn't missed out by not visiting the Ashmolean.

Ffion gave him a suspicious look before continuing. 'It now holds the largest collection of Raphael drawings in the world, as well as extensive archaeological collections from prehistoric Europe, Ancient Egypt, Classical Greece... I could go on if you like.'

'No, there's no need. I get the picture.'

He turned the car into Beaumont Street and pulled into a parking space outside Oxford Playhouse. A coach waiting in front of the museum was disgorging a stream of primary school children clutching clipboards under their arms and chattering excitedly while a harassed-looking teacher ticked them off on her register. Jake and Ffion darted around the children, just making it to the revolving doors of the grand neo-classical building ahead of them.

On entering, Ffion made straight for the information counter and presented her warrant card to the attendant on the desk.

The woman looked at them in some alarm. 'Police? Is there a problem?'

'On Friday afternoon a journalist called Alexia Petrakis had an appointment with one of your staff – Dr Philippa Atkins. We'd like to speak to her.'

Ffion's abrupt request did little to put the attendant at ease. 'Dr Atkins is our curator of Phoenician Antiquities,' she said nervously. 'Would you like me to see if she's in her office?'

'Please.'

While they waited for her to make the call, Jake glanced around the building's imposing entrance space. He had to admit that the museum was certainly very popular – there was a steady stream of visitors coming and going through the revolving doors. Running off to the left was a long gallery of Greek and Roman statues, half of them with their noses missing. The unfortunate schoolchildren were being shepherded through the gallery, hopefully on their way to somewhere more interesting. In front of him he caught a glimpse of a room that confirmed his worst fear – a display of broken pots was proudly presented, next to some lumps of rock. He shuddered.

The attendant finished speaking and put the phone down. 'Dr Atkins is on her way down now.'

After a few minutes a middle-aged woman with long grey hair descended the stone staircase that led to the upper floors. She wore a baggy blue shirt with the sleeves rolled up and a pair of red reading glasses on a multi-coloured cord around her neck. She held out her hand. 'Dr Philippa Atkins. I understand that you're from Thames Valley Police. Is this about Alexia Petrakis?'

'It is,' said Ffion.

Dr Atkins looked worried. 'I heard on the news that she'd been murdered. What a terrible thing to happen. You'd better come up to my office.'

She led them up the stairs and into a small room overflowing with papers, boxes and archaeological artifacts. 'Please excuse the mess,' she said. We're in the process of reorganising some of our collections of antiquities.'

'Not a problem,' said Ffion, taking a seat on a window sill.

Jake stood next to her, surveying the chaotic state of the office. It reminded him of his own cramped and cluttered apartment in Cowley. Except that in his case, the boxes that covered every available surface had once contained pizzas, not ancient treasures.

'We've been told that Alexia Petrakis had a meeting with you on Friday afternoon,' said

Ffion. 'Is that correct?'

'Yes, she did,' said Dr Atkins. 'She phoned me earlier in the week to arrange the meeting. She was very keen to see me.' She looked from Ffion to Jake and back to Ffion. 'Do you think that this might be connected to her murder?'

'That's what we'd like to find out. What did she want to see you about?'

'That's the strange thing,' said Dr Atkins. 'She had a very specific request. She wanted to talk to me about one of the pieces on display here at the museum. It's one of our most important exhibits, in fact. A Phoenician votive statue.'

'Sorry to interrupt,' said Jake, 'but you just said two words I didn't understand. Phoenician and votive.'

Dr Atkins smiled at him indulgently. 'Sorry. I'm the head of Phoenician Antiquities here and I'm used to speaking with other experts. You must stop me if I start to use jargon. The Phoenicians were an ancient Mediterranean civilisation originally from the Levant – that's modern-day Lebanon, northern Israel and parts of Syria. They spread as far west as Carthage in North Africa and Cadiz in Spain between 1500 and 300 BC. They were peaceful traders, which is perhaps why they're not as well known as the more warlike civilisations of the ancient world like the Greeks and Romans. But you shouldn't underestimate their significance. They invented the first phonetic alphabet, for instance.'

'Got it,' said Jake. 'And a votive statue is?

'Ah, yes. A votive offering is an object, usually of some significant value, placed in a sacred location with the intention of gaining favour with the gods or other supernatural beings. Sometimes they were destroyed as a sacrifice, but very often they were buried with wealthy individuals to secure their safe passage and protection in the afterlife.'

'Great,' said Jake. 'Thanks.'

Dr Atkins smiled warmly at him.

Ffion was displaying considerable impatience at this diversion. 'You said that Alexia was interested in one particular votive statue?'

'Yes,' said Dr Atkins, turning back to her. 'In fact, I have it right here in my office. It was put into storage while we rearrange the display cases and I retrieved it to show to Ms Petrakis.' She took a wooden box down from a shelf and removed the lid. Nestling in a bed of straw was a carved figure, about fifteen inches tall. Dr Atkins put on a pair of gloves and very carefully lifted the statue up for them to see.

'She's rather beautiful isn't she?' she enthused. 'She's a Phoenician deity from the middle of the first millennium BC – almost three thousand years old. This is an extraordinary piece of art. Look at the detail in the face, which has been carved with a half smile and look of such serenity. You can see the quality of the workmanship in the pleats and folds of her robe, and see here,' – she pointed to the figure's hand – 'how she's fingering a beaded necklace around her neck. The slightly protuberant abdomen and breasts suggest pregnancy, an obvious symbol of fertility and fecundity.'

Jake was willing to concede that there might be more in the museum than just bits of old broken pottery. Maybe when the case was over he'd ask Ffion to give him a quick tour of the museum's highlights. He caught Ffion's eye. It was clear that Dr Atkins would wax lyrical on the subject of Phoenician artwork all day if they let her.

'Where did the statue come from?' asked Ffion.

'From the city of Byblos, which is now in Lebanon.'

'And how did the statue end up in this museum?'

'Well, it's a relatively recent addition, by museum standards. It was donated to us some thirty years ago by Dr Brendan Harper, the warden of Merton College.'

Jake and Ffion exchanged meaningful glances. 'What exactly did Alexia want to know about the statue?' asked Jake, trying to keep the growing sense of excitement out of his voice.

'Well, in fact she didn't seem especially interested in the statue itself. She was mainly interested in seeing the export licence. I have it right here.' Dr Atkins laid the statue back in its box and picked up a piece of paper from her desk. 'As I mentioned, the statue was discovered in an archaeological dig led by Dr Harper and was brought back to this country in 1987.'

Ffion took the document from her, her eyes flicking rapidly over the details.

'What exactly is an export licence?' asked Jake.

'Every ancient object exported from one country to another has to have an export licence,' explained Dr Atkins. 'It proves that the article is genuine, and also enables the government to control a country's cultural assets. In the case of this statue, Dr Harper managed to bring it out of the country just in time.'

'What do you mean?' Jake asked.

'In 1988 the government of Lebanon passed a law making it illegal to export any kind of antiquity out of the country. This was quite possibly the last item of any significance to be exported.'

'That was lucky,' said Jake.

'In more ways than one,' remarked the curator with a faint smile. 'Dr Harper was still only a young man when he began digging at Byblos. Unearthing this statue launched his career. You could say that it was the discovery of a lifetime.'

'You need to tell us exactly what Alexia Petrakis wanted to know about this export licence,' said Ffion urgently.

Jake cringed at the abruptness of her demand. Ffion could be unbelievably crass at times. When he'd first got to know her, she'd been openly rude to him on several occasions. He wondered if she was even aware of how insensitive she was to other people's feelings.

Dr Atkins regarded her with obvious irritation.

'Miss Petrakis didn't ask me anything directly. She just wanted to see the licence.'

'Did she take a copy?'

'I told her she could take a photograph if she wanted to, but her main interest seemed to be the signature on the form.'

Jake peered at the scribble of ink at the foot of the document. The illegible scrawl was even worse than his own unruly handwriting 'Whose signature is it?'

'Just a ministry official.'

Ffion was studying the document intently. She held it up to the light, examining the paper, then replaced it on the desk where she continued to pore over it. 'Could this licence be a fake?'

Dr Atkins looked aghast at the suggestion. 'A fake? Certainly not.'

Ffion turned her emerald eyes on the curator. 'Why not?'

'Dr Harper is one of the country's most distinguished archaeologists.'

'Maybe,' said Ffion. 'But that's not what I asked. Could this document be a fake?'

'No,' declared Dr Atkins coldly. 'Categorically not. It has all the required details and has been stamped with the official ministry seal. I must say, I don't like the implications of your question. Dr Harper has been a very generous benefactor and supporter of the museum, as well as being much admired for his work on the ancient Near East.'

Ffion handed the licence back.

'Now, was there anything else you wanted to know?' asked Dr Atkins.

Jake sensed that they had used up all of the museum curator's goodwill.

'No,' said Ffion.

'Thanks very much for all your help,' said Jake. He smiled broadly, but his attempts at reconciliation were not returned.

'We'll see ourselves out,' said Ffion shortly.

Jake hurried after her as she marched down the stairs and out of the museum. He caught up with her at the exit. 'Why the hell did you act like that? That was unbelievably rude.'

'Hmm,' she said distractedly. She ignored him as they made their way back across Beaumont Street.

Back in the car he turned to her in annoyance. 'All right, are you going to explain to me what's going on? Why were you so rude back there?'

Ffion seemed surprised at his accusation. 'Rude? Was I?'

'Of course you were! Didn't you even realise?'

'I didn't mean to be. I was just busy thinking.' She sat motionless in the car, looking into the distance, obviously still deep in thought.

It was almost as if she had forgotten he was still there. He stared at her for a full minute, trying to puzzle her out. After a while he decided that she probably hadn't deliberately set out to offend their host. Perhaps she hadn't even realised what kind of impression her direct words and abrupt behaviour had on people. In a way, that made it easier to accept, if there was no malice intended. And yet, if they were ever going to move beyond friendship to a more serious relationship, he wasn't the only one who was going to have to work at becoming more sensitive.

Eventually she seemed to return to the real world. 'Why are we still here?' she asked. 'You need to drive us back to the college.'

'Not just yet. First you can tell me what you were pondering so deeply. What did we actually achieve by coming here? Apart from offending one of the museum's curators, I mean. I don't think I really learned anything.'

'Well,' she said in her sing-song accent, exaggerating it in the way she always did when she was teasing him. 'It looked to me like you learned plenty. Two new words in one day.'

'Ha, very funny,' he said. It was hard for him to stay cross with her for long. 'But I meant about the case.'

'I'm not quite sure. The export licence looked above board to me, but Alexia must have had a good reason for wanting to see it. She may even have been murdered because of it. Come on, we'd better get back to Merton College before Baxter offers us as a sacrifice to the gods.'

CHAPTER 25

From across the table in the interview room at Kidlington, Greg Baxter regarded the butler of Merton College with a sense of satisfaction, knowing that he was now very close to uncovering the truth. The man still denied killing the three women – had even claimed not to have known them – but how long would he be able to maintain his charade of ignorance under continued close questioning?

It should have been obvious from the beginning that the butler was at the centre of everything. Who else had access to the college's wine cellars? Who had been in charge of serving at the college dinner? Why, it had been the butler himself who had carried the warden's soup to high table and had removed the silver dome that covered it, with a dramatic flourish. It was clear now that he had been taunting the police the whole time.

'Let's start again from the beginning, shall we?' said Baxter. He had all the time in the world to crack this nut wide open. Twenty-four hours, to be more exact, but that would be plenty to force a low-life crook like Nick Kernahan to spill his secrets. The man was sweating profusely in his plastic chair, looking as scared as a rat in a trap. He might still be dressed in his black waistcoat and bow tie, but Baxter knew what kind of man he was dealing with. Beneath his fancy uniform, Nick Kernahan was scum. A vicious criminal with a violent past, and a long and unpleasant future behind bars to look forward to, if Baxter had anything to do with it.

It was true that no obvious motive had yet emerged, but Baxter was confident that after a few hours he would get to the bottom of that. For the time being it was clear that the butler had both the means and the opportunity to carry out his sick and twisted killing spree.

He opened his file at the beginning and lifted out a page. 'Five years ago you were involved in an altercation between yourself and the college chef at the time, a Mr George Flynn. Is that correct?'

'You know it is,' said the butler. 'I've answered your questions once already.'

The suspect was growing impatient, but Baxter was in no hurry to speed things along. An interview with a prime suspect was like one of Mrs Baxter's steak and kidney pies. It took time to bake, for the juices to thicken up and the pastry to turn golden. You couldn't rush it.

Baxter consulted the page before him. 'The unfortunate Mr Flynn received a brutal beating at your hands. He was taken to the emergency department at the John Radcliffe hospital where he was treated for' – he read aloud from the loose page – 'two fractured arms, severe bruising to his face and chest, concussion, and corneal abrasions to one eye. A nasty business. You were arrested at the scene and convicted of assault occasioning actual bodily harm.'

'I don't deny it,' said the butler. 'I've already been punished by the courts for beating up George Flynn. Justice has been done.'

'Hardly. It seems that the judge took pity on you and gave you a suspended sentence. An unusual course of action. Very unusual. I wonder why he did that?'

'You know why he did. The college warden spoke on my behalf at the hearing. He promised the judge he'd keep me in employment as one of the conditions of my suspended sentence.'

'How fortunate for you,' said Baxter. 'And how good of the warden to do that on your behalf.' He lowered his palms to the chipped formica desktop and leaned towards the suspect. 'Why did the warden protect you? What hold did you have over him?'

'I didn't have any hold,' protested Kernahan. He's a good man, the warden. He appreciates loyalty and he repays it in kind. I won't say a word against him.'

Baxter leaned back in his chair and steepled his fingers in triumph. 'That's an interesting expression. "He repays loyalty." What debt was Dr Harper repaying to you?'

The butler squirmed in his chair. 'Nothing. I didn't mean anything by that.'

'No?' Baxter let his gaze wander briefly around the interior of the shabby incident room. It was a grotty, dilapidated little corner of the world, and yet it was his domain. He had interviewed countless criminals across this very desk, looking directly into the eyes and the souls of rapists, robbers and murderers, and he felt more at home here than he did in his own house. Now he had sensed an opening and he wasn't going to allow anything to stop him. 'What did you do for the warden? Did he ask you to beat up the chef?'

'Why would he do that?'

'That's what I'm wondering. What could possibly make a civilised man like Dr Brendan Harper, warden of an Oxford college and famous archaeologist and television presenter, want to send such a brutal message to a lowly college chef? Why did he feel threatened? Let's see. Might the chef possibly have shown rather too much interest in Mrs Harper, a very good-looking woman, if you don't mind me saying?'

Baxter knew as soon as he'd made the accusation that he'd struck gold. A light seemed to flicker out in the butler's eyes. Baxter recognised that sign for what it was – an end to the defiant lies that Nick Kernahan had poured out since being arrested.

When the butler spoke again, it was as a man who knew the game was up. 'George Flynn was a dirty bastard, always chasing women. He had countless girlfriends on the go. They were practically falling over themselves to be with him. You know how it is with men like that. They don't know any boundaries. When he started showing an interest in the warden's wife, I warned him he was out of line, but he wouldn't listen. He was used to getting his way with women.'

'And what was Mrs Harper's reaction to this show of interest?'

'She was taken in by him. I couldn't understand what a classy woman like her saw in a man like that. But Flynn had a kind of magical charm over women. He wasn't all that much to look at, but he had a way of talking that made women fall head over heels. Even Mrs Harper wasn't immune to him.'

'And so you spoke to Dr Harper about your concerns?'

'Yeah. I did. I felt it was my duty.'

'And he asked you to send the chef a warning. Perhaps payment was discussed?'

'I didn't do it just for the money. I wanted to teach that bastard a lesson. But yeah, Dr Harper asked me to put a stop to things.'

'George Flynn was in hospital for almost a month.'

'I'm not sorry. He got what he deserved.'

'And yet you didn't.'

'I admitted what I'd done and I went to court. The warden put in a good word for me. Like I said, he's a good man.'

'A good man who paid for another man to have, if you'll excuse my language, the shit kicked out of him?'

'George Flynn deserved everything he got.'

'And in return you protected the warden's reputation and kept his secret. What other secrets have you kept?'

Now the butler looked really frightened. 'You can't pin those murders on me. I don't know a thing about them.'

'Really?' said Baxter. 'That isn't exactly true, is it, Mr Kernahan? In fact, you were the one who presented the soup – the gazpacho – to Dr Harper, knowing full well that it contained the eyeballs of your first victim.'

'I didn't know that!'

'You were the one who stole college cutlery from the kitchen to use as tools in your butchery of the three women.'

'I didn't!'

'You were sending a signal to the warden, weren't you? Threatening to bring his reputation crashing down and wrecking his chances of being elected vice-chancellor. What had he done to deserve that? Threatened to throw you out of your job? If he did that, you risked being sent to prison, didn't you?'

'No! He didn't do anything!'

'But,' said Baxter, 'your biggest mistake was to use a bottle of college Madeira wine to poison Tina Mackenzie. If you hadn't been careless enough to leave your own fingerprints on the bottle, we might never have found out about your criminal past. Not only that, but you also failed to realise that as the only person in the college with access to the wine cellars, it would be immediately obvious that you were the poisoner. You're not exactly a criminal genius, are you?'

'You've got it all wrong. That's not what happened.'

The butler was nearly in tears now, the big man reduced to a quivering wreck. A gentle push would topple him over the edge of the precipice and into a full confession. Baxter had seen it happen right here in this very room, time and time again. It was his favourite part of the job.

'Tell me the truth, then,' said Baxter softly. 'Tell me what really happened.'

CHAPTER 26

'We really must stop meeting like this,' said Vik
as he emerged from Meg's room and saw Bridget
waiting on the landing at the top of the staircase.
Inside the room, the white-clad SOCO team was
still busy scouring the scene of the third murder
for evidence.

'It is becoming something of a habit, isn't it?'
said Bridget grimly. 'How's it going in there?'

'It's slow work, but we're making progress.'

'Anything you can share with me yet?' Bridget
knew that it was only a matter of time before
Baxter showed up again and she would have to
make herself scarce. She had missed Dr Sarah
Walker this time. The medical examiner had
already been and gone. But Bridget doubted she
could have told her very much she didn't already
know. With an axe embedded in her chest, the
cause of Meg's death couldn't have been more
obvious.

'Not much to report,' said Vik. 'Forensics
haven't found anything useful from the second
murder scene apart from a fingerprint on the
bottle.'

'The butler's, I hear.' As Dr Irene Thomas had explained, college servants had an important part to play in a drama of this kind. Bridget shook her head. This was not a drama, but real life. She must keep reminding herself about that.

'I see that you're keeping yourself well informed,' said Vik. 'Baxter thinks he's caught his murderer.'

'And what do you think, Vik?'

'It's not my job to have opinions. All we do in SOCO is search for stuff to send to the lab.'

'Was there nothing else in Tina's room? No hair? No clothing fibres? I find that hard to believe.'

'The problem was that we found too much. There were hairs and fibres everywhere. My missus would have had a fit if she'd seen the state of the place. To be frank, some of these college rooms are a bit filthy.' He pulled a face.

Bridget could imagine that a SOCO team leader might be somewhat sensitive to household dirt. By the sound of it, Mrs Vijayaraghavan kept a clean house. Cleaner than Bridget's, at any rate.

'I thought that dirt was your trade, Vik.'

'I guess that's true. But it's going to take an age for the lab to analyse everything we found. Actually, the latest murder scene looks a lot more promising.'

Bridget was pleased to hear that. 'In what way?'

'Well, although there were no prints on the

murder weapon or on the brush that was used to paint the message on the wall, we have managed to retrieve a hair that we've sent for analysis.'

Bridget brightened at the news. 'You think it might have been the murderer's hair?'

Vik raised his hands in a gesture of acquiescence. 'As I say, I'm not paid to think, but it definitely didn't belong to the victim, and it was caught in the blood that had leaked onto the bed linen.'

'How long before you'll be able to get a DNA match?'

'A couple of days, I'd say.'

'Okay.' Bridget was grateful to the technological miracles that Vik and the forensics team were able to work, but it was always frustrating that their tests took so long to yield results. 'In the meantime, can you tell me the colour of the hair?'

'Grey. Another interesting point is the nature of the murder weapon.'

'You mean the axe.' Bridget tried to recall the details of its appearance. 'It looked like a pickaxe if I remember rightly.' She wondered if the weapon belonged to the college, since all the previous tools used by the murderer had been.

'A pickaxe, right. The experts have been trying to find out what kind.'

'You mean that there are different kinds of pickaxe?'

Vik gave her a wry smile. 'Of course. You didn't expect this to be easy, did you?'

'I suppose that would be too much to ask. So what kinds are there?'

'Well, we wondered at first if it was the sort that mountaineers use, but they're usually constructed from special lightweight materials – aluminium alloys, Kevlar or carbon fibre. They tend to be brightly coloured too. The British Army issues pickaxes, but they follow strict regulations – their handles have to be exactly three feet long.'

Bridget knew better than to ask Vik why that might be. She didn't need a mini lecture on the history of the British Army pickaxe. She tried to hurry him along to the point. 'So if it's not one of those...'

'The people who know more about these things than I do inform me that it's not a mattock, which is the normal kind of tool used by builders for digging, but is something a little more refined.'

'Please just put me out of my misery, Vik.'

'So, it seems that the axe is quite small, with a traditional construction of a steel head and a wooden shaft, and the head has a pointed tip at one end and a small flat blade at the other. We think it's the kind of tool an archaeologist would use for breaking up compacted soil during an excavation.'

'An archaeologist? Are you sure?' Bridget's brain began to make connections.

'We're pretty certain. You see, the brush that was used to paint the message on the wall also looks like an archaeological tool. It's the type that's used when an item has been recovered from the ground and needs to have fine particles of sand and soil removed.'

'You're saying that Meg Collins was murdered using an archaeologist's toolkit?' There was only one archaeologist that Bridget knew, and his name was Dr Brendan Harper, warden of Merton College, the man who for some unknown reason had taken such a close and unusual interest in the careers of all three victims.

She was just absorbing this latest bombshell when she heard footsteps running up the stairs. They sounded far too energetic for Baxter, who went everywhere and did everything at a steady plod. Sure enough, Ffion and Jake soon rounded the corner at the top of the staircase, Ffion in front, wearing her trademark emerald green leather jacket, and Jake panting slightly at the rear.

'I'm glad we've found you, ma'am,' said Ffion. 'Could we have a word, please? Before DI Baxter finds out we're here,' she added with a wink.

★

'You did what?' Baxter felt his anger rising. Was this man playing him for a fool?

'I have contacts in the trade you see,' explained Nick Kernahan. 'All the college butlers do. I work with the college's wine suppliers and importers, as well as local wine merchants. It's not hard to find a buyer, even for rare vintages.'

'You're telling me that you stole cases of wine from the college and sold them for personal gain?'

'I'm ashamed to admit it,' said the butler. 'Like I said, the warden's been good to me. It's a terrible way to repay his kindness. But I had no choice.'

Baxter had heard enough. 'I'm not interested in why or how you stole bottles of wine. I'm trying to solve a murder case. Three murders. I don't have time for your babbling.'

But Nick Kernahan hadn't finished, not by a long way. Now that he had started to talk, it seemed that he couldn't confess enough. 'What happened was that after my previous trouble with the police –'

'When you assaulted the chef.'

'– I started to gamble. You know, online betting. It's so easy these days. I was betting on the horses, the dogs, at bingo, at roulette. Well, it gets addictive. You can even place in-game bets, like on which team will score the next goal, or which player will get a yellow card. It's a bit crazy, to be honest. Sometimes I won, sometimes I lost, but after a while I realised I was losing more than winning.'

'What a surprise,' said Baxter unsympathetically.

'So I needed to get hold of some cash, quickly. I couldn't think of anything else to do.'

'Of course you couldn't.'

'That's when the new chef, John Bradley, started blackmailing me. He said he'd tell the police about what I'd done. I threatened him, but I could see he wasn't scared. He knew I'd lose my job and go to prison. I was desperate. I didn't know what to do.'

'Of course you didn't,' said Baxter. 'Do you know why that is?'

'No.'

'Because you are a total waste of space. Did anyone ever tell you that? I'm not surprised you've made such a complete and utter balls-up of your life. First you punch a man all the way to hospital, then you lose your shirt gambling, then you start stealing to fund your habit. And now' – Baxter was working himself up to fever pitch. He knew he shouldn't. His doctor had warned him about this kind of behaviour. Liable to raise his already high blood pressure and put his health in jeopardy. Blah, blah, blah. His wife had warned him too. Nagged him to lose weight, and ease off the booze and the bacon sarnies. But how could he not get mad, when faced with such blatant and overwhelming stupidity? – 'and now you've wasted valuable police time while a serial killer is at large and every minute counts! I'm going to throw the book at you. I'll charge you with every bloody offence I can think of. Theft. Breaching the conditions of a suspended sentence. Wasting police time. You'll be going to prison, son, and no more butlering or fine wines for you. And no more bloody bingo either!'

He stormed out of the interview room leaving Nick Kernahan behind. A police constable was wandering down the corridor, carrying a mug of tea from the canteen. He looked at Baxter's red face in alarm and stopped. 'Is everything all right, sir?'

'No, it bloody well is not,' yelled Baxter. 'What's your name?'

'Rushton, sir. PC Rushton.'

'Can you drive, Rushton?'

'Yes, sir. Of course, sir.'

'Then get me back to Merton College as fast as you bloody well can!'

★

'You get a very nice view from here, ma'am,' said Jake, as he peered out across Merton Field from her window in the Grove Building.

'Just as long as you don't mind ghosts,' muttered Bridget. She still hadn't seen any spectral visitors wandering along Dead Man's Walk at night, despite what Dr Irene Thomas had said about ghosts being an essential element in any revenge play, but the number of ghosts inhabiting the college was growing by the day. Three of her friends were now dead. Four, if you counted Lydia Khoury. She prayed that no more would join them.

'Ma'am?'

'Sorry, nothing. Now, what was it you wanted

308

to talk to me about?' Bridget sat down on the room's only chair, while Jake stood by the window and Ffion sat on the desk with one leg crossed over the other, her ankle boots dangling mid-air. 'Any news from Kidlington about the college butler?'

'Baxter's just finished questioning him. Apparently he's extracted a confession.'

'A confession?' Bridget could scarcely believe it. 'But why would the butler want to kill off college guests? That doesn't make any sense.'

Ffion and Jake exchanged glances. 'No, that's not what he confessed to, ma'am.'

'Then what?'

'Stealing wine from the college cellars. Apparently the cellars hold thousands of bottles of vintage wines, champagne, port, sherry and other fortified wines. Some of them date back more than fifty years. Baxter can't believe the college has such lax security.'

'This is ridiculous,' said Bridget.

'We agree,' said Ffion. 'So, Jake and I have just paid a visit to the Ashmolean Museum.'

'What?' Was the world going mad? While Baxter was busy arresting wine pilferers, Jake and Ffion had been out visiting a museum. 'I take it that you didn't just go to see their latest exhibition?' The special display about Rembrandt's early years was one that Jonathan had told her about. She was hoping to go and see it with him, if he recovered from his injuries in time.

'No. Andy did some background work and discovered that Alexia Petrakis came to Oxford on Friday, one day before the gaudy, and had a meeting at the museum with an expert in Phoenician archaeology.'

'I wonder why she did that,' said Bridget. As far as she knew, Alexia had no particular interest in archaeology, Phoenician or otherwise. But this was the second time that the subject of archaeology had been mentioned in the past half hour.

'We wondered the same,' said Ffion. 'So we went to see the museum curator. It seems that Alexia was very interested in a particular votive statue that was discovered by Dr Brendan Harper in Lebanon back in the eighties.'

Bridget's interest in this new angle was growing steadily. 'Of course. Alexia was writing an article about Dr Harper. It was going to be a bombshell.'

'Dr Harper unearthed the statue at a city called Byblos. Apparently it was the archaeological find that catapulted him to stardom and got him his first television deal. He brought the statue to Oxford in 1987, one year before it became illegal to export ancient artifacts out of Lebanon.'

'I wonder why Alexia wanted to see it. Did you find out?'

'She was interested in the export licence for the statue.'

'Did you see the licence yourself?' asked Bridget.

Ffion nodded. 'Yes, it looked perfectly legitimate to me. But there has to be some reason why an investigative journalist like Alexia wanted to see it. She must have been onto something.'

Bridget thought for a moment. 'I wonder if this has anything to do with Lydia Khoury.'

'Who?' asked Jake.

'An old friend from a very long time ago.' Bridget took a deep breath and settled back in her chair. 'There were six of us in total. We were studying different subjects, but we became good friends in our first year when we were living in college. During our second year we decided to live out, and we rented a house together in East Oxford. It was a total dump. The landlord was so mean he never paid for anything to be fixed properly. In the middle of winter the central heating broke down and we had to walk around wearing three layers of clothes before he eventually arranged for a mate of his who was a plumber to come and fix it. But that didn't matter. We had an amazing time together.'

A recollection of how they'd been those twenty years ago suddenly washed over Bridget as she recounted her story. 'We were all just nineteen or twenty years old. Young, carefree, desperately excited to be sharing a house together. It felt like we had finally become adults and claimed our freedom. Alexia was the most outrageous member of the group. Half-Italian, half-Greek, she was like some exotic bird flown in from a hot land. I'm not sure the rest of us really knew what to make of her. She certainly shook us up and opened our eyes to a more exciting world. She would bring home bottles of wine and cook impromptu meals for us – Greek or Italian dishes, supposedly family recipes that had been handed down for generations. But you never knew with Alexia whether she was telling the truth. She had a gift for making up stories. She always had a new boyfriend, or two, or three. And she was always breaking up with them, and sometimes making up again. It was impossible to keep track of her.'

She let the happy memories flow. 'Meg was a wild extrovert who dressed in bright colours and never stopped talking. She was a party animal who loved to say outrageous things to shock people. But she had a serious side too. She was always talking about how she would change the world one day through science. Then there was Tina. She was quieter than Meg and Alexia, but just as ambitious. Tina spent most of her time working, but she could be fun too, especially after a few drinks.

'Next was Bella. You wouldn't believe it when you see her now, but Bella was stunningly beautiful when she was younger. She had lovely long hair and was incredibly slim. But she never had a boyfriend. I think she was too shy, or perhaps just too busy with her studies. Of all the group she was probably the most dedicated. We all believed that she would stay on at Oxford and end up as a professor one day. And then there was Lydia. Lydia was an immigrant to this country. She was born in Lebanon but her family travelled to Britain during the early 1980s when the civil war in Lebanon became too dangerous for them to stay. Her first language was Arabic but she also spoke fluent English, French and Aramaic. She came from a strict Maronite Catholic background.'

'Maronite?' queried Jake.

'The Maronite church is an eastern Catholic church,' explained Ffion. As usual, Ffion seemed to know her facts, so Bridget let her proceed. 'The leader of the church is based in Beirut, but most of the church's members now live outside Lebanon. It's a very strict church, even by Catholic standards. In fact, when the current patriarch was asked for his views on gay rights, he said that homosexuality is a disease and is abnormal.'

'I think I get the picture,' said Jake.

'Yes.' Bridget picked up where she'd left off. 'Lydia had a very rigid upbringing and she was extremely devout. But she was full of fun and we all got on really well together.'

'I'm beginning to get the feeling that something went wrong,' said Jake.

Bridget nodded. 'After a year living out together, we moved back into college for our final year. That last summer in Oxford was very hot. Studying for Finals was hell, especially for Meg who suffered from dreadful hay fever. We were all looking forward to finishing the exams and being able to relax. But then the first of a series of terrible events unfolded.'

She paused, wondering if she was being too melodramatic. But no, on balance she didn't think she was.

'The day after I finished my last exam, my younger sister Abigail who was sixteen and still living at home was abducted. She went missing after school and the police began a search. Her body was discovered three days later in Wytham Woods near Oxford. She'd been strangled.'

Bridget kept her voice level as she related the story. The bare facts summarised the case well enough, but scarcely began to touch on how she felt about them, even now.

'Obviously I left Oxford and returned home to Woodstock to be with my parents and my older sister. I stayed there for the rest of the summer, waiting for news. But the police never found Abigail's killer.'

Jake's expression had become doleful as he listened to the story of her own personal tragedy. He clearly had no idea what to say. Bridget saved him from having to say anything by pressing on. 'But that was just the first horrible incident. The next catastrophe hit Lydia. She was studying Archaeology and Anthropology, and her tutor was Dr Brendan Harper. In fact Dr Harper was the reason Lydia had applied to study at Merton. She'd always wanted to visit her homeland one day, and Dr Harper was famous for his excavations at the city of Byblos, which was where Lydia was born. It seemed like the perfect fit. So in her final year she travelled to Lebanon and took part in a dig there. It was that work that formed part of her final dissertation.

'But there was some kind of problem with Lydia's fieldwork in Byblos. I don't know what exactly, because by this time I was back in Woodstock with my family and I had enough problems of my own to deal with. But it seems that she had done something wrong and she ended up failing her dissertation. It was the end of all her hopes and dreams.'

'Lydia isn't at the gaudy this weekend, is she?' asked Jake.

'No. After I left Oxford, the others stayed on until term ended. During those last few days, Lydia committed suicide.'

The room fell silent. 'There must have been an inquest into her death,' said Ffion eventually.

'Yes, there was. I didn't attend because of my own circumstances, but the verdict was suicide.'

'There was nothing suspicious about it?'

'No,' said Bridget. 'But now I'm beginning to wonder.'

'Could there be a link between Lydia's suicide and the article that Alexia was planning to write about the warden?' asked Jake.

'I don't know,' said Bridget. 'Alexia was interested in the statue at the Ashmolean. But the only real connection between that and Lydia's death is Byblos. If the statue was discovered in 1987, that's nearly two whole decades before Lydia worked on her dissertation.'

'But suppose there was a connection,' said Ffion. 'If the warden was somehow responsible for Lydia's death, might he also have murdered the other three to stop them from talking?'

'Well,' said Bridget. 'he certainly has a lot to lose right now. If any scandal emerged about his past, it would scupper his chances of being elected vice-chancellor.'

'If that's the case,' said Jake. 'Might you and Bella also be in danger?'

'I don't think I am,' said Bridget, although she was touched by her sergeant's concern for her safety. 'As I explained, I left Oxford before all this happened, so I don't know anything more than what I've told you. As for Bella, I've already asked Ryan to keep watch over her.'

Ffion's eyes suddenly widened.

'What is it?' asked Bridget.

'Ma'am, DI Baxter ordered Ryan to leave Bella and to return to the kitchen.'

'He did what?'

'He said that he was the one running this investigation, not you.'

They were interrupted by a loud knocking on the door. It flew open to reveal Baxter standing there, a look of cold fury on his face. He looked angrier than Bridget had ever seen him.

'I thought I might find you two here,' he shouted, addressing Jake and Ffion. 'What the hell are you doing?'

'Sir,' said Jake, 'we came to tell DI Hart that –
'

Bridget rose to her feet. 'They have just informed me that you ordered DS Ryan Hooper to leave Bella Williams, even though I specifically asked him to provide her with protection. Is that true?'

'That's correct,' said Baxter. 'You are not, as I have repeatedly said, part of this investigation, and if I find you interfering anymore with this case then I shall arrest you on grounds of obstructing a police enquiry. Now stay in your room! Do I make myself clear?'

Before she had a chance to reply, he rounded on Jake and Ffion again. 'Now you two, get back to the dining hall! We still have a murderer to find!'

CHAPTER 27

Bridget remained in her room after Baxter had gone, taking Jake and Ffion with him. They had given her a lot to think about.

She moved to the window where Jake had stood, and stared out of it gloomily. Before her, across the college gardens stood the old stone wall, following the line of the original city wall, with Dead Man's Walk running along its length. In the distance a group of schoolboys were playing rugby on Merton Field. And beyond that stretched Christ Church Meadows, leading all the way down to where the River Cherwell flowed into the Isis.

The voices of the schoolboys carried across the open field, reminding her inevitably of Chloe. Bridget was missing her daughter desperately after three days of separation, but at least she knew she would be safely in school, where Vanessa would collect her in her Range Rover later in the day. Not like Abigail, who had set off on foot from school that sunny June afternoon, never to be seen alive again.

The corpses were piling up in her mind like a

grim funeral pyre. Abigail. Lydia. Alexia. Tina. Meg. What was it that Meg had said so flippantly that night in the college bar? And then there were four. Now just two of the original group remained – herself and Bella, and Bridget wasn't going to lose another friend.

Baxter had presented her with a clear choice – to comply with his instructions and remain in her room, leaving Bella unprotected, or to deliberately disobey him. The choice was an easy one for her to make.

She waited long enough to be certain he had left the building, then slipped from her room and crept downstairs. At the exit to the Grove Building she peered outside and, seeing that the coast was clear, made her way quickly through the college grounds, passing the chapel, the library in Mob Quad, the dining hall and gatehouse, before eventually reaching Bella's room in St Alban's Quad unseen. She listened carefully, but there was no sound of voices or movement from within. She rapped smartly on the door, waited a moment, then knocked again louder. There was no reply and she was seized by a sense of cold dread.

She had played this scene twice already, first at Tina's door, and then at Meg's, like a grisly drama that insisted on repeating itself over and over again. Both previous times, on finally gaining access, she had been confronted by a dead body.

She tried to open the door, but it was locked.

Without Jake to help her, she didn't fancy her chances of kicking it down. Instead she spun on her heels and walked briskly to the porter's lodge, keeping one eye out for Baxter. A uniformed police officer was stationed in the gatehouse, clearly under orders to prevent anyone from leaving. Bridget marched up to the desk where the porter sat reading his newspaper. 'I need the key to Bella Williams's room. Quickly, please.'

The porter regarded her with an unfriendly scowl, perhaps remembering her earlier remark about the warden being able to creep around the college unseen. 'I'm not in the habit of giving out keys to people, especially not when the police are investigating three murders.'

'I am the police.' Bridget flashed her warrant card at him in annoyance. 'Now give me the key.'

Having got what she needed, she headed back to St Alban's Quad and knocked on the door one last time. 'Bella! It's Bridget! Are you in there?'

Nothing. She fitted the key in the lock, her hands trembling. She turned it and pushed the door wide open.

The room beyond was dark. She had a heart-stopping moment when she fully expected to see Bella's dead body lying on the bed or on the floor. It was only once she'd switched on the light and ascertained that the room was empty that she breathed again. She looked around, searching through the bedside locker, and scanning the room for anything that might give her a clue to where Bella had gone, but the room was almost bare, save for a book left open on the desk.

★

Back in the temporary incident room in Fellow's Quad, Baxter was sounding off again. Jake stood at the back of the room, his hands clasped firmly behind his back, half-listening to what the DI had to say, half his mind on what Bridget had said about Lydia Khoury. There had to be a connection between Lydia's suicide, the warden's discovery of the votive statue in the ancient city of Byblos, and the present series of killings. Twenty years separated each of these events, and yet they must be linked in some way. Jake knew it. He just couldn't see how.

Baxter pointed to his noticeboard. 'Right, this is what we have so far. Three murders. Several persons of interest. No solid evidence. The times of death of the second and third murders do little to rule out any of our suspects. Tina Mackenzie was killed in her room on Sunday afternoon. During that period, a significant number of the college guests were being interviewed by teams of detectives, and I interviewed the warden myself. But none of those interviews lasted for longer than thirty minutes. There was ample opportunity for anyone in the college to have visited Miss Mackenzie's room and tricked her into drinking the poisoned wine. The fact that the butler's fingerprints were found on the bottle we are now treating as unconnected with the investigation.'

Baxter glowered at those present as if daring them to challenge his decision to waste time arresting and interviewing the butler. No one did.

'Ms Meg Collins was released from police custody at around midnight on Sunday and was killed in her room during the early hours of Monday morning. Her body was discovered at approximately eight o'clock. The medical examiner's initial estimate of the time of death is sometime between three and four o'clock. Although our officers were stationed throughout the college throughout the night, none of them reported seeing any suspicious activity at any time. Although, I note that DI Bridget Hart was spotted walking through the college during the early hours of that same morning.'

Jake glanced around at his colleagues. It was obvious from their body language that none of them believed for a moment that Bridget Hart was on a killing spree. Not even Baxter himself showed any real inclination to believe it.

'So every single person in the college had the opportunity to commit all three murders,' growled Baxter.

Jake mulled over the fact that so far, all Baxter had achieved with his strategy of retaining everyone in the college for three days was presenting the murderer with the perfect opportunity to continue their activities unhindered.

'Let's look again at the murder weapons used,' continued Baxter. 'In Alexia Petrakis's case, a length of wire was used to garrotte the victim. We know that the wire was stolen from a college storeroom. We also know that the knife used to remove the victim's eyes was taken from the kitchen. In the case of Tina Mackenzie, potassium cyanide was added to Madeira wine, and the victim's ears were cut off. The wine was sourced from the college cellars, and once again a college knife was used to butcher the body. We don't yet know the source of the cyanide. Obviously that's not something that is left lying around the college, but in a university environment there might be any number of possible sources for the poison. It could have been bought, stolen or made by the murderer.

'Thirdly, Meg Collins was killed with a pickaxe, and her tongue removed. As before, a college kitchen knife was used to cut out the tongue, but the pickaxe may give us a new lead. Forensics believe it to be an archaeological tool, as is the brush that was used to write the message in blood on the wall of the room. This provides us with an obvious link to the warden of the college, Dr Brendan Harper, who is himself an archaeologist.'

Ffion's hand shot up. 'Sir, do you think we should consider Dr Harper to be a suspect in the case?'

Baxter turned his bull's head to face her. 'I hardly think that is likely, do you, DC Hughes? It's hard to imagine a more respectable man and one with so much to lose. With the warden currently standing for the position of university vice-chancellor, why would he possibly risk becoming embroiled in a triple murder case? No, it seems far more likely to me that somebody is deliberately trying to destroy his reputation in order to stop him from being elected.'

'But sir, we know that Alexia Petrakis planned to write a damaging article about the warden. She's now dead. Isn't it likely that Dr Harper is using the gaudy as an opportunity to remove anyone who might threaten him in some way?'

'No,' said Baxter. 'If anything, it's more likely that whoever is behind this is using the gaudy as a smokescreen. So far we've been concentrating our attention on the dinner guests, but the warden is far more likely to have made enemies among the academic staff of the college. I want to interview every tutor, lecturer and professor in this place, and find out where they were throughout the past three days. We'll work in pairs and make a start right away. DS Derwent, I'd like you to go and see the warden and find out if any of his archaeological tools have gone missing. Let's see if we can identify where the killer got hold of this pickaxe. Any questions?'

Jake braced himself for Ffion to raise her hand again, but it seemed that she had nothing more to ask.

'At least,' said Baxter, 'now that the perpetrator has delivered their three messages – see no evil, hear no evil, speak no evil – I think it's safe to assume that no further murders will take place.' He searched the room for anyone who might want to disagree with him. 'All right then, let's get cracking.'

CHAPTER 28

Much to her dismay, Ffion found herself once again teamed up with Ryan, this time to conduct interviews with the college's academic staff. Their brief: to discover which one of the crusty old lecturers and professors hated the warden so badly that they were willing to commit three murders in order to stop him becoming vice-chancellor.

They returned to high table in the dining hall to begin their task. On the way, Ryan stopped briefly to chat to one of the serving staff, a very attractive young Polish woman. Their body language didn't suggest to Ffion that the subject of their discussion was the murder enquiry.

'Making plans for this evening?' she asked, when he took his seat at high table.

'If we ever get out of this place. Come on, let's make a start.'

The first tutor who came to be interviewed was a grey-haired woman who, despite her obvious age, carried herself perfectly straight. She took a seat opposite Ffion, and sat unblinking, a trace of a smile on her lined features.

'Name?' said Ryan.

'Dr Irene Thomas.'

'Subject?'

'Modern History.'

Aha, thought Ffion. Bridget's former tutor. Ffion knew enough about Oxford degree courses to understand that Modern History referred to everything that took place after the fall of the western Roman Empire in 476 AD. Anything that had happened before that was deemed the domain of the Ancient History faculty. In Oxford, the word "modern" was always a relative term.

'Where were you on Saturday afternoon, between the hours of three and seven o'clock?' asked Ryan.

'In the college library in Mob Quad. I was studying a text relating to Sir Francis Throckmorton, one of the many conspirators who plotted to overthrow the queen and restore a Catholic monarchy to England. Sir Francis was educated at Oxford, though not, I'm happy to say, at Merton College.'

Ffion wrote it down. 'I assume that when you say "queen", you're referring to Queen Elizabeth I?'

Dr Thomas's gaze swung from Ryan to Ffion like the beam of a lighthouse. 'Correct. The Elizabethan Age witnessed a multiplicity of plots and conspiracies directed against the throne. It was a most fascinating period of history.'

'Did you see Alexia Petrakis at any time during

that day?' asked Ryan, steering the interview back to his list of questions.

'No. I spent the day working in the college library in Mob Quad.'

'Where were you on Sunday afternoon between the hours of two and six o'clock?' This was the time in which Tina Mackenzie had met her end.

'I was working in the college library in Mob Quad.'

'And on Monday morning between two am and six am?'

Ffion readied herself to write down "working in the college library in Mob Quad" but instead Dr Thomas gave a somewhat unexpected answer.

'At two am I was in my room enjoying a glass of sherry with DI Bridget Hart.'

Ryan looked puzzled. 'And how long did that go on for?'

'I would think until around three a.m. We worked our way through a considerable volume of sherry, and had plenty to discuss.'

'So it would seem. And after that?'

'I turned out my light for the night shortly after three, then rose again at my usual time of six o'clock.'

'You only had three hours' sleep?' queried Ryan.

'I assure you that's not unusual, Sergeant. At my advanced age, I have precious little time remaining to me. I can't afford to waste it on sleep.'

'Right,' said Ryan, stifling a yawn.

'If you're attempting to pin down everyone's movements at the times of the three murders, I feel that you're wasting your time,' said Dr Thomas. 'With more than one hundred and fifty guests in the college, how can you possibly hope to narrow the field sufficiently to identify potential suspects? I would suggest that this is an impossible task.'

'We're just doing our job, madam,' said Ryan.

'Then it's no wonder that the murderer has been able to carry out three murders already without you being able to catch them.' The old woman turned her attention to Ffion. 'A more intelligent approach would be to identify those with some kind of connection with the deceased and to focus your efforts on them.'

'What kind of connection do you have in mind?' asked Ffion.

It seemed that Dr Irene Thomas had been waiting to be asked just this question. She offered Ffion the ghost of a smile. 'It is said that murder always boils down to one of three essential motives – love, lust and loathing. I use the word lust here in its widest sense, you understand – the desire for money or power, not just sex. Ask yourself who knew all three victims. Then ask what they stood to gain from their demise.'

'What do you think they stood to gain?' asked Ffion, ignoring Ryan's evident irritation at being side-lined.

'Well, let's consider each candidate in turn, shall we? In a broad sense, most of the people here in college had some casual acquaintance with the three victims. A college environment is a closed community where strong and powerful bonds are forged. But casual acquaintances do not normally kill each other, at least in a civilised place such as Oxford. Now, the two people most obviously connected to all three victims must surely be DI Bridget Hart and Miss Bella Williams. I'm sure I'm not telling you anything new. Let's take each in turn. Bridget was good friends with all three murdered women, but hadn't had any contact with them in nearly twenty years. On the face of it, that in itself seems suspicious, as if there may have been some falling out between Bridget and the others. But once we take into account Bridget's own personal tragedy, I think we can easily explain her lack of contact.'

Ryan shot Ffion a questioning look at this reference to Bridget's past, but Ffion ignored him. It wasn't her place to share confidential information about her boss's personal life with Ryan.

Dr Thomas pressed on. 'I think it's fair to conclude that Bridget had nothing to gain from their demise. Bella Williams, on the other hand, may have had a motive – loathing, or more specifically jealousy. For while her three contemporaries shot to greatness in their respective careers, poor Bella's intended career didn't even get off the starting blocks. Instead she was forced to watch the others' successes from afar, while her own achievements remained a mere shadow of what she had hoped. For almost two decades she endured this painful injustice, and now, faced with the reality of just how far her peers had risen, wouldn't she be justified in feeling, at the very least, a certain anguish? And, being unable to do anything to improve her own circumstances, might she have considered the option of bringing down those who had risen so far?'

Ffion nodded encouragingly. It seemed that the History tutor had followed her own line of reasoning, painting out exactly the same scenario that she had arrived at. 'So you think that Bella is the most likely suspect?'

'Hardly,' said Dr Thomas shortly. 'Could jealousy really have motivated an intelligent woman like Bella to take the lives of three old friends? I doubt it very much. If we are going to get to the bottom of this mystery, I think we need to look for a much stronger motive than that.'

Ffion felt the disappointment of having her theory summarily dismissed like a physical blow. But she allowed herself to consider the facts calmly. Dr Thomas was probably right. Jealousy was surely far too petty a motive for a woman like Bella to exact such extreme retribution against three innocent people. 'What then?'

'Let's throw our net a little wider, shall we?' said Dr Thomas. 'Let us next consider the warden of the college, Dr Brendan Harper. He was also strongly connected with the three women. In each case, he took a close personal interest in each one's career.'

'We know that he introduced Alexia Petrakis to influential contacts in the media world,' said Ffion. 'And that he persuaded the college to invest money in Meg's company. In what way did he help Tina?'

Dr Thomas seemed surprised that Ffion didn't already know the answer to her question. 'Why, by persuading a highly-respected professor of jurisprudence to give her a glowing reference. He fast-tracked her career in law, there's no question about it. You can take it from me that his behaviour in this regard was not normal. The senior tutor is not expected to provide a personal career service to every graduate of the college. Yet he went out of his way to help each of the three murdered women. Now, why did he give his help so generously?'

'It must have been for repayment of some kind of debt,' speculated Ffion. 'But what?'

Dr Thomas's face remained inscrutable. 'I think that you may find that the answer lies with his former student, Lydia Khoury, and the inquest that was held into her death. The inquest that, I'm sure you already know, returned a verdict of suicide.'

'Are you suggesting her death wasn't suicide?'

'No. I know nothing for certain, and I will say no more about it. But there is one more person I think you ought to place on your list of suspects. The warden's wife, Mrs Yasmin Harper.'

'Why would she be involved? Did she know the three victims?'

'If the warden is involved, it is entirely logical – indeed obvious, if you don't mind me saying – that the wife may be too. Have the police interviewed her yet?'

'We really can't reveal any of the details of the investigation,' said Ryan, stepping in before Ffion could say anything.

'Then I take it that you haven't,' said Dr Thomas. 'I would advise you to rectify that as soon as possible. Mrs Yasmin Harper is a very interesting individual. She was born into an extremely wealthy and powerful Egyptian family, and might have expected to make an advantageous marriage in her home country. She could literally have chosen any husband she desired. And yet she married an almost penniless English archaeologist. Why did she do that?'

'Love?' suggested Ffion.

'That's always a possibility,' said Dr Thomas in a tone that suggested that the notion had never once crossed her mind. 'It is said that Dr Harper is a good-looking man. It is certainly true that he possesses a natural charm. He may have turned a young girl's head. Or perhaps Yasmin Harper saw potential in this young man with such a bright academic future ahead of him. After his celebrated discovery of a Phoenician artifact in Lebanon, he was already attracting a certain amount of media attention. Maybe this beautiful, highly intelligent – and, shall we say, ambitious – woman saw an exciting opportunity for herself in the shape of Dr Brendan Harper. If so, she was proven right. Dr Harper's career rose magnificently, first as senior tutor, then as warden of Merton College – not to mention his appearance as a presenter of popular television shows – and now he stands at the threshold of becoming vice-chancellor of the university. How might Mrs Yasmin Harper react if someone now threatened all that?'

'Threatened in what way?'

'I merely refer you to my previous answers,' said Dr Thomas. 'Love, lust and loathing. You will find the reason for these murders in one of the three.'

Ffion took a moment to digest all the information that Dr Thomas had shared with them. It seemed she was not short of opinions on the case, despite having apparently spent most of the past three days shut away in the library in Mob Quad. One fact that was clear was that the History tutor said nothing casually, and that everything she had told them was potentially significant. One particular remark that she had made at the beginning of the conversation stuck in Ffion's mind – how the Elizabethan Age had witnessed a multiplicity of plots and conspiracies directed against the throne. Was that how Dr Thomas pictured the recent events in college? And if so, what plots and conspiracies might she be secretly aware of, directed against the college warden?

'There is of course one other person who might be involved in all of this,' said Ffion, 'and who was around at the time of Lydia Khoury's death. Someone who knew all the people involved, and who would have a vested interest in directing suspicion towards the warden and his wife.'

'And who might that be?'

'You,' said Ffion.

'Ah, yes, of course. How very astute. There is always me.'

CHAPTER 29

There were two ways of getting from the main college buildings to the warden's lodgings – through the gardens around the back, or via Merton Street itself. Jake could see no reason to go skulking around the back way like an intruder. Instead he left the college through the main gatehouse, acknowledging the uniformed constable on duty there as he went. The life of a detective sergeant could be dull and tedious at times – for instance when carrying out door-to-door enquiries or interviewing a hundred and fifty dinner guests at an Oxford college – but it beat hanging about, guarding entrances and exits, or pacing the streets in all weathers. He was glad not to have to do that job.

He left the gatehouse and turned right up Merton Street, once again asking himself the unanswerable question – why cobbles? Merton Street was a quiet backwater, almost completely devoid of traffic, even though it was adjacent to the busy High Street, which was almost permanently clogged with double-decker buses, taxis and cyclists. It wasn't hard to understand why Merton Street was so quiet. No sane motorist would ever want to bring their vehicle down here.

He passed the Subaru, giving it a friendly pat as he went and checking its bodywork for scratches, then continued on down the road to the warden's lodgings.

From the street side, the appearance of the building was very unobtrusive. Jake had expected some great Gothic mansion with turrets and gargoyles. Instead the lodgings took the form of a modest, white-painted house. He would never have guessed that the head of a prestigious Oxford college lived there had it not been for the plaque fixed next to the front door, announcing the fact to the world. He strode up to the house and rang the doorbell.

After a short while the door was opened by the warden's wife. It was the first time for Jake to meet her and he was taken aback by her beauty and elegance. Mrs Harper was younger than her husband, and had the poise and grace of a queen, perhaps a modern-day Cleopatra. She wore a plain white dress that showed off her lightly-tanned skin and jet-black hair. A silver necklace adorned her slender neck, and long earrings dangled from her ears. Like the building itself, she was nothing like what he'd expected.

For a second he was so astonished by the sight of her that he struggled to remember her name. Jade? Jasmine? Yasmin. That was it. Yasmin Harper.

'Good morning, Sergeant. How may I help you?'

'Morning, madam. Mrs Harper, that is. Sorry to bother you, but is your husband at home?'

She hesitated a moment before replying. 'Brendan? No, I'm afraid he's not here.'

'Do you know where I might find him?'

'No. I don't know where he is right now.' Yasmin Harper stood in the doorway, not moving away, but not closing the door either. Her dark eyes held a faint glimmer of unease.

Jake lingered on the doorstep, sensing that she had more to say.

According to Baxter, the butler claimed Mrs Harper had once had an affair with the college chef. Looking at her now, Jake wondered whether the story was true. Could such an accomplished and self-assured woman really have risked embarking on such a reckless act? And if so, had she more secrets to hide?

'Look,' she said, seeming to come to a decision, 'maybe you'd better come inside. I have something I need to tell you.'

★

Bridget left the staircase on St Alban's Quad, wondering which way to turn next. She could go left into the college gardens, where she had found Tina on Sunday morning. But Bella had never been one to seek solitude in nature. She had always loved the soaring architectural beauty of Oxford's spires and quadrangles, preferring the feel of stone beneath her feet instead of grass. Yet Bridget was wary of returning to the dining hall or wandering about the quads in case she bumped into Baxter. She lingered in St Alban's, not knowing where to go.

If only Baxter hadn't been so pig-headed, refusing to believe that the last of her former housemates might be at risk. When all this was over she would speak to the Chief Superintendent about Baxter's disrespectful and bullying behaviour.

The bell on the chapel tower began slowly to chime the hour and Bridget checked her watch. Midday already, and the sun was high in the sky. It was as the bell completed the last of its ponderous chimes that she suddenly had an idea where Bella might be.

Although Bella had never been particularly religious, as a student she'd been a member of the college's campanology society. When the pressure of work became too much, Bella had sworn that there was nothing better to relieve stress than to join in with the regular bell-ringing at the chapel. She'd even travelled to other churches in Oxfordshire, ringing the peals at weddings and at Sunday services. Perhaps she had returned to the chapel now.

Bridget crept quietly through the arch that led to Front Quad, and from there hurried through Patey's Quad and Mob Quad. Fortunately Baxter was nowhere to be seen. She passed through the final archway leading to the chapel lawn, then entered the antechapel at the south transept.

The chiming of the bells had now ceased and the church stood still and quiet. Bridget's steps rang out loud and clear as she crossed the flagstones that led into the main body of the chapel itself. Above her the square tower of the belfry appeared to be deserted, although it was impossible to be sure from down here. Bridget covered the space quickly, shuddering as she recalled the horrific discovery of Alexia's sightless body stuffed rudely into the wooden cupboard in the north transept. She wondered what kind of hate might lead a killer to disfigure someone so coldly and brutally.

She passed up the aisle leading to the great Gothic eastern window. Just before the altar she turned right towards the sacristy. She knocked hurriedly on the door and, when there was no reply, she pushed it open and entered the room beyond. The chaplain had not made good on his promise to tidy the room, and it was just as messy as it had been when she'd come here to speak to him about his meeting with Alexia. She left the room, pulling the door closed behind her and returned to the antechapel.

A small scrape echoed around the tall tower and made her look up.

'Bella? Is that you? Are you up there?'

She stopped and listened, but there was no answer and no more sounds from the belfry.

Instead she left the building the same way she had entered and stopped outside the chapel.

What now? She could continue to wander the college in the hope of finding her friend, but she would be just as likely to encounter Baxter before she discovered wherever Bella had vanished to.

On impulse she turned instead to the side of the chapel and the door that led up to the tower. The wooden door was always kept locked, but in the old days, Bella had owned a key, allowing her access to the belfry. Bridget took hold of the iron ring fitted to the door and twisted it. To her surprise it turned easily in her hand and the heavy door swung open to reveal a wooden staircase beyond. Stepping inside, Bridget began to climb the tower.

★

The interior of the warden's lodgings resembled something out of a style magazine. Jake hurriedly removed his large boots before daring to set foot on the pale carpet that lined the hallway.

Yasmin Harper invited him through to the elegant lounge. 'Please, take a seat, Sergeant.'

There were so many sofas and armchairs available that he stood momentarily bewildered by the choice.

'Perhaps we could sit together by the window,' suggested Mrs Harper indicating a window seat.

Jake swallowed nervously. The arrangement seemed altogether too intimate, but it would be rude to decline. 'Yes,' he said. 'That would be nice.' He took a seat where she had indicated.

A low table near the window was dominated by a display of freshly-cut roses. Their scent added a heavy perfume to the room. Mrs Harper stood behind them. 'Would you like a coffee? I have some in the cafetière.'

He had the impression that she wasn't yet quite ready to tell him whatever it was she wanted to say. He was happy to give her the time she needed to compose her thoughts. 'Please,' he said.

He waited while she went to the kitchen and came back with two delicate china cups and saucers on a tray with a small jug of cream and a silver dispenser filled with sugar cubes. The tray shook slightly as she set it down on the table next to the flowers.

She sat down beside him, very upright, her hands folded in her lap. Jake added two lumps of sugar to his cup of coffee and topped it up to the brim with cream. He hesitated, then added a third sugar cube. It would be a shame not to, since she'd gone to so much trouble over its presentation.

Yasmin Harper stared in the direction of the floral display, as if examining it for imperfections. He followed her gaze, letting his eyes rest for a moment on the long green stems and densely-packed flowers that adorned them. The deep pink petals looked flawless to him.

'You said that you had something to tell me?'

he prompted. 'Is it about your husband?'

She lifted her dark eyes to his. 'This is rather difficult for me, Sergeant, but I'm worried about Brendan. You see, I think that the three messages left by the murderer – see no evil, hear no evil, speak no evil – may have been intended as a warning.'

Jake stirred his coffee with a silver spoon. 'What makes you say that?'

'I believe they relate to an event that took place some seventeen years ago, not long after Brendan and I were married and I came to live in England.'

Jake sipped his coffee, waiting for her to go on.

'My husband was senior tutor at the time, and lectured in Archaeology and Anthropology. One of his students was a Lebanese woman called Lydia Khoury. She was a gifted student with great promise. Sadly in her final year she failed her dissertation and took her own life a few days later. There was an inquest, naturally. Several of Miss Khoury's friends from college gave evidence at the inquest.'

Jake pricked up his ears. 'Would that be Alexia Petrakis, Tina Mackenzie and Meg Collins, by any chance?'

'Yes. An allegation surfaced that my husband had abused his position. Alexia, Tina and Meg all spoke in defence of Brendan, who was completely exonerated. But a fourth student – Bella Williams – accused him of deliberately failing Lydia's dissertation in order to protect himself.'

'Protect himself from what?'

Mrs Harper didn't answer his question directly. 'Bella made a number of accusations. But the girl was very clearly distressed by the death of her friend. She didn't seem to be a credible witness. The coroner didn't take her seriously. Neither did I, at the time.'

'I see,' said Jake. 'But now you do?'

'Let's just say that I have my concerns.'

'And how exactly do you think this relates to the three murders?'

Yasmin Harper turned the full force of her gaze on Jake. 'As I explained, Sergeant, this is extremely difficult for me to say, but I'm afraid that my husband may have murdered them to guarantee their silence.'

Jake stared at her in astonishment.

'Much as it pains me to say it, I have always known that Brendan had something to hide. Although he publicly denied it, it was apparent to me that he had done something he was secretly ashamed of. Why else would he have gone to such lengths to help those three women get started with their careers? He bought their silence. Now, perhaps with him coming so close to being chosen as the next university vice-chancellor, they believed they had an opportunity to extract something more from him. I think they may have been blackmailing him. That would explain the three messages at the crime scenes and the removal of the body parts. See no evil, hear no evil, speak no evil. They were made as a warning to the others.'

'But the eyeballs were placed in your husband's soup. Why would he have done that?'

'To divert attention from himself. To make it appear that someone was conducting a campaign to discredit him. But the women involved would have understood that the warnings were meant for them.'

'But in that case, why three warnings? With all three women dead, who else was there to warn?'

'Don't you see, Sergeant? The fourth woman, Bella Williams. I believe that she may be in grave danger.'

Jake swallowed, processing the new information. Bridget, too, had been worried about Bella's safety. She had placed Ryan to watch over her. And Baxter had sent him away.

He remembered then why Baxter had asked him to come to the warden's lodgings in the first place. 'The weapon used to carry out the third murder was a pickaxe. Our forensics team think it might be the kind of tool that an archaeologist would use during an excavation. The brush that was used to paint a message on the wall might also be the type used by an archaeologist.'

Yasmin Harper nodded. 'My husband's toolkit contains those items. When he's at college he always keeps it in his office here in the house. I searched for it this morning, but it wasn't there. And now my husband has gone out and isn't answering his calls.'

345

'All right,' said Jake, removing his phone from his pocket. 'Your husband's toolkit. What else did it contain?'

Now Yasmin Harper looked genuinely fearful. 'All kinds of tools. Spades, brushes, trowels, sieves, measuring tape. But also needles, spikes and knives.'

CHAPTER 30

The wooden flight of stairs that led up inside the tower was steep and narrow. Bridget was quite out of breath by the time she reached the level of the belfry. She really must find time to do more exercise. But at least her instincts had proved right. Bella was up there, not far from the top of the stairs, leaning against the railing that overlooked the antechapel, some thirty feet below. Her back was turned to Bridget.

On the floor of the belfry was a black leather holdall a few feet long. It looked like a tool bag of some kind. Metal objects glinted from inside.

'Thank God I've found you,' gasped Bridget. 'I was so worried.'

The balcony of the belfry ran all the way around the inside edge of the tower along a path just two or three feet wide, and the railing that Bella was leaning against looked old and rickety.

Bridget tentatively stepped onto the walkway and peered gingerly over the edge. From up here, the floor of the antechapel seemed a very long way down. 'Why don't you come back downstairs with me?' she suggested to Bella. 'We can talk in the chapel.'

'I don't think so,' said Bella, turning around. 'I like it up here.' As she turned, an object in her hand emerged from the shadows and flashed briefly in the light. It was a knife.

Before Bridget could work through the implications of that, her phone began to ring. The sudden sound ricocheted off the walls of the bell tower. She could see that it was Jake calling. 'I need to take this.'

'No,' said Bella. 'Give the phone to me.'

'What?' Bridget's thumb hovered over the screen. The phone continued to ring. If she didn't answer it in the next five rings it would go to voicemail.

'I said give me the phone!'

Bella raised the knife, which Bridget now saw was more like a ceremonial dagger. She lurched forwards with the blade and grabbed the phone from Bridget's hand. Then she backed away again and flung the phone over the railing. It crashed onto the stone floor below with a crunch of shattering glass. The ringing ceased.

Now that Bella had moved, Bridget could see that they were not alone on the balcony. Behind her was a man tied to a chair. The warden. His hands and feet were bound tightly with short lengths of cord. One of the bell ropes had been wrapped around him several times, securing him to the chair. He'd also been gagged with his own shirt which had been ripped off, exposing his chest. In his eyes Bridget saw nothing but naked terror.

Everything suddenly became clear. Bridget had followed the trail of clues to its end, but had failed to spot the final twist. Bella was not a victim, but a murderer. She had pulled all the strings and Bridget had allowed herself to be deceived, blinded to the truth by her old friendship.

But she would make up for it now. She stood firmly on the balcony, planting her feet to stop her legs from shaking. 'It's over, Bella,' she said, trying to sound braver than she felt. 'Don't do anything stupid. Drop the knife.'

Bella smiled. 'It's far from over, Bridget. You've arrived just in time to witness the grand finale. In fact, I'm glad you're here. You deserve to know everything.' She retreated along the walkway until she was standing immediately behind the warden. She pointed the tip of the knife towards his bare chest. 'I came to the college this weekend in search of retribution. Each of my victims has made a repayment for their crimes. First I took a pair of eyes, then a pair of ears, and then a tongue. See no evil. Hear no evil. Speak no evil. Do no evil. Now it's the warden's turn to settle his debt. Since his crime was the greatest, he must pay for it with his own heart.'

★

Jake ran out of the warden's lodgings the back

349

way, through the garden. After what Yasmin Harper had told him, he knew he had to find the warden, or Bella, or both before there was another death.

When he reached St Albans's Quad he rushed over to Bella's room and pounded the door with his fist, shouting her name at the top of his voice. But there was no reply. He turned and set off again.

He tried calling Bridget as he ran, but only managed to reach her voicemail. Baxter wasn't answering his phone either. He stopped for breath when he reached Front Quad and was about to try Ryan's number, when to his immense relief he found Ffion running from the other direction.

'Have you seen Bella or the warden anywhere?' he shouted.

'No. I've been looking for them myself.'

'The warden's on his way to kill Bella,' he blurted. 'We have to stop him!'

'No,' said Ffion. 'It's the other way around. Bella plans to kill the warden.'

He stopped, breathless after his exertion. 'What? Why do you think that? His wife just told me she thinks Harper murdered the three women to stop them revealing some kind of dark secret about his past.'

Ffion nodded. 'I guessed he had something to hide. That's why he failed Lydia Khoury's final dissertation. She discovered something when she was out in Byblos. Something to do with the votive statue that he'd found there on a previous dig.'

'But wasn't Alexia Petrakis planning to publish an article about that?'

'She was. But I don't think the warden knew about it. Or Bella, for that matter.'

'So why would Bella want to murder her three friends and then the warden?'

'It was Dr Irene Thomas who explained it to me.'

'Who?' yelled Jake. He was fed up of being told about people whose names he'd never heard of.

'Bridget's old History tutor.'

'What on earth does she have to do with any of this?'

'Nothing. But she told me that murder is always down to one of three motives – love, lust or loathing.'

'And which is it in this case?'

'Once I'd turned over all the facts in my mind, it was obvious,' said Ffion. 'We've been looking at everything from the wrong angle. It isn't lust, and it isn't loathing that's driving the killer. It's the most powerful emotion of all – love.'

'Love?'

'I'll explain later. But first we need to find Bella.'

★

'Put the knife down, Bella. You don't want to do this.' Bridget tried to keep her voice calm and level, the way she'd been trained to defuse difficult situations. But her thoughts and emotions were a turbulent maelstrom.

How could she have failed to see what was right in front of her? She'd never suspected Bella for one moment, but if she had then Tina and Meg might still be alive. She felt their deaths on her conscience.

'That's where you're wrong,' said Bella, her eyes glinting in the dim light of the belfry. 'I want to do this very much. I've never wanted anything more.'

All traces of the depressed and lethargic woman Bella had been at the beginning of the weekend had vanished. She was now much more like the person Bridget remembered from her younger days – driven, animated and alive. 'I've been waiting a long time for this. Seventeen years in fact.'

'But why?' Bridget knew that if she could keep Bella talking, there was a good chance that help would arrive. Sooner or later someone would notice that she and the warden had gone missing. Jake would be worried by the fact that she hadn't answered his call. Ffion was smart too, and might realise that something was wrong. She wasn't holding her breath that Baxter would appear like a knight in shining armour. 'Why did Alexia, Tina and Meg have to die? What crime did they commit?'

In Bridget's experience, when someone in Bella's position was given an opportunity to talk, their stories would often come gushing out. Like Irene Thomas had said, it was being denied a voice that led people to take drastic action. If you could relieve the pressure by letting them talk, then there was a hope that you could prevent them harming someone else or themselves.

'I'm doing this for Lydia,' said Bella. She pointed at the warden with her knife. 'He killed her.'

The warden tried to say something, but the gag in his mouth prevented him from forming any coherent words.

'Lydia committed suicide,' said Bridget.

The blade flashed. 'Because of him! Because of what he did to her!'

'And what was that, Bella?'

'He failed her dissertation. He did it deliberately, so that no one would take her claims seriously.'

'What claims?' asked Bridget, although she suspected she knew half the truth already.

'When Lydia was doing her fieldwork in Byblos she spoke to local workers who told her a secret. Back in 1987, this man' – she jerked the curved knife again at Dr Harper, this time scratching his skin and drawing blood – 'bribed an official to obtain an export licence for a rare and valuable statue. He knew that if he didn't obtain the licence very quickly, the law that was about to be passed by the Lebanese government would prevent him from bringing his trophy back to Britain. His moment of triumph would be snatched away forever. And so he bought himself a licence from a corrupt official.

'When Lydia found out, she wanted to tell the world the truth. She cared about the people and the communities in her home country. She would never have pillaged archaeological sites for their treasures. But Harper shut her down in the cruellest way possible – by taking away her dreams of becoming an archaeologist. After all, who would take the word of a failed undergraduate against a celebrated academic?'

Bridget took a step forward along the narrow balcony. 'All right. I believe you. Lydia's death was a tragic waste. I feel angry about that just like you do. She was my friend, too, remember? But what had the others done wrong?'

'They protected him!' roared Bella. 'At the inquest into Lydia's death, we had an opportunity to speak the truth, to explain what Lydia had discovered, and to expose everything that this man did. But instead, they said nothing, pretending that they'd seen and heard nothing. I was the only one who spoke the truth, but no one listened to me. Instead, they were rewarded for their lies, and the warden made sure that my application to study for a doctorate degree was turned down.'

Bridget took another step toward Bella and the warden. 'Is that why you're doing this? Because the warden ruined your hopes of a life in academia? Is this an act of revenge?'

'No! Of course not. Haven't you guessed the

truth yet?'

'What truth?' Bridget inched forward again.

'Lydia and I were lovers.'

Bella's passionate declaration brought Bridget to a halt. 'Lovers?'

'In secret, of course. Attitudes to things like that were very different then. Lydia had a strong religious upbringing. She had been taught to feel ashamed of what she was. If her parents had found out about the two of us, they would have disowned her as their daughter.'

Bridget slowly nodded her agreement. It was just two decades ago, yet for Lydia it might as well have been the dark ages. Society in general had been much less liberal, and Lydia's own religion held strongly intolerant views on homosexuality. Small wonder that she and Bella had kept their love a secret, even from their friends.

'I'm sorry,' said Bridget. 'I had no idea.'

'I'm doing this for love,' declared Bella. She began to draw a circle with the tip of her blade around the warden's heart. Drops of blood welled up wherever the sharp point punctured the skin.

Bridget moved forward again. 'No, please Bella. Stop. This isn't love. It's revenge, that's all. It will achieve nothing. Lydia was a caring person who never hurt anyone. She would never have wanted you to do this.'

'How do you know? She's dead. This man didn't ever stop to think what she wanted. He was willing to destroy a young woman's life to protect his own reputation. Bridget, the system failed Lydia. This man – who was given the duty of looking after her – chose instead to betray her. The legal system had a chance to find justice, but that failed her too. So I have no choice.'

'There is always a choice, Bella.'

'Then I choose this.' Bella looked up from her grim work to issue a challenge. 'What about your sister, Abigail, and the man who murdered her?'

Bridget was startled by the unexpected question. 'What about her?'

'Was her killer ever found? Did the legal system punish him for what he did?'

'No.' The word was a whisper.

Bella pointed the knife in Bridget's direction. 'The system failed you, too, Bridget. If you had the opportunity to avenge Abigail's death, wouldn't you take it? Wouldn't you make the same choice as me – an eye for an eye, a tooth for a tooth?'

Bridget stopped in her tracks, all thoughts of stopping Bella suddenly gone.

Hadn't she spent countless hours awake in bed at night, thinking of all the terrible things she would do to Abigail's killer if she ever found herself alone with him? In the recesses of her mind was a dark basement, dank and mouldy, filled with instruments of torture – red hot pokers, thumb screws, a rack, an iron maiden. It was terrifying how the longing for revenge lurked just beneath the surface of our civilised façades, like a primeval urge that could never be laid to rest. At times it felt as if grim retribution was the only rule that made sense. She recalled the words of Irene Thomas. The act of revenge must invariably be in excess of the original crime.

But then she saw the blade in Bella's hand and came to her senses.

'No. I became a police officer because of what happened to Abigail. I want to uphold the law, not take it into my own hands. Without the law we're just savages. You should understand that the intention of the Biblical eye for an eye principle was to limit retribution to the value of what was lost, and to prevent people taking excessive vengeance. What you've done, the revenge you've enacted, is wholly disproportionate to the original crime. You've left a trail of butchery and wrecked lives. Please stop now before you do any more senseless damage.'

'I can't,' said Bella. 'I passed the point of no return a long time ago.' She pressed the tip of the blade deeper into the warden's flesh and a fresh trickle of blood appeared.

'No!' shouted Bridget. 'It's never too late to choose a different path. Alexia had a change of heart. Did you know that? She was planning to write an article about the warden and expose the truth of what he'd done in Byblos, and how his actions had led to Lydia's death. She was even willing to reveal the part she had played in the deceit. She wanted to repent.'

357

'You're lying!'

'No, the chaplain told me. Alexia arranged to meet with him here in the chapel on Saturday afternoon to discuss her article. By killing her, you prevented her from publishing the truth.'

'I don't care,' spat Bella. 'She was seventeen years too late to save Lydia.'

At that moment the door to the antechapel crashed open and footsteps pounded hard against the flagstone floor.

'Ma'am? Are you in here?'

The voice was Jake's. Bridget risked taking her eyes off Bella for a second to peer over the railing. Jake and Ffion were standing in the middle of the antechapel next to her smashed phone.

'Up here,' she shouted.

Out of the corner of her eye, she saw a flash of metal, and heard an agonised groan. Bella had stabbed the warden.

*

The blade of the dagger was buried deep in the warden's chest right up to its handle. Bella pulled it out, and a spurt of blood followed. The warden let out a muffled shriek.

Bridget launched herself at her friend. Heedless of her own safety she threw herself forward, seizing hold of Bella's arm. Close up she could see that the hilt of the knife was elaborately carved with metal engravings. But this was no time to stop and admire its craftsmanship. Bella's eyes were wild with madness. She twisted out of Bridget's grasp and pushed her away, yelling triumphantly as she struck out again. The dagger bit into the warden's flesh for a second time.

Bridget aimed a sharp kick at Bella's shin and she fell back, sprawling against the railing that ran around the balcony's edge. The dagger was still in her hands.

Bridget had no idea what Bella would try next, but she moved to position herself in front of the warden. 'If you want to kill him, you'll have to kill me first,' she said.

Bella groaned. 'No. You can't stop me.' But she backed away into the corner of the narrow balcony, clutching the knife in front of her.

Bridget hoped that Jake and Ffion would make it up the tower before Bella did anything else. For now she seemed docile, crouching on the floor and keeping her distance.

Bridget carefully untied the warden's shirt that had been used to gag him. She pressed the fabric against the wound, struggling to stem the flow of blood pouring from the warden's chest but the crisp white cotton soon turned into a sodden mass of red rag. Dr Harper's face had taken on a sweaty sheen and he was fast losing consciousness.

Bridget heard Jake and Ffion's footsteps coming up the stairs behind her, and by the time they appeared in the belfry, Ffion was already on the phone calling for an ambulance and police back-up.

'Help me untie him and get him into a horizontal position,' said Bridget.

While she and Ffion worked to free the warden and lower him into the recovery position, Jake moved past her to where Bella was cowering in the far corner.

'Give me the knife,' he said in his soft northern accent which was usually so good at eliciting trust from wary suspects and recalcitrant witnesses.

Bella responded with an incoherent wail.

Leaving Ffion to tend to the warden, Bridget rose to her feet and moved to Jake's side. Bella was crouched in the corner of the belfry like a frightened animal, the knife still raised in her trembling hand.

'There's still time to give yourself up, Bella,' said Bridget. 'You might be able to plead manslaughter on the grounds of diminished responsibility.'

'No!' screamed Bella. 'I don't want to give myself up. Don't you see? Getting away with it was never part of the plan.' She pointed the blade of the knife at her own throat.

The chilling words of Dr Thomas came back to Bridget again. The revenger always ends up dead.

'I wouldn't do that if I were you,' said Jake. He launched himself at Bella.

She slashed at him with the knife, but he

grabbed hold of her outstretched arm and twisted it behind her back, forcing her to drop the weapon. It clattered to the floor, and Jake kicked it over the edge of the platform where it landed on the floor of the antechapel.

The struggle was over as quickly as it had begun, and Bridget felt herself breathe again, unaware that she had even been holding her breath. For a few agonising seconds she had pictured Bella thrusting the dagger through Jake's heart, killing him outright.

Now she lay helpless on the floor. 'That knife belonged to Lydia,' she wailed. 'It was a traditional Lebanese knife. It was the only thing I had to remember her by.'

Bridget stepped forward. 'Bella Williams, I am arresting you for the murders of Alexia Petrakis, Tina Mackenzie and Meg Collins, and for the attempted murder of Dr Brendan Harper.' The groans coming from a few feet behind her told her that the warden was still hanging in there, just. 'You do not have to say anything, but it may harm your defence if you do not mention when questioned something which you later rely on in court. Anything you do say may be given in evidence. Do you understand?'

She took Bella's sobbing moans for agreement. Outside she could hear the wail of an ambulance in the distance.

CHAPTER 31

Back at Thames Valley Police HQ in Kidlington, Bridget finished typing her official complaint against Baxter. She had toned down her anger at the way he had treated her, but her list of grievances was still substantial. She printed the document ready to take with her to her meeting with Detective Chief Superintendent Alex Grayson.

After the ambulance had arrived to rush the warden to hospital, and a police car had taken Bella away to be put safely under lock and key in a police cell, Bridget had considered going straight to Vanessa's house to see Chloe. She was missing her daughter terribly and longed to hold her in her arms. But it was still only early afternoon and it would be another couple of hours before Chloe finished school. Instead, Bridget had quickly phoned both Vanessa and Jonathan to let them know she was safe, and had then returned to work, keen to put her aggrieved thoughts into writing while the unfairness of her treatment by Baxter was still fresh.

The Chief Superintendent had agreed to meet

her as soon as he had been briefed on the conclusion of the case by Baxter. Bridget watched the two men talking through the glass walls of Grayson's office. It was obvious that at least part of the discussion taking place related to her, and she was glad that she had come to the office to make her position clear and fight her corner. After all, it was she who had finally arrested the killer, putting her own life at risk to do so. And it was she who had made many of the key breakthroughs in the investigation, even though it had taken a joint effort with Jake and Ffion to finally make an arrest. After fifteen minutes, Baxter stalked out of the office, avoiding eye contact with her, and the Chief Super called her in.

'DI Hart, please take a seat.'

The Chief was never one to waste words, and Bridget was well used to his clipped, spartan way of speaking. A photograph of the Chief standing next to his wife – both of them unsmiling – stood on the edge of his desk and Bridget wondered if conversation at home with the Graysons was just as terse as in his office. The fact that he had used the word "please" indicated that he was in a relatively good mood following the arrest. He sat behind the broad expanse of his desk reading from a report as Bridget took a seat opposite.

His opening gambit took her by surprise. 'DI Hart, DI Baxter has submitted an official complaint about your conduct during this investigation.' He picked up the typed sheet of paper he'd been reading and brandished it before her. 'Baxter alleges that you obstructed his inquiry, undermined his authority, and wilfully and repeatedly disobeyed his orders as senior investigating officer on the case. He cites more than' – Grayson waved the report angrily in his hand – 'a dozen specific examples of your alleged misconduct.'

'May I see the report, sir?'

'No. I see that you have also brought me a document to read.' He indicated the form she held in her hand.

'Yes, sir. It's an official complaint about DI Baxter's behaviour.'

'I thought it might be.'

Grayson accepted it from her without looking at it and placed it on his desk, next to Baxter's own report. 'DI Hart, how long have you been a detective inspector in this department?'

'Almost six months, sir.'

'Six months, yes. Do you know how long DI Baxter has been in his position?'

'No, sir.'

'Just over twenty years.'

Bridget felt her anger beginning to grow again. It had taken her a long time to reach the rank of detective inspector, held back by being a single mother with a young daughter to look after, plus the fact that she had never spared the time to engage in office politics or to join in with after-work drinks at the pub with her colleagues. If Grayson was going to hold that against her and take Baxter's side simply because he'd been in his job for longer, she would fight this all the way to the top. 'With respect, sir, I don't see why that's relevant.'

Grayson drummed his fingers on the desk before continuing. 'DI Baxter is one of my most experienced detectives, with a solid track record of arrests behind him. He's a valued member of the team.' He paused. 'But experienced detectives sometimes get stuck in a rut. They develop their own way of doing things, and they don't take kindly to newcomers. They become complacent.'

'Yes, sir.'

'I like you, DI Hart. I like the way you carry out your work. You have potential.'

Bridget raised her eyebrows. She had never heard the Chief deliver such effusive praise. 'Thank you, sir.'

'In this latest investigation, you arrested the perpetrator and saved a man's life.'

'Yes, sir.'

'Even though Baxter told you not to.'

Was that a glint of amusement in the Chief Super's eye? Bridget had never seen one there before, so couldn't be sure.

The glint, whatever it was, didn't last long. 'DI Hart, I don't like detectives who can't obey instructions. It concerns me when officers follow their gut instincts and don't play well as members of the team.'

'No, sir.'

'But I do admire detectives who stick to their guns and get the job done, against all the odds.'

'Yes, sir.' It seemed to Bridget that Grayson liked to have his cake and eat it. To be fair though, she'd never met anyone who didn't.

'This was a good outcome,' continued the Chief. 'In the end, at least. Let's not spoil everything with a dispute between two of my best detectives. If Baxter agrees to withdraw his complaint, will you withdraw yours?'

Bridget thought for a moment. Part of her wanted to take Baxter to task and prove to him that she'd been right all along. But what would that really achieve? She had seen for herself that a desire for revenge and retribution led nowhere. 'Yes, sir. I agree.'

'Good. I absolutely bloody hate paperwork.' Grayson ripped the two complaints in half, scrunched them into a ball and launched them with perfect aim into his waste paper basket.

'Don't you need to check with DI Baxter before you withdraw his complaint, sir?'

'I don't think that will be necessary. I've given the matter serious consideration and have decided to treat his grievance with the seriousness it deserves. I think we're done here, DI Hart.'

'Yes, sir. Thank you, sir.' Bridget wasn't entirely sure what she was thanking him for. It felt more like a draw than a win. Baxter had got away with his bullying and mistreatment, and she knew that her rivalry with him would continue whenever they worked together in the future. He was just too pig-headed to change his ways. But at least it felt like she had Grayson on her side now. And Baxter would know that too.

She stood up, taking one final look around the large space of the office. Grayson sat in the middle, like a slightly malevolent octopus, surrounded by his golfing photos and his trophies. 'By the way,' he said. 'I've just had a phone call from Mrs Harper. She phoned to say that her husband will pull through, but that he's decided to withdraw from the vice-chancellorship race. There'll almost certainly be an enquiry into his behaviour seventeen years ago with regard to Miss Lydia Khoury's dissertation, and probably also into the export licence that he obtained to bring a statue to this country from Lebanon. I imagine he'll be forced to resign his position as warden of Merton College before these enquiries get underway.'

'Good,' said Bridget. 'Then Lydia will get some kind of justice after all. It's just a shame that it came at such a high price.'

Grayson swivelled a pen between his thumb and forefinger. 'I know these last few days must have been very stressful for you.'

'Yes,' admitted Bridget. 'They have. I was expecting a nice relaxing weekend, but instead I found myself in the middle of a blood bath.'

'Well, take a few days off,' said Grayson gruffly. 'You deserve it.' He dismissed her with a wave of his hand.

'Thank you, sir.'

★

Jake had just finished typing up his report of the events in the belfry. He was no fan of paperwork, but it was best to get these things done while they were still fresh in his mind. Besides, the case had ended well, the way everyone always hoped for – with the perpetrator behind bars and ready to face justice.

The Chief had praised him for his quick and brave action in disarming Bella and stopping her from turning the knife against herself. The other guys in the office had congratulated him too. In fact Ryan, Andy and Harry had promised to take him out for a celebratory drink.

'You ready, then, mate?' asked Ryan. 'I reckon we might even buy you the beers tonight.'

'Yeah, maybe,' said Jake. 'There's just something I need to check first.'

Ryan followed his gaze across the office to where Ffion sat, still typing at her keyboard, a plume of steam rising gently from her Welsh dragon tea mug. 'Ah, yes, the fire-breathing Welsh dragon. Don't worry, mate. You go and do what you have to do. Just be careful you don't get burnt. Me and the lads will be down the King's Head if you need something to put the flames out.'

'Yeah, okay, right,' said Jake distractedly. 'Thanks.'

He packed up his gear and went over to Ffion's desk. 'You still working?'

'Nearly finished.' Her long fingers continued to fly across the keyboard. 'Is there something bothering you?'

'There's one thing I'm still not sure about,' he said. 'Did you really work out that Bella was the murderer just from what Bridget's old History tutor told you about love, lust and loathing?'

'Well, not entirely from that, obviously.'

'Obviously.' He waited.

'There was also something Meg Collins said when Baxter interviewed her. When asked about the cyanide, she said that a school chemistry lab would have everything you needed to manufacture it.'

'And Bella was a school teacher.'

'Yeah.' She saved her report, powered off her computer, and lifted the mug of hot tea to her lips.

'You planning to join the others down the pub, then?' Jake ventured.

'No, I don't think so. It's not really my scene, you know. Boys, beer, football.'

'No, I didn't think it was.' He watched the steam curling from her mug, wondering what kind of weird witch's brew it contained this time. Jake couldn't imagine drinking any of that stuff himself, whatever health benefits it was supposed to impart. He preferred a flat white coffee with a few sugars to sweeten it, or a mug of builder's tea himself. Or a good pint of beer for that matter.

You couldn't go wrong with a pint. He wondered if he ought to have joined the lads down the pub after all.

'You going beer-swilling with the boys, then?' asked Ffion, the exaggerated Welsh lilt in her voice teasing him.

'No, I don't think so. Actually, I was wondering if you'd like to go somewhere with me?'

'Where?'

'I don't know. Where would you like to go?'

'That depends on what you have in mind when we get there.'

'Um...' He could feel himself growing hot under the collar and knew that very soon his ears would be turning a bright pink. If they hadn't already. Why couldn't he just talk to Ffion without embarrassment? He wasn't usually tongue-tied with girls. 'I...'

'Are you asking me out on a date?' Ffion lowered her mug to the desk and turned her piercing emerald eyes directly on him.

'Um... yeah. I suppose I am. So, would you like to?'

'You still haven't said where.'

'Does it matter?'

Ffion's face was unreadable. 'It might do. So if I were you, I'd give the matter some careful thought.'

'Uh, yeah. I suppose.' He realised that he had no idea what Ffion liked to do with her time. She was a long-distance runner, of course, and went to Taekwondo classes, but those weren't the kind of activities he had in mind. She liked to ride her Kawasaki bike, but what might a woman like Ffion do socially, if anything? 'Well, would you like to show me around the Ashmolean museum? I had a look at their website. The Egyptian section actually looks quite interesting.' Hell, he'd even look at broken Greek cooking pots if he had to. 'I expect it's closed now, but maybe we could go this Saturday?'

Ffion regarded him over the rim of her mug. 'Is that really what you want to do?'

'Not really, but...'

'Where would you like to go?'

'Well, there's a comedy gig on tonight at the O2 Academy on Cowley Road. It's a local guy who's starting to get a good reputation. We could go for a curry afterwards, maybe. Or grab some beers from the Irish pub opposite my place.'

He waited for her reply, wondering if he'd just totally blown his chances. He had no idea whether Ffion would enjoy the kind of evening he'd just described. For all he knew, it might be her idea of hell. But if so, then any kind of relationship between them just didn't stand a chance.

She rose to her feet and pulled on her green leather biker's jacket. 'I think I'm done here.'

'Oh,' said Jake in disappointment. 'Are you leaving?'

'Of course,' she said. 'I'm leaving with you. A gig and a curry sounds lush.'

It was getting late by the time Bridget finally arrived at her sister's house in North Oxford to collect Chloe.

Vanessa opened the door with her usual sense of melodrama. 'Bridget! We've all been worried sick about you. You could have been killed in that madhouse! I've been hearing the most horrendous things!'

Rufus the dog bounded over, doing his level best to knock Bridget sideways. She gave the Golden Labrador a friendly scratch behind the ear.

'Well, I'm here now, and I'm perfectly okay,' she said, trying to calm Vanessa down.

Despite the efforts of the police to keep the more lurid details of the murders under wraps, it was inevitable that they would slip out. Soon they would be on all the news headlines, no doubt, but they were obviously already spreading along Oxford's tightly-knit grapevine. She wondered just how much Vanessa had heard, and whether it was accurate. But she had no desire to talk about any of that now.

'Mum?' Chloe rushed out of the lounge and threw her arms around Bridget, hugging her tight. 'I'm so glad you're all right. It sounds like the gaudy was more like a horror show.'

'Well it certainly wasn't a joyful occasion,' said Bridget. 'How are you? Did Aunt Vanessa look after you well?'

'Of course, Mum. Everything's good.'

'Come and sit down,' said Vanessa. 'I'll put the kettle on.'

'Thanks,' said Bridget. 'But I really must get home.'

'Nonsense. What are you going to eat? I bet you don't have a thing in the fridge back home, and not much in the kitchen cupboards either.'

Her sister knew her too well. 'I can easily pick up a takeaway.'

'Don't be silly. Come on in. I'll cook you a proper meal. Besides,' she added, 'there's someone here who wants to see you.'

Curious, Bridget followed Vanessa into the lounge. Sitting in a reclining chair with his feet up on a stool was Jonathan.

'Bridget.' He tried to get up when he saw her, but she could see that it still caused him a considerable amount of pain to move.

'Jonathan? What are you doing here?'

'I sent James to bring him over when I heard that you'd been released from the college,' said Vanessa. 'Now, I'm off to rustle something up in the kitchen. You two have some time together.' She closed the door to the lounge and withdrew to her domain. Bridget knew that when Vanessa promised to "rustle something up in the kitchen" she could expect to be treated to a gourmet meal.

'Don't get up,' she said to Jonathan, pulling up a pouffe and sitting down beside him.

'Thank God you're not hurt,' he said, taking

her hand in his.

'I survived,' she said. 'Just.'

'Do you want to talk about it?'

'Not really.' It seemed that every time she and Jonathan tried to get together, work got in between them, and sometimes in life-threatening ways. Jonathan had been lucky to escape alive after her last murder case, and even though his injuries had been serious, they could have been so much worse. She knew just how precious life was, and how easily it could be snatched away. She had lost three friends to murder and one to the justice system this weekend. It was going to take some getting used to.

'Well,' said Jonathan brightly. 'I've got something that might cheer you up.'

'Oh?'

He reached inside his jacket pocket and produced a pair of tickets. 'They're for Hamlet, at the Oxford Playhouse. I bought the best seats.'

'Oh,' said Bridget, trying unsuccessfully to mask the dismay in her voice. 'Revenge tragedy.'

Jonathan's face fell. 'Oh God. Have I done the wrong thing? If you don't want to go, I quite understand.'

The expression on his face was so grave she couldn't help laughing in response. She wrapped her arms around his neck, being careful not to disturb the wound on his abdomen, and gave him a kiss. 'Jonathan, with you, I'll go anywhere.'

In Love and Murder (Bridget Hart #4)

Deception. Death. A Deal with the Devil.

When Dr Nathan Frost, a lecturer in German literature at Oxford University, is invited to a lavish party at the country house of a wealthy businessman, he knows there'll be a price to pay. After all, as an expert on the legend of Faust and Mephistopheles, he can recognise a deal with the devil easily enough. But even he's not expecting such a sinister end to the evening.

Called to investigate a suspicious death at a country house, Detective Inspector Bridget Hart is surprised to find a government minister among the party guests. Her team must navigate powerful interests to find the truth. But in a world of favours, backhanders and corruption, nothing is as it seems and nobody can be trusted.

Set amongst the dreaming spires of Oxford University, the Bridget Hart series is perfect for fans of Elly Griffiths, JR Ellis, Faith Martin and classic British murder mysteries.

 Scan the QR code to see a list of retailers.

Bridget Hart series (large print ISBNs)
Aspire to Die (978-1-914537-01-1)
Killing by Numbers (978-1-914537-03-5)
Do No Evil (978-1-914537-05-9)
In Love and Murder (978-1-914537-07-3)
A Darkly Shining Star (978-1-914537-09-7)
Preface to Murder (978-1-914537-11-0)
Toll for the Dead (978-1914537134)

About the author

M S Morris is the pseudonym for the writing partnership of Margarita and Steve Morris. Together they write the Bridget Hart series of crime novels set in Oxford. The couple are married and live in Oxfordshire. They have two sons.

Thank you for reading

We hope you enjoyed this book. If you did, then we would be very grateful if you would please take a moment to leave a review online. Thank you.

Find out more at **msmorrisbooks.com** where you can join our mailing list.

Printed in Great Britain
by Amazon

38031167R00219